PRAISE FOR *LIGHT BURNED*

"The thrilling, captivating conclusion to Jayci Lee's Realm of Four Kingdoms series will make you gasp, cry, and swoon in the best way!"

—Abigail Owen, #1 *New York Times* bestselling author

"Love aches on every page of this romantic and riveting conclusion to the Realm of Four Kingdoms series, and *Light Burned* is immensely satisfying for readers of epic romantasy. Sunny Cho is timeless, a modern sarcastic badass, and also a hero of ages. This saga is the action-packed, swoony adventure you've been waiting for!"

—C. B. Lee, *New York Times* bestselling author

"*Light Burned* is the absolute perfect ending to one of my all-time favorite romantasy series. Packed with humor, heart, and nonstop action, this finale will have you laughing one minute and crying the next. I was on the edge of my seat waiting to see how my favorite characters would tackle the final boss, and Jayci Lee did not disappoint. An epic conclusion to a fantastic series!"

—Falon Ballard, *USA Today* bestselling author of *Something Wicked*

PRAISE FOR *KING FORETOLD*

"Imaginative, clever, and drawing upon Korean folklore/fantasy to deftly craft a distinctive and original action/adventure romantic fantasy, *King Foretold* by Jayci Lee is an extraordinary, memorable, and fun read from cover to cover. An ideal and recommended pick."

—*Midwest Book Review*

"Breathless adventure blended with fierce, forbidden love in an entrancing world will keep readers turning the pages in this captivating Korean mythology–inspired romantasy!"

—Abigail Owen, #1 *New York Times* bestselling author

Praise for *Nine Tailed*

"Urban fantasy readers will adore the smart-mouthed, sword-wielding fox spirit at the heart of this fast-paced tale full of magic, secrets, and romance."

—*Booklist*, starred review

"Jayci Lee has gifted us with the best kind of romantasy—a wild ride with a sexy, protective hero, a spunky protagonist, a fast-paced plot sprinkled with the perfect amount of sexual tension, and world-building so layered and rich you can sink your teeth into it!"

—Lexi Ryan, #1 *New York Times* bestselling author

"*Nine Tailed* is a wild, scorching, compulsively readable romantasy that delivers it all—characters who leap off the pages, fast-paced adventure, romance with all the feels, and a fascinating, magical world to die for. You won't be able to put it down!"

—Abigail Owen, #1 *New York Times* bestselling author

"Fast paced, heartwarming, and heartbreaking—my new fave fantasy romance! *Supernatural* meets K-drama vibes, immigrant globe-trotting immortals, and an epic battle between destiny and fate. *Nine Tailed* stole my heart with an explosion of fireworks and a wonderfully compelling gumiho. A stellar start to what promises to be a swoon-worthy series. I cannot wait to get my hands on the next one!"

—A. Y. Chao, *Sunday Times* bestselling author

"An absolute thrill ride! *Nine Tailed* is brimming with action, humor, and smoldering tension. Lee spins a fantastically original tale filled with cool magic and swoony romance you don't want to miss."

—Juliette Cross, author of the Stay a Spell series

"Jayci Lee's *Nine Tailed* gives Janet Evanovich–meets-Buffy vibes in a vibrant fantasy setting full of Korean mythology. If you're in the mood for some spicy, magical fun, this is the book for you."

—Megan Bannen, author of *The Undertaking of Hart and Mercy*

"I have been dying for a Korean-inspired romantasy, and Jayci Lee has come through! *Nine Tailed* is a sexy, fantastical adventure that reminds me of mythical stories of my youth while fulfilling the romance-loving heart of my adulthood. Finally, a kickass Korean heroine who feels familiar and who has me fist-pumping 'Yes!' as she tackles the darkness that chases her all while fighting for her HEA. Sunny and Ethan are my new OTP, and I demand a K-drama adaptation starring Go Youn-jung and Rowoon immediately!"

—Susan Lee, author of *Seoulmates*

LIGHT
BURNED

OTHER TITLES BY JAYCI LEE

Stand-Alone Novels

Give Me a Reason

That Prince is Mine

Realm of Four Kingdoms

Nine Tailed

King Foretold

A Sweet Mess

A Sweet Mess

The Dating Dare

Booked on a Feeling

The Heirs of Hansol

The "I Do" Dilemma

The Not So Secret Crush

The Enemy Entanglement

Hana Trio

A Song of Secrets

One Night Only

Just a Few Fake Kisses

JAYCI LEE

This is a work of fiction. Names, characters, organizations, places, events, and incidents are either products of the author's imagination or are used fictitiously. Otherwise, any resemblance to actual persons, living or dead, is purely coincidental.

Published by Montlake, Seattle

www.apub.com

EU product safety contact:
Amazon Media EU S. à r.l.
38, avenue John F. Kennedy, L-1855 Luxembourg
amazonpublishing-gpsr@amazon.com

ISBN-13: 9781662538636 (hardcover)
ISBN-13: 9781662532238 (paperback)
ISBN-13: 9781662532221 (digital)

Cover design and illustration by Elizabeth Turner Stokes

Printed in the United States of America
First edition

To hope eternal that shines brightest in the darkest night.

Hope that . . .
love is more powerful than hate,
good will prevail over evil, and
the light will always dispel the dark.

Shine.

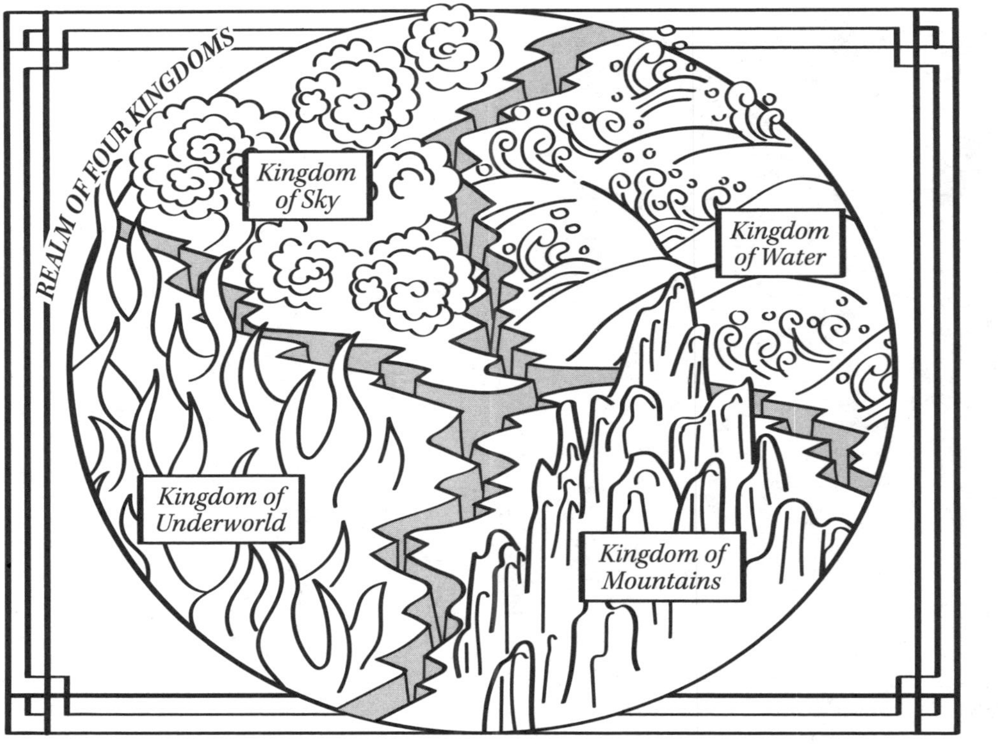
REALM OF FOUR KINGDOMS
Kingdom of Sky
Kingdom of Water
Kingdom of Underworld
Kingdom of Mountains

QUICK AND DIRTY GUIDE TO PRONOUNCING ROMANIZED KOREAN

Pronouncing romanized Korean words is really hard, even for those fluent in Korean. In *Light Burned*, I try my best to be consistent in romanizing Korean words, following the Revised Romanization of Korean system currently used in South Korea.

The consonants are pretty straightforward. The way you intuitively sound them out in your head will be close enough not to trip you up while you read. But there are a few tricky vowels that you might need some getting used to.

I think these are the most helpful ones to note:

a is pronounced "ah"

ae is pronounced "eh"

eo is pronounced "uh"

i is pronounced "ee"

o is pronounced "oh"

u is pronounced "oo"

The cool thing about these vowels is that they will always sound the same no matter what consonants you combine them with. So the word for *nine-tailed fox spirit*, *gumiho*, is pronounced "goo-mee-ho";

the word for *the world of gods, Shingae,* is pronounced "sheen-geh"; and the name for *the god of Underworld, Yeomla,* is pronounced "yum-la"; and so on and so forth.

Now, if I haven't confused you more, go forth and read *Light Burned* with confidence. You got this! Welcome back to the Shingae.

CHAPTER ONE

ETHAN

The sky deepens into a silky indigo as night falls across the Kingdom of Mountains. The battle has been raging hard and brutal for hours. Exhaustion envelops me like an ominous shadow, but I crack my neck and swing my axes with sharp flicks of my wrists, flinging the blood off the blades. The enemy soldiers flinch and scurry back, and I flash them a menacing grin.

Captain Ha, the head of the royal guards, plants his feet wide at my left and crosses his tree-trunk arms over his chest. At my right Jihun, my brother in every way that matters, wipes his long sword on his armguard, then stabs the tip into the dirt ground.

The soldiers jump and scamper some more. The poor fools have no fight left in them, but they still outnumber us fifty to one.

I locked up my father, the former King of Mountains, mere hours ago. It didn't take long for his loyal general to lay siege on the Shinsi Palace in his name. And Jihun and I joined the royal guards to hold the line outside the audience hall.

A part of me wishes I hadn't, damn my duties as the King of Mountains.

I left Sunny in the dungeon with my father, and I haven't seen her since. While I'm glad she isn't caught up in the fray, it's not like her to shy away from a fight.

Where is she?

My skin tightens with a growing sense of wrongness. If she had a choice, she would be by my side right now.

"Do you surrender, General Shin?" I shout across the vast courtyard.

"Not until I have your head on a spike." He waves his fist in the air, then in a fit of temper, he kicks and screams at the soldiers around him. "Go kill him, you worthless fools. All of you. Go!"

"Your Majesty"—Jihun half turns toward me, keeping his eyes on General Shin—"please retire to the audience hall and get some rest. We will subdue this uprising when reinforcement arrives."

"How long until they reach us?" I subtly shift my weight from leg to leg to relieve the aches in my battle-worn body.

"They are a half day's ride away."

"I don't have half a day," I growl. Something went wrong in the dungeon. I need to get to Sunny.

"Your Majes—" he begins.

"I am ending this *now*." I cut him off. "Are you with me, Jihun?"

"Always." He doesn't hesitate to give his support, even as a muscle jumps in his clamped jaw, frustration in every line of his face.

"Thank you." I clap a hand on his shoulder. What I am about to do will sap me of what strength I have left, and he knows it. But I need to find Sunny before I lose my mind. I turn my grim gaze on the enemy. "Give me some room."

Captain Ha backs up without question and orders his men to keep their distance. After a mutinous pause, Jihun walks away to stand with the royal guards. When my people are safely behind me, I cross my axes—one golden, one silver—in front of my chest, then slash them down, drawing an *X* in the air. They vanish before my fists fall to my sides.

I wouldn't want to misplace the true crown of the King of Mountains.

With a deep inhale, I step toward the enemy soldiers. Many of them look too young to be twenty-four years old, the age the Shinbiin come into the peak of their powers and become nearly immortal. I don't want to hurt these young soldiers, but I don't have the luxury of second-guessing myself.

I need to find Sunny, and I have to get past them to go to her. They will fall, because she always comes first.

The gi of Mountains rushes through my veins and sings in my blood. I close my eyes and coax the vibrant life force toward my heart's center, concentrating the gi into a single point. Sweat beads on my forehead, and my body trembles as I struggle to contain the growing power.

Almost there.

"What's going on?" The anxious question bursts from a soldier at the front and spreads like wildfire across their formation. "What is he doing?"

When my entire chest beats with power, I open my eyes at last, casting a green glow on their terrified faces. The silver gi of Sky swirls within me, fortifying the magic, but it's the green gi of Mountains that pounds to be released, burning in my eyes. I press the base of my open palms together and extend my arms out in front of me.

With a shout, I discharge the power in a pulsating stream through my hands, even as I grit my teeth to hold back its full might. The magic grows and spreads like a green tidal wave and rams into General Shin's army. Silently, the soldiers fall, row after row, like a well-arranged domino set.

I grunt as I abruptly cut off the stream of magic. That couldn't have taken more than five seconds, but it wasn't a second too soon. My arms shake as I lower them back to my sides, my chest heaving with labored breaths.

I stare across the sea of unconscious soldiers. *Unconscious*, not dead. I want to crow with triumph. I don't know how I dampened my magic—gut instinct and desperation probably had something to do with it.

Either way, I did it. I spared the lives of my enemies. Brute strength without control doesn't make you powerful. It makes you a brute. With both strength *and* control, I feel truly powerful for the first time—like I'm worthy of this power.

It's ironic that I can hardly stay upright as my head spins violently. I almost plant my hands on my thighs, seeking purchase to drag air into my lungs. But I can't show weakness. Not now.

I left General Shin standing because he cannot concede defeat if he's unconscious. Unfortunately, I see the flaw in my plan too late as the edges of my vision darken.

Well, shit.

I can't accept his surrender if *I'm* unconscious.

"I got you." Jihun is at my side before my knees can buckle, his grip firm on the back of my arm.

"Perfect timing." I lean imperceptibly against him, inhaling a proper lungful of air, and the vertigo passes.

"General Shin." My voice sounds firm and steady, if not as loud as before. "Do you—"

The general falls to his knees before I finish my question. "Please show mercy, Your Majesty."

Ah, that's right. General Shin doesn't know his soldiers are alive. I doubt he cares much about his men's well-being. But he thinks I killed them all and will do the same to him if he doesn't yield. *I'll take that.*

"Captain Ha, show General Shin"—I jerk my chin toward the sniveling general—"to his new accommodations."

"With pleasure, Your Majesty." The captain bows low, then motions for two of the royal guards to follow him. They stumble after him, throwing frightened glances my way.

Confusion lines my forehead until I realize that the royal guards also think I killed the soldiers. Can I blame them? They've been under my father's ruthless regime for centuries. How can they be sure I'm not like him? I have to earn their trust.

"Captain Song"—I address Jihun formally for the benefit of the guards—"have the enemy soldiers restrained before they regain consciousness."

"Yes, Your Majesty." He doesn't look surprised—just proud. I nod at him, my chest tight with gratitude. Then he faces the royal guards and commands, "Secure the soldiers. Work quickly."

Across the courtyard, Hailey, our resident jeoseungsaja, clips Captain Ha's shoulder as he leads General Shin away from the royal audience hall.

"I'm sorry," she pants, but she doesn't slow down to hear the captain's reply, instead making a beeline toward me. My heart gives a sickening lurch when she reaches me, clutching her side. "Your Majesty—"

"Catch your breath first," I interrupt her, not ready to hear what she has to say. Sunny is not with her. It can't be good news.

"Are you okay?" Jihun has the wherewithal to ask.

Hailey nods as she gulps in more air. "But I don't think this could wait."

"What happened?" I brace myself.

"Sunny's gone." She bites her trembling lip, then blows out a shuddering breath. "She went to the Mortal Realm to stop Daeseong from killing the thousand humans he has kidnapped."

Everything goes out of focus, and my ears ring with the high-pitched sound of someone flatlining. I lock my knees so they don't buckle under me.

"Where?" My voice is unrecognizable, harsh and feral.

"I took her to the entrance to the Gray Void." Hailey hikes her chin up. "I couldn't stop her, so I helped her."

I take a stumbling step forward, and Hailey backs away. With an impatient shake of my head, I squeeze her shoulder to let her know I'm not angry with her. Sunny is a force of nature. She cannot be stopped. I know that, and yet . . .

She might still be here. I have to find her. I take a calming breath and blink hard to clear my vision. Taking down General Shin's army depleted me, but I dig for whatever dregs of power I have left.

Lend me your strength, Mountains.

"Where is the Gray Void?" I manage to rasp.

"Just outside the city walls . . ." Hailey shoots a panicked glance at Jihun.

I don't wait to hear what he has to say. The gi of Mountains flares in my veins and flickers over my skin as I run until I'm a blur in the streets. I don't know what I'll do if I find her.

I can't leave and abandon my kingdom . . . my people, but she can't stay. The very fate of the worlds is at stake. She is the only one who has a fighting chance of stopping Daeseong and the Amheuk, an ancient force of darkness.

I'll think about that when I find her. In this moment, all I want is to hold her in my arms and tell her I love her.

I love you more than anything, Sunny.

A growl rips out of my throat as I push myself faster, and a teardrop slides across my temple and flies into the air. I streak past the city gates, and I hear her—a cry of pain.

"Sunny," I roar, and I race toward her voice.

My neck muscles strain tautly, near their snapping point. I taste blood in my mouth as my lungs burn. I don't need to fucking breathe. Sunny is hurting, and I have to find her. She needs me.

But I feel myself slowing down, no matter how I urge my body faster. I'm too weak. I've pushed myself too hard. I stumble as I force my legs to keep moving. Pain rips a low moan out of me, but I don't stop—I won't stop until I'm at her side. I have to tell her.

I love you more than life.

I see her at last. She stands in the distance—a speck on the moonlit hill. With the last of my strength, I stumble toward her.

"Sunny," I shout, but only air rattles past my lips. I watch in horror as she takes a faltering step toward the Gray Void. Then another. My hand reaches out for her as my legs give out, and I fall to my knees. "Please. Stay."

But . . . she is already gone.

EVEN THEN

Fire burns everywhere. Rivers run dry. Trees wither. The earth hardens and cracks. The very life forces of Mountains, Sky, Water, and Underworld feed the fire. Together they are infused with all the colors of light, and a blinding white gi—full and wild—is born.

A female stands in the midst of the fiery ruin with her arms spread wide. Her snow-white hair billows around her head as though she's floating in water. Her eyes are closed, her expression serene, as though she is soaking in the warmth of the winter sun.

Suddenly, she opens her eyes, and white fire burns in them. Her face hardens even as tears stream down her pale cheeks. She clenches her fists and screams, a piercing sound of sorrow and defeat. White light bursts from her chest.

I welcome the fire as everything I know burns around me. I welcome her even as the fire consumes me. I am awed and terrified by her beauty, by her power.

I burn until I am nothing.

Even then . . . I love her.

CHAPTER TWO

ETHAN

"Sunny!" I jerk awake with a hoarse whisper, my hand grasping at air. With wakefulness comes the ache, and I dig the heel of my hand against my chest, just to the left of my sternum.

Where is she? Is she okay? Her cry of pain as she disappeared into the Gray Void still rings in my ears. Is she hurt? Or . . . worse? *No.*

Sunny heals faster than even the Shinbiin. She's okay. She has to be. I would know if anything happened to her. But I won't be able to take a full breath until I'm holding her in my arms again.

I rub one bleary eye, then the next and scan my surroundings. Even in the dim glow of the light orbs, the royal audience hall of the Shinsi Palace oozes opulence. The dark, gleaming floors, the thick wooden columns with their intricate etchings, and the imposing throne—carved from a thousand-year-old tree—with gold branches and jade leaves stretching toward the ceiling and to the ends of the wall. All of it screams wealth and power. The former King of Mountains, my father, would never have held audience anywhere . . . *less.*

Now *I* am the King of Mountains, but I can't even make myself sit on the throne. My father killed my mother, and made numerous attempts on my life, to cling on to it. I think it understandable that I'm hesitant to sit on the blood-tainted thing.

Instead, I slept on the floor, with my back against its arm. Now, I straighten away from the throne, then cringe when my shirt clings to me, soaked with sweat and splattered with blood.

Not mine.

It could have been, with the right weapons, though. I don't know how many weapons my father made with the sacred tombstone of Dangun, the god of Mountains, or who has them. But I can't fall back on my invincibility to protect me, with those still out there.

I rub at the ache in my chest again. I don't know if Sunny would be any safer here, but I want her by my side. She would never let me shield her from danger. *My beautiful, ferocious warrior.* But at least we can fight together.

"Your Majesty." Jihun approaches the dais, dressed in his brass-scaled battle armor.

"Must you call me that?" I glance up at him with a bad-tempered scowl.

"Yes." His lips don't so much as twitch, not that he smiles often, but his expression softens when he asks, "How are you feeling?"

"Swell." I push to my feet and stretch out my stiff back. "I should be *doing* something, not hiding out in here."

Jihun reaches down to the floor and retrieves the viridian robe of the King of Mountains, the gold bear emblem embroidered on each shoulder and on the chest and back. He shakes it out with great care, then offers it to me. I hesitate, grimacing in distaste, before I snatch the silk robe out of his hands.

"You subdued a rebellion two days ago, then fought off a deadly assassin last night. I would argue *that* constitutes doing something," my royal guard remarks as I shrug into the robe with sharp, impatient tugs. "And the soldiers are preparing to fight for the Kingdom of Mountains and their new king. Your place is on the throne. That is what your people need."

"Don't you get tired of always being right?" I lower myself onto the throne with a weary sigh. My body sinks into the comfortable seat, even as a shudder of distaste runs through me. This throne—this entire *kingdom*—belongs to me now. I have to stop thinking of them as my father's.

"It's a blessing and a curse." This time, one corner of his mouth quivers for a split second.

I chuckle but quickly sober. "Do we know who sent the assassin? My father? Or my grandfather?"

Why do all the males in my family want to kill me? I've come to terms with my father's longtime aspiration to see me dead, but I recoil from thinking about my grandfather's betrayal. It's too new, too raw.

"We chased her down, but she killed herself before we could question her." Jihun hisses a frustrated breath. "But when she used magic to evade capture, her eyes burned with green fire."

"She's a being of Mountains, and her suicide fits the tyrant's MO." I rub my forehead, too tired to be angry. "How did my father send an assassin when he's locked up in the dungeon?"

"We will get to the bottom of it, Your Majesty," my royal guard vows.

I nod curtly. "Have you heard from Captain Seo?"

The captain is one of the best trackers in the Order of the Suhoshin. Shouldn't she have found Sunny by now?

"She has only been gone a day." A muscle bunches in Jihun's jaw.

So that's a no. I drag both hands down my face. "Sunny's been gone for two."

"I'm well aware," he all but growls.

My surprised gaze shoots toward him at his uncharacteristic flash of temper. His expression remains stoic, but he must feel as frantic as I do. He's in love with Sunny. My fists clench around the arms of the throne, but I slowly unfurl my fingers. *She is mine.* I have no reason to be jealous, especially not now.

She went after the dark mudang on her own, while I got sidetracked subduing an uprising. I wish I had waited for her outside my father's prison like I'd promised. I wish I'd stormed back in there and gotten her the hell away from that insidious bastard. But the lives of a thousand humans—perhaps the fate of the Mortal Realm itself—depended on her extracting Daeseong's location from the tyrant.

Nevertheless, I wish I hadn't left her side. Whatever my father told her sent her running to the Mortal Realm without so much as a goodbye. I went after her as soon as I heard—only to catch a glimpse of her back as she disappeared into the Gray Void.

In that desperate moment, I would've gone after Sunny if Jihun and Jaeseok hadn't found me. I would've plunged into the Gray Void if they hadn't delivered the devastating news of General Bak's betrayal. My grandfather, a general of the Kingdom of Sky, plans to exact his revenge and wage war on the Kingdom of Mountains, even though the tyrant no longer sits on the throne.

Even then, a part of me still wanted to follow her to the Mortal Realm. I considered leaving my people to face the Kingdom of Sky's invasion on their own—an invasion I brought down on them.

Shame burns through me, but my love for Sunny burns brighter. In the end, I didn't abandon my people, because I love her. I stayed to defend the Kingdom of Mountains because she would never want me to do anything that would make me hate myself. Even so, it took every ounce of my willpower to resist the call of my heart, telling me to run to her—telling me *she* comes before all else.

"It has been a taxing few days," Jihun says by way of apology, pulling me out of my thoughts.

"Try a taxing few months." I offer him a wry half smile.

Before she left, Sunny told Hailey that she had mastered the magic of the Yeoiju, a gift of the Cheon'gwang. And Jaeseok relayed that Draco and Minju had left for the Mortal Realm to bring Sunny the sword of light, a weapon powerful enough to stop the dark mudang. With the added help of Minju's intelligence and the might of Draco's dragon, Sunny had to have defeated Daeseong.

Then why aren't they back yet?

I claw at the collar of my shirt as the cold hand of fear wraps around my heart and squeezes. It has been two days since Sunny, Draco, and

Minju went after the dark mudang—and a long, silent day since I sent Captain Seo to the Mortal Realm to find out what happened to them.

Why haven't any of them sent word?

"We should—" I bolt to my feet when the doors to the audience hall burst open.

At the same time, Jihun draws his long sword and places himself directly in front of me. I finally understand why Sunny yells at me every time I shield her with my body. It's aggravating as hell. I deliberately walk around him to stand at his side.

"Your Majesty." Jaeseok stumbles toward the dais with his hand wrapped around his shoulder, blood seeping through his fingers.

"Jaeseok, what happened?" I take a step toward the dokkaebi, my heart pounding against my ribs and echoing in my ears. "Speak, Lieutenant Cha."

I briefly indulge in the fantasy that he comes bearing good news—news that Sunny is safe. But I don't need to see the pallor of Jaeseok's face and the dread in his eyes, not to mention his injured shoulder, to know that he brings no such news.

"It is worse than we anticipated," he says in a hoarse rasp. "General Bak has invaded with the entire might of the Kingdom of Sky."

My grandfather does not want a war. He wants a massacre.

CHAPTER THREE

Sunny

One of the glorious things about Las Vegas is that there is every imaginable color and flavor of margarita available, twenty-four seven. It is gloriously disgusting. But considering the atrocities I've committed, I deserve to suffer this level of hell.

I'm on a mission to drink myself into oblivion. I've been stumbling from one bustling casino to the next, replenishing my yard-long plastic cup at every overcrowded stop. Thank goodness for humans and their unwavering skepticism. Nothing muddles magic traces better.

"Humph." If I have enough sense left to remember that I'm hiding from the Shingae, the world of gods, then I must not be drunk enough. *That won't do.* Or maybe I'm just falling back on old habits.

"Sunny," someone calls me from behind.

I lurch to a stop and sway in spot for a second. Once I regain enough balance not to keel over, I turn around to face the person who said my name. I really should be shivering in my breeches. Because if someone from the Shingae found me, then I'm a sitting duck. Even if I'm not too drunk to hide, I'm way too drunk to fight.

I am a drunk duck in breeches.

I snort. With admirable restraint, I refrain from quacking and focus my bleary gaze on the muscular, flannel-clad chest in front of me. Then I look up—and up—until I meet warm hazel eyes smiling down at me. I blink to make sure I'm not seeing things, but the mop of red hair is hard to miss even at my advanced level of inebriation.

"Ford?" I cringe at the loudness of my own voice. I'm not happy to see my old friend. The squishy feeling inside me is just margarita slushing around. "What are you doing here?"

His smile morphs into a frown. "I work here, Sunny."

"Since when?" We used to work in the same shitty casino. Did he move jobs? I squint in confusion—and also because he's swaying back and forth. The second part might be on my end, though.

"Longer than I've known you." He throws his hands up. "What are *you* doing here? Are you okay? I haven't seen you in months."

"You work here?" I'll catch up to the rest of the stuff he said later.

"Yes, like you used—Never mind." He plows his fingers through his hair, then narrows his eyes at my neon-green cup. "What the hell are you drinking?"

"Oh, this?" I beam at him. Ford is a bartender—a cocktail connoisseur, if you will. He will understand the depth of my suffering. "It's a green-apple margarita."

He barely manages not to gag. "You don't touch that shit."

"I'm not the same person you used to know." I deserve to drown in revolting margaritas. "I drink it in every flavor. If Las Vegas concocts it, then I drink it. It is my only source of sustenance."

"Jesus." He rubs his hand over his jaw and whips off the neatly folded white towel from his shoulder. Then he cranes his neck toward a petite blond with a gorgeous tattoo sleeve at the other side of the bar. "I'm taking my break now, Charlotte."

I vaguely register that I'm standing at the bar of my former place of employment, a small casino off the Strip. *What am I doing here?* I shrug, jostling the margarita in my hand, which reminds me of my main objective. *To get shit faced.*

I open my mouth wide to catch the straw to my treacly drink and bob my head every which way because it's a slippery little sucker. I snicker at the unintentional pun, then resume my chase for the elusive straw.

I come perilously close to sticking the thick straw up my nose before I finally manage to wrap my lips around it. I take a long, syrupy sip, and the ache in my chest eases for a brief second at my self-inflicted punishment.

"Let's go." Ford takes a gentle hold of my upper arm and leads me toward the back of the casino, through a crowd of tourists and regulars.

The chime of slot machines and the clink of chips fade away, and a different din hits my ears. Knives clack like woodpeckers as the prep cooks chop mountains of vegetables, and fat cuts of steak sizzle as the line cooks throw one after another onto the flaming grills.

"Where we going?" I mumble around the straw. I'm not taking it out of my mouth again after all the trouble I went through. "Not somewhere quiet, I hope. I need to be around a bunch of humans."

Something niggles at the back of my mind. I shouldn't be telling Ford this. Beings of the Shingae like me must abide by its rules even when we're hiding from it. First, we can't expose the world of gods. Second, we must protect the magic. Hence, I shouldn't be explaining why I need to mingle in a crowd of humans to hide my magic . . . to a human. But the third and most important rule inconveniently flashes past my alcohol-dulled mind.

Keep the Amheuk at bay.

"Oopsy daisy." I drink more margarita to suppress unwanted memories from surfacing. "Pretend you didn't hear that last part."

"Oopsy daisy?" He pinches the bridge of his nose, reminding me of a stern seonnam I don't want to think about. I quickly take another sip of my adult slushy, and Ford mutters, "Christ on a cracker."

He takes me through the kitchen and out the back door. Inside the casinos, time seems suspended at the peak of night, but a new day is awakening outside. Fortunately, the faint wash of dawn hasn't reached the dim alleyway yet. *Good.* I'm not ready to face the light of day.

I crinkle my nose. The stench of the overflowing trash bins competes with my margarita for the title of the most disgusting thing in the alley. I took myself out of the running to keep things fair.

"What happened to you, Sunny?" Ford gingerly props me up against the building. "Where's Ethan?"

I spin away from Ford in the nick of time and hurl rainbow-colored vomit like a fucking unicorn.

Where's Ethan?

Somewhere I can't be . . . In a realm I've sentenced to a fate worse than death by destroying its one defense against the Amheuk. *I don't want to remember.* A scream builds in my chest, but it doesn't get a chance to escape as I throw up some more.

Ford gathers my hair into a fist and rests his warm, meaty hand on my back. I shove him away and stumble back from him. His gentle touch is too much to handle. The Yeoiju makes a keening, worried noise inside me. *The Yeoiju?* I haven't heard its voice in days.

For a fleeting moment, I'm deeply relieved not to be completely alone. But then, I shove away the Yeoiju, too—deep down until I can't hear it anymore—because I don't deserve its solace.

"Oh goody. I didn't drop my marg." I take a sip of the melted green liquid and gargle my mouth with it. Then I chug down the remainder. "I need a refill."

Ford grabs a hold of my shoulder when I turn to walk away. "What's going on, Sunny?"

I spin on him, dislodging his hand, and snarl, "It's none of your business."

"Then why are you here?" He arches a thick red eyebrow, unfazed by my antagonism. "Of all the casino bars in Vegas, why did you walk into mine?"

Because I'm scared. Because I needed to see a friendly face. Because I don't really want to be alone.

"Don't flatter yourself." I narrow my eyes at him. "I was too drunk to see where I was going."

"Yeah, right." Ford snorts. "How long has it been since you've eaten? Food, not that abomination."

I recall a crowded PC bang in a Korean fishing village, where I ate my last meal. And just like that, the memories come crashing back. *Oh gods. No.* The tyrant tricking me into a blood oath to leave the Kingdom of Mountains and to never return. Leaving Ethan without saying goodbye. Tracking down Daeseong in Santorini. Battling the dark mudang at the caldera. Running toward the kid . . .

Draco.

The tears I've kept at bay rush out of me in torrents. They were so brave, so strong. *I'm so sorry I couldn't protect you.* But I avenged them. Daeseong died at my sword like he deserved.

I stabbed him in his black heart, then I bewitched him to force the truth out of him. I needed him to admit that I am not his daughter. With my darkest power, I robbed him of his free will—violated him in the worst possible way—only to find out that he *was* telling the truth.

I am the dark mudang's daughter. And I killed him. My own father.

Monster. Abomination.

Gripping my head in both hands, I scream until my stomach clenches tightly enough to curve my back. I glance at Ford through my tears. *Help me.* My eyes plead with him to make it stop hurting, even though he can't. *No one can.*

I broke my promise to my mother and used the vilest magic anyone could use on another being. I deserve to suffer. Ford steps toward me with his hand outstretched.

"Take another step, and you forfeit your life," an icy voice says in a crisp British accent from somewhere behind me.

Run, Sunny.

My gumiho pushes against my skin, urging me to shift. But it's too late. The Shingae has found me. Again.

CHAPTER FOUR

Sunny

Like everything she wears, Captain Seo makes mortal clothes look effortlessly chic—even the dungarees she inexplicably donned for this occasion. But my plastic margarita cup slips out of my limp grasp when Minju steps around the captain in a white strapless dress the size of a headband.

I need to sober up to understand the situation—or the dress code at the very least. *Wait.* What am *I* wearing? I glance down at myself and slump in relief. I'm wearing a pair of black jeans with a black T-shirt.

I don't remember changing out of my torn, bloodied clothes from Santorini, but I'm glad I did. I hardly even mind the *Vegas, baby!* emblazoned across my boobs in sparkly gold letters.

Meanwhile, Ford stands like a statue, with his hand still outstretched toward me, but his eyeballs jump back and forth between the two seonnyeos. Even glamoured to dampen their celestial beauty, Captain Seo and Minju are drop-dead gorgeous.

The poor man might have stopped breathing. I squint one eye to check his gi. His colorless life force trickles faintly around him. But that's normal for humans. He'll live.

"I was so worried about you, Sunny." The historian hurtles herself at me and wraps her arms around my waist in a freakishly strong grip.

"I thought I told you to go back to the Realm—" I bite my tongue and shoot a glance at Ford. Based on his expression, he doesn't hear a word I'm saying, but I still rephrase my accusation to Minju. "I told you to go *back*."

"And I told you I'm not leaving until you tell me what happened." Minju raises her chin.

"Why don't we continue our conversation somewhere less"—Captain Seo wrinkles her nose—"*ripe*?"

"Sunny." Ford regains his faculties and comes to stand beside me. "Who are these people? Are they here to hurt you?"

"I could ask the same of you." The captain executes a perfect eyebrow arch.

"Stop it," I say hoarsely. "I would trust all three of you with my life."

"Even so, we have much to discuss." Minju sends a curious glance toward Ford. "And we cannot talk in front of your friend."

"Why not?" my mouth blurts before my mind catches up. But when it does, the answer comes to me like a clap of thunder. If things had gone differently in Santorini, then the Mortal Realm would have been annihilated by the Amheuk. "Why ever the fuck not?"

Once the Amheuk finishes destroying the Realm of Four Kingdoms—I flinch away from the thought, bile rising to my throat—it will come for the Mortal Realm to plunge it into darkness. I dig my nails into my palms to stop my hands from shaking.

Humans need to know about the ancient force of darkness, even if it exposes the Shingae to them. They have the right to defend their world.

I slap my palm against the wall of the building to fight off a dizzy spell. *What am I thinking?* I don't give a damn about the Realm of Four Kingdoms. And I don't care about the Mortal Realm. Even if I cared, getting involved would only make things worse for everybody. Because I can't be good, no matter how hard I try. What happened in Santorini proves that.

"Sunny." Ford wraps his arm around my shoulders. "You okay?"

"I'm fine," I lie, not meeting his gaze.

Minju takes a step toward me, and I glare at her in warning. I can't let her console me. If I unravel, I won't be able to put myself together again. After a considering look, she gives me a solemn nod, then turns her attention to Ford.

"Hello, I am Minju," she says shyly. "What is your name?"

"I'm Ford." He stares at her for a second too long, then gives his head a sharp shake. "Nice to meet you, Minju."

"Well, *Ford*." Captain Seo crosses her arms over her chest without introducing herself. "Is there somewhere private we can talk?"

"Sunny said she needed to be around a crowd of people." Ford sticks out his massive chest and narrows his eyes at the captain. Yet she holds the upper hand on the intimidation factor.

"It did make her nearly impossible to track down," Minju murmurs.

Ford frowns, his eyes jumping between the three of us.

"Fair enough." The captain shrugs. "How about just somewhere people can't overhear us? Preferably a locale with a less pungent aroma?"

"I know exactly the place." Ford gingerly lifts his arm off my shoulders, but his hand hovers behind my back. "Can you walk, Sunny?"

"Of course I can." I step away from the wall and, with intense concentration, manage not to take a nosedive.

I follow Ford through the kitchen and back into the casino, flanked by Captain Seo and Minju. They think I'm a flight risk, but they needn't worry. The earlier dizzy spell passed, but the weight on my chest makes it difficult to breathe. I'm in no condition to run—and I can only crawl so fast.

Ford leads us past the five-dollar slot machines, with the captain wearing a pinched look the entire time. I can't tell if she disapproves of the migraine-inducing lights and the nonstop bells and whistles or the eye burning cigarette smoke, laced with the sickly candy-shop smell of vapes.

Minju, on the other hand, is wide eyed and delighted. While technically a part of the Order of the Suhoshin, the historian doesn't need to visit the Mortal Realm to carry out her duties. It's a shame, really. There is nothing she loves better than discovering new things to study and understand.

Distracted, and still far from sober, I don't notice where we are until Ford scans a key card to a door in the back corner of the casino.

"We're going to talk in the haunted storage room?" I squeak.

He gapes at me like I've lost my mind. "What idiot said this room is haunted?"

"All the idiots who work here." I throw my hand out to encompass the whole casino floor. "They said no one ever uses the storage room because it's haunted."

I believed them because ghosts in fact exist. Stranded souls roam the worlds, kept from moving on to their next life by their han—grief twisted into an unhealed scar. The stranded have always given me the heebie-jeebies. But after the Gray Void, I don't know what to think of them.

In fact, I don't want to think about the stranded at all, or the Gray Void. *Especially the Gray Void.* My heart races uncomfortably fast. I need to stop thinking about anything that matters.

Existing hurts.

Shaking his head at me, Ford opens the door and stands back to let the rest of us through. Minju and I stare at Captain Seo, silently begging her to take the lead. The captain only hesitates for a second before she bravely steps inside. I follow next, grabbing Minju's hand and tucking her behind me. Ford comes in after us, muttering about ghosts and idiots, then closes the door.

"This is not a storage room." I can't help but state the obvious.

"What makes you say that, genius?" He smirks. "The gilded crystal chandeliers or the Italian marble floors?"

I'm too busy gawking at my surroundings to come up with a respectably acerbic retort. Instead, I give him an uninspired middle finger as I run my other hand over a brand-new blackjack table. "Why is there a secret high-limits room?"

"It wasn't meant to be a secret." He rubs the back of his head. "The boss wanted to lure high rollers here."

"High rollers?" I scrunch up my face. "No self-respecting whale would come to this crappy, run-down casino."

"Exactly," Ford says with a grimace.

"Wait a minute." I side-eye him. "How do you know about this room?"

He glances away and clears his throat. "I helped design the bar."

I lean wearily against the blackjack table and flap my hand in a *whatever* gesture. There's obviously more to it than that, but exhaustion dulls my curiosity. I yawn long enough to make tears leak from the corners of my eyes. I haven't slept in days.

Ford watches with a grim press of his lips, then he walks over to the fancy bar and turns on the espresso machine. I perk up when it whirs, gurgles, and hisses with the promise of caffeine, but I deflate again when Captain Seo and Minju ambush me.

I just want to dissociate and drink a double espresso. *Is that too much to ask?* Apparently, it is.

"Sunny, we really must talk." Minju lays a hand on my arm. "Like I said, there is much to discuss."

"But first, are you certain you want to burden your friend with the knowledge of the Shingae?" Captain Seo glances over her shoulder. "He won't be easily convinced, and you'll be risking his sanity."

"No, I'm not certain." I scowl at her. "But what's the alternative?"

"You can destroy the Amheuk and stop it from ever invading the Mortal Realm," Minju states matter-of-factly.

"Sure." My chest constricts with fear. Defeating Daeseong, a mere servant of the Amheuk, nearly destroyed me. Asking me to stop the *actual* ancient force of darkness is like asking a fruit fly to take down a tiger. "Easy peasy."

"She never said it will be easy," Captain Seo grits through her teeth. "But it *is* possible, Sunny."

"You don't understand." I cup my forehead, averting my gaze.

None of it matters. They won't want my help if they find out whose daughter I am. They won't trust me if they find out what I've done. How could they when I'm capable of taking away their free will at any time? I don't even trust myself anymore. I never thought I would bewitch someone, but now I know that I'll resort to my worst self if I'm desperate enough.

"Double espresso and water." Ford sets both down on the bar and sends a meaningful glance toward the captain. "Now I'll get out of your hair."

Captain Seo has the grace to nod her thanks, finally letting down her guard by a millimeter.

"Ford, wait." He's already at the door by the time I catch up with him. "Thank you. I'll come find you when we're done."

"Take care, Sunny." He gives me a wistful smile.

The door closes behind him with a soft click. I'm tempted to run after him and have him pour me shot after shot of tequila—anything to avoid this conversation. But I don't deserve tequila, unless it's mixed into a gross, overly sweet margarita.

"I'm not coming with you," I say with my back to Minju and Captain Seo. Then, taking a ragged breath, I turn toward my friends and summon the sword of light with a snap of my wrist. I'm counting on the hordes of humans outside to hide the brief flare of magic. I hold out the sheathed sword toward them. "But you can take the Shin'gwangdo."

"What is the sword of light without you?" Captain Seo asks quietly.

"You can wield it better than I ever could." I keep my gaze trained on the captain's face to avoid looking at the blue dragon scales on the sheath. "And with Ethan's axes, there's a chance—"

"Stop." Minju all but growls the word, her expression fierce. "Draco didn't die so you can hide in Las Vegas, drinking until you can't even walk straight."

"Shut up," I rasp. *"Shut. Up."*

I don't remember unsheathing the Shin'gwangdo, but I'm gripping the hilt of the sword, with the glowing blade pointed at Minju. She stares at me, her face slack and pale, and Captain Seo leaps between us, summoning her twin swords.

"Stand down, Cadet Cho," she commands, but her voice is reedy with shock.

What the fuck am I doing?

"I-I'm so sorry, Minju." I lower the Shin'gwangdo, horrified with myself. "I would never hurt—"

The door to the high-limits room bursts open, cutting short my woefully inadequate apology. I spin around, raising my sword again, just in time to block a ball of fire coming for my face.

"Did you think the Jaenanpa was done with you, gumiho?" The scraggly blond sneers, pushing his glasses up his nose. His minions enter behind him, snickering like assholes. "Even dragon spirits can't kill us, because of the might of our magic."

The last magic thief to enter the room shuts the door behind him, and the twelve of them form a semicircle behind their scrawny leader. Of course Blondie survived. Draco freed all the human hostages from Akrotiri without killing a single corrupt shaman. It wasn't the might of their stolen magic that saved them. It was the kid's mercy.

I swallow a faint moan. *Draco.* I want to reach in and rip my heart out. Anything to make it stop hurting.

"Aww, you followed me all the way here from Santorini?" I flash Blondie a bloodthirsty smile, and the coward practically turns blue with fear. "I'm touched, but you really shouldn't have."

I swish my sword in the air with lazy flicks of my wrist, stepping between my friends and the Jaenanpa. Why do these depraved pieces of shit deserve to live when Draco is dead? The answer is simple. They don't.

The kid was good through and through. *But I'm not.* There is nothing holding me back from killing these bastards.

With a battle cry, I rush toward them.

CHAPTER FIVE

Sunny

"Not so mighty now, are you?" My nose is an inch away from Blondie's as I press my sword against his throat. His Adam's apple bobs, and a single drop of blood wells on his pasty skin and rolls down his toothpick neck. "Careful there. You might hurt yourself."

A brave soul at one end of the semicircle begins murmuring under her breath. I glance down at the hands curled at her sides. It's subtle, but she is tapping the tips of her fingers on the pads of her thumbs as though counting something in her head. *Ooh, sneaky.* She's incanting a spell.

"Nuh-uh," I chide with indulgent annoyance and dig the Shin'gwangdo deeper into their leader's throat. Blood slides down the blade of my sword, pooling above the hilt. "No using magic that doesn't belong to you. Obviously, that goes for all you psychopaths. Or else your leader will die before you can utter another syllable."

"Sunny," Minju gasps. "This isn't you."

"I hate to break it to you, my friend"—my smile takes on a desperate edge—"but this is *exactly* who I am. The sooner you accept that, the better."

I can hasten the process by sharing that I bewitched Daeseong to confirm he was my father. I can tell her I'm capable of violating her in a terrifying way if it served my needs. Then . . . why don't I?

I don't want to lose her. I don't want to lose my friends.

"I can't move," the sneaky mudang suddenly yelps. The other shamans mimic her squirming and join in her panicked cries. "Why can't I move?"

Even Blondie strains against the invisible binds, careful not to jostle his head, and pales even more, until he resembles nonfat milk. Keeping my blade firmly against his throat, I aim an accusatory glare at Captain Seo.

"Still tempted to slaughter the lot?" The captain pierces me with a steely glance. She thinks I'm not far enough gone to kill helpless humans.

I'm not so sure about that.

I redirect my gaze to the fire-slinging mudang. He boasted about torturing a child to steal his elemental fire magic. He would've killed Draco without hesitation in Santorini if he'd had the chance. Rage burns in my stomach and rises up my throat, but I hiss out a long breath as the Shin'gwangdo trembles in my hand.

If I slit his throat, there will be no going back for me. *Who am I kidding?* It's probably already too late. But do I want to seal the deal for the fleeting satisfaction of ending this coward? Am I willing to erase even a shadow of hope?

I bare my teeth at the piece of trash in a savage snarl, and his khaki pants grow dark around his crotch. *Gods, he's pathetic.* My anger drains out of me. He makes me sick, but his irritating existence means nothing to me in the grand scheme of things.

"You're not worth it." I step back from him, withdrawing my sword, and glare at Captain Seo. "Happy now?"

She grunts. "What exactly about this situation do you think makes me happy?"

"Nothing." I'll give her that. "But I think I found a silver lining."

I don't know how. I just know.

Blondie flinches when I face him again, and I drawl, "You have something that doesn't belong to you, thief."

I close my eyes and summon a small white orb on my palm. A shuddering sigh escapes past my lips. The warmth of the white light soothes all the jagged edges of my shattered soul. The Yeoiju hums deep inside me. It doesn't hate me. It didn't leave me. Relief shivers through my body. I open my eyes, revealing the white fire I can feel burning in them.

"What are you doing, beast?" The corrupt mudang struggles against the captain's invisible binds.

I hold out my hand, and the light of the Yeoiju floats between us, pulsating and glowing bright. I call to the stolen elemental magic—a magic born of the Cheon'gwang—trapped inside the thief, suffocating in darkness.

The magic swirls to the surface of his body in tendrils of red gi, pooling at his torso, then surges out of his chest in a stream of fire. The mudang screams in outrage, thrashing against the binds, and a blood vessel bursts in his eye.

"It's my magic. It's mine," he shrieks, face contorting with outrage. "You can't take it. How are you doing this?"

The white orb expands, embracing the fire magic and its life force, and my heart beats in rhythm with it. The magic once belonged to a young girl, and I can feel the sorrow in her lingering life force.

"You are free," I rasp past a tight throat. In a burst of white light, the elemental magic and the poor girl's gi are released back to nature. "Be at peace."

I reabsorb the light of the Yeoiju and bank the white fire from my eyes. My friends stare at me, their faces frozen in shock—closer to delight for the historian. I clear my throat, and Minju clacks her mouth shut.

"We need to leave." She grabs the captain and me by our sleeves and drags us toward the door.

"How about if you take the captain and leave?" I tug my arm out of her hold. "I had no trouble staying hidden until you two came along."

"Are you sure about that?" Captain Seo digs her heels in, and Minju drops her arm with a sigh. "It only took a day for us to find you, and the Jaenanpa had to have been close by to drop in on us like this."

"Now that you have unleashed the Yeoiju, your magic is too powerful to hide." Minju lays a gentle hand on my shoulder. "You are not safe on your own. The Jaenanpa won't stop until they have your magic."

"You don't have to worry about me," I say gruffly, not shaking her hand off for some reason.

"We're more worried for the Jaenanpa," Captain Seo deadpans. "They have no idea who they're dealing with."

"Stop being funny." I scowl. "I am dangerously close to liking you."

I scrub my hands up and down my face, then shake my head like a dog drying its fur. I wish I had more margarita. Too bad I can't hide from reality forever, spewing pretty rainbow vomit.

I can't make myself regret freeing the girl's magic, but wielding my Yeoiju right now might not have been the wisest move. I just sent out a beacon to all the Jaenanpa and beings of the Shingae alike, broadcasting my location. More importantly, I've put my friends in danger with my recklessness.

Getting blissfully drunk can no longer be my primary objective. I need to keep Minju and Captain Seo alive. My inner turmoil can fucking wait its turn.

Time to flex my avoidance muscles with a side of compartmentalization.

"Let's go." I head out the door. "We have a plane to catch."

We could have flown anywhere. Nothing muddles magic like technology, and an airplane is a shit ton of technology. The destination doesn't matter as long as we're airborne in a hunk of human-created metal.

But we are flying to Korea. Are my seraphim companions planning to drag me back to the Realm of Four Kingdoms from there? To be fair, they would never drag me anywhere. They would probably ask me nicely. *Assholes.* It doesn't matter. I am focused *solely* on keeping them alive. I can't think about anything beyond that without frying my brain.

I don't even let myself regret leaving Ford without so much as a *see you later*. It's probably for the best I disappeared on him. I might already have put him in danger. I can't give the Jaenanpa any more reasons to connect him to me. I hope those thieving mudangs are too preoccupied with stealing my powers to concern themselves with a human bartender.

You're thinking. Stop it.

I cross my arms and sulk—salty that I didn't get the solo window seat. While it has the unfortunate side effect of making me look like a petulant child, glomming on to superficial feelings is much safer than behaving like a grown-up with an ever-increasing load of emotional baggage.

Captain Seo insisted we share the two seats in the middle row—first class, courtesy of the Suhoshin black card—because she continues to believe I am a flight risk. I roll my eyes for the tenth time. There is nowhere to run on an airplane—even a huge one like the Boeing 747—especially while it's flying thirty thousand feet above sea level. Is she afraid I'll lock myself in one of the tiny bathrooms?

Minju, the occupant of the coveted window seat, has her nose buried in a romance novel she bought at the airport bookstore. She hasn't looked outside her window once, but I can't work up the resentment to begrudge her the seat.

The historian is anxious to return to her tomes and scrolls in the Kingdom of Sky. She believes she can find a way to increase our chances of defeating the Amheuk, besides just throwing me at it. My Yeoiju and the Shin'gwangdo might be our best bet against the eternal darkness, but they won't be enough.

I won't be enough.

My avoidance muscles flex to shield me from further thoughts on . . . that. Anyway, I feel for Minju. Actively waiting for something is exhausting, nerve racking, and bone-achingly *tedious*. I'm glad she managed to lose herself in a book.

I catch a glimmer of metal from the corner of my eyes as Captain Seo slips out a shallow copper bowl from one of her dungaree pockets. Apparently, the captain and Minju moon shifted to Las Vegas, wearing a dobok and a hanbok, respectively. And they swiped their current outfits from a clothesline behind a trailer home on the outskirts of town to "blend in."

I didn't point out that neither attire helps them blend in. In her tiny white dress, Minju looks like an angel made for sin. And Captain Seo has no business looking that hot in freaking dungarees. Rather than blending in, the two of them attract more hungry eyes than is good for us.

Captain Seo sighs down at the bowl in her hands.

"What is that?" I ask.

"My cell phone," she answers glumly.

"Fine, don't tell me." I sniff, leaning into my spoiled-brat era. I play my role so well that I want to smack me on the back of my head. "I don't really want to know anyway."

"It is a small, sturdy bowl I can carry around." With another sigh, the captain tucks it back into her pocket. "It's difficult to communicate between the realms, but it is impossible without the moon's reflection."

"Like for moon shifting?" I cock my head to the side.

"To an extent, yes." She nods. "But when you moon shift, you leave the bowl behind. With a message, you don't shift away from it."

"The bowl is reusable, and you can carry it around." I grin, perking up a little. "Like a cell phone."

"Yes." The captain huffs a frustrated breath. "An incredibly inconvenient, unreliable cell phone."

Grown-up Sunny pokes her head out before I can stop her. "Did you tell Ethan you found me?"

"No." Captain Seo rubs her temples, not bothering to deny my assumption. Of course he sent her. She wouldn't have left his side unless he pulled rank on her. "We were rather busy with the Jaenanpa, weren't we?"

I don't even let myself *attempt* to decipher my reaction to her answer. That would be the opposite of focusing on surface emotions. It's bad enough I let myself think about him . . . even for a second. *Ethan.* My head buzzes and vibrates like a jack-in-the-box ready to pop.

"I'm hungry," I blurt, louder than necessary.

"I'm glad to hear you brought your appetite." The flight attendant chuckles, handing me an in-flight menu.

I blink in surprise as I accept the menu. He has impeccable timing, and I consider hugging him. *Thank you for saving me from grown-up Sunny.* But I settle for giving him a dazzling smile.

Only thanks to her lightning-fast reflexes, Captain Seo narrowly escapes being impaled in the eye by the sharp corner of a first-class menu. Pressing back into her seat, she gingerly takes her menu from the dazed flight attendant.

I turn off my smile, regretting my uncharacteristic behavior. And after a bumbling apology at the captain, the poor man makes his way down the aisle, glancing back at me every two steps.

"You should be careful where you flash that thing." Captain Seo's lips curl in wry amusement.

Her familiar teasing sends unwelcome warmth through me—warmth I mentally shove away. I don't want our friendship to thaw out my numb dissociation. I stare a hole into my menu and resolutely ignore her. But her considering gaze makes the side of my face prickle and itch.

I clench my jaw until my back teeth creak in protest. She wants to figure out what's wrong with me? *Fine.* Call me Lumière—because she can be my guest.

I sure as hell won't risk a catastrophic meltdown to figure it out myself, especially since there is no fixing me.

CHAPTER SIX

Ethan

I stare at the small bowl in the back corner of the dais, listening with half an ear to the generals and high officials gathered in the audience hall. They've been making the same argument on loop for over an hour.

Where are you, Sunny?

The stitches of my sanity are snapping one by one, every minute I'm apart from her. Yesterday, we received word from Captain Seo. *Found Minju. Daeseong dead.* A longer message would have been scrambled while crossing the realms, but the cryptic note made me want to punch my fist through the wall.

Why aren't Sunny and Draco with Minju? Why didn't the three of them come back once they killed the dark mudang?

"Enough," I growl. The officials standing before me have burned through what little remained of my patience. "I will not sit idly by while the enemy ravages my kingdom."

General Bak and his army from the Kingdom of Sky are raining down death and destruction everywhere their feet fall.

"Please withdraw your ire, Your Majesty," General Im intones. "Your humble servants only wish to protect you."

"We beg of you, Your Majesty," the generals and officials drone as one. "Please keep yourself safe."

"Am I to stand back and watch innocent people lose their homes, their farms, *their very lives*?" The arms of the throne creak under my grip. "Am I to do nothing? Is that what you are telling me? My father might have gladly hidden behind this throne, but I am not him."

"Forgive your humble servant." General Im drops to his knees and presses his forehead against the hardwood floor.

Then everyone joins in the fucking fun and falls to the ground. "Forgive your humble servant."

"Assemble the soldiers guarding the capital. I will ride out with them." I need to do something before I go mad. "And open the gates to Shinsi for those seeking refuge."

"But, Your Majesty, we cannot have you come to harm." General Im raises his head, eyes wide with panic. "We also cannot risk a security breach to Shinsi. The capital and its palace must not fall. They are the symbols of—"

When I slash my hand through the air, the general shuts his mouth so fast that his teeth clack together from the force. I breathe through my nose to get a grip on my anger.

"They will symbolize *nothing* if I stand by while the Kingdom of Sky annihilates my people." Frustration roars through me. *Why can't they understand?* "There is no Kingdom of Mountains without its people. I will fight to protect them."

"Your Majesty." Jihun breaks his silence next to me.

"If you say my place is on the throne," I snap at him in English, "I will kick your ass."

He raises his eyebrow by a millimeter, expressing his skepticism at my ability to kick his ass. My surprise elicits a bark of laughter out of me.

"I will ride by your side, Your Majesty." Jihun bows his head with restored deference.

"You . . . will?" This time, the surprise silences my laughter. "I mean . . . I am glad to hear it."

"We will not leave Shinsi unprotected, General," Jihun continues. "His Majesty will lead a battalion to the front lines, but the rest of your division may remain and protect the capital."

"As you say, Lord Adviser," General Im says with a resigned sigh.

Lord Adviser? I arch a brow at Jihun. He gives me a nearly imperceptible shrug. I guess we're rolling with it. It's no secret he's my right-hand man. Besides, there is no one else in all the realms I would rather have as my royal adviser.

"Now that we are in agreement"—I hold General Im's gaze until he fidgets—"shall we discuss strategy?"

"Of course, Your Majesty." He bows low.

"Good." *Thank the fucking gods* is more like it. I am drowning in helplessness. There is nothing I can do to keep Sunny safe from here, but I will do everything in my power to protect my people. "Generals, you may remain, but the rest of you are dismissed. I entrust every one of you with the care of our people."

"If I may, Your Majesty." One official—Lord Song, I believe—steps forward. I nod for him to proceed. "It is an honor to serve a king who encourages us to help our people, rather than punish us for it."

The rest of the high officials murmur and nod in agreement. I swallow thickly. My father might have been a greedy, despicable king, but the core of the Kingdom of Mountains's government remains just.

"While it is highly irregular for a king to risk his life on the battlefield, we will pray for your safe return." Lord Song presses his lips into a determined line. "And we will follow your example and do our best to put the needs of our people ahead of our own."

"It is my honor to lead this kingdom with you," I say with solemn sincerity. "With every one of you."

"We are not worthy, Your Majesty," the officials cry in unison, bowing deeply from their waists.

I didn't mean to trigger more bowing. I shoot a panicked glance at Jihun. The corners of his mouth curve for a split second.

"Thank you for your service, my lords." He diplomatically urges the high officials to depart. "The royal guards will be available to assist you with any preparations."

As they file out of the audience hall, the officials quietly discuss opening up their grain storage to feed the hungry. I could do with a little less bowing and platitudes, but they are good people. I hardly know them, but they have already made me proud. And now it's my turn to make them proud.

I beckon Jihun, and he leans close. "I gather General Im is the one in charge of defending the capital?"

"Yes, Shinsi and the rest of the southwest quadrant." His lips barely move.

"Thanks." After flashing him a sheepish grin, I arrange my expression into stern lines and turn my attention to the three generals in front of me. "General Im, I may not be well versed in warfare, but I do not expect you to throw open every gate to Shinsi all at once."

The general sags with relief, and I come *this close* to rolling my eyes. The male must think I'm either hopelessly unintelligent or utterly irrational.

"I will leave the specifics of protecting the southwest quadrant up to you," I continue in my most reasonable voice, "but you will accept as many refugees as you can, without unduly risking the capital."

"And General . . . ?" I cock my head at a wiry young male, who could be anywhere between twenty-four and two hundred forty.

"My family name is Jo, Your Majesty," he promptly supplies.

"General Jo, I received reports that your troops are overstretched."

"Yes, Your Majesty." He nods grimly. "My division defends the northwest quadrant, but we have deployed more than half of our soldiers to the northeast. The Kingdom of Sky invaded through the portal between the kingdoms, which lies in the easternmost region of that quadrant."

"Did our portal keepers survive the invasion?" I interrupt.

"They killed the keeper on duty as soon as they crossed over. Our remaining keeper tried to reach the portal to seal it off, but too many enemy soldiers had already come through, and Keeper Yoon couldn't make it past them." General Jo exhales through his nose. "Our soldiers managed to rescue her before the enemy killed her, too, but we do not know whether she will recover from her injuries."

"Please keep us apprised of Keeper Yoon's progress, General." My brows dip into a frown. "But going back, you deployed more than half of your soldiers to the northeast quadrant, leaving your quadrant vulnerable. Why so many? Is the northeastern division so outnumbered that they cannot hold their ground against the enemy?"

Has my grandfather amassed forces too great for us to defeat?

"Yes . . . and no," General Jo replies as the other generals exchange uneasy glances. "The northeast quadrant has the biggest military unit in the Kingdom of Mountains, but the division was led by General Shin."

"Since General Shin has been captured and imprisoned for leading the insurrection"—I pinch the bridge of my nose—"the northeastern division has no direct leadership."

"Regretfully, no." General Jo breathes a weary sigh. "The soldiers who aided General Shin in the insurrection are either dead or imprisoned, and those who refused to join him are scattered throughout the kingdom."

"In other words, our primary military unit—and our first point of defense—is in shambles." Then I mutter under my breath, "Talk about a perfect shitstorm."

"The majority of the enemy's forces are marching straight for Shinsi, cutting across the northeast quadrant toward the southwest quadrant," General Jo continues. "Our troops are doing their best to slow the enemy's progress, but we are quickly losing ground."

"General Hong, Your Majesty." A tall, broad male steps forward and executes a sharp bow. "I command the southeastern division. I have sent five thousand soldiers to the northeast quadrant, but, unfortunately, I cannot spare any more because . . . May I approach the throne?"

"Your Majesty?" Jihun asks, even as he gives me a minute nod to communicate his assent. He trusts these generals, and if need be, he could take down all three without breaking a sweat.

"Approach, General Hong," I say with a sardonic glance at my royal adviser.

Coming to stand next to Jihun, General Hong unrolls a map of the Kingdom of Mountains and holds it out for both of us to see.

"We found signs of an enemy brigade approaching the southeast quadrant from the north." He traces a finger in a half circle from the top right of the kingdom to the bottom right. Then he repeats the movement on the left half. "We anticipate additional combat brigades to move around the western outskirts of the Kingdom of Mountains to launch a coordinated attack on the capital."

"I wouldn't expect anything less from General Bak." My hands fist on the throne. "He would have all grounds covered."

"With our remaining troops, General Jo and I must defend the northwest and southeast quadrants to prevent Shinsi from being hit from every direction," General Hong continues. "But the northeast quadrant remains our weakest point."

My brows furrow into a frown. "Would the enemy forces be able to moon shift past our defenses?"

"It is difficult to moon shift in mass numbers, but dividing their units risks weakening their forces," the general explains patiently. "Furthermore, it is too dangerous to moon shift into a hostile territory without knowing what awaits them on the other side."

"That makes sense." I'm in way over my head. My mortal college education didn't cover magical warfare. "Thank you, General."

I resist the urge to drag my hand down my face, and I push aside the wave of uncertainty. I can't afford to be embarrassed by my inexperience. I have a lot to learn, but I have the generals and Jihun by my side. I am not fighting this war alone.

Unlike Sunny.

The quiet accusation lands on me like an anvil, and my lungs seize up, cutting off my air supply. I promised her we'd face whatever lies ahead together. I promised her she would not be alone. My heart screams at me to run to her. I don't know how much longer I can resist its plea.

My gaze drifts back to the bowl. *Come back to me, Sunny.* I close my eyes and exhale a long, slow breath. She will come. We are bound by the threads of fate. I feel it in the depth of my soul. We *will* be together again.

For now, I must focus on what I can control.

"Generals, where am I needed most?" I shoot my palm out when General Im opens his mouth. "Where can I be of the most use *in the battlefield*?"

"You are most needed in the northeast quadrant, Your Majesty." Despite General Im's death glare, General Jo continues staunchly, "It is where the fighting is the fiercest, and the morale is the lowest. And perhaps, with you there, the soldiers dispersed by General Shin's revolt will return to fight at your side."

"Then that is where I'll go." My tone brooks no argument.

I am done watching people die for me. It is long past time I protected my people . . . even if it means taking down my own grandfather.

CHAPTER SEVEN

Sunny

Captain Seo, Minju, and I land in Korea just before sunset. I'm proud of myself for eating and sleeping my way through a thirteen-hour flight without once thinking about anything more complicated than chicken or beef.

And the captain let me. In fact, she doesn't poke and prod me, neither literally nor figuratively, even *after* we get off the plane. Maybe she gave up on trying to figure out what happened to me. I shrink in on myself. Or maybe she thinks I'm beyond help. I shrink even smaller.

I don't give a fuck.

Besides, this situation has a calm-before-the-storm vibe. The captain doesn't give up on anything. A slow, dull ache spreads in my chest. Even if I give up on myself, she won't give up on me.

Stop it, Sunny. Hope is stupid.

Once we step out of the hectic bustle of the airport, the three of us move faster and talk less. Without the protection of the airplane, we're fair game for anyone who wants to track us.

I wave down a taxi. When a middle-aged woman cuts in front of me as though she has every right to *my* taxi, I shoulder her away. After a brief tussle, the ajumma scoffs at me in affront and immediately cuts in front of a sucker who doesn't know any better.

While I indulge in a smug grin, Captain Seo gets into the front seat of the taxi *I* hailed before I can call shotgun. *Who's the sucker now?* Grumbling under my breath, I shuffle in after Minju into the back seat.

"Eurwangni Beach, please," the historian promptly tells the driver.

I don't ask how she knows the closest beach to Incheon International. *Whatever.* I shouldn't be surprised by her vast knowledge of . . . well, everything. *But why Eurwangni Beach?* I shrug and go along for the ride. As long as the two seonnyeos do nothing to interfere with my one and only objective of keeping them alive, then I officially do not care.

Moreover, I heard Eurwangni Beach has a killer seafood restaurant right by the water. They grill fresh clams and scallops over lump charcoal until the shells open to reveal the tender meat inside, bubbling in their juices. Saliva pools in my mouth just imagining the sweet, briny goodness.

Captain Seo pays for our fare with the black card, and we get off the taxi at the beach. The sun hovers just above the horizon, casting a shimmering stretch of golden light across the water. We don't speak for a long moment, entranced by the beautiful sunset.

"Today is Hangawi," Minju murmurs, breaking the melancholy silence.

"Really?" My eyes widen, and butterflies flutter in my stomach. "We should eat some songpyeon for good health."

First of all, I love the sweet, half moon–shaped rice cakes. Second, I haven't celebrated Mid-Autumn Festival in over a hundred years, and a small, often unheeded part of me misses the holiday that celebrates family and abundance.

"Okay." Minju smiles distractedly. "We have quite a bit of time until the road turns silver."

"Until the what turns what?" I ask, exchanging a bewildered glance with the captain.

But the historian doesn't answer and crosses the street toward a row of single-story structures facing the beach. My gaze snags on a small hut that stands sandwiched between two modern buildings, looking woefully out of place.

When Minju heads straight for it, the captain and I jog across the street to catch up with her. The hut appears to be a restaurant, and from the delicious smells wafting through the windows, a very good one.

"Huh." A smile quirks Captain Seo's lips. "The restaurant is your namesake."

The sign outside the hut says, **Minju Ne**, which means "Minju's Place" in Korean.

"All the stores are probably closed for Hangawi . . ." I trail off when Minju pushes open the restaurant's door and walks right in. "Okey dokey then."

"After you," the captain says with a sweep of her arm.

I step past her with a mocking bow but come to an abrupt stop. "Whoa."

Minju stands in the middle of the restaurant, embraced by two strangers—a tall, broad man and a diminutive woman, both middle aged and exceptionally attractive. And the three of them are weeping elegantly—tears falling silently down their cheeks with no snot in sight.

"You're blocking the way." Captain Seo nudges me to the side and walks inside the restaurant. "Whoa."

I don't care. I don't care. I don't—

"What the hell is happening?" I croak. *Damn it. I care. But only to the extent of keeping my friends alive.* "Minju, do you know these people?"

"I do." The historian steps back from the strangers, sniffing delicately. "They're my parents."

"Guh." My brain vibrates with curiosity, but I shut that nonsense down. All I have to know is whether her parents will kill us or not. Anything else will get me too close to giving a fuck.

I focus my magic gi goggles on them. Minju's mother glows with the vibrant red gi of Underworld—a dokkaebi. As for her father, I don't need to see his silver gi, the life force of Sky, to know he's a seonnam. His exquisite bone structure is a dead giveaway.

Her mother takes out a handkerchief from the apron tied around her waist and dabs away the tears on Minju's face, while her father watches the scene with a heartbreakingly tender expression. I blink away an inexplicable tear, clearing my throat.

Okay. They probably won't kill us.

"Nice to meet you, Mr. and Mrs. Ha." Captain Seo, with her fully functioning brain, bows respectfully from her waist. It seems like a good idea so I mimic her. Just because I care about nothing doesn't mean I have to be disrespectful to Minju's parents.

"Are you friends of our darling daughter?" Mrs. Ha doesn't give us a chance to respond and pulls us into a hug, one in each arm. She is surprisingly strong for someone so small—not that I'm much taller.

Before I can force myself to squirm out of her embrace, she drops her arms and steps back from us. "Oh my. What am I thinking? You girls must be hungry."

Again, we don't get a chance to object as she bustles away and disappears into what I assume is the kitchen. In the brief lull, I study the small restaurant with round eyes—to scope out a potential escape route, of course. I don't actually care about any of it.

The walls are covered with rustic hanji, and a menu, handwritten on a wood plank, hangs on one side. The simple wooden tables and chairs crowding the front hall add a perfectly haphazard and cozy feel to the quintessential mom-and-pop restaurant. It's so *human*. I can't believe two shinbiins run this place.

"Come sit down. Please." Minju's father beckons us to a table close to the kitchen. He grabs three paper cups from a neat stack at the corner of the table and pours cold roasted-barley tea into them. "You, too, daughter. Rest your feet while I go help your mother."

"It seems like they were expecting us." Captain Seo sits down with her gaze trailing after Mr. Ha's retreating back. "How did they know?"

"They were expecting *me*." Minju tugs me down next to her and faces the captain. "I visit my parents every year on Hangawi."

"Wow, what a coincidence." I bite my lip, because it can't be a happy one.

Minju must be exhausted from tracking me down. Not to mention everything that happened before I ran away to Las Vegas. And now, we're on the run from the Jaenanpa because of me.

"I'm sorry I ruined your visit," I whisper.

"You did nothing of the sort. If it weren't for you, I would still be in the Realm of Four Kingdoms." She squeezes my hand over my lap. "Besides, I'm glad my parents finally get to meet some of my friends."

"It's an honor to meet them." Captain Seo tilts her head to the side. "Did your parents come to the Mortal Realm so they could be together?"

Her loaded question is characteristically efficient. With one sentence, she conveys that she recognized Mr. Ha as a seonnam and Mrs. Ha as a dokkaebi and she understands their union is forbidden under the Code of the Realm—beings of two different life sources cannot marry. And with her lack of censure, she reassures Minju that she's not passing judgment in any way.

That's impressive, even for the captain.

"My mother was a suhoshin stationed in the Kingdom of Sky when she met my father. They fell in love and married in secret." Minju stares down at her hands. "They kept their secret safe for over two centuries . . . then I came along. They couldn't risk anyone finding out that I'm of both Sky and Underworld, because they wanted me to have a normal life in the Realm of Four Kingdoms." She sighs heavily. "My parents came to the Mortal Realm to protect me."

"They just left you behind? All by yourself?" I accuse. Being together matters so much more than *normal*. It could never be worth the cost of being alone. "Why couldn't they bring you with them?"

"Living in the Realm of Four Kingdoms is her birthright." Mrs. Ha steps out of the kitchen with a tray laden with a feast, but her expression is grim. "We couldn't take that away from her."

"What's so great about the Realm of Four Kingdoms?" I persist. "What's more important than family?"

"Life," Mr. Ha says, coming to stand next to his wife. "If shinbiins leave the Realm of Four Kingdoms, they become mortal."

CHAPTER EIGHT

Sunny

My mouth drops open. "What?"

"It's true." Minju's mother walks the rest of the way over to our table. "When shinbiins live in the Mortal Realm for long enough, they begin to age at the same rate as humans."

I want to ask why that happens but hold my tongue because it's starting to feel too much like caring about shit.

"We fall to illness, and it takes time for us to heal from our injuries." Mr. Ha transfers the plates from the tray until food covers every inch of the tabletop. "We couldn't force such a fragile, fleeting life on our daughter."

"But it would be worth it to be with you," Minju whispers, making her parents gasp.

"What are you saying?" Her father shakes his head.

"Once all this is over, I'm coming here to live with you." She juts her chin. "This is Minju's Place, after all."

Her mother opens and closes her mouth several times, twin grooves forming between her brows. "Let me start with this question. What do you mean, *all this*? Once what's over?"

The historian pales, her bravado draining out of her, and her panicked gaze jumps to meet mine.

"You should tell them." I take her hand under the table. "Your parents chose mortality for you. They have a right to know."

If Minju goes back to the Realm of Four Kingdoms to fight the Amheuk, she might not live to see the next Hangawi. *Hell.* None of us might.

"The Kingdom of Sky has waged war against the Kingdom of Mountains." Minju starts with the less horrifying part of *all this*, but her parents' eyes widen with horror regardless.

"To stop the tyrant?" her mother whispers.

"No, a new king has taken the throne." Minju smiles faintly. "The true heir to the Kingdom of Mountains."

"The Queen of Mountains's son?" Her father gasps. "The King Foretold?"

Captain Seo, Minju, and I gasp in return.

"How do you know about the King Foretold?" the captain demands, then remembers her manners. "That is . . . could you tell me how you know about the King Foretold, Mr. Ha?"

"The same way we found out about a secret group sworn to serve him." Mrs. Ha clicks her tongue when Captain Seo chokes on her saliva. She sits next to the captain and pats her back until she stops coughing. "Gossip, child."

"Gossip?" A vein pulses on the captain's forehead, her patience waning. "What gossip? Please explain, Mrs. Ha."

"Don't fret." Minju pats Captain Seo's white-knuckled fist, lying on top of the table. "They'll explain everything. Just give them time to get there."

"Your parents give convoluted answers that jump all over the place?" I snort. "I didn't know that was a family trait."

"Oh hush." Minju crinkles her nose at me.

"We only recently found out about the prophecy of the King Foretold." Mr. Ha pulls up a chair for himself at the short end of the table and takes a seat. "The Queen of Mountains was a legendary diviner, but there are diviners here in the Mortal Realm as well."

"All of them have been bombarded with the same prophecies these last few months." Mrs. Ha seamlessly picks up where her husband left off. "The beings of the Shingae in the Mortal Realm are a tightly knit group. We watch each other's backs and share information."

But my mother and I were always alone . . . It doesn't matter. Nothing matters. *Why do I keep forgetting that?*

"Ah yes." Captain Seo huffs a tired laugh. "Gossip."

"Exactly." Minju's mother punctuates her word with her index finger in the air. "The best source of intel."

Wait. My face scrunches up in confusion. *Did she say* prophecies? *There's more than one prophecy?* I shake my head to dislodge the pesky question. I. Don't. Care.

"Well?" Mr. Ha glances between the three of us.

"*Well*, what?" I blink at the distinguished seonnam, the whole not-caring thing taking a toll on me.

"Is the Queen of Mountains's son truly the King Foretold?" Mrs. Ha answers for her husband. It's like the two of them share a hive mind.

"Yes," I say simply. When Captain Seo and Minju look at me with twin expressions of affront, I shrug. "What's the point of keeping it a secret? The diviners in the Realm of Four Kingdoms must have seen the prophecy as well. Everyone will find out soon enough, if they don't already know."

"The point is we must keep the king safe at all costs. The realm needs him for the fight against the Amheuk—" The captain catches herself and claps a hand over her mouth. So much for delivering the horrifying news gently.

I halt the direction of my thoughts. *What horrifying news? I do not know of what you speak.*

"The Amheuk?" Mr. Ha bolts to his feet, his chair screeching against the floor, and plants his palms on the table with a loud thwack.

"Oh yes," Minju murmurs sheepishly. "That's the other part of *all this*. The Amheuk has breached the Realm of Four Kingdoms."

La la la la la, I shout in my head, *I can't hear you.*

Her mother makes a choked sound as her hand flies to her throat. “You are definitely staying with us. A fragile, fleeting life is better than certain death.”

“Mother.” Minju puffs a small sigh. “I will come live with you *after* all this is over. For now, my place is in the Realm of Four Kingdoms.”

“Your place is—” Mrs. Ha’s words come to an abrupt stop when her husband places his hand on her shoulder.

“Yeobo,” he says, “we didn’t raise our daughter to turn her back on the people who need her.”

“But . . .” Mrs. Ha’s bottom lip trembles.

“You know she won’t be safe here for long.” He gently cups his wife’s cheek. “The Amheuk will not be satisfied with conquering the Realm of Four Kingdoms. The Mortal Realm will be next unless it is stopped.”

My heart pounds at every pulse point. I don’t want to hear this—to face this. I want to tear off my skin. I want to disappear. I don’t want to save the worlds. I can’t choose to be good. *I can’t.* I’m no good.

Don’t think, Sunny. Stop thinking.

“You’re right, yeobo.” Minju’s mother presses her lips into a firm line. “We should be helping her, not holding her back.”

“And we will help.” Mr. Ha looks around the table with a determined smile. “But first, let’s celebrate Hangawi with our daughter and her friends.”

Thank gods.

My avoidance muscles were beginning to cramp from the strain. A short reprieve from the tension sounds like heaven.

“Yes.” With a matching smile, Mrs. Ha mimes putting food into her mouth. “Please eat. There’s plenty more in the kitchen.”

“There’s *more*?” Captain Seo squawks in surprise.

I can see why the captain’s iron composure cracked. The table is filled with japchae, jeon, galbi jjim, and a dozen different banchans. And our rice bowls are piled so high that they’re shaped like long capsules.

I’ll worry about *all this* later. Or maybe never. *Never* sounds like a better plan.

For now, I'm going to stuff my face with extraordinary amounts of homemade food. I go for the japchae first. It's my number one favorite food. Soy sauce, garlic, and toasted sesame oil coat each strand of bouncy vermicelli. And the strips of marinated beef and the rainbow of sautéed vegetables—spinach, carrots, shiitake mushrooms, and onions—are perfectly seasoned. Every bite of japchae explodes in my mouth in a symphony of flavors and textures.

"It tastes just like how my mother used to make it," I whisper.

Before sentimental tears sting my eyes, I grab a giant piece of braised short rib and bite into it. The meat falls off the bone and melts in my mouth. I nearly moan from the richness of the galbi jjim and the burst of umami flavor. Then I make sure to taste each kind of jeon—bites of egg-battered fish, oysters, and gray squash, pan-fried to a golden brown—dipped in a tart, sweet, and nutty seasoned soy sauce.

These foods transport me back to my childhood, where I took love, comfort, and safety for granted. And sharing this Hangawi table with my friends is a privilege I don't deserve but will cherish forever.

I manage to swallow past my tight throat, thanks to the savory beef and taro soup. *Focus on the food, Sunny.* I take my own advice and eat like there's no tomorrow. *Shit. Bad choice of words.* I ignore the slip and clean off the last grain of rice in my bowl.

Mrs. Ha looks at my bowl and smiles. "My cooking wasn't to your liking?"

"This is the best meal I've had in a century." I grin back at her. I might have secretly unbuttoned my jeans in the middle of the feast.

"I have to agree with Sunny." Captain Seo leans back in her seat with a hand over her flat stomach. "This was amazing. Thank you so much, Mr. and Mrs. Ha."

Mr. Ha doesn't respond right away, his gaze turned toward the night beyond the windows. "Oh, yes. Of course. We are so happy to meet Minju's friends. It would've been unthinkable for us to send you off on your journey without filling your stomachs first."

"We will definitely need the energy." Minju exchanges a loaded glance with her father.

"Girls, can you help me clear the table while Minju chats with her father?" Mrs. Ha asks in a shaky voice, standing from the table.

"Please sit down, Mrs. Ha." Captain Seo bolts to her feet and jerks her chin at me. I struggle to my feet, feeling like I ate my weight in food. "You've already done too much. We will take care of cleaning up."

"That's lovely of you to suggest." She piles empty dishes onto a metal tray. "But I won't understand a word of what they're talking about. That's what happens when both your husband and your daughter are renowned scholars."

My gaze shoots toward Minju and Mr. Ha, who have already moved to a corner table near the front of the restaurant. They bend their heads toward each other as they speak in low voices, their faces shining with twin expressions of passionate curiosity and determination. Whatever lies ahead, they will consider every possibility and make sure we're as ready for it as we will ever be.

We? Who is this we?

"Please promise to stand back and tell us what to do," I concede to Mrs. Ha. "The captain and I'll do all the work."

"You girls are very sweet." Mrs. Ha puts one last plate on the tray and clasps her unsteady hands in front of her. "Come this way."

Picking up the tray full of dirty dishes, I follow the older female into the kitchen and get to work. I haven't washed dishes since we—I course correct my thought—since *I* left Las Vegas the night the red assassin attacked me in my apartment. The rush of warm water, the soft suds, and the clack of plates and saucers soothes the open wound inside me, like a cool hand on a feverish forehead.

I pass a clean dish to the captain, and she dries it, frowning down at her hands with intense concentration. It's adorable. She's a warrior with zero experience in domestic endeavors. I tuck my chin to hide my smile and slow down with the washing so she doesn't feel rushed.

Mrs. Ha is quiet as she puts the clean, dry dishes into the cupboards. I can't see her face, but her shoulders droop as though an aching sadness weighs them down. The coming of the Amheuk will do that to a person. But I have a feeling her worries are more immediate.

What exactly are Minju and her father talking about that has Mrs. Ha so scared?

When all the dishes are cleared away, the three of us step out from the kitchen. Minju looks up and gives the captain and me a solemn nod, but she avoids her mother's eyes. My stomach tightens with nerves. I'm worried for my friends, especially since I won't be going with them.

How will they get back to the Realm of Four Kingdoms? The question sneaks past my firewall before I can stop it. *Shit.* Now I can't unthink it, and more questions rush into my consciousness.

Does the Amheuk still lie in wait at the entrance to the Realm of Four Kingdoms? Or has the darkness already seeped inside the realm? Is everyone . . . okay?

I reach behind me for a handhold as the corners of my vision darken. *Oh gods.* My frantic fingers feel the back of a chair, and I grip it tightly.

Are you okay, Ethan? Please be safe.

The sound of Mr. Ha's chair scraping across the floor jolts me back to the present before I spiral out of control. Minju gets to her feet as well and switches places with her mother, so the three of us face her parents. She slips her cold hand into mine, and I squeeze it without thinking.

"Girls," Mr. Ha says in a voice that reminds me of Optimus Prime, "are you ready to walk the moonglade?"

CHAPTER NINE

Sunny

Mrs. Ha claps a hand over her mouth to silence her sob, and Minju's hand tightens around mine until my bones creak in protest. I hold back a wince with gargantuan effort, but after five long seconds, I squirm in pain.

"What is the moonglade?" Captain Seo asks warily.

Thankfully, Minju drops my hand and answers, "Every year on Hangawi, when the harvest moon hangs low in the sky, a silver road appears in the ocean."

"Isn't that just an elongated reflection of the moon?" I flex my hand to make sure none of my fingers are broken.

Mr. Ha smiles at my question. "On any other day, yes."

"But it becomes more than that on Hangawi." Minju wanders away from us to pace the length of the small restaurant. "When people all around Korea celebrate under the brightest full moon of the year, their joy and gratitude imbue the moon's reflection with more power."

"What kind of power?" I try to wrap my head around a magic road in the ocean.

I am a being of the Shingae. Magic isn't new to me. But some of the things I've had to come to terms with these last few months have been wild, even for me.

"The moon's reflection becomes real . . . in a way." She stops pacing to search for words. "It solidifies into a silver road for beings of the Shingae."

"Where does it lead?" Icy dread tickles down my spine. I have a feeling I know the answer.

"To the Realm of Four Kingdoms." Minju resumes pacing.

But why do we need to walk the moonglade to get back to the realm? A faint moan slips past my lips because I know the answer to that as well.

"Why have I never heard of this?" The captain shakes her head, her mouth slightly agape.

"It is an ancient magic, forgotten by many." Mr. Ha sighs wistfully, as though saddened by the loss of any knowledge.

"And also, because no one dares to walk the silver road," Minju adds.

I cinch my lips together. I don't want to know.

But Captain Seo opens her big mouth. "Why is that?"

"We don't know." The historian cringes. "There are no recorded accounts of anyone who survived the walk across the moonglade."

Damn it all to fucking hell.

"So those are our options," the captain says grimly. "Fight our way past the Amheuk to enter the Realm of Four Kingdoms. Or walk across the moonglade, which no one has ever survived?"

A high-pitched ringing pierces my ears, and I clasp the sides of my head.

"Please, daughter." Rushing to her side, Mrs. Ha grabs both of Minju's hands. "This is suicide. Give us time. Your father and I will think of another way."

"Time is the one thing I cannot give you." Minju pulls her mother into a hug. "Besides, just because no one ever made it across does not mean we won't."

"She's right, yeobo." Mr. Ha wraps his arms around both females, heartbreak and hope warring on his face. "They have better odds of making it across the moonglade than getting past the Amheuk."

The walls I've built around my mind shatter, and my knees buckle. I reach for a chair at my side and try to sink into it, but I miss the seat and fall on my ass, bringing the chair crashing down with me.

Some things I'd forgotten in the endless struggle to stay alive. While others I'd deliberately pushed to the back of my mind because it was . . . too much. But there is no more hiding from the shitstorm *I* set in motion.

It's all my fault.

"Sunny." Captain Seo reaches my side in a split second. "What's wrong?"

Minju grasps my arm from the other side. "Are you okay?"

"Is the Amheuk still hovering at the entrance to the Realm of Four Kingdoms?" I ask in a trembling voice, as my friends help me to my feet.

"Yes, it is." The historian absently turns me around and dusts off my ass. I'm not a toddler, but I'm too wrecked to protest.

"I made it into the Mortal Realm seconds before the Amheuk reached the entrance." The captain shudders. "I flew faster than I'd ever flown to get away from it and landed way off base. But even from gods know where, I could see it coiled in the sky beneath the Realm of Four Kingdoms."

"That's why we can only return to the realm by walking the moonglade." I glance between Minju and her father for confirmation.

"I'm afraid so," Mr. Ha says. "There is no other way."

"But what is the Amheuk waiting for?" This time I look behind me to make sure I don't miss the chair and sit down before my legs give out. "Why hasn't it invaded the Realm of Four Kingdoms yet?"

"Our best deduction is that it is recuperating," Mr. Ha answers. "We don't know how it escaped from its prison beyond the abyss, but it must have depleted its powers doing so."

"Ah." I nod and . . . nod.

"The Amheuk is not without limits." Captain Seo holds my gaze. "That means it can be destroyed."

I stop nodding because I'm getting dizzy. I do my best to pull myself together and ask, "How long do we have?"

We? *Why do I keep saying* we?

"There is no way of knowing." Frustration laces Minju's words. She hates not knowing the answer. "But I think it's safe to assume that we don't have much longer."

"Then we better get on with it and walk the moonglade," I mutter. "Whatever the hell that means."

There I go with the we *again.*

My knees bounce haphazardly like drops of water on a sizzling pan. I thought I wanted to stay the hell away from all of this. But how can I turn my back on the Realm of Four Kingdoms when *I* put it in danger?

I can't run from this anymore. *I* destroyed the Gray Void. I flinch at the thought, but I grit my teeth and face the stark truth. I didn't understand it at the time. I was only trying to survive the Gray Void as it tried to annihilate the dark magic from the ancient rune on my back.

I would have died, but the light of the Yeoiju saved me from being torn in half by the dark magic and the Gray Void. Even though I didn't know how to wield the Yeoiju yet, it eradicated the word of power from my body. But somehow, the white light also destroyed the Gray Void, the only thing that stood between the realm and the endless dark.

I am responsible for the destruction of the Gray Void. I signed the death warrant for everyone I hold dear within it.

My knees stop bouncing, but my insides continue quaking. I wrap my arms around my midriff, resisting the urge to rock back and forth on the chair. I can't regret freeing the stranded from their prison. But was it worth endangering the lives of everyone I care about? I don't know. I'm glad I didn't have to make a conscious decision in that moment.

But those stranded souls . . . There were so many of them, all of them *suffering*. Why were they trapped in the Gray Void in the first place? I shake my head. It doesn't matter. I know in my gut I did the right thing. Now I just need to clean up the mess I created.

Too bad I have no idea how.

I sink my teeth into my bottom lip and tighten my arms around my stomach. Whatever darkness lies within me, I also bear the light of the Yeoiju. It stayed with me even though I am the literal spawn of the devil. And it didn't leave me when I bewitched and killed said devil.

I don't believe the Yeoiju stayed with me because I'm deserving of its light. Maybe it didn't abandon me because I have some uses left. I am not worthy of Ethan—the pain hits me like a rib-shattering punch—and I'm not worthy of my friends.

But . . . what if I can still protect them?

It won't change who I am. That doesn't matter. Besides, it might be better that I'm no good because now I can do *anything* to keep them safe. Since I can never deserve them, nothing will hold me back from playing dirty. Yet something inside me recoils from the thought.

As my panic recedes bit by bit, I notice the somber silence in the restaurant, each of us lost in our thoughts.

"It's time." Mr. Ha sighs, looking out the window at the moonlit night.

"I . . . Please give me five minutes," Captain Seo blurts and hurries out of the restaurant with a fleeting glance my way.

She's sending a message to Ethan.

I jump to my feet and chase after the captain. I catch up to her just as she reaches the beach. She takes out the copper bowl from her dungarees and walks to the edge of the water. She returns to my side with the bowl halfway filled, then kneels on the sand. I wordlessly drop to my knees beside her.

Captain Seo gathers a small mound of sand in her palm and pours it into the bowl. Then she positions the bowl of water and sand in front of her so it catches the full moon on its surface. She pulls out a rumpled square of paper along with a stubby pencil. I make out the word *casino* etched on the side of the pencil, but her fingers hide which one she nabbed it from.

"What are you going to say?" The soft breeze carries away my whisper.

Why am I setting myself up for heartbreak?

"Very little." The captain sighs and glances at me with eyes full of sympathy. "Like I said, communicating between the realms is difficult and unreliable. Anything more than a few words will become jumbled, making the whole message incomprehensible."

I can only nod, because my pounding heart is lodged in my throat. Captain Seo smooths out the small piece of paper on her thigh and writes carefully on it so the pencil doesn't rip through the paper. I don't look away even as tears sting my eyes.

Found Sunny. Coming back.

"I can't go back to the Kingdom of Mountains," I choke out.

"I know. Minju told me. I meant we're coming back to the Realm of Four Kingdoms." She lays the piece of paper on top of her palm. "We will explain everything to him once we get there."

I'm not sure I want to explain any of it, but I keep that to myself—as well as the fact that I can't decide whether to go to the Realm of Four Kingdoms with them or not. I have no idea what I'm going to do.

The captain closes her eyes and speaks an incantation under her breath. The note levitates off her palm and floats over the bowl. She continues the soft chant until the paper combusts in a burst of silver flames, leaving behind an afterimage of the message in the air. Then the silvery traces of the words sink into the water and disappear.

Did the message find Ethan on the other side of the abyss? I wish I could chase after the words and reach his side in my next breath. I miss him so much. I feel hollow—like every essential organ inside me is gone. I am empty without him.

For the first time, I let myself think about how Ethan must have felt when I left him to chase after Daeseong—how he must feel not knowing what happened to me. I close my eyes as my throat and chest tighten painfully.

I almost lost my mind when he disappeared from the mountain cave with the yellow assassin. Not knowing he was safe almost wrecked me. He must feel the same way—desperate, helpless, scared.

I'm sorry, Ethan.

The message will at least reassure him that I'm safe. I hope that will be enough for now.

CHAPTER TEN

Ethan

We ride at the back of the battalion at Jihun's insistence. Although impatience crawls over my skin, my royal adviser made the right call. After hours on horseback, every muscle in my body screams with pain. I would never have been able to keep up at the front of the line.

Yet I am strangely comforted by my limitations.

The gi of Mountains floods me with power. I am invincible. But all this might and magic feel too big for my body. And the normalcy of sore muscles quietens the dissonance within me. No matter how immense my powers—I stretch my back with a groan—I cannot last on this horse much longer.

I am still me.

"Don't get me wrong," I murmur to my horse, as though he overheard my inner musings. He's a beautiful animal, muscular and sleek with a brown coat so rich that it almost looks black. "You're an impressive warhorse. My body just needs to get accustomed to riding on your back for hours on end."

The horse neighs in reassurance, and I pat his neck and glance up at the darkening sky. When I hear the gallop of another horse approaching, I straighten in my saddle.

"We made good progress." Jihun reins in his ride to trot beside me and points at a line of trees ahead of us. "We'll set up camp for the night in that forest."

"Got it," I say casually, holding back a hoot of relief. Even sleeping on the cold ground sounds like heaven at this point.

Jihun covers his almost smirk with a cough. "Your tent should be ready by the time you arrive."

"My tent?" My brows draw together. "Will the soldiers be sleeping in tents?"

"No." He shakes his head once. "The rest of us will sleep under the stars. We need to be prepared to mobilize quickly."

"Then I should too." I set my jaw, bearing down for an argument. I didn't ride into battle to be pampered. "I'm not more deserving of comfort than any of these soldiers."

"While I appreciate the thought"—Jihun crosses his arms—"you will do no such thing."

"I will do"—I narrow my eyes into dangerous slits—"as I see fit."

"My apologies, Your Majesty." He sighs and wipes a hand down his face. "I want you in a tent for selfish reasons. If I ward your tent, I won't have to stay up all night guarding you. I could use some rest. It's been a long time since I've ridden this long and hard."

"Yeah. It's no joke." I deflate, my righteous indignation leaking out of me. "Of course you need rest."

"If it's any consolation"—my royal adviser scratches the side of his neck—"your tent is not exactly suitable for glamping."

"What?" I rear back in mock outrage. "Do you mean to tell me there won't be copious amounts of silk and shearling for me to drape my royal body over?"

Jihun snorts. "Now there's a mental image I never wanted to have."

I grin and urge my horse toward the forest. We ride in comfortable silence until we reach our bivouac. Even after a long day's march, the soldiers laugh and talk among themselves as they gather firewood and prepare to settle down for the night.

I know the exact moment they notice our arrival. They drop everything they're doing and come to stand at attention. Then they exchange panicked glances, some bowing from their waist and others falling to their knees.

I realize these foot soldiers have never met the king before and have no idea how to greet me. *Hell.* I don't know how to greet a king either. I nod and motion for them to rise. They stay put, sneaking glances at each other.

"Where's my tent?" I whisper to Jihun.

"Your tent is this way, Your Majesty," my royal adviser says loudly for the benefit of the floundering soldiers, then leads me to the edge of the camp.

The round tent, reminiscent of a Mongolian yurt, with a tall, pointed roof, stands in a clearing in the woods. I step into the spacious shelter and look over my shoulder at Jihun as he follows me inside.

Several light orbs float beneath the high ceiling, lighting the interior in a warm glow. A sleeping mat, complete with a silk comforter, takes up one side of the tent, while a low table with seat cushions occupies the other. There's even a small washing station tucked behind the sleeping area.

"You don't consider this glamping?" I gape at Jihun.

"We don't provide breakfast in bed," he deadpans.

"Have you been moonlighting as a stand-up comic?" I chuckle. The lively chatter picks back up outside, and I breathe a sigh of relief. "I guess this tent has many uses. I didn't realize how uncomfortable the soldiers would feel around me."

"They aren't so much uncomfortable as they are awestruck," Jihun explains. "They are honored to have you ride with them."

I rub the back of my head. "All this will take some getting used to."

"I hope you don't have to get used to the battlefield aspect of your reign." He sighs. "Your grandfather—"

"No." I slash my hand through the air. "The moment General Bak invaded the Kingdom of Mountains, he stopped being my grandfather."

"Do you really believe that?" Jihun asks quietly. "He has always been a tough son of a bitch, but he's . . . family. I still can't believe he would do this."

"He *is* doing this." My lip curls back. "He wants revenge, no matter the cost."

Even if the cost is killing his only grandson. I clench my fists at my sides. I didn't choose to have the tyrant's blood running through me. And I am as much his beloved daughter's son as I am my father's. Why can't my grandfather see that?

"He plans to lay waste to the Kingdom of Mountains because the tyrant killed my mother." I shake my head. "But my people already suffered so much when they lost their queen. I can't watch them suffer more because of my father's sins. I have to stop General Bak."

"*We* will stop him, my king." He presses his fist to his chest.

I clap him on the shoulder, then blow out a long breath. "But tonight, I could use a stiff drink."

I remember the makgeolli Sunny and I shared at her childhood home. But the fleeting warmth of memories is not enough. I want her in my arms. I shift my eyes toward the tent flap, wondering if it is dark enough for the moon to have risen.

"Captain Seo might have sent word," Jihun murmurs, following my gaze and train of thought.

I don't know if I want another short, cryptic message. *Who am I kidding?* Any news will be like a sip of air to a drowning man. It just can't be bad news. *It won't be.* Hanging on to hope, I fill a small bowl with water and step outside the tent.

I quickly make my way around to the back so the soldiers can go about their business. Jihun stays close behind me. The full moon shines brightly in the night, and I crouch to the ground and pour a fist of soil into the bowl. When the water calms and the moon's reflection stares up at me, I murmur a chant, and silvery-green fire sparks above the bowl.

I hold my breath as the flame splits into strands and swirls in the air. Then my eyes widen when they converge into letters. With my heart pounding against my ribs, I trace my fingers above the precious message, careful not to touch.

Found Sunny. Coming back.

My relief doesn't have a chance to solidify because a fire-tipped arrow flies by my head and embeds itself next to the bowl, scattering the letters into the air.

"No," I rasp, my hand reaching heedlessly for the words now gone.

I swipe my hand over my head, pitching a protective dome over Jihun and me, and a barrage of fiery arrows falls impotently to the ground. When I glance over my shoulder, I can make out enemy soldiers in the distance, hiding in the trees.

I take my time rising to my feet, fury roaring in my ears, then I turn to face the archers. My voice is a low growl, but my magic carries the words to my enemies. "You picked the wrong time to interrupt my evening."

These assholes took something priceless from me. I've been waiting days for that message. I don't care if the words would have dispersed in a few seconds. They were *my* few seconds to see Sunny's name lit up in the silver-and-green flames of *my* magic. It was mine.

But Sunny is okay. *Thank the fucking gods.* I knew she would be. I knew and yet . . .

I want her here. I need to bury myself inside her. She is mine, but I want to hear her say the words and sip them from her lips. I want to claim her and be claimed by her. We belong together.

Just a while longer.

I blow out a measured breath. Sunny will be here soon, and I hope to never endure the torture of being apart from her again. But first, I have to teach these enemy soldiers a lesson.

"Shall we?" I raise my brows at Jihun, gripping an axe in each fist.

He nods, silver fire glinting in his eyes. "We should beat some manners into these assholes."

I head toward them with a deadly smile, my axes hanging deceptively loose at my sides. Subduing these archers shouldn't take long, but I don't plan on stopping there. I will keep going until I have General Bak on his knees, even if I have to fight every soldier from the Kingdom of Sky myself.

I won't have Sunny come back to a war-ravaged kingdom. Not if I can help it.

CHAPTER ELEVEN

Sunny

"We better say goodbye here," Mrs. Ha says, with a tremulous smile at her daughter. "If I go to the beach with you, I won't be able to stop myself from bodily dragging you away from the moonglade. I can't . . . watch."

"I think that's a good idea." Minju's face crumples as she falls into her mother's open arms. "We will have a more leisurely Hangawi next year. I promise."

People shouldn't make promises they can't keep.

I told Ethan I'd see him in five minutes. That turned out to be a complete lie. No one knows what future awaits them. They don't know what choices they will make when thrown into impossible situations. They don't know who they are capable of becoming. No one knows that five minutes could become forever.

People shouldn't make promises at all.

"I know you will do everything in your power to come home. And I will pray for your safe return with all my heart." She leans back and cups Minju's cheek. "You are an extraordinary person, daughter. Your intellect has always astounded me, but it is your big, courageous heart that will help save the worlds. I know it."

Minju nods, biting her wobbling lip to hold her tears at bay. "I love you, Mother."

"I love you too." Mrs. Ha pulls her into a hard, fast hug and pushes her away. "Now go."

Captain Seo and I bow to the older female, but she gives us a chiding look before hugging each of us in turn. "You girls take care of each other."

"We will, Mrs. Ha." The captain bows again, then follows Minju out of the restaurant. Mr. Ha waits outside with his hands clasped behind his back, facing the ocean across the street.

"I should join them . . ." I trail off when Mrs. Ha looks at me with heartfelt concern.

"I see such pain and sorrow in your eyes." She clutches my cold hands in her warm ones. "Whatever happened—and no matter what happens in the future—you cannot exist without living. You must live, child."

I turn away from her kind face, my throat working to swallow. The warmth and wisdom of Mrs. Ha's words remind me of my mother.

"If you can't do it for yourself, then do it for your friends." Sorrow tinges her soft laugh. "I'm asking for selfish reasons. My daughter believes in you. She needs you, Sunny."

"But . . ." I meet her gaze. "I'm so afraid."

"That just means you are not a fool." She gives my hands a squeeze and gently releases them. "I don't know what role you are meant to play in all this, but remember you don't need to be perfect. Just live to the fullest and strive to do better. That is all any of us can do. And that is *enough*."

I stare wide eyed at Mrs. Ha, her words converging with my mother's in my head.

No one is perfect, and you are no exception, daughter. But I love you, imperfections and all. I only ask that you always try to do better. Learn from your mistakes and grow. That is all any of us can do.

My eyelashes flutter as I suck in a heaving breath, and I can see clearly for the first time in days. Maybe for the first time in over a century.

Life isn't black and white. No one is all good or all bad. We falter. We make mistakes. We disappoint ourselves and one another. Yet everyone has a choice—not to be perfect, but to choose to do better.

Goodness isn't an immutable state of being. It's about every choice we make, countless times in our lives. One good choice doesn't make you a good person. And one bad choice doesn't make you a bad person. Neither are we the sum of our choices. *Because who the hell is keeping score anyway?* The worst thing we can do is to give up—to stop caring—when we have the choice to do better.

"I can do better." For Ethan. For Draco. For my friends. Most of all, I will do better for myself, because I am not a lost cause. I am *not* a monster. No matter what happened, I deserve a chance to do better. "Or I sure as hell will try."

"Language, child." Mrs. Ha scrunches her nose, exactly like her daughter, but her eyes sparkle with pride. "But that's the spirit."

"Thank you." I bow low from my waist. My entire body tingles, like life is circulating through my veins, awakening from a forced slumber.

"Go, before I'm tempted to snatch my daughter." The older female lightly nudges me toward the door. "*Live*, Sunny."

I press my lips together and nod. Closing the restaurant door behind me, I exhale shakily and swipe my forearm across my eyes. Then I jog across the street and catch up with Captain Seo and Minju. Mr. Ha is already at the edge of the water. My friends must have lingered behind, waiting for me to join them.

"Hey." I can't quite meet their eyes, feeling ridiculously shy for some reason. "I, uh, I'm coming with you."

"I know," Minju chirps with a little hop. Next to her, the captain slumps ever so slightly, relief in the lines of her body.

"How could you possibly know that?" I grumble, nonplussed. "I literally decided like a minute ago."

"I can see it on your face." The historian smiles guilelessly.

"See what on my face?" I press my hands against my cheeks.

"That you decided to rejoin the world of the living," Captain Seo says in a husky voice.

"Is it that obvious?" I wrinkle my nose, hoping to frown away my blush.

"Yes," my friends answer as one.

They know. I don't need to explain that I'm going all in to save the Realm of Four Kingdoms from the Amheuk. They don't need to hear that I will fight to the death at their sides—not for the fate of the worlds, but for them. Because they already know. *Thank gods.* Just the thought of saying those things out loud makes me squirm.

"What gave it away?" I flash them a picture-day smile that shows both rows of my teeth. "My sunny personality?"

The captain stares straight ahead like she feels squirmy too. "Your eyes don't look cloudy and lifeless like a dead fish anymore."

"Uh, thanks?" I'm too giddy to be offended by the dead-fish reference.

I might be walking to my death right now, but I'm doing it with my friends. *For* my friends. Even if I can never be good, I can always do *better*. It is fucking exhilarating to feel hope again.

"Before dawn, girls," Mr. Ha drawls like an indulgent headmaster. "If you please."

"Sorry, Father." Minju cringes. "We're coming."

Properly chastised, we pick up our pace and hurry to his side. The gleaming reflection of the Hangawi moon really does look like a solid silver road stretching across the surface of the ocean. It's hard to believe something so peaceful and beautiful is most likely deadly.

"Ready to become the first beings to cross the moonglade in one piece?" Worry flashes in Mr. Ha's eyes as he glances at his daughter, but he hangs on to his determined smile.

"You seem knowledgeable about the moonglade and all." I suck air in through my teeth. "Do you have any pointers on how to stay alive?"

"When you moon shift, you defy the laws of time and space to step *past* the abyss. Magic allows you to do that." He pauses to meet each of our eyes. "Walking the moonglade, as the name suggests, involves less magic and more . . . walking. It is far from a magicless endeavor, but it will take time and endurance to travel *across* the abyss."

"How far is it to the Realm of Four Kingdoms?" Captain Seo pulls her shoulders back as though bracing for his answer.

"In scientific measurements, I would estimate that it is approximately two million light-years away," Mr. Ha says in all seriousness, and I choke on my own spit. "But like I said, there is magic involved, which distorts the physical distance."

"Then can you tell us how long it would take to cross the moonglade?" The captain might appear calm to a casual observer, but the tightness around her eyes is a dead giveaway that she is absolutely freaking out. "Your best guesstimate."

"Time is a funny thing." He chuckles nervously.

"We know virtually nothing," Minju explains, patting her father's back in wordless comfort. If he's anything like his daughter, he hates not having the answers for us. "Our only hope is . . ."

"Let me guess." My stomach plunges to my toes. "My Yeo—"

"Sunny." The historian cuts me off. "We will discuss that on the road."

"Is the secrecy necessary at this point?" I let my head fall back on a weary sigh. "All hell has literally broken loose."

"It is for my parents' safety." Minju's voice is tight with concern, her gaze darting to her father. Mr. Ha diplomatically takes a few steps away, whistling tunelessly under his breath.

"I'm sorry." I drop my head, appalled at myself. It's already hard for her to leave her parents like this. I can't believe I almost added to her worries. "I am a giant asshole."

"Revolting." Captain Seo grimaces.

"All is well, Sunny." Minju smiles at me, and I feel like a teeny, tiny asshole.

I don't deserve her. I shake away the defeatist thought. I will do better to deserve her—to deserve all my friends.

"So what were you saying about our only hope?" I ask her when her father meanders back to our side. I hope he didn't overhear anything, especially the giant asshole part.

"Our only hope?" The historian blinks myopically. "Oh, that's right. As I was saying, our only hope is synchronicity."

"Come again?" I stretch my neck out and point my ear toward her.

"Synchronicity," she repeats obligingly. "We found you just in time for Hangawi when moonglading is our only means of returning to the Realm of Four Kingdoms."

Captain Seo sputters incoherently, while I open and close my mouth a dozen times. I finally get my voice to work and bellow, "Our only hope is reading way too much into a random coincidence?"

"I'm with Sunny on this," the captain says in a more moderate tone.

My jaw drops despite the hopelessness tugging at me. "You're *agreeing* with me?"

"Don't get used to it," she mutters.

"Now, now," Mr. Ha says, unease tugging down his lips. "Let's hear Minju out before we dismiss her opinion."

"Thank you, Father." Minju scrunches her face, looking for the right words. "*Synchronicity* means different things to different people. Humans sometimes give significance to two unrelated incidents out of desperation, or fear. But it also takes an open mind and courage to reflect on—and even act based on—the deeper meaning."

"No, thank you." I cross my arms. "I do not want to start a crystal collection."

Captain Seo elbows me in the ribs and nods at Minju to continue.

"For beings of the Shingae, we should recognize that there are no such things as random coincidences." Minju spreads her hands. "The three of us were guided to this moment by the hands of fate. We are meant to make it across the moonglade."

"Have you ever considered that fate is a fucking sadist?" My upper lip curls with bitterness. "And that they guided us here to *die*?"

"Of course I've considered that possibility." Minju snorts delicately. "That's why I said synchronicity is our only *hope*. It is far from a certainty. Maybe not even a probability. But nothing can stop us from hoping."

Fate and destiny have done nothing but screw me over. That might be a good thing, though. Since fate shit on my life nonstop, maybe it's time for some good things to happen. *Fuck.* Now I'm clinging on to the gambler's fallacy? *I've been losing all night, so I'm bound to win the next round.* That's pretty pathetic. Minju's "synchronicity reflects the hands of fate" theory sounds much better in comparison.

"Fine. Let's do this"—I tilt my chin up—"and hope like hell that fate isn't a total bastard."

CHAPTER TWELVE

SUNNY

"So how does this work?" I toe the water, but the moonglade doesn't so much as flicker against the ripples. The silver road is literally solid.

"We just . . . walk." Minju glances over her shoulder at her father.

He nods reassuringly and waves us on. We've already said our goodbyes to him. Lingering will only make leaving harder for her. I'm here to help my friends, aren't I? I suck in a sharp breath and step onto the moonglade, then I peek open one eye. *What the hell?* When did I even close my eyes?

With an impatient tsk, I open them wide and look down. I'm standing on the silver road, and I haven't been struck down by lightning or anything. *Cool.* I'll take that as a win.

"Come on." I wave Minju and Captain Seo over. "I thought we were in a hurry."

The captain joins me first and, again, no death by lightning. She meets my eyes and shrugs. "So far, so good."

I look toward the distant horizon, and my shoulders droop. It's going to be a long, long walk. Perhaps the true challenge of walking the moonglade is enduring the torture of cardio.

Minju hesitates in front of the silver road, lifting and lowering the heel of her right foot. I try to give her an encouraging smile, but she squints at me in confusion.

"Oh never mind." I let my features settle into a comfortable scowl. "Let's go. We haven't got all day." Then I turn to the captain and quip, "This walk is going to be worse than cadet training, isn't it?"

"If it is, then I haven't done my job." Captain Seo smirks, drawing a chuckle from me.

But when Minju gingerly steps onto the moonglade, I choke on my laugh as Eurwangni Beach disappears and darkness swallows me whole.

"What the—" I'm tossed around like a lonely wet sock in the dryer—spin, drop, spin, drop. I can't see which way is up and which is down in the pitch black.

"Oh shit!" I shout as the darkness suddenly bottoms out beneath me.

I fall until I have no air left in my lungs to scream. But my stomach swoops again and again, and my toes flex and squirm against the sheer terror of free-falling. At some point, my voice returns to me, and my scream pierces my ears.

How long have I been falling?

Longer than a jump from the Empire State Building, five times over. I feel my sanity unraveling when my body finally goes limp, reaching its limit, and my eyes roll back. *Thank gods.* But before the sweet oblivion of a dead faint claims me, I hit the ground with a resounding thump.

"Ow." Pain lances through every inch of my body, but I don't care. Nothing can be worse than falling . . . and falling. Laughter trickles out of me in unhinged relief.

"Daughter."

I stop laughing. I stop *breathing*. Keeping my gaze lowered, I push against the ground—a distant part of me recognizes the silver road—and get to my feet. Even after I stand, swaying on unsteady legs, I don't dare look up.

"Come, daughter," my mother says. "Let me hold you."

My breath comes in short, unsteady pants, and I finally raise my head. The dark surrounds me, but I see her in the ghostly glow of the silver road. She is only a few yards away, wearing a plain beige hanbok, with her hair in a neat, low bun.

"Mother?" Tears blur my vision. I wipe them away with an impatient swipe of my hand. I can't see her if I'm crying.

"Yes, Mihwa." She nods and holds her arms open with a warm laugh. "Come, daughter."

I take a step, then falter, my eyes narrowed in confusion. "But how?"

"Does it matter?" Her smile is sad but beautiful.

"No." *Gods, I missed her.* "I guess it doesn't."

I run toward her but stumble to a stop again. This can't be my mother.

But she's right here.

Why shouldn't I get to hug her—to feel her arms around me—one more time? I work so hard. Don't I deserve this one thing?

I take one step, then another—faster and faster until I'm sprinting. She's so close. *Almost there.* I stretch out my hand. My fingertips nearly skim hers, when I'm yanked back, like I have a bungee cord wrapped around my waist, and I crash onto the ground where I started.

"Mother," I scream, straining against the invisible hold.

"Behave, Mihwa." Daeseong steps behind my mother and wraps his hands around her throat.

"You," I snarl. "Get away from her."

"Mi—" My mother gags and gurgles as her fingers claw at the dark mudang's hands. "Mihwa, bewitch him. Make him stop."

"But Mother, I swore never to use that despicable power. *You* made me swear it." I slowly shake my head. "I c-can't. I won't. I don't want to be a monster like him."

"Please, daughter. Bewitch him," she cries. "Save me. Please."

"It's . . . not right," I croak. "I . . . I have to try t-to do better."

"He's *killing* me." Her eyes glow red.

"Wh-what . . ." I bury my fingers in my hair. "What's happening?"

"Sometimes, you have to do bad things for the right reasons." My mother's eyes are back to the warm brown they have always been, and they glisten with unshed tears. "I don't want to die, Mihwa. *Bewitch him.* Don't let him kill me."

I blink. *But Daeseong already killed her.* I draw in a shuddering breath. *Mother is dead.* A wail rises to my throat like I've lost her again, but I fist my hands, my nails digging into my palms. This isn't her.

"Mother would *never* ask me to condemn myself to save her." She isn't real. But I miss her so much that I still want to run to her. "Who are you?"

"Me?" She points at herself, another sad smile curving her lips. Blood blossoms like crimson poppies over her hanbok until it stains the fabric red. "I am your mother. The one you let die to keep your hands clean."

I shiver from the memory of my mother's gumiho rearing up on her hind legs to shield me from Daeseong's dark magic. I remember her crumpling to the ground as her life bled out of her—and how she died in my arms. The female standing in front of me is *not* my mother.

"Besides, you've already used your dark power once." Daeseong releases her throat and steps around her. "What's the harm in doing it again?"

"You're not him," I rasp, my blood pounding in my ears. "I killed him."

"You did, didn't you?" The fake Daeseong tuts his tongue as dark blood soaks through his gray dopo from a gaping wound in his chest. "You killed your own father. *Twice.* How could you redeem yourself from that?"

"With every choice I make." I stand tall and face my demons. "I will choose to do better."

"You will fail." My fake mother's voice sounds sibilant.

"Then I will try to do better the next time." My Yeoiju hums with pride. "I will try and try again until my last breath."

My fake mother rakes her fingers down her cheeks, and her skin slides down like melted wax, exposing a layer of raw flesh. She tugs and pulls at her face until I can see her eyes bulge and swivel in their sockets, the muscles pulsing and twitching.

Daeseong's replica mimics her grotesque performance, peeling away the skin of his head like a hood. I gag on the bile rising to my throat. Then he emits a piercing screech, stretching his jaw open past his chest.

I clap my hands over my ears and watch in horror as their limbs elongate and bend like gangly spider legs. The monstrosities launch themselves at me, their movements jerky and freakishly fast. I duck my head under my arms, a silent scream tearing out of me. Scared out of my mind, I don't even think about fighting them off.

My Yeoiju, however, is made of sterner stuff than that.

It sings inside me, and warmth spreads through my body. My fear recedes by a fraction, clearing my mind. But before I can gather myself and figure out a plan, a stream of white light bursts from my chest, arching my back.

The demons' screeches hit a fever pitch, and I press my palms harder against my ears.

My limbs begin to quake, and panic slices through me. If I don't stop the Yeoiju, it will deplete my magic, then draw power from my very life force. With a roar, I call back the white light before I lose control and raise my Shin'gwangdo to fight off the demons.

But they're . . . gone. The Yeoiju defeated them.

My arm falls limply to my side, with my sword dangling by my thigh. Panting into the heavy silence, I finally look around me. In the fading white light, I see a wall of fire surrounding me in a mile-wide radius.

It should be sweltering where I stand, but I don't feel any heat emanating from the towering inferno. Unfortunately, the countless naked bodies floating and writhing in its depths certainly do.

Dear gods.

We're not walking through the abyss. I fall to my knees. We are walking through the depths of hell.

CHAPTER THIRTEEN

Sunny

"M-Minju," I shout, whipping my head left and right. "Captain, where are you?"

My teeth clack together from the force of my tremors. I can't stop shaking, and a whimper slips from my mouth.

I can't hear the screams of the tortured people floating in the wall of fire surrounding me. But their eyes roll back in agony as their mouths gape wide, their bodies thrashing. I can *feel* their screams.

"Ch-Cheyun!" I shout from the top of my lungs, my body curling in on itself. "Minju! Where are you?"

Then someone whimpers, "Please."

I run down the silver road, toward the fractured voice, and skid to a halt in front of Captain Seo.

"Please." She sobs on her knees and buries her face in her hands. "Let me just stay by your side."

I crouch down in front of her. "Who are you talking to?"

"You don't need to return my love," the captain continues as though I haven't spoken.

"Cheyun." I put my hand on her trembling shoulder, but she doesn't seem to notice. "It's me. Sunny."

"I know I'm hard and cold." She drops her hands from her face and plants them on the ground. "I was raised to be a suhoshin—to fight and protect. I don't know how to be anything else."

"Come on." I shake her by her shoulders. "Snap out of it, Cheyun."

"That's not true. I *do* have feelings." She clutches at her chest with one hand. "My love is real, Jihun."

I rear back. Captain Seo is in love with Jihun? But whoever she's talking to isn't him. She's stuck in her own personal hell.

"But I don't know how to be soft and pliant. That's not me." She weeps. "I can't pretend to be someone I'm not."

"And you don't have to, Cheyun." Gods, I hope she can hear me. "Besides, you're not hard and cold. You are capable and honest. That's different. There are so many lies and half-truths in the worlds. We need your brand of blunt honesty. And you're always fair and kind when it counts."

"He doesn't love me." She responds to me in a small, broken whisper. *Thank gods.* I'm getting through to her. "He wants me to change."

"The real Jihun would never ask you to change. He respects and trusts you," I say with absolutely certainty. "He thinks you are strong, brave, and loyal. We all do."

Captain Seo pushes off the ground and rises to her knees.

"Also, you can't blame him for not seeing what's right in front of him." I scoot closer to her. "Males are dumbasses that way."

Her eyelashes flutter like she's struggling to wake up. *Come on, Cheyun.* She's strong. She can fight this.

"I admire you so much." I clear my throat. "You never have to change yourself to win someone's heart, because you're amazing as you are."

Her eyes shoot open on a gasp, and she whips her head around in terror.

"Hey." I grab her arms and squeeze. "Hey, you're okay. It's me, your favorite suhoshin cadet. You're okay, Cheyun. It's over."

Her face crumples, and she drops her forehead onto my shoulder. I'm not sure about the "over" part. We *are* trapped in hell, but I feel better having found her. It's still terrifying as fuck, but at least I'm not alone. I pat her on the back.

She sniffs and returns the awkward pat, then she sits on her haunches and takes in our surroundings. "Hell."

I don't know if she's cursing, or identifying our current location.

"I . . ." Her gaze suddenly shoots back to me. "Did I . . . say something?"

"You said a lot of things." I huff a resigned sigh. I respect her too much not to tell her the truth. "From which I gathered that you're in love with Jihun."

"Fuck." She drops her head.

"It isn't as bad as that. I obviously won't tell anyone. I have zero interest in your love life. Ugh." I pretend to gag. When she looks up to arch an annoyed brow at me, I continue in a serious tone, "But let me make one thing clear. If Jihun doesn't realize how fucking lucky he would be to have you, then it is *his* loss, because you are the biggest badass I have ever met."

Captain Seo's bottom lip trembles, and she bites down on it with a scowl. I swiftly glance away with a matching scowl. But after an embarrassed second, I gasp and scramble to my feet.

"Have you seen Minju?" I look around wildly, but all I see is fire and agony.

"Oh gods." The captain jumps to a stand. "We have to find her."

"Minju!" I shout. "Damn it. Where are you?"

We call for her, running up and down the silver road, until our voices turn into reedy rasps.

"I can't find it," Minju whimpers, and my stomach lurches.

"That way." I sprint toward her voice with Captain Seo at my heels.

We find her digging in the hard ground, her nails torn and bloody. "I can't find it."

"Minju." I fall to my knees and pull her into my arms. "Wake up, Minju."

"I have to find the answer." She pushes away from me and digs frantically. "Everyone will die if I don't find the answer."

"Do not place that burden on yourself." The captain kneels beside the distraught historian. "No one expects you to find the answer to save us all. We will do it together. The Sentinels will fight for the worlds *together*."

"You are not alone, Minju." I press my wobbling lips together and gather her wrecked hands in my own. "You will never be alone."

And neither will I.

"What if I fail them?" She tugs on her hands, but I hold on tight. "I can't fail them. What if I ruin everything?"

"We'll be right by your side, picking up the pieces," I tell her, and she blinks slowly. *Am I finally getting across to her?* "After we clean up the mess, we can try again. All of us."

"It's *my* job to find answers." Her voice breaks on a shrill note. "I don't know how to fight like everyone else. What use am I if I can't do this one thing?"

"Minju . . ." My hold on her hands slackens, and she wrenches them back to claw at the silver road.

"I have to find the answer," she mutters, digging and digging. "It's the only way I can help them."

Then she screams in anguish and bashes her forehead against the ground.

"Stop it," Captain Seo yells, jerking Minju up by her shoulders. The historian thrashes against the captain's hold, spittle flying from her mouth, and scratches at the captain's arms, drawing blood with her broken fingernails.

"Enough." I shove Cheyun aside and deliver a resounding slap across Minju's cheek.

Shocked silence descends on all three of us.

I can't believe I slapped my friend, but I had to get through to her somehow. I needed to stop her before both of them got hurt.

With a heaving breath, Minju opens her eyes and looks around her. *Thank gods.* The worst is over. She will need a minute to process the fact that we are in literal hell, but she's awake.

I prepare to tug her into my arms to console her but stop myself short. *What if she remembers I slapped her?* The corners of my mouth dip into a grimace. Then again, she did stab me in the heart once.

"Wow," Minju breathes in wonder.

"What was that?" I squint.

"There are no written accounts of hell." Her eyes jump from point to point in near manic curiosity. "This is truly an extraordinary opportunity."

"Fuck me." I clap my hand over my eyes.

Captain Seo scoffs at my side. "I second that."

"All right. Up we go." I hoist Minju to her feet. "We need to get out of here. There's a reason why there are no written accounts of hell. It's because no one makes it out alive. Or is it because no one makes it *in* alive?"

"Oh my word," Minju squeaks and covers her mouth. "Yes, we must leave."

I almost stomp my foot when I realize the flaw in my plan. "But *how*?"

"I think we have to keep walking the silver road," she says.

"Which way, though?" The captain scratches her forehead. "I can't even remember which direction we came from."

"I don't know about you guys, but I didn't walk here." I gulp. "I *fell*."

Captain Seo and Minju agree with a sharp nod.

"Even so, we have to keep walking the moonglade," the historian insists. "Out of all the convoluted scraps of information about the silver road, that is the only clear, consistent fact my father and I discovered. We have to 'walk the moonglade' in order to reach the Realm of Four Kingdoms."

"We have to pick a direction, then." The captain sighs.

"Fine. Let me try something." I search for gi—any gi—but there is no life here. Only death. "I can't see anything."

"Try again." Minju slips her hand into mine. "Take your time."

I don't want to stay here a second longer than necessary, but I listen to her advice. Spinning slowly in a circle, I peer into the wall of fire, trying and failing to ignore the writhing bodies.

There is no life force for me to discern.

I'm about to turn back to my friends when something flickers at the corners of my eyes. I spin back, zeroing in on it. A speck of red gi glows in the distance.

The life force of Underworld.

CHAPTER FOURTEEN

Sunny

It seems counterintuitive, but the Kingdom of Underworld is not for the dead. After all, Underworld is one of the four life sources created by the Cheon'gwang.

"Does hell lie in the Kingdom of Underworld?" I ask Minju, not letting the smudge of red gi out of my sight.

"Every King of Underworld has been less than frank when it comes to that question." She purses her lips in annoyance. "But it is not outside the realm of possibility."

"Good." I stalk toward the life force of Underworld. "Because I think I just found an entrance to the Kingdom of Underworld."

The red gi veers to the left of the moonglade, but I have a feeling we shouldn't get off the silver road. I'll worry about that when we get closer to the entrance. For now, we walk.

"What do you see?" Captain Seo shortens her stride to match mine.

"I see the gi of Underworld over there." I point toward it even though she can't see it. I'm the only one in both realms who can.

I stare at the red life force ahead of me, because it might be our only way out of hell. But I also do it to keep my eyes averted from the wall of fire that surrounds us, rising without end, with countless emaciated bodies jerking and twitching inside. Their silent screams scrape against my skull, and cold dread slithers down my spine.

I wonder if my friends can see it too. Their steps seem steady enough, but their eyes are intensely focused on the moonglade a few paces ahead of them. Minju is wringing her hands raw, and a muscle tics uncontrollably beneath the captain's right eye. *Yup.* They see it.

"How much farther?" Captain Seo clips out.

"Not very far," I murmur.

But the entrance to the Kingdom of Underworld—at least, I hope it's the entrance—is much farther away than I'd thought. I press a hand against the stitch in my side and pant as I put one foot in front of the other. On the plus side, the red smudge is getting bigger as we march on. We are definitely headed in the right direction.

I catch Minju by the arm when she stumbles and ask, "Do you need to take a break?"

"No." Her gaze flits up toward me. Then with a gasp, she tucks her chin into her chest. She must've accidentally gotten an eyeful of the burning bodies. "No break."

"Okay." The glowing red gi arches like a doorway in the distance. I wrap my arm around Minju's shoulders. "Let's keep going."

To my relief, the silver road curves slightly to the left as we get closer to the archway. *Good.* We can keep walking the moonglade *and* get the hell out of . . . hell. I snort. *That's one hell of a pun.* I snort harder.

"What's so funny?" The captain keeps her gaze pointed down.

"Nothing." I shrug. "Deadly peril always makes me a little loopy."

"That's adorable." Minju peeks at my face for a split second before lowering her eyes to the road again.

I snatch my arm away from her shoulders. "If you have enough energy to utter such blasphemy, you can walk without my help."

Captain Seo and Minju laugh at my expense. I bite my cheeks to hold back a smile. I'm happy to share my loopiness with my friends. We could all use a distraction from the tortured souls floating around us.

They must have done some horrible shit to be in there, but it still doesn't sit right with me. I actually feel sorry for Yeomla, the god of Underworld. Deciding who gets punished, how much, and for how long seems like a heavy burden to bear. But who am I to pity a god? They probably don't give us regular folks a second thought.

"Wait. Look over there." I point toward the red gi again. The life force appears arched because there is a physical door framing it. "You guys can see that now, right?"

They both look up from the road and follow my line of sight.

"There's an arched entryway," Minju gasps.

"Thank the fucking gods." The captain pushes her hair off her forehead. "Let's get the hell out of here."

Laughter sputters out of me even though I clap a hand over my mouth. Minju and Captain Seo blink at each other.

"I get it now." A slow smile spreads across the captain's face. "You really are adorable."

"Well, fuck," I mutter. Cutesy is definitely not my vibe.

"I still don't get it." Minju blinks big round eyes at me. "What's so funny?"

"You know, because we're in hell . . ." I clamp my mouth shut when the traitor dissolves into giggles.

"Sunny is just *precious*, isn't she?" Captain Seo says with a shit-eating grin.

"So precious." Minju sighs. "I want to tuck her inside my pocket and carry her around with me."

"I highly doubt that scrap of fabric you're wearing even has a pocket," I jeer to hide how vulnerable I feel.

I don't mind being teased, but I do mind how much I enjoy it, coming from these two. I'm trying . . . I'm trying really hard . . . to move on from Santorini. But I'm not ready for soft, squishy feelings yet.

"You're right." Minju's smile droops, and I feel like a dick. Well, at least, a dick isn't *precious*. "I miss my hanbok."

"I'm sure the Kingdom of Underworld has plenty of hanboks." Captain Seo narrows her eyes at me, and I look down at my toes. "Just hang on a little bit longer. We're almost there."

"And you look lovely in that dress, even though it's microscopic." I mumble my version of an apology. When Minju's face shifts into an *aww* expression, I point a warning finger at her. "If you call me anything resembling 'cute' or 'sweet,' I will take that back so fast."

The captain coughs to cover her laugh, and Minju wisely says nothing. But her smile tells me she's *thinking* "cute" and "sweet" in association with me. *Oh well.* I guess it's fine as long as I don't have to hear it.

"What do you know?" I stop in front of the entryway. "We made it."

I blink and shake my head to dispel my magic gi goggles so I can take a proper look at the physical obstacle we're up against.

"It's just a door," I say, sounding almost disappointed. The double-leafed door, made of rough black metal, stands about eighty feet tall, with long, vertical handle bars in the same material. But still, it's just a door. "I'm not asking for Cerberus—I bet he's busy guarding Hades or something—but there should at least be a brutish horned dokkaebi standing around with a giant spiked club."

"I take offense at that stereotype." Minju, a half dokkaebi, pouts.

"Are you upset this door won't be challenging enough to get through?" Captain Seo gapes at me. "I'm not certain twenty people could push it open."

"Do you think we need to *push* or *pull*?" I tap my chin with my finger, remembering the iconic comic about a kid at genius school pulling on a door with all his might when it says *push*. We can't afford to make the same mistake. "It's important to figure that out before we waste all our energy pushing or pulling the wrong way."

With an inquisitive hum, Minju approaches one end of the door and peers at the hinges, then she walks the width of a basketball court to reach the other end and repeats her inspections. She hums again and returns to our side.

Captain Seo and I look expectantly at her, but she shrugs. "I can't tell."

"That's okay." I swallow my frustrated groan and nod encouragingly at her. "We'll figure it out together."

"From a logical perspective, the door should open toward us." The captain rubs her jaw. "It presumably leads to the Kingdom of Underworld, where people reside. If the door opens outward, people could be hit by it. As opposed to in here, where no living beings should be roaming around."

"But if it opens inward, shouldn't there be scratch marks on the silver road?" I walk a half circle in front of the door. "Because I don't see any. The door is too heavy not to leave a mark."

"Then it's magic," Minju offers unhelpfully. But of course, she's right.

"Maybe if we—" With a sharp hiss, Captain Seo snatches away the hand she'd pressed against the door. "Shit."

"What happened?" I rush over with Minju. The captain's palm is an angry red with blisters popping up one after another. "The door seared your hand."

"I can see that." She grimaces, holding her wrist.

Luckily for her, Captain Seo is a shinbiin. Her healing power rapidly pulls the heat out of the burn, and she breathes a relieved sigh after a minute. The burn will take longer to heal completely, but her pained expression smooths out.

"How do we open a door we can't touch?" Minju waves her hand, murmuring an incantation. "As I suspected, it is heavily warded by powerful magic."

"Fuck my life." I kick the door, and the tip of my combat boot sizzles and melts off, revealing my big toe. I groan, curling my fingers into claws, but I refrain from scratching and kicking the door because it'll hurt me more than it will hurt the door.

"You should be glad your toe didn't melt off." The historian pinches her lips to one side. "Hmm."

"Hmm?" My withered hope perks up again. "*Hmm* what?"

"Oh . . . that is . . ." Minju shakes her head and tries again. "Your toe didn't melt off."

"You already made that observation. What about it?" I reel my hand in a circle, trying to draw out the rest of her thoughts.

"I think that means you can touch the doors without being burned."

"What? How? Why?" I ask intelligently.

"I'm not sure." Then her eyes widen. "You know how you extracted that mudang's fire magic? It must have something to do with that power. Do you remember how you did it?"

"Hell if I know." I cringe. "Not helpful. Sorry."

"Well, I think you can undo whatever magic that's guarding the doors and open them."

"You *think*?" The captain throws her hands up. "We can't risk melting Sunny into a puddle on a half-baked hypothesis. No offense."

"None taken," the historian says quietly, clearly offended.

Captain Seo's apologetic grimace disappears as she summons her twin swords. "We have company."

Demons.

Not just any demons, but the ones from *my* nightmare, limping toward us on wrecked, uneven legs. At least they don't have spider legs anymore. Unfortunately, they brought company—monstrous versions of Jihun and the rest of the Sentinels, even Draco.

CHAPTER FIFTEEN

Sunny

That's not Draco.

I know this logically. Like the rest of the demons, their face is half melted off, and they advance on us with the distinct gait of a zombie. Then why is my stupid heart twisting like this?

It. Isn't. Them.

Minju whimpers, and I snap out of my grief and confusion. *That isn't Draco.* Minju is the one I need to protect right now. I push her behind me and summon the Shin'gwangdo. I call on the Yeoiju and push the light into the sword. At least, I try.

"Shit." The blade has the feeble glimmer of a day-old glow stick.

My heart pounds uncomfortably fast as I force more light into the Shin'gwangdo. I must have depleted my magic when I took down the wannabe Daeseong and my un-mother the first time.

The demons pick up speed, closing the distance between us every time I blink. I hold up my sword. A light tremor starts in my arms, then my legs, and my chest seizes, drawing a choked gasp from me.

The Yeoiju is siphoning what remains of my life force. My body spasms. *No.* I withdraw the white light from the Shin'gwangdo, stumbling back from the effort. Minju catches me by the arms before I fall on my ass.

"Sunny, you mustn't wield the Yeoiju here," she says in an urgent whisper. "Life doesn't exist in this place. There is no gi for you to draw from except your own."

"I gathered that," I pant. "I'll just have to stop these fuckers the old-fashioned way."

"I'm not sure you can," Captain Seo says grimly.

"But we have to try." Ethan and our friends need us. We will *not* die in hell. "Wannabe Daeseong and Un-Mother are from my nightmare. I'm guessing the anti-Jihun is from yours, Captain? Are the rest of the fake Sentinels from your nightmare, Minju?"

"Y . . . yes." She releases my arms when I pat her hand, signaling I'm okay now.

"All right. We got this." I raise the Shin'gwangdo in a two-handed grip and widen my stance. "Stay behind me, Minju."

Anti-Jihun reaches us first, and Captain Seo slices his head off in a single swing. Before I can finish wondering if the head will reattach itself to the body or if the body will regrow a head, the captain stabs the fake Hailey in the chest.

In the span of seconds, Anti-Jihun regrows his head and rushes us, with the demon Jaeseok at his side, their mouths snarling and snapping. Captain Seo meets them halfway, swinging her swords with deadly precision. Minju claps a hand over her mouth when the captain cuts Demon Jaeseok's legs off at his knees. I squeeze her shoulder, then run into the fray.

I cleave Wannabe Daeseong from his shoulder to waist and kick him to the side as Fake Hailey comes at me. I slash her across the chest in a slanted X. But when the not Draco lunges at me, I freeze and stare at their distorted face, searching for what . . . I don't know. I scream when a blade bursts out of their chest and their face goes slack.

"Sunny, you need to keep it together." Captain Seo pulls her sword out of Not Draco, and they slump to the side. "They're demons. Only demons."

I come to my senses with a gasp—just in time to kick Un-Mother away from Minju. But the demons keep coming, everything about them grotesque and wrong.

"This isn't going to work." I nudge Minju toward Captain Seo. "Take care of her, Cheyun. I have to get this fucking door open."

I run to the door leaf closest to me and hover my hands over it. With a bracing breath, I press my palms against it, squeezing my eyes shut. The door feels hot, but not enough to burn. I crack one eye open. *Yup.* My hands show no signs of melting off.

"What did we decide on?" I yell over my shoulder. "Pull or push?"

The captain cuts down one demon and jumps over its limp body to slash another, while Minju smacks one—Wannabe Daeseong, I think—over the head with her romance novel. I don't think they heard me.

"Shit." I look up at the handle bars. My fingertips would barely graze the bottom of the handle even if I took a running leap. They must be decorative. "Push, it is."

I brace my shoulder against the door and push with a roar. My feet slip on the silver road, but I step forward and push harder. I shift into my gumiho form, flaring my nine tails behind me. Now the size of a full-grown lion, I give the door a mighty heave. It doesn't budge an inch.

Use your head, Sunny.

An amused snort escapes my snout as I imagine ramming the door with my head. I guess even my gumiho isn't immune to my morbid loopy humor. The situation is more dire than I thought.

What did Minju say about the stolen magic? I shift back to my human form and stop straining against the door.

Think, Sunny. Think.

How did I draw Blondie's magic out of him? I step back and summon an orb of white light to my palm. It flickers, threatening to fade away. *You know what?* Thinking is overrated.

I let instinct take over.

I close my eyes and *sense* the magic warding the door. Many people contributed to protect this entryway—many powerful beings of Underworld. The black metal is knit together by magic. I can't parse out the spells, but I can sense each life force powering the magic.

When I open my eyes again, I see the strands of red gi swirling around the door, forming intricate runes. My Yeoiju hums in my chest, calling to the magic, and the surface of the door shimmers, dimly at first, then glows brighter and brighter.

My physical senses vaguely note the captain's grunts and labored breathing, her sword whooshing and ringing through the air. I faintly hear Minju's squeaks of alarm followed by dull thwacks. But I turn my mind inward again. This is where my focus belongs.

I don't force the magic from the doors. I coax it out. *You aren't needed here anymore.* The white orb on my palm shines—no longer weak and flickering—as the red gi flows into it in a gentle ribbon. *You can return to your life source.*

The white light burns bright, and my lungs expand on a full, satiating inhale. For a fleeting second, I wonder if my Yeoiju wants to cling on to the life force of Underworld—it's so powerful and beautiful. But when I release a flowing exhale, the glowing orb disperses the red gi into the air, and everything, including my white light, returns to where it belongs.

My Yeoiju hums softly in my chest, warm like a banked fire, and I blink away the white flame from my eyes. Disappointingly, the door is still just a door. A big, heavy door that I can't open. I slap my palm against it, dropping my head in defeat.

"Oh shit." I barely catch myself before I fall flat on my face.

When I regain my balance, the right half of the door stands ajar. I nudge it with the tips of my fingers, and the door opens wider without resistance. With an excited squeak, I spin around to face my friends.

"It was *push*, you guys," I squeal with a huge-ass grin, but my smile dies a quick death.

Captain Seo falls to one knee, crossing her swords above her head, and the entire Bizarro Sentinel crew bears down on her—their misshapen faces obscenely hungry. And Minju swings her book with wild eyes as my fake parents close in on her.

Doom threatens to buckle my knees. *I couldn't reach Draco in time.* I close my eyes. I can't watch more of my friends die. *Then don't.* I force my eyes open, my nails digging into my palms. I can't reach them in time, but the light of the Yeoiju can.

I won't let them hurt my friends.

My body clenches with fury, and I scream as white light explodes out of my chest. I feel heat coursing into me from behind. It feels different from the warmth of nature's gi in the Mortal Realm, but I don't have the bandwidth to decipher what that means.

I focus on my desperation to save my friends. I don't hold back. I let the white fire pour out of me. Captain Seo and Minju shield their eyes as the demons disintegrate fleck by fleck, like dry kindling on a log fire.

"Sunny," the captain calls out. "Sunny."

Her hoarse shout reaches me as though from far away. I don't know how long she's been calling my name, but bit by bit, I return to the present—to the edge of hell. The demons are gone, and my friends cringe against the Yeoiju's light, their eyes squeezed shut.

"Fuck." *I have to douse my magic.* Before I can try, the gi fueling the Yeoiju abruptly shuts off, and the white light sputters out on its own. I don't worry about the how, and instead run to my friends. "Are you okay?"

"Yes, we're fine," Captain Seo reassures me as I help her to her feet. "Thanks to you."

"How did you summon the Yeoiju?" Minju asks in a small voice. "Did you deplete your gi?"

"I . . . I don't think so." I shake my head. "I didn't have very much left in me."

"If you didn't use your own life force, then—"

"The gi of Underworld," I breathe. "I felt heat coursing into me, fueling the Yeoiju. I must've somehow absorbed the life force I released from the magic warding the door. I thought I sent the gi back to its life source, but maybe I unconsciously called it back?"

Minju bites her bottom lip, something like fear in her eyes.

"What's wrong?" Dread curls in my stomach. "You're scaring me."

"What?" The historian blinks rapidly then pffts with a flap of her hand. "It's nothing. *Wait.* You opened the door?"

Is she trying to distract me? Well, it works. "I sure did."

"So?" Captain Seo grins. "What are we waiting for?"

"Nothing at all," I say, then race the hell out of . . . hell.

CHAPTER SIXTEEN

Ethan

I don't mow down the enemy archers with a blast of magic. I need the physicality of hand-to-hand combat. Captain Seo found Sunny. But these fuckers scattered the precious message—the first connection with my fated love in days—and I am *not* inclined to forgive them.

Violence, impatience, and desire course through my veins. *Sunny is okay.* And I want her—no, *need* her—in my arms. For now, I will subdue these archers from the Kingdom of Sky with pleasure. With a vicious smile, I dispel the protective dome from around Jihun and me.

We descend on them with weapons drawn, knocking aside their fiery arrows like gnats, until we are too close for them to shoot. The panicked soldiers scramble for their swords, and I tut at their clumsiness. They are archers, not swordsmen. This won't be as satisfying as I'd hoped.

With leisurely slashes of our weapons, Jihun and I disarm the archers within seconds and bring them to their knees, just as our soldiers come running.

"Do not be alarmed." Jihun raises his voice. "Our king is safe."

"We came as soon as we heard the fighting." An officer addresses Jihun, confusion and worry lining her face.

"You didn't take long," he reassures her. "These bastards merely fell too quickly."

"Tie them up and question them." I snarl down at the enemy soldiers, my fury yet to be banked. "The rest of their battalion must be nearby."

"Yes, Your Majesty." Our soldiers execute sharp bows, then roughly bind the enemies, all the while sneaking glances at me. But this time, they don't look at me with nervous awe but with genuine respect.

I guess I earned some street cred with them. I nod at them and walk back toward my tent with Jihun at my side.

"That wasn't much of a fight, was it?" He meets my gaze, a corner of his lips curling.

"Not even a proper warm-up." I grin back. "Now, about that drink."

"Say no more." My royal adviser inclines his head in a wry bow. "You have more than earned a stiff drink, Your Majesty."

"And we have reason to celebrate." I'm practically skipping.

"Yes, we do," Jihun says with the biggest smile I've ever seen on him.

I want to punch it off his unreasonably handsome face. But only for a split second. *Sunny is mine.* I'm not being a possessive asshole. It's the simple truth. She belongs to me. And I belong to her.

I glance at Jihun from beneath my lashes, my chest clenching with regret. I don't want his heart broken, but it is unavoidable. I just hope it mends quickly and without scarring. He is my brother. I cannot do this without him.

The archers from the Kingdom of Sky speak to Jihun because he's a fellow seonnam, and also because they are none too happy with General Bak. They feel that they're nothing more than cannon fodder to the general. He doesn't value them or their lives. Not in the least.

If the general doesn't value his own men, then the lives of my people will mean nothing to him. My grandfather must be stopped, and fast.

Moving in the dead of night is risky, but we have no other option. If the enemy battalion suspects we captured their archers alive, they will realize their location might be compromised. We have to get to their camp before they can relocate.

This time, Jihun and I head our battalion on foot, rather than riding in the back. With the element of surprise on our side, I might be able to subdue their entire battalion in a silent heartbeat and avoid spilling blood—both ours and theirs.

The seraphim soldiers are not to blame for this war. They're just following orders. All the blame lies at General Bak's feet. The pain of his betrayal stabs at me, but I push it aside. I can't let my emotions distract me. The lives of my people depend on it.

Jihun raises his fist, and I jerk to a stop. At first, I don't see it. But I scan the woods surrounding us and the clearing ahead. *There.* The enemy's bivouac stands at the edge of the forest, with its soldiers sleeping in clusters.

I step forward, but Jihun stops me with a hand on my arm. "It is impossible to see how far their bivouac spreads out."

"I'll extend my magic as far as I can." I jut my jaw.

"That is exactly what I do *not* want you to do." My royal adviser levels me with a glower. "We need to fight a *war*. You can't expend all your gi on a single battle."

"What's the alternative?" I cross my arms over my chest armor. "Battle to the death?"

"I'm glad you asked," he says in a wry whisper. "We can infiltrate their camp, find their commanding officer, and extract their surrender."

"And how will you find this commanding officer?" I peer anxiously at the enemy camp. We don't have time to bicker.

"The same way they found you." Jihun arches an eyebrow. "Look for the tent. I can bind a dozen people at once, so I should be able to handle the guards without a ruckus. Then you can go and have a nice visit with the officer."

"Huh." I nod. "That might actually w—"

I draw in a strangled breath, and my gaze slowly drops to the arrow sticking out of my chest. It somehow got past my armor. But more shockingly, it got past my invincibility.

My knee buckles, but Jihun catches me before I fall, spinning around to put himself in the line of danger. *Gods damn it.* He needs to stop using his body as my shield.

"Your Majesty," he rasps, half carrying me behind a tree. "Lean on me."

"How . . . ?" Only weapons made with Dangun's tombstone—a sacred artifact in the Kingdom of Mountains—can pierce me. "How did General Bak get his hands on . . . ?"

"Don't speak." Jihun grips my shoulder. "You won't be able to heal until this comes out. Ready?"

I grunt when he rips the arrow out without waiting for my response, and I press my palm against the gush of hot blood. "Fucking hell."

"I need to inspect your wound." Jihun lowers me to the ground. "I couldn't push the arrow through without risking your internal organs, but pulling it out might have torn more tissues."

"I'll heal. It didn't hit my heart." But I grip his hand when he begins unbuckling my armor. Contrary to my assurance, the arrow might have *grazed* my heart. Still, there is no time for him to fuss over me. "The gi of Mountains heals me faster than the other shinbiins. The bleeding already slowed."

"Thank gods." Then he looks back at our soldiers and barks, "Stay back."

"Do you think this is a trap?" I lean my head against the tree, breathing through the pain. I *will* heal. It just hurts like a son of a bitch for the time being.

"No." Jihun shakes his head. "The camp hasn't stirred. It must be a lone assassin."

"Whoever it is must have night vision," I mutter. "Their aim is deadly."

My royal adviser beckons one of the officers from the company nearest us.

He approaches us on quick feet, low to the ground. "Yes, Lord Adviser."

"Form two squads of your best trackers and find the assassin," Jihun orders succinctly. "Do it quietly. I want them alive."

"Yes, Lord Adviser." The officer's gaze flickers toward me, and I give him a thumbs-up. He frowns at me for a second, then bows his head. "With your leave, Your Majesty."

"Go right ahead." I slur my words, and Jihun's sharp gaze focuses on me.

"I thought you already stopped bleeding?" he accuses and reaches for my armor again. I slap away his hand.

"Almost but not quite." I shift on the ground and groan. "And I have to admit it stings more than a paper cut."

"Fuck, Ethan." Jihun almost runs his hand down his face but stops when he sees my blood all over it. "You better not be lying."

I need to stop fucking around. I close my eyes and breathe, focusing on absorbing the gi of Mountains. I feel the tear in my heart healing first. Then, slowly, the wound on my chest mends itself.

I open my eyes again. "Let's go find that tent."

"Like hell you will," Jihun says through clenched teeth.

"I'm not taking this armor off, but my wound is completely closed." I push up to my feet before he can object. "Trust me."

He narrows his eyes at me with a distinct lack of trust. "Can you at least give our trackers a five-minute head start to capture the assassin? Or do you really want another arrow through your heart?"

"Not *through*," I grumble. "It just scratched my heart."

"I knew it." Jihun points a finger so close to my face that my eyes cross. "The arrow *did* hit your heart."

I walked right into that one. Maybe I do need that extra five minutes to get my head in order. I clear my throat and muster as much dignity as I can. "We will set out in five minutes, Lord Adviser."

"As you say, Your Majesty." He bows his head without a trace of irony.

But I know it's there.

I lean back against the tree trunk and sigh. I wish I had some Slim Jims to make up for the blood loss. They seemed to work wonders for Sunny.

I allow myself a wistful smile. *She's coming home.* Now that I know she's safe, nothing seems as dire. Not even the war. I can do anything with her by my side.

And the things I want to do *to* her when I get her to myself. *Gods.* I grow lightheaded for a reason entirely unrelated to an arrow to the heart. I chuckle under my breath. I'm hiding in the woods from an enemy battalion, and I have a hard-on for her. Having been inside her once, I don't think I could ever get enough.

I surreptitiously adjust my pants and turn my thoughts toward less arousing topics. Such as a sullen teenage dragon. My lips curve into a fond smile. I miss that kid. It'll be good to see them. I know they are one of the reasons Sunny is coming back to me.

Draco is utterly devoted to her. I know they did everything in their power to keep her safe. They are such a good kid, and I'm grateful they went after her. But I am ready to have Draco and Sunny back by my side, where I can keep them safe. They would both balk at the idea, but I will die protecting them, whether they like it or not.

"Has it been five minutes?" Adrenaline prickles across my skin. I can't stand around for another second.

"Not y—" Jihun goes still when there's a dull thud and a groan in the distance. "Sounds like they found the assassin."

"That's our cue." I step away from the tree and head toward the enemy bivouac with careful steps. Jihun follows close behind, without argument for once.

The soldiers of the Kingdom of Sky are not spread out too far from one another. We soon determine the periphery of their camp and move stealthily around it. But we reach the opposite end of the bivouac with no tent sighting.

Jihun circles his index finger in the air, suggesting we make our way around the other side. He leads the way, pulling out a pearlescent white plaque.

"You're going to flash your suhoshin captain emblem at them?" I whisper.

He deigns to glance over his shoulder, but the seonnam is much too dignified to roll his eyes. "The tent is likely warded. This emblem will emit a faint glow when it detects a ward."

"Awesome." I grin. "It's a two-in-one."

Jihun frowns and raises a finger to his lips. I wisely stop talking. With the weight of Sunny's disappearance lifted from my chest, I'm too giddy for my own good—for any of our good.

As we approach the midpoint of their camp, the emblem glows a ghostly white in the night. Jihun comes to a standstill and slowly pivots with the plaque. I watch silently at his side. I feel something too. A whisper of powerful magic.

Jihun tilts his head for me to follow and makes his way inward, flitting from point to point like a shadow. I do my best to mimic his movements, but I am not a seasoned suhoshin like him. My stomach clenches with nerves that I'll give us away.

Gods, I wish I was invisible.

The number of sleeping soldiers increases as we near the center of their camp. Then we discover the shimmering outline of a tent ahead of us. Enemy soldiers stand guard around the entirety of the tent, with their arms locked together, forming an impassable circle.

My brows draw low over my eyes. This isn't the tent of a commanding officer. They have someone inside that they don't want to escape—a prisoner. Jihun turns toward me with a grim set of his mouth, then he jolts, a gasp slipping past his lips. He freezes in place until he's certain no one heard him before swiveling his head left and right.

What the hell?

I can't dare ask him what's going on. But when his eyes widen with panic, I clamp a hand on his shoulder. For some reason, that scares the shit out of him. His extensive training is probably the only thing that stops Jihun from scrambling away from me, screaming his head off—that and his nerves of steel.

His Adam's apple bobs as he tries and fails to swallow, then he takes a measured breath and reaches out a hand. He pats my face, and I shove his hand away, glaring at him. But he blows out a sigh, his whole body sagging for a second. Then he looks toward me again, an odd smile spreading across his face.

I side-eye the seonnam. He needs food and rest. He is unwell.

Jihun gives his head a sharp shake and scans the area around the tent. Then he points at a diminutive seonnyeo sitting cross-legged near the entrance to the tent, two soldiers flanking her. Glancing in my direction, but not quite meeting my eyes, he presses one forearm over the other in an *X*.

I rear back. *He wants me to kill her?*

I take a closer look at the seraph. She wears a hanbok with a long overcoat made of a patchwork of blue, red, yellow, and white fabrics. Her eyes are closed, and her hands rest over her knees, her thumb and middle finger pressed together. It's difficult to be certain in the dark, but her lips quaver as though she is talking to herself.

The seonnyeo is casting a spell. The tent isn't protected by stagnant wards. She is continuously reinforcing the wards. A memory—my mother's—sparks in the back of my mind, and I recognize the female as a spell maiden, a rare shinbiin whose affinity lies in spoken spells rather than elemental magic.

Jihun stands patiently at my side while I figure it out on my own. He wants me to entrap her under a dome and cut off her magic. I have to stop her from casting her wards on the tent for us to get inside. I nod at Jihun, but his gaze stays on the spell maiden.

I extend my arms in front of me, pressing my wrists together, and fire a stream of gi from my palms toward the seonnyeo and the two soldiers guarding her. When my magic engulfs them, her eyes snap open, and her guards spin from side to side, their mouths gaping with shock.

Before the soldiers circling the tent can alert the rest of the camp, Jihun binds all of them—hands, feet, and mouths.

"Is it done?" A muscle tics in his jaw.

"Yes, I've trapped the spell maiden and her guards," I whisper.

With a nod, he heads for the tent entrance, glancing over his shoulders. The bivouac remains quiet. I follow Jihun inside and bump straight into his back. *What the . . .* I step around him to find his face slack, and I trace his line of sight.

A female sleeps on a mat in the center of the tent, her long braided hair lying over one shoulder. She's beautiful, but I see her pallor in the dim glow of a light orb, and her lips have a faint purple tint to them.

Gods. She isn't asleep. She has been poisoned.

"Who is she?" I ask in a wary voice.

"She is"—Jihun blinks and drags himself out of his stupor—"the Queen of Sky."

THE FOUR GODS

The Cheon'gwang bestowed divine life force on the four gods—the god of Heavens, the god of Earth, the god of Water, and the god of Underworld—to protect the worlds and all the beings within them.

When the time came, the Cheon'gwang sacrificed itself to imprison the Amheuk beyond the abyss—for only true light can defeat eternal darkness—and the Endless War was no more. But in its absence, the four gods grew arrogant and selfish.

Ungnyeo, a bear with a noble spirit, saved the god of Earth, Hwanung, from losing his way like the other gods. She taught him love, humility, and selflessness, and the fated mates watched over the Mortal Realm with generosity and benevolence. Their happiness was complete when they were blessed with a son, Dangun, who was good, through and through.

But Hwanin, the god of Heavens, thought Ungnyeo—a mere mortal and a bear spirit—beneath his divine son and asked Hwanung to return to the Kingdom of Sky. He even offered to take in his half-blood grandson, as long as they left Ungnyeo behind. Hwanung refused.

The god of Heavens bitterly resented his son's happiness with his mortal wife—called it obscene and wrong. To justify his own vile heart, Hwanin convinced himself that Ungnyeo schemed to steal his son away from him—that she destroyed his family. He spread his vitriol in the Realm of Four Kingdoms by convincing the Shinbiin that animal spirits were lying, deceitful creatures.

But even that proved insufficient to satisfy Hwanin's hate. And the god of Heavens vowed to have vengeance on Ungnyeo.

CHAPTER SEVENTEEN

SUNNY

I glance at the menacing black door a few steps behind us. My friends and I finally made it out of hell, but we didn't get very far.

"Fuck my life," I sigh as very tall, very broad males—dressed in tailored black suits of all things—swarm us, brandishing caveman clubs covered with inch-long spikes. I glare at Minju. "I thought dokkaebis didn't use spiked clubs. You said I was being *offensive*."

"I will allow this *once* that I was mistaken," the historian says primly, even as she presses up against me.

"Ya think?" I yell.

"Perhaps we should shelve that discussion for another time." Captain Seo stands with her back against mine and raises her twin swords.

"Right." I sandwich Minju between myself and the captain, then hold out the Shin'gwangdo, taking a defensive stance.

The ten mountainous goblins sprint headlong toward us. My blood pounds in my ears. I bounce on the balls of my feet to stop myself from paralyzing in fear. A battle cry rips out of my mouth when they're almost on top of us. Then . . . the males rush right past us, like they don't even see us.

What in the ever-loving hell?

The dokkaebis collectively heave the black metal door shut, inch by arduous inch. It seems much heavier than when I pushed it open with next to no effort. My friends and I can't help but flinch when the door shuts with an ominous thud.

Gods, I never want to go back in there.

It occurs to me too late that maybe we should've made a run for it while they were distracted. Because with the door to hell shut, the dokkaebis swiftly surround us in various threatening poses. They move awfully fast for such ginormous people. They would actually be intimidating, if it weren't for their ridiculous sunglasses.

"I appreciate the nod to *Men in Black*," I drawl, gripping the hilt of the Shin'gwangdo with both hands. "But are the shades really necessary in the middle of the night?"

I can't tell where we are. Dull, gray fog surrounds us as far as even my magic gi goggles can see. There are no trees, buildings, or anything at all, except for hell's door behind us and the towering goblins looming in front of us.

I *can* see the night sky above us, though. The moon seems impossibly far away, as small as my pinky nail, but it *is* nighttime, so no sunglasses necessary.

"Sunny." Minju tugs on the sleeve of my T-shirt. "Goading them might not be the best idea."

"We can remove the sunglasses, if you prefer," the biggest of the big dokkaebis says in a smooth, dark voice. He steps toward us and takes off his sunglasses with one hand, angling his head just so.

"Oh my," Minju breathes.

Oh my is right. The move is so blatantly sexy that I bite my index finger, considering asking him to do it again . . . mostly to aggravate him but also because I wouldn't mind seeing him do that again.

The saucy request, however, dies on my lips when he raises his head and meets my gaze. A chill runs down my spine, and this time, it isn't the good kind.

His eyes are completely black. No pupils, no irises, no sclera. Just *all* black.

"Please don't trouble yourself on our account." Captain Seo clears her throat, not quite meeting the male's eyes.

"Thank you. That is very thoughtful of you." The goblin gives her a crooked grin as he puts his sunglasses back on in a reverse striptease.

I swear the captain *sighs* like a smitten teenage girl when the sunglasses slide back in place. I gleefully tuck away the moment as future teasing material. *Absolute gold.*

"Now then," the biggest dokkaebi continues, "shall we discuss what brings you to our kingdom?"

"Why don't we start with a round of introductions?" I quip. "You go first."

I feel another tug on my sleeve. I ignore her, but she tugs again. I turn to Minju with bulging eyes. "What?"

"I know who they are," she whispers, sneaking a peek at them. "They are the Judges of Ten Hells."

I study the ten males consideringly. Sure, they have chilling eyes—I focus my magic gi goggles on them—but their life force, while powerful, is not god level. As a matter of fact—I squint and look more closely—something depleted a chunk of their gi recently, but they are recovering quickly. Either way, they are mighty as they come and should not be trifled with.

But trifling is so much fun.

"Hmm." I lower my sword a smidgen. "I'm not familiar with the Judges of Ten Hells. Are they special or something?"

Captain Seo makes a choking sound from behind me, and Minju covers a scandalized gasp with her hand. The sexy dokkaebi chuckles darkly, the sound rumbling in his chest. I start to fan my face, but I catch myself and pretend to scratch my neck.

"I still think introductions are necessary." I dig my heels in because I am a gumiho of conviction. "Do you guys go by numbers or names?"

Minju emits a high-pitched squeak, and the captain kicks my calf with her heel. I ignore them both.

"I am the Judge of Tenth Hell." He dips his head in a gallant bow. "My friends call me Gyun."

"And my friends call me . . ." I remember the nickname Haesan, my suhoshin-cadet buddy, gave me. *Stormy.* I suddenly miss the massive merman so much that my breath hitches. "I'm Sunny."

"Why are you here, Sunny?" The Judge of Tenth Hell cocks his head to a tantalizing angle. "And how did you escape the Tenth Hell?"

"That was Tenth Hell?" It's an honest question since I had no idea that was *Tenth* Hell. And also, I'm stalling. "Is Tenth Hell the worst hell? With First Hell being the nicest? Or is it the other way around? Although, I can't imagine *any* hell being nice—"

"Sunny," he says my name so softly that I barely hear him, but his tone scares me enough to shut me up. For a second.

"Now would be a good time to help," I hiss at my friends from the corner of my mouth.

Do we tell him the truth? How much of the truth do we tell him? My gut tells me he isn't our enemy, but that doesn't make him our ally either.

"We walked the moonglade from the Mortal Realm to return to the Realm of Four Kingdoms," Minju explains succinctly.

I guess we're going with the truth.

Surprise rumbles through the judges, but they grow silent when the Judge of Tenth Hell holds up a hand. "Why did you choose that deadly path instead of entering past the Gray Void?"

"Because the Gray Void no longer exists, and . . ." Minju takes a bracing breath. "The Amheuk now lies in its place."

There are no surprised murmurs this time around. The judges simply lose their *fucking shit.*

"The Amheuk?" cries one judge.

Others whip their heads around every which way, as though the ancient force of darkness is descending on them right this second.

"But how could that be?" another yells, shaking the poor dokkaebi next to him by the shoulders.

Maybe the *whole* truth wasn't the best idea.

I shrug with a tilt of my head. Who can stay calm when somebody basically tells you that you're all going to die? Their alarm is to be expected. What I *didn't* expect was for them to take Minju at her word.

People tend to become angry when they're scared. And when they're angry, they start pointing fingers to cast the blame on the easiest scapegoat. I expected them to accuse Minju of lying, of trying to trick them for her own gain. They should be vilifying her—punishing her—to hide from their own fears.

But apparently, the Judges of Ten Hells don't point fingers and cast blame on others. They feel and express their fear authentically. That is a sign of true strength. I respect them for it, and maybe I can even . . . trust them.

When the Judge of Tenth Hell raises both hands, the other judges finally fall silent, even as they continue exchanging alarmed glances past their sunglasses.

"We have many questions, but I believe the most pertinent one is this." The Judge of Tenth Hell looks at Minju, Captain Seo, and me in turn. "Why did you risk your lives to return to the Realm of Four Kingdoms when you knew the Amheuk has breached the realm?"

"To stop it from destroying the worlds." The captain offers Minju and me a solemn nod of solidarity. "Or die trying."

The dokkaebi's eyebrows rise over his sunglasses. "Is that true for all of you?"

"Yes," Minju and I answer as one.

"Huh." The Judge of Tenth Hell turns to me. "May I ask why you would do that?"

I open my mouth to tell him I'm doing it for the adrenaline rush, but I hear myself saying, "To protect the one I love, because he is my beating heart. And to save my friends, because they are my family. I will give my life for them, because there is no life without them."

My eyes do their best to mimic saucers, and I clap a hand over my mouth, hard enough to sting.

Did I just say those things out loud?

"You can only tell the truth to the Judges of Ten Hells." Minju runs a soothing hand down my back. "They can't decide the fate of a passing soul based on lies, so it is literally impossible to lie to them."

"I guess sarcasm counts as lying," I mutter, shaken from baring my fucking soul to total strangers. In front of *my friends*. I don't know which part is more embarrassing.

Also, the judges decide the fate of the passing souls? Not the god of Underworld?

"Please, call me Gyun," the Judge of Tenth Hell says with a warm, open smile, oblivious to my monumental mortification and confusion. "There is no reason more noble than yours, and I would be proud to call you my friends."

"I might not want any more friends." Loving the ones I already have is overwhelming enough. "But I guess it's better than being bludgeoned to a pulp with a spiked club. Wait. If we make friends with one of you, does that mean we have to be friends with *all* of you?"

"I'm afraid so," a younger looking dokkaebi says with laughter in his voice. "Hi, I'm Jun. I'm the Judge of First Hell—the nicest hell."

He's teasing me. We really must be friends.

"Sunny gets loopy in dangerous situations. It's her coping mechanism," Captain Seo explains on my behalf. "Hi, Jun. I'm Cheyun, and this is Minju. Now that we're all friends, can one of you show me the quickest way to the Kingdom of Mountains?"

His smile dims by a fraction of a watt. "Why are you in such a hurry to go to a war-ridden kingdom?"

"So General Bak followed through with his plan," Minju murmurs in toneless dejection. "He waged war on the Kingdom of Mountains—against his own grandson."

My molars grind together as my entire body clenches with helpless rage. If the general hurts Ethan—if *anyone* hurts him—I might set the whole world on fire. It kills me that I can't go to him when he needs me. But it's my own fault for foolishly letting the tyrant king trick me into the blood oath, keeping me away from Ethan.

For a split second, I consider going to the Kingdom of Mountains anyway. But I stare down at my left palm and trace the circle of blood branded on the mound beneath my thumb. If I break the oath, I will bleed from the circle until I die a quick but painful death.

I am not afraid of pain or death, but I am no use to Ethan or my friends if I'm dead. I need a chance to do better. I owe it to them. I owe it to myself.

"That war is why I have to return to the Kingdom of Mountains without delay." Captain Seo answers Jun's question. "I need to help them stop the Kingdom of Sky's unprovoked assault—to end a senseless war waged to satisfy one male's thirst for vengeance. Only then can the four kingdoms unite to fight the real war against the Amheuk."

Captain Seo is right. The four kingdoms must unite. If they can't work together, we might as well hand over the realm to the Amheuk.

I draw a sharp breath, goose bumps blanketing my skin. Ethan must unite the four kingdoms and defend the realm from the eternal darkness. *That* is his destiny as the King Foretold.

"I will take you to the portal," a soft-voiced dokkaebi says. "I'm Mun, the Judge of Fourth Hell."

"They really should go by numbers," I murmur without thinking, still reeling from how the prophecy of the King Foretold will be fulfilled. "There's no way we'll remember all these na—"

"Thank you, Mun." Captain Seo raises her voice over my blabber, then glares at me.

I cringe sheepishly. *Right.* I probably shouldn't insult the only beings who can take us where we need to go. But where do *I* go from here? I can't return to the Kingdom of Mountains without dying. Maybe I can help Ethan from the Kingdom of Underworld.

"I am a historian with the Order of the Suhoshin." Minju pulls back her shoulders, determination in every line of her lovely face. "I need access to the nearest Suhoshin library. I must do my part to defend against the Amheuk."

"It would be my honor to escort you to the Kingdom of Underworld's Suhoshin headquarters." Jun executes a gallant bow.

"Is there anywhere *you* need to be, Sunny?" Gyun asks dryly.

"As a matter of fact, there is." My heart pounds in my chest with half nerves and half determination. I know how to help Ethan. "I need an audience with the King of Underworld."

CHAPTER EIGHTEEN

Sunny

The foggy, gray place outside hell's door is not the Kingdom of Underworld. I, in fact, do not know where this place is, and the Judges of Ten Hells insist on keeping it that way.

"You want us to put *these* on?" I stare down at the black-on-black sunglasses in my hands, while Minju and Captain Seo do the same. "Wouldn't blindfolds be more secure?"

Judge Number Eight mutters about the flimsiness of cloth blindfolds, and Judge Number Three clucks his tongue and nudges the other judge with his shoulder.

"Trust us." Jun, the judge of the nicest hell, grins encouragingly at us. "These work much better."

Flexing her nerves of steel, the captain puts hers on first. "Whoa."

"What? What is it?" Minju's curiosity gets the best of her, and she rushes to put hers on. "Goodness. It's like someone snuffed out all the stars and the moon. I can't see *anything*."

"No." Captain Seo brings her palm up to her nose. "Not even a vague outline."

"If you please." Gyun, the Judge of Tenth Hell, gestures for me to put on my sunglasses. "We cannot let anyone discover the location of the Ten Hells."

I shrug and put mine on, then sigh ponderously. I consider not telling them for a brief second, but trust matters between friends. "I can see through these."

"No, you cannot," Mun, the Judge of Fourth Hell, states with absolute certainty. "No one other than the Judges of Ten Hells can see through these sunglasses."

I roll my eyes behind my sunglasses, then wonder if I look cool in them. They're a lot like classic Ray-Bans.

"I thought I couldn't lie to you guys." I cross my arms over my chest and wait patiently for him to realize he's wrong.

"No, you cannot," Mun concedes. "Then I do not understand."

I fully understand his confusion. My best guess is that I can see through these because of my magic gi goggles. But that's going to be a long explanation.

"Please don't ask us to explain." Minju clasps her hands together. "It is a rather long story, and time is of the essence. One of your ties will work nicely as a blindfold, and Sunny will promise not to peek. Won't you?"

"I pinky promise." I smirk and hold up my pinky, thinking no one will take me up on it. But Jun bounds up to me like a golden retriever and links his pinky through mine. I can't help but smile. "Do you want me to stamp it too?"

"Do I ever." He presses his thumb against mine. "There."

"Please allow me." Gyun tugs on the knot of his tie.

Holy mother of Dangun.

I watch mesmerized as the Judge of Tenth Hell takes off his tie. I'm hopelessly in love with Ethan. The Realm of Four Kingdoms faces imminent annihilation. Yet . . . I cannot look away from the smoking-hot judge.

He tilts his head this way and that, exposing the strong column of his neck. And his sleeve slips down to expose a strip of his wrist. It is positively *indecent,* even with his shirt buttoned up to the top.

Gyun finally tugs his tie free and holds it out to me. It couldn't have taken more than seven seconds, but I swipe a hand across my mouth in case I drooled.

"Thanks," I warble, taking the tie from him. I quickly wrap it over my eyes to hide my fluster. "Who's taking me to the Jeoseung Palace again?"

"That would be me," Gyun murmurs at my side, and I squeak a little.

Oh for fuck's sake.

"Can I take these sunglasses off for a moment?" Minju asks.

"Of course." Jun consents without hesitation.

A second later, I grunt as I'm tackle hugged by a small seonny-eo-dokkaebi. "Be safe, Sunny."

I wrap my arms around her and hug her back. "I'll see you soon, Minju."

"And I will see you soon as well." Captain Seo squeezes my shoulder, and I give her an awkward bro hug.

"The dead wait for no one. Not even the Amheuk." Gyun speaks in a grim voice. "Judges, with the exception of Mun and Jun, please return to your posts. And keep an eye out for the dead entering the First, Fourth, and Tenth Hells. We will be back as soon as we escort our new friends to their destinations."

I hear a series of whooshes. *Damn.* I wish I could've seen how the judges made their exit.

"So . . . how do we do this?" I reach out with my hand until I feel a solid wall, which I assume is Gyun.

"With your permission, I will carry you," he says.

"Of course you will." I sigh. "I mean, you have my permission."

As soon as the words leave my mouth, I'm lifted off my feet and something weird happens. I can't feel myself—like I don't . . . exist.

Am I dead? Is Gyun a bad friend? Did he kill *me?*

Suddenly I smell smoke, warm and fragrant like a Yule log burning in the fireplace. *Okay, I must not be dead.* I sniff again, the tip of my nose pressed against the side of someone's—I assume Gyun's—neck. He's the one who smells like a burning log.

"We're here." He sets me down on my feet. "Welcome to the capital of the Kingdom of Underworld."

I tug Gyun's tie off, and my jaw drops as I take in the city. We're standing on a hill, looking down on . . . a metropolis.

It's not flashy like the Las Vegas Strip, or Times Square, but several tall black buildings jut into the sky, and streetlamps dot the concrete roads winding through the city. Granted, there are no cars on the road but—A fucking motorcycle rushes by below us.

I fling my arm out so fast that Gyun jumps back to avoid getting smacked. Then I flap my hand wildly in an effort to encompass all . . . that.

"How?" I sputter. "Technology . . . Magic . . . How?"

"It is *technically* not technology in the way you're thinking. No pun intended." Gyun shrugs a big shoulder. "It's what humans would call 'analog.' Our machinery is made of cogs and gears, but powered by magic. And we build everything by hand, using principles similar to somok woodworking, where precise joints are created to interlock and fit together."

"That is *not* wood." I jab an accusing finger at the tallest building, made with some kind of gleaming black material.

"No, the Jeoseung Palace is built with volcanic stones." He tilts his head, admiring the dark high-rise.

"Are you saying your people cut joints and grooves into volcanic stones?" I lower my hand, unclutching my figurative pearls.

"It took many years of hard work and dedication, but we wanted the Jeoseung Palace to symbolize our kingdom's commitment to advancement."

"*Commitment to advancement*?" I repeat like a parrot.

"The rest of the kingdoms in this realm believe that magic should be stagnant." He shakes his head. "But the Kingdom of

Underworld studies magic to develop ways to move forward with the rest of the worlds."

"How is that not science?" I think science is spectacular. Magic defies logic, but science achieves magical results, following the rules of logic. I just don't understand how magic can coexist with it. "How are your advancements not *technically* technology?"

"We are still figuring that out." He looks out at the city. "But we do know that the crux of the conflict between magic and technology comes from digitization and the type of energy used to power the machinery."

"Fascinating," I breathe. "So this is the capital of the Kingdom of Underworld?"

"Yes." Gyun sticks out his huge chest, like a proud father. "The rest of the kingdom isn't as advanced, but we'll get there."

I want to gawk and ask more questions about magical advances, but that will have to wait.

"Do you hear that?" I cup my ear and pretend to listen. "I think I hear the tortured souls of Tenth Hell calling for you."

"Not funny." A corner of his mouth tics up. "But I do need to get back. Are you ready?"

"To meet the King of Underworld?" I gulp. "Heck yeah."

"He's a nice guy." Gyun wraps his hand around my arm. "You'll like him."

Then something tries to vacuum my soul out of my body—or at least, it feels that way—and we're standing inside a sleek black lobby on the top floor of what I'm guessing is the Jeoseung Palace. A female with a pinched face sits behind a black reception desk in a trim black skirt suit.

So much black. I might like this kingdom.

"We need an audience with the king," Gyun tells her without preamble.

The female's eyes widen, but she gathers herself. "Do you have an appointment, Your Honor?"

"No." He shakes his head once. "Regardless, please inform the king that I need to speak with him urgently."

"Will your . . . guest wait outside for you?" Her nose crinkles ever so slightly.

"No, she will accompany me." An eyebrow arches above his sunglasses. "Have no doubt. He will see us."

"Of course, Your Honor." The female rises to her feet and rushes to a tall double door, guarded by two grim reapers, then she murmurs, "Your Majesty?"

"Yes," a voice answers from behind the doors, and the floor vibrates beneath me.

Holy shit.

I have never heard a single more intimidating sound. I'm not sure if I want to meet the King of Underworld anymore. I am literally quaking in my combat boots. I might want to gouge my eyes out, magic gi goggles and all, if the king looks as scary as he sounds.

"Forgive me for disturbing you. But the Judge of Tenth Hell has an urgent matter to discuss with you." She glances over her shoulder at me. "And he has brought a guest."

I roll my eyes. I'm not suppressing my magic. She knows I'm a gumiho, and she obviously doesn't approve of my existence. *I change my mind.* I don't like this kingdom any better than the other three.

"Send them in." The whole lobby rumbles at the king's voice.

I gulp as anxiety washes over me, but I pull my shoulders back. How hard can it be to convince the King of Underworld to send troops to aid the Kingdom of Mountains, then bend his knee to Ethan?

Hard. It will probably be very hard.

CHAPTER NINETEEN

Sunny

I refrain from sticking my tongue out at the snooty receptionist as Gyun and I walk past her into the breathtaking throne room of the Jeoseung Palace.

Three of its walls are floor-to-ceiling glass with a spectacular view of the glittering city below. An onyx throne with an impossibly high back—edgy, both figuratively and literally—stands on a dais at the opposite end of a black carpeted path. But no king sits on the throne.

"This way," Gyun says close to my ear.

We find the King of Underworld working over a cluttered desk strewn with glittering cogs and gears, nuts and bolts, and a thousand other bits and pieces I don't recognize. He's wearing a rumpled black T-shirt and loose black jeans, muttering at an intricate contraption in his hands. His onyx crown rests atop a riot of shiny, black curls, tipping precariously to the side.

The King of Underworld is *nothing* like I expected. The male standing before me can only be described as a hot nerd, both endearing and weirdly sexy. Not intimidating at all.

"Your Majesty." When the king doesn't respond, Gyun smiles with indulgent affection and repeats, "Your Majesty."

“Gyun.” The King of Underworld looks up with a wide smile and trips in his hurry to give the Judge of Ten Hells a hug. “It’s been too long. You have to look at this calculator I’m working on . . .”

“The calculator might have to wait,” Gyun interjects when the king takes a breath. “This is Sunny, Your Majesty. She has something to tell you.”

“Wow. You’re a gumiho.” The king focuses his gaze on me with disconcerting intensity. At least he stopped using his earthquake-inducing voice. “If it isn’t an imposition, I would love to see your fox form. I imagine you are quite glorious.”

“Your Majesty.” Gyun rests his hand on the king’s arm. “That will also have to wait. I’m afraid this is quite urgent.”

The chaotic energy around the king abruptly settles into an intense quiet. He nods once to the Judge of Tenth Hell and turns toward me again. I didn’t see it before, but he truly is the King of Underworld. Beneath the mess of curls and disheveled clothes, he is all power and authority.

“Tell me.” His command reverberates through me.

I might not have his full attention for long, so I go straight for the kill. “The Gray Void has been destroyed, and the Amheuk has breached the Realm of Four Kingdoms.”

“Gyun.” The king keeps his narrowed eyes on me. “Please question her for me.”

Of course. He wants to make sure I’m telling the truth. Considering the gravity of the situation, I’m not too insulted.

The judge complies with the king’s wishes in an even tone. “Has the Amheuk breached the Realm of Four Kingdoms?”

“Yes.” I level an acerbic look at the king. I should probably be more respectful, but I’ve had a long day.

“Ask her what destroyed the Gray Void,” the king says.

“*I* did.” I slash my hand across the air when he turns to Gyun. “Stop wasting my time. I am telling the *truth*.”

"But why did you destroy the Gray Void?" the judge asks in genuine confusion.

"It wasn't a conscious choice. I entered the Gray Void with a word of power branded on my back, and it tried to destroy the rune's dark magic, which would have killed me." I harden myself against the onslaught of memories. The unforgiving cold of the Gray Void. The fire of the ancient rune burning through me. The pain as the two forces threatened to tear me in half. "But my survival instinct kicked in, and I somehow destroyed both the ancient rune and the Gray Void."

Then I remember the desperation of the stranded and their heartfelt gratitude at being freed.

"The Gray Void contained countless stranded souls. They were all trapped there . . . suffering," I murmur past numb lips. "When I destroyed the Gray Void, I ended up releasing them from their captivity."

The Judge of Tenth Hell pales, horror filling his eyes, but the King of Underworld simply looks resigned.

"You knew about the stranded." I don't pose it as a question—it's a sharp-edged accusation and condemnation—but he answers anyway.

"Yes." His Adam's apple bobs.

"Your Majesty." Gyun's voice breaks. "To exist in a timeless void with no agency, no hope, no end in sight . . . That is a fate worse than any punishment in the Ten Hells. Their very existence must have been *pain*. You knew? Yet you did nothing?" Disappointment bleeds into his words. "How could you, Taeyoung?"

"I have no excuse." The king drops his head. "Ever since I took the throne and inherited that bloody legacy, I have been doing everything in my power to find a way to free the stranded without destroying the Gray Void. But I couldn't figure out how any of it works. I don't even know where those stranded souls came from . . ."

Curiosity and impatience war inside me. I want to understand the truth of the Gray Void. I want to make sense of all that suffering. But . . . the stranded have already been freed. Saving the Realm of Four Kingdoms has to come first.

"Now isn't the time to seek absolution." I cut him off.

"You're right." The king offers me a solemn nod. "If the Amheuk has truly breached the Realm of Four Kingdoms, we have no time to waste."

"One last question, Sunny." The Judge of Tenth Hell scrubs his hands over his face. "*How* did you destroy the Gray Void?"

"I have . . ." *Have* seems like such a passive word to describe the connection between the Yeoiju and me. But I don't have a thesaurus on me, so I continue, "I have the Yeoiju."

The king and the judge exchange a startled glance, and Gyun murmurs, "The prophecies are coming to pass."

The prophecies in the plural again. I only know about the prophecy of the King Foretold, and the Yeoiju doesn't come into it. What does the second prophecy have to do with the Yeoiju? With me?

I rub my forehead. "*What* prophecies?"

"Both the prophecy of the King Foretold and the prophecy of the End of Days," the judge answers.

"How do you know about the prophecy of the King Foretold?" I ask to hide my ignorance about the other one.

"Our diviners have been barraged with visions of the two prophecies for the last few months." The King of Underworld has that eager, nerdy excitement back on his face. "If you truly hold the Yeoiju, and you must, since you cannot lie to Gyun, then you are part of the prophecy of the End of Days. But I disagree with the prevalent interpretation—"

"Th-that's not important right now." I take a choked breath. I don't want to know about the prophecy of the End of Days. "But if you know about the prophecy of the King Foretold, then you must know what must be done."

"The four kingdoms must be united under the King Foretold in order to defend the realm against the Amheuk," the king answers without hesitation.

"Then will you help stop the Kingdom of Sky's invasion on the Kingdom of Mountains?" Pleading enters my voice. I don't care if I'm begging if I can help Ethan. "Will you bend a knee to the King of Mountains?"

"If I make this quick and easy"—the King of Underworld smiles wanly—"do you think there will be time for you to give me a glimpse of the Yeoiju's power?"

"Taeyoung." Gyun shoots a startled glance at his king. "This is not a decision to make lightly."

The King of Underworld slowly faces the Judge of Tenth Hell, straightening to his full stature. The two of them are about the same height, but the king suddenly seems to tower over the enormous judge.

"You do not know me if you believe I make this decision lightly." His voice rumbles like thunder, and I clap my hands over my ears. I definitely should be more respectful toward him.

"Forgive me, Your Majesty." The judge bows low, well and truly chastised. "Wherever you lead, I will follow."

"I know you will." The king's expression softens. "Assemble the generals. We have a war to win and a realm to protect."

"Yes, Your Majesty." With a quick nod my way, Gyun hurries toward the doors.

"Gyun, wait," I call out and run up to him. "Tell the Judge of Fourth Hell . . . What's his name? The one taking Cheyun to the portal to the Kingdom of Mountains? By the way, you guys really should go by numbers."

"Mun." Gyun, a.k.a. Number Ten, arches an eyebrow.

"Yes." I hold out both hands. "Can you ask Mun to tell Cheyun to wait? She can guide the Kingdom of Underworld's army to the Shinsi Palace."

"Understood." With a sharp grin and a two-fingered salute, the Judge of Tenth Hell rushes out the door.

I return to the King of Underworld's side and belatedly remember my manners. "Um, thank you, Your Majesty."

"I am merely doing what is best for my kingdom and this realm." The king seems back to his disheveled, nerdy self. "So about that glimpse . . ."

I don't fully understand this powerful yet endearing king, but my instinct is to trust him, as I trust Gyun. Trust isn't something I give easily, because it makes me vulnerable. But I'm starting to understand that it also makes me stronger.

"With all due respect, Your Majesty." I shake my head in teasing resignation. "You are kind of a nerd."

"I will own that proudly." The King of Underworld offers me a lopsided grin.

Rolling my eyes at him, I summon a small white orb to my palm. My smile falters when the light flickers, a dull ache squeezing my heart.

"Fascinating." The king leans in, unaware of my discomfort, and stretches out a hand toward the light.

"Careful with that." I fist my hand and extinguish the light before he hurts himself, and to stop hurting myself.

"My apologies," he says sheepishly. "I get carried away when I encounter something unique."

"Sounds like a friend I know." *I hope Minju is doing okay at the Suhoshin headquarters.* "May I ask you a question?"

"Certainly."

"Are you on relatively good terms with the King of Water?" I know the four kingdoms have been in some sort of a feud for centuries.

"Queen," he murmurs. "The Queen of Water. And we are not exactly on good terms."

"Like mortal-enemies 'not good'?" I worry my bottom lip. "Or different-tastes-in-literature 'not good'?"

"She and I . . . do not get along." A muscle bunches in his jaw.

"So there is no way for me to get an introduction?" I ask weakly.

By some miracle, we have the Kingdom of Underworld on our side, but we need the Kingdom of Water as well. I was able to convince the King of Underworld that everything I said was true, because we had a living, breathing lie detector in the room. I don't know how I'm going to convince the Queen of Water. I was hoping the king could put in a good word for me.

"Not from me, I'm afraid." The king cocks his head to the side. "Do you know anyone from the Kingdom of Water? Preferably a friend?"

"Yes," I breathe. "I do have a friend from the Kingdom of Water."

I don't want to put that annoyingly kindhearted in'eo in danger, but Haesan might be my only hope of enlisting the Queen of Water to our side. Besides, everyone in the Realm of Four Kingdoms is already doomed. What's a little more mortal danger?

CHAPTER TWENTY

Ethan

"Is she okay?" I ask Jihun, who presses his fingertips against the Queen of Sky's wrist.

"There's a pulse." His lips thin into a grim line. "A weak one."

"What do you think she's doing here?" I study her pale face. *My aunt.*

"After your mother died, General Bak forced his younger daughter to marry the King of Sky, who was nearly a thousand years old." Jihun pats her cheek lightly, trying to make her stir. "The general wanted her to convince the king to wage war against the Kingdom of Mountains. But even after the king passed away, the war never came because the queen held her ground against her father."

"How convenient for the general that she suddenly changed her mind." My mouth twists with bitterness.

"*Too* convenient." he says meaningfully.

"You mean General Bak poisoned his own daughter to usurp her army?" Nausea churns in my stomach.

"That seems to be the most likely explanation." Jihun gently shakes the queen's shoulder. "Your Majesty, can you hear me?"

"The general couldn't leave her in the Kingdom of Sky, because he was afraid someone would find her and discover what he'd done." It all makes sense now. "So he brought her to the Kingdom of Mountains and hid her in the middle of a battlefield."

"And he needed her close to keep poisoning her to prevent her from regaining consciousness. I don't think he intended to kill her, but he might have poisoned her one too many times for her healing powers to save her." Jihun meets my eyes. "She needs a physician. It might already be too late . . ."

The Queen of Sky is the only blood relative I have that doesn't want me dead. Unfortunately, she might pay for her nonmurderous nature with her own life.

I won't let that happen.

"We need to get her out of here." I glance toward the entrance. "How long can you keep the soldiers bound?"

"Not much longer." His voice is strained but steely. "But you cannot take down the entire battalion."

"You're right. At least, not until we get her out of harm's way," I say grimly. "We'll just have to see how long my shield lasts with hundreds of soldiers attacking us."

"Well, actually"—Jihun's lips curve in an unexpected smile—"you can test your endurance another time."

"What?" I side-eye him. "You have a better idea?"

"I do, as a matter of fact." He sounds positively smug. "We can simply walk out . . . after you turn us invisible."

"What have you been smoking?" I sputter.

"Earlier, when we were approaching the tent"—he holds my gaze—"you turned invisible."

If he were anyone else, I wouldn't have believed him. But this is Jihun. He is much too dignified to fuck around with me.

"Whoa," I breathe. "Is that why you freaked out and palmed my face?"

"You can't blame me. You suddenly . . . disappeared." He huffs a silent laugh. "I had to make sure you didn't evaporate into thin air."

"Fuck." My thoughts spin, struggling to come to terms with my newfound power. "Invisibility, huh?"

Jihun quickly sobers. "Do you remember how you did it?"

"I move like a clumsy orangutan compared to you," I mutter. "I wished I was invisible so I wouldn't give us away. I didn't know it would happen literally."

"Good." Jihun wraps the Queen of Sky in a light blanket and lifts her into his arms. "Just do that again."

"Yeah. Sure. Piece of cake," I grumble under my breath. "Wait. What about you two?"

"You can expand your protective dome to shield other people. I believe your invisibility works the same way," he says with confidence. "It is a new power, but it is still yours, Ethan."

"You have enough faith for the both of us." I walk to the entrance and reach for the tent flap. "It's do-or-die time."

"Let's aim for *do*." Jihun steps outside with the queen in his arms, and I follow him with a hand on his shoulder.

My heart pounds as the gazes of the bound soldiers shoot toward us. *Shit.* They saw the tent flap open and close.

But did they see us?

Cold sweat runs down my back, and anxiety tightens my muscles. This is how I felt the first time I turned invisible—desperate and scared.

Jihun sets a steady pace away from the tent. "Are we invisible?"

I have to get Jihun and the Queen of Sky out of the enemy's camp. Once the queen regains consciousness, she can stop this war—end this whole nightmare. I might even get to have an aunt.

"Yes," I say, more from hope than conviction.

"Good, because I can't hold the binds anymore," he groans.

The moment of truth.

I glance behind me at the recently unbound soldiers. They're running in and out of the tent and gesticulating wildly. Relief rushes through me. They don't see us.

But I strain to hold the dome over the spell maiden as we move farther away. She casts spell after spell to break through, and a sharp pain pierces my chest. With a grunt, I let the dome dissolve. Invisibility has top priority.

"The spell maiden is free," I warn Jihun quietly.

He nods without looking back and continues taking measured steps until the tent is lost in the shadow of the woods. After what feels like hours—but it couldn't have been more than thirty minutes—Jihun juts his chin toward the dense trees ahead.

Our soldiers are hidden well, but I glimpse two of them stationed at the front. My knees go weak with relief. *A few more steps.* But just as I let my guard down, dirt and leaves hit the back of my head and rain down my back. The assholes figured it out.

"Shit." I shove Jihun toward the trees. "Go. Take her to safety."

"Ethan." He looks over his shoulder for the briefest second, conflict clenching his features.

"That's a command." My low voice rumbles through the forest. *"Go."*

Jihun runs, his feet barely touching the ground, with the Queen of Sky pale and unconscious in his arms. When they reach our troops, I cast aside my invisibility and face the enemy battalion.

"Well, come on then." I summon my axes, then pivot to the side, raising the golden axe over my head and the silver in front of my chest. "I don't have all day."

Standing in the midst of the magnificent trees, I am surrounded by an army mightier than theirs. The gi of Mountains streams in through my very pores, and my magic swells and grows.

The archers let loose their arrows with high-pitched screams. I block every one of them as though they come at me in slow motion. Then the infantry runs headlong toward me. I plant one foot in front and bend my knees, bracing for the impact I'm about to deliver, then cross my axes over my chest. With a roar, I send out a wave of power, my feet skidding back from the force.

The enemy soldiers ram against the wall of gi. When one falls, another replaces them, battering endlessly into my magic. I send out another pulse, then another, until the soldiers pile high on the ground—the opposing force of my power the only thing stopping them from toppling to my feet in an avalanche of bodies.

Only two more rows of infantrymen remain beyond the wall of magic and the dam of fallen seraphim. Then a wiry male steps out from behind the soldiers still standing—a general, based on his brass scaled armor and reinforced helmet.

"Are you feeling mighty, young king?" He sneers. "I would have thought taking out foot soldiers with your high magic would be beneath you. Or has your common upbringing failed to teach you what it means to fight with honor?"

"Was it honor that made you hide behind your soldiers while they fell by the hundreds?" I cock my head to the side. "Or has your noble upbringing failed to teach you how to value the lives of others?"

"I challenge you to single combat," the general says abruptly, his fragile ego faltering in the face of my condescension. He jerks his chin toward a soldier, who promptly draws a large circle in the dirt with his sword. "The first one to step out of the circle loses."

"And what would that loss signify?" I keep my tone nonchalant while I struggle to keep up the wall of gi.

"The loser will surrender this battle." The general rubs his hands together, hardly able to contain his vile glee.

The blood drains from my face. He intends to kill my soldiers—every last one of them. I see it in the sadistic glint of his eyes.

"You are down to less than two hundred men, General," I drawl, hiding my revulsion. "I can easily end this right now, rather than wasting my breath on you."

"I will not allow my soldiers to yield while they have life in them." A sinister smile lifts the corners of his mouth. "Do you really want the blood of a thousand beings on your hands? More, if you count your own soldiers, who will inevitably fall."

The bastard is threatening me with the lives of my soldiers, as well as his own. I can see why General Bak entrusted the queen's imprisonment to this male. He is as savage as he is ruthless. A dangerous combination for a person in a position of power.

My fists clench around the axe handles before I lower them with a grunt. My magic cuts off, and the unconscious soldiers tumble to the ground in an avalanche. I leap back from the bodies, and my legs nearly give out as they hit the ground. But before I stumble, a firm shoulder props me up.

"The queen is safe, Your Majesty," Jihun says close to my ear. "We will moon shift her to the Shinsi Palace tonight for the royal physician to tend to her."

"Thank you." I lean against him.

"Please allow me to be your champion," he whispers. "I know General Gim. The sick bastard will employ every known dirty trick to take you down. He craves glory more than anything."

"More reason why I can't risk having you fight him on my behalf," I argue, even as I struggle to catch my breath. My limbs jiggle like fucking Jell-O. The only times I enjoy feeling boneless are when Sunny is involved.

"With all due respect"—Jihun blows out a beleaguered sigh—"please stop being a stubborn ass. I can anticipate his moves ten steps ahead of him. There's no need for you to waste any more time or energy on him."

"Fine," I concede less than graciously. "But will he agree to fight you instead?"

"You need to accept his challenge, then assign me as your champion," Jihun explains. "Per the Code of the Realm, the general cannot back out once you accept his challenge. And the fighter has the right to select a champion."

"General Gim." I project my voice, hoping I sound stronger than I feel. "I will accept your challenge under one condition. If you win, swear to spare the lives of my soldiers."

"I swear it," he says much too swiftly for him to mean it. "Do you accept my challenge, Your Majesty?"

"I do." But before the general can gloat, I add, "And Captain Song Jihun will fight as my champion."

"That pup doesn't stand a chance against me." General Gim's face turns splotchy with anger. "Isn't that right, Captain Song?"

"You can console yourself any way you wish." Jihun sounds almost bored, the cocky son of a bitch.

I chuckle when the general sputters, and I turn to Jihun with a sardonic grin. "You got this, right?"

"Right." A corner of his mouth curls up. "Now kindly remove yourself to the spectator zone."

"Asshole," I say with gruff affection, then do as I'm asked. Two of my soldiers flank me as soon as I step into the woods.

"Since your soldiers have collapsed over your ring, why don't I draw us a new one?" Jihun suggests.

Without waiting for the general's response, my royal adviser extends two of his fingers and spins in a slow circle, using his power of wind to clear out a ring in the ground, about fifteen feet wide. Then he stands to one side, clasping his hands loosely behind his back.

"Per code, I presume?" Jihun asks casually. When the general responds with a curt nod, Jihun inclines his head in a mocking bow. "Whenever you're ready, General."

General Gim leaps lightly into the circle in front of Jihun and draws his sword, his movements almost too fast to follow. My eyes narrow in accusation at my sneaky adviser. The general is much more formidable than I was led to believe.

He attacks without delay, and Jihun evades his blade at the last minute with a nerve-rackingly slow shift of his torso, his hands still clasped behind him.

"All right, show-off," I mutter under my breath.

With a frustrated growl, General Gim swings his sword in quick succession, and Jihun at last frees his hands and dodges the blade like he means it. Then in a lightning motion, he drops to the ground in a low, sweeping kick, throwing the general off his feet.

The general lands on his back with an oomph but immediately flips to a stand. "Enough. I'm done with games."

"Watch ou—" Before I can get my warning out, the male throws a handful of dirt at Jihun.

"By *games*, I assume you mean *fighting fair*?" Jihun drawls.

The dirt falls to the ground two feet away from his face. His wings of wind glimmer in the faint light of early dawn, and his shoulder-length hair flutters as he draws his wings away from his face. Then he finally summons his long sword with a twist of his wrist.

"Now then." He smirks. "Where were we?"

"You arrogant bastard," General Gim snarls.

Sparks burst as their swords meet in the middle of the ring, one warrior to another, and they battle in a dance of brutal beauty. Jihun blocks the general's blade over his head, spins out of its trajectory, and slashes his sword down the general's side in a long, diagonal line, cutting open his armor.

General Gim stumbles back, a hand pressed to his side, before Jihun can mark an *X* on him. His palm comes away bloody. "You little fuck."

"I don't appreciate being called *little*," Jihun murmurs.

He has definitely upped his comedy game. I shift restlessly on my feet and notice that my legs feel stronger. I clench and unclench my fists and grunt softly in satisfaction. My strength is returning.

I'm jumping into the ring if anything goes wrong. To hell with the Code of the Realm. I will not watch another brother die.

Silver flames burst to life in the general's eyes, and I think I hear Jihun say, "There it is." Then General Gim slashes his sword through the air and sends lightning hurtling toward Jihun. He leaps to the side, but the lightning bolt sears a jagged line down his arm.

"Jihun," I shout, taking a step forward. Everything happened too quickly for me to react, but even I know that use of magic in single combat violates the code.

My royal adviser gives me a subtle shake of his head. I stop advancing toward the ring, even as magic gathers in my chest.

"You have violated the Code of the Realm." Jihun shifts his shoulder with a wince.

"Who is to know? I will kill you and every one of your soldiers." The general flashes a slimy grin as the smell of ozone fills the air and electricity sparks along his body. "As for your king, I shall spare him, since he might prove useful. But he wouldn't need his tongue for what we have planned for him."

"Even if your violation of the code wasn't punishable by death, you signed your death warrant with that threat against my king." Steel glints in Jihun's eyes as he sheathes his sword. "A coward like you doesn't deserve to breathe the same air as him."

I hear the flap of his wings as wind gusts from them, gaining power until I have to shield my eyes. Jihun spreads his arms wide, and a dust storm rises in the woods.

"Y-you can't use magic," the general stutters like the hypocrite he is. "It . . . it's against the code."

"You forget, I am a suhoshin. I am better versed in the Code of the Realm than you." Jihun's voice echoes through the woods. "The moment you used magic, you gave me the right to protect myself by any means available to me."

Jihun slowly draws his hands together, his lips peeling back from the effort, and gathers the wind and dust between his palms until a churning, basketball-sized sphere forms in front of him.

Fear flashes across the general's face before he throws his head back and releases a shrill battle cry. Electricity zapping through his body and in his eyes, he raises his sword high and funnels the current into his blade. With another shriek, he brings down his sword, and lightning streams out of its tip and blazes straight toward Jihun.

"No." The roar of the wind swallows my cry. Covering my face against the flurry of dust, I take a step toward the ring, only to be pushed back by a powerful gust. *"Jihun."*

Teeth clenched, I shoulder through the barrage of wind by sheer force of will. My eyes tear up as I squint to see past the dust storm.

Jihun launches the ball of wind and dust at the lightning bolt, swallowing and neutralizing it in the air. But the ball's trajectory doesn't slow as it spins and expands until a twister whips toward the general.

General Gim's mouth parts in horror, but I don't hear his scream as the tornado surrounds him and lifts him into the air. Electricity bursts and crackles inside the cyclone, lighting up the twister like an inverted Christmas tree, and the smell of burning flesh fills the air.

Jihun strains to hold his arms up in the air, silver fire blazing in his eyes. And he steps one leg behind him, both knees bent and shaking. A guttural shout explodes out of him as he leans his torso forward, and his back leg slides until his knee hovers mere inches above the ground.

At last, the lightning slows to sporadic bursts. I hold my breath until the sparks die out altogether. With a faint moan, Jihun drops his arms and falls to his knees. The tornado dissipates, and the general's charred body lands on the ground with a dull thud.

I run toward Jihun and help him to his feet before pulling him into a tight hug. "Don't ever pull a bullheaded stunt like that again."

"Yes, Your Majesty." He weakly pats my back.

I step away from him and turn to face the last standing enemy soldiers.

"General Gim has colluded with General Bak to poison and imprison the Queen of Sky." I project my voice, and uneasy whispers rise from the soldiers. "If you are loyal to the Kingdom of Sky and your queen, put down your blade and surrender."

A soldier steps forward, flipping a dagger around and around in his hand. "I'm afraid my orders were to put my blade . . . inside you."

Shit. He's an assassin.

I throw a shield over me and Jihun, and not a second too soon. The blade embeds itself into the dome, less than an inch away from my right eye. Then the shield flickers and dissolves. My gi hasn't recovered enough to form a proper dome. And Jihun can hardly stand on his own.

But our soldiers pour out of the woods and surround us, and our archers aim their arrows at the assassin, stopping him in his tracks. Air rushes past my lips in relief. But the unconscious enemy soldiers stir on the ground. I can't let this turn into an all-out battle.

"Soldiers of the Kingdom of Sky," I shout. "I can end this war without any more bloodshed. Surrender now, and your lives will be spared. I swear it."

The enemy soldiers steal uncertain glances at us, their nervous murmurs growing louder. When we make no move to attack, some of them cautiously help their dazed comrades to their feet.

This just might work.

CHAPTER TWENTY-ONE

Sunny

"Stormy?" Haesan says as he steps through the doors of Jeoseung Palace's throne room. "Why are you in the Kingdom of Underworld? Come to think of it, why was *I* summoned here?"

I can't help myself. I take off in a run and launch myself at the in'eo. The mountainous merman doesn't so much as stumble and wraps his arms tightly around me. His chuckle starts quiet, then grows into a full belly laugh as he spins me around in the air.

"You're alive." He carefully sets me back on my feet. "Gods, I can't believe it."

"Yeah, me neither." I grin. "How are you, Gang Haesan?"

His smiling face suddenly crumples. "Hana . . . She's dead."

I haven't forgotten about Hana, my cadet roommate, but I'd buried the memory of her tragic death deep inside me. After Santorini, I couldn't bear to carry more grief. But for Haesan, who had been at the Kingdom of Sky all this time, Hana died, and I disappeared, then a war broke out in the span of days.

"I know," I croak. "I'm so sorry."

I wonder if the former King of Mountains made himself useful from the dungeon and took care of Shim Duna, his spy and Hana's murderous twin sister. He had been furious when I told him that she divulged the truth of his "illness" to me. But with time and distance, I feel a twinge of regret for indirectly sentencing her to death.

"Hana was the sweetest person I knew." Haesan clears his throat, glancing away. "I . . . uh . . . the suhoshin cadet training is in shambles. It's no wonder with Captain Seo gone."

I let him change the subject. "I can imagine."

"And you won't believe the rumors flying around." He leans closer.

"What rumors?" I lower my voice.

"About Duna being a spy for the King of Mountains." He peeks at me from beneath his lashes. "And some nonsense about the coming of the end of days."

Like a long-forgotten dream, images of a weeping female standing in the midst of white fire flicker in my mind. *Am I somehow involved in the prophecy of the End of Days?* I grit my teeth and avoid the hell out of the sudden question. Besides, the Amheuk is the one hell-bent on destroying the worlds, not me.

Now all I have to do is break the news to Haesan that the apocalypse is *not* some nonsense . . .

"At any rate"—the merman shakes his head, setting his golden barbels swaying—"who has time for rumors now that the Kingdom of Sky and the Kingdom of Mountains are at war?"

"And that brings us to why we invited you to Jeoseung Palace." The King of Underworld smoothly interjects himself into the conversation.

Haesan starts, his eyes flying to the king's onyx crown. "Forgive me for my insolence, Your Majesty. I should have paid you my respects first."

"You're fine." I flap my hand, then remember it's not my place to forgive the in'eo. The King of Underworld seems cool, but I can't forget he is also scary powerful. "Right, Your Majesty?"

"Right." He smiles distractedly. "But about why he is here . . ."

"Oh yes." I turn to Haesan. "Do you want the good news first? Or the bad news?"

"Bad news. Always the bad news first." He gulps. "Unless it's really bad . . . Never mind. I want the bad news first."

"The Amheuk has breached the Realm of Four Kingdoms." I'm getting sick of repeating that gods-awful sentence.

"Gah." Haesan draws back, clawing at the air like he wants to climb up a tree and hide. "What possible good news could follow that?"

"Well, we're planning to fight back." I pop up to the balls of my feet. "So . . . yay."

"I need to sit down." The in'eo sways on his feet, and I'm tempted to yell, *Timber*. I'd forgotten how *big* he was. "I have to throw up."

"Don't," the King of Underworld commands in a deep, rumbling voice.

"Yes, Your Majesty." Haesan straightens and comes to attention, his nausea royally intimidated out of him. He blows out a long breath. "Okay, Stormy. I'm ready to hear what part I have to play in this."

"You need to get me an audience with the Queen of Water and help me convince her to send troops to the Kingdom of Mountains." I watch for signs of renewed nausea from him. "There is no time to waste on a war between the kingdoms. The Realm of Four Kingdoms has to unite to fight the Amheuk."

"And you assume because I'm from the Kingdom of Water that I know the queen?" He side-eyes me.

Fair point. What was I thinking?

I hide my cringe with a scowl and cross my arms. "Well, do you?"

"I do, in fact." He grins, and I'm too relieved to be annoyed at him. "My aunt is the jimil sanggung to the Queen of Water. But still, you shouldn't assume things. You just lucked out this time."

"Sure. Anything you say." I cup my forehead, limp with relief. Besides, I am due some good fucking luck. "Okay. We need to leave now."

"There is one small problem . . ." Haesan raises a finger. "You can't breathe underwater."

"The Kingdom of Water is . . . underwater?" My jaw drops.

"I don't understand why you are so surprised." He frowns. "You would think it is rather obvious. It is the Kingdom of *Water*."

"I guess when you put it that way," I grumble.

"To be fair, the kingdom itself is beneath a watertight dome," Haesan allows. "But we have to traverse by water to get to the Kingdom of Water and the Dragon Palace."

"I can assist with that problem." The King of Underworld raises his index finger in all his nerdy glory. "I invented an apparatus that allows you to breathe underwater. It never failed me when I used to visit Bora—That is, I've tested it numerous times to great success."

"If it's good enough for a king, then it's good enough for me." I follow him to his cluttered desk. I have no idea how he can find anything there, though.

"I know it's here somewhere." When the king can't find the apparatus on his desk, he haphazardly opens drawers that are filled to the brim with what appears to be junk. "But I haven't used it since . . ."

"Did you find it?" I ask, leaning over to peek inside the drawers.

"Not yet." He straightens and taps his chin with his finger. "Ah yes."

The king drags out an overflowing chest from beneath his desk. *Good gods.* He will *never* find it in there.

"There you are." He greets what appears to be a wooden clothespin like an old friend. Then he holds it up in the air with a triumphant grin. "This is what you need."

"It is?" I expected something . . . bigger. Something that can hold or make oxygen.

"I thought you needed to breathe underwater." The king's brows knit in confusion.

"I do. Is . . . that supposed to help with that?" I point at what I am now certain is a clothespin.

"Absolutely." The King of Underworld reaches out and pinches my nose with it. "There."

"Thank you, Your Majesty." I promptly remove the offending clothespin and tuck it into my jeans pocket. "I'll put it on when I get there. If you can point us toward the portal, we'll be on our way."

The corners of the king's mouth droop. "So there is no time for you to show me your fox—"

"Your Majesty." The Judge of Tenth Hell storms into the throne room with two males and two females in tow. "I have gathered the generals."

"Very well." The king glances at me and sighs forlornly. I consider taking my gumiho form because I feel bad for him. But then, he draws his shoulders back and says with dignity that belies the puppy dog face he was making a minute ago, "Gyun, this is Gang Haesan. He will arrange an audience with the Queen of Water for Sunny. Please escort them to the portal and have the keeper let them through to the Kingdom of Water."

Gyun takes stock of Haesan before he nods. "Yes, Your Majesty."

"Who is that?" the in'eo asks me from the corner of his mouth.

"He's the Judge of Tenth Hell," I say, also out of the corner of my mouth.

"Of course he is." Haesan almost sounds cheerful. He might be going into shock.

"Sunny." The king turns to me. "Once the Kingdom of Sky is subdued, will you arrange for Bora . . . I mean . . . the Queen of Water and me to meet with the King of Mountains?"

"I . . ." *Ethan.* Suddenly, I can't breathe.

"You do know the King of Mountains, do you not?" The King of Underworld cocks his head to the side. "It seems unlikely that anyone would risk their life to help someone they don't even know."

"I do know him." Even if I can't return to the Kingdom of Mountains, the Sentinels will know what to do. "The King of Mountains will meet with you and the Queen of Water gladly."

I can only hope that the Queen of Sky will be cooperative once the war ends. We need all four kingdoms united, not just three. I knead the back of my neck. *One thing at a time.*

"Ready?" Gyun arches a thick eyebrow at me.

"Yes." I tug on Haesan's sleeve. "Let's go."

"With your leave, Your Majesty." The Judge of Tenth Hell bows to the King of Underworld.

"Thank you for everything, Your Majesty." I bow low from my waist, and Haesan mimics me at my side.

"Till we meet again," the king says to me with a courtly bow.

"Come with me." Gyun rushes us out of the throne room. Then he reaches out for Haesan and me, his hands hovering behind our backs. "If I may."

I nod, and Haesan shrugs. The judge wraps his arms around each of us, and we're standing outside the Jeoseung Palace. I squint, surprised to see the sun out.

Morning has dawned in the capital of the Kingdom of Underworld. *Another day apart from Ethan.* I push aside my longing. Moping because I miss him isn't going to help Ethan. I have to send him reinforcements so he can end a war he never asked for—a war he tried so hard to stop.

"This city looks peculiar," Haesan murmurs. "But not in a bad way."

"Thank you." The Judge of Tenth Hell looks amused.

I put a hand on the judge's arm. "Were you able to reach Mun?"

"Yes." Gyun nods. "He will escort Cheyun to the Jeoseung Palace to confer with the generals."

"Good, thank you." But I gasp, gripping his arm tighter. "Will you please let Minju know where I've gone?"

"I will be sure to tell her." Gyun clasps his hand over mine in reassurance.

"Thank you." Then I catch Haesan's eyes, and he nods. "I think we're ready to go."

"Taking both of you at once, I can only teleport short distances." The judge rubs the back of his head apologetically.

"I've heard the Judges of Ten Hells can do that." Haesan looks at Gyun with something like awe. "Make as many stops as you need. It'll be amazing no matter what."

"We're not here to get a tour of the Kingdom of Underworld." I roll my eyes at the in'eo. "But do what you need to do, Gyun."

The Judge of Tenth Hell wraps his arms around our waists, and I'm hit with the sensation of being sucked out of my own body. Just as quickly, I feel solid ground under my feet again. This time, we're at the edge of a more traditional hanok village. Before I can appreciate its quaint charm, we teleport again.

We stand in the middle of a black-sand desert, hot wind blowing in our faces. I blink and hold a hand up. "Give me one second. My brain needs to catch up."

Haesan nods in agreement, looking green around the gills. He pats his body down from chest to thighs, then he stares down at his hands, flipping them over, back and forth.

"Okay, good." He sighs. "I'm still here."

"Teleporting works differently than moon shifting," Gyun says sympathetically. "It'll be easier if I carry you, but with two of you . . ."

"Don't worry about it." I take a deep breath. "Ready, Haesan?"

A choked gurgle escapes past his lips, but he manages to nod. I'm proud of the big softy.

"We're almost there." Gyun wraps his arms around our waists and tucks us extra close. I think he's trying to make us feel less disembodied. "This will be the last jump."

The in'eo nestles himself against the judge's side, like he's snuggling a teddy bear. I shrug and do the same.

Being pressed against Gyun does make the teleportation less disorienting, and in a blink, I'm back on solid ground. My throat constricts halfway through a sigh of relief when blazing heat blasts my face.

"What the fuck?" I rasp. We're standing at the bottom of a volcano, complete with trails of sizzling lava sliding down its sides.

"Are we in . . . hell?" Haesan hugs his midriff.

"Gods no." The judge snorts, then coughs to hide his amusement. "No, Haesan. We are nowhere near hell."

"Yeah." I laugh nervously. "You do *not* want to know what real hell is like."

"Well, well, well." A tall, willowy female sashays toward us in a skintight leather jumpsuit. "Fancy meeting you here, Gyun."

"Keeper Bang." The judge addresses her formally. "I have brought you two travelers. The king bids you to allow them passage to the Kingdom of Water."

"Neither of them is a being of Underworld." She crosses her arms, accentuating rather perfect breasts. "Do you have the appropriate documents with you?"

"They are both guests of the King of Underworld." Gyun's voice softens terrifyingly. "And time is of the essence."

"It is not easy to prepare passage to the Kingdom of Water." The keeper pouts in displeasure, then a cunning smile curls her lips. "And I am out of water. I can't prepare a token to the Kingdom of Water without water."

"Will this work?" Haesan cups his palms, and water swirls to the top.

"Are you going to claim to have run out of vials, too, Keeper Bang?" A muscle tics in Gyun's jaw.

"As a matter of fact—" she begins snidely.

"Do *not* test me," the judge says through gritted teeth.

"Oh fine." Two glass vials each the size of my thumb appear in her hand, and she tips them into Haesan's palms and fills them with water. "There was a time you would've grasped at any excuse for one more minute with me."

"There *was*."

Sadness flickers across the keeper's face before it's replaced by haughty disdain. "Excuse me while I go do my job."

"So Gyun, you're single now?" I quip to break the tension in the air.

"Yes." A ghost of a smile touches the judge's lips. "Why do you ask?"

"If we survive the apocalypse, I might have the perfect gal for you." I wink, then abruptly sober. I miss Hailey so much.

Is she okay? Is everyone okay?

"How long do you think she'll keep us waiting?" Haesan tips his chin toward the keeper, who has her back turned to us a few yards away.

"Not long," the judge says. "She is good at her job once she puts her mind to it."

As soon as the words leave his mouth, Keeper Bang walks back to us. "Come with me."

"And I'll take your leave here." Gyun gives my arm a gentle squeeze. "Good luck, Sunny. You have more good in you than you believe. Trust yourself."

What does he mean? How could he know? But the Judge of Tenth Hell is gone before I can ask him.

"Well, are you coming?" Keeper Bang asks over her shoulder as she climbs up the volcanic mountain.

"Sunny?" Haesan swallows.

"Coming," I yell and tug on his arm. "Stop being a baby. It's not like she's going to push us into the volcano."

Famous last words.

CHAPTER TWENTY-TWO

Sunny

"Okay." Keeper Bang turns toward us at the top of the volcanic mountain, lava bubbling behind her, and hands each of us a vial of water. "Throw the tokens into the volcano and jump."

Haesan shoots me an accusatory glance.

I attempt a nonchalant shrug. "She's not *pushing* us. We have to jump."

The merman narrows his eyes at me even more. I don't glare back at him because I have to admit it's a very slight difference.

"We can do it together." I take the vial from him and hold his hand tight. "On three. One. Two. *Three.*"

"Wait." Keeper Bang waves her hands in alarm. "You don't actually have to . . ."

I don't hear the rest of her sentence as I throw the vials into the molten lava and jump in after it. And Haesan has no choice but to follow because I have an iron grip on his hand. Luckily, a swirly blue portal opens up inside the volcano, and we fall through it.

Shit.

We hit the water with a sizzling splash, and I scramble to get the clothespin out of my pocket. But my jeans are plastered against me, thanks to the water, and I struggle to stick my hand inside the pocket.

I arch my back the best I can to give my hand better access to my pocket, and I barely get the tip of my middle finger inside. The skintight jeans seem to have fused onto my legs. *Where did I even buy these?*

I glance around the water, but I don't see Haesan. I start to panic as my lungs burn, and I kick my legs a little too hard.

"Sunny." Haesan grips my shoulders. "I'm right here. You're okay."

I have no idea how he's talking underwater, but I came to terms with knowing nothing when it comes to this fucking realm. *Gods, the water is so cold.* I nod at him and dig into my pocket.

Jagged pain splinters through my chest as I use up the last of my oxygen. I rush to fish out the clothespin with numb, fumbling fingers, only to lose hold of it in the water. Air escapes from the corners of my lips. The clothespin floats away from me, and my vision narrows as I fight for consciousness, my body begging me to inhale.

Haesan lunges for the pin and pinches my nose with it—just as I take a heaving breath, not caring that I'll inhale a lungful of water. But it's . . . air. *Thank gods.* I greedily gulp in more air, but my limbs flail like I'm drowning, my panic still not spent.

"Gang Haesan, did you bring a sinker to the Kingdom of Water?" an amused voice drawls.

"Don't be an asshole, Ahn Seongho. My friend can swim like a fish," Haesan snaps as he hoists me into his ginormous arms and gathers me against his chest. Then, he whispers for my ears only, "Please tell me you know how to swim, Sunny."

"What?" *I can talk, and not in that underwater bubbling voice like in cartoons.* I take another full breath. *I can breathe through my mouth without gulping down water.* It's all actually pretty cool. I finally stop flailing. "I . . . I know how to swim."

"Hmm." Haesan doesn't sound convinced.

"What business does she have in our kingdom?" Ahn Seongho asks in a more official tone.

I notice the tall, pretty male for the first time. He is wearing a flowing blue robe, similar to the silver robes worn by the portal keepers at the Kingdom of Sky, with a man bun on top of his head.

"None of your business," Haesan grumbles.

"I am a portal keeper. It is precisely my business." The keeper smirks.

I glance between the two males. I've never seen my friend so rude to anyone before. While Keeper Ahn comes across as a little cocky, he doesn't seem all that bad.

"She needs an audience with the queen." Haesan relents. "It is a matter of great urgency."

The keeper frowns at his earnest words, then he nods decisively. "Then make haste, Haesan. I won't hold you up any longer."

"Th-thank you, Seongho." Haesan seems a little taken aback. "M-maybe we can get a drink sometime, and . . . catch up."

"I would like that." Keeper Ahn smiles, the corners of his eyes wrinkling. "Now, go and take care of that urgent business."

With a nod goodbye, Haesan swims out toward our destination, still carrying me.

"Who was that?" I ask.

"We grew up together," he says, propelling us forward with powerful kicks of his legs. "He was my childhood nemesis."

I side-eye the in'eo. "He doesn't seem so bad."

"Yeah," Haesan concedes. "He seems to have grown out of his bratty stage. Maybe I should've given him another chance sooner."

He leaves unsaid that he might never get that chance now. And I can't in good conscience assure him that he will. I can hope and try my best, but I can't promise him a better future. Or any future at all.

We swim on in somber silence. I shiver after a while.

"How far is the Dragon Palace from here?" The clothespin lets me breathe, but the water is freezing cold. I'm not sure how long I can last.

"Not too far." My friend pulls me closer, and I burrow into his warmth. "We're almost at the capital."

"Thank gods." I crane my neck and squint my eyes, then I see it—a pearlescent walled city. *Hmm.* Something looks . . . off, but I can't put my finger on it. *Whatever.* I drop my head against Haesan's chest again. I couldn't care less at the moment. I just want to get dry and warm.

He swims us to the bottom of the fortress and knocks on the big mother-of-pearl gates. Two guards swing them open from the inside. But something still isn't right. I feel like I'm watching them on TV.

Curious, I reach toward them, but my fingers skim across an invisible barrier. *That's why everything looks weird.* The capital of the Kingdom of Water is enclosed in something, like it's inside a giant snow globe. I press my fingertips against the barrier, and this time, there is a little give. *Interesting.*

With startled shouts, the guards jump back and point their spears at us.

"Wh-what's their p-problem?" My teeth clack like castanets.

"I am Gang Haesan," he says quickly to the guards. "I am here to see my aunt, Gang Sanggung."

"That female just b-breached the barrier." One of the guards waves his spearhead at me.

"Impossible," the other guard rasps.

I blink at them and belatedly notice the water splashes on their uniforms.

Well, shit.

I should probably say something in my defense. My Yeoiju is usually the explanation for all the weird shit I can do, but that will probably freak them out more. "I d-didn't mean t-to."

"She's my friend—one of the good guys." Haesan takes a step toward the open gate, and both guards point their spears at us. "Please let us in. She's a being of Mountains. She won't survive much longer in the water."

The guards exchange uneasy glances but don't budge.

"Let the child through," a female chides from behind them. "He practically grew up in the Dragon Palace. Do you really want to risk Gang Sanggung's ire?"

"But the female—" one guard insists, as the other slowly lowers his spear.

"Is his *friend*." The female's voice takes on a steely edge. "Do you want to deal with the diplomatic headache of letting a being of Mountains die from hypothermia?"

"No, Jo Sanggung." The guard finally relents and steps back from the doors, but he points a naggy finger at me. "You can come in, but don't make any sudden moves."

I gape at the male as I shiver uncontrollably. *Do I look like I'm capable of making any sudden moves?*

"Hold your breath," Haesan says close to my ear. "And try not to move."

I do my best not to shiver too hard as he steps through the gates in slow motion. It literally feels like he's pushing through a giant blob of Jell-O. But he steps out on the other side to a mild autumn day, and I sag with relief.

Haesan walks past the guards with a glare, then bows to the female who stands across from us. She is wearing a turquoise hanbok chima with a navy blue dangui on top, the attire of a high-ranking court lady.

"Thank you, Jo Sanggung," he says when he straightens.

"I thought you were busy training to become a suhoshin." She tuts her tongue and waves her hand, whipping the moisture out of our wet clothes. "Does the beauty in your arms have anything to do with you playing hooky?"

The dry clothes feel like heaven. Warmth seeps back into my body, and my teeth quiet down enough for me to think straight.

"Uh." Haesan shifts on his feet, glancing from the court lady to me, then back. "Actually, yes."

I squeak in outrage and wriggle in his arms. He sets me gently on the ground, then smiles proudly when I don't keel over. It's not easy being mad at someone so sweet, but I manage to scowl at him. "I am *not* the reason you skipped out on your suhoshin cadet training."

"But you are, Stormy." His brows pull low, then after a second, his eyes widen, and he waves his hands frantically at the court lady. "No, no, no. Not in the way you think. She is my friend—a friend that I am a little afraid of. It is not what you think at all."

"Why are you here, child?" She smiles indulgently at the bright-pink in'eo.

"We came to speak with my aunt." His expression sobers, worry replacing embarrassment. "We need an audience with the queen. It is a matter of great urgency. The lives of everyone in the Realm of Four Kingdoms are at stake."

"Surely you exaggerate." Jo Sanggung chuckles uneasily.

"No, my lady." I shake my head. "He does not."

She studies my face for a long moment, then she nods as though coming to a decision. "The queen will hold her daily assembly soon. The Dragon Palace is only a short distance away. I will escort you to the royal audience hall."

The court lady walks exceptionally fast, and we hurry to keep up with her. I turn to Haesan and whisper, "Who exactly is she?"

"Jo Sanggung is in charge of the royal kitchen," he answers. "And a good friend of my aunt."

The palace really is close by, and we're able to enter through the main gate without a fuss, thanks to Jo Sanggung. The Dragon Palace resembles the Celestial Palace, with its grand hanok structures and manicured lawns and gardens—but without the creepy vibe. I glance up at what should be the dark depth of water, but the blue sky and cotton candy clouds greet me. *Cool.* We're inside a magical version of a biodome.

My stomach growls as we follow Jo Sanggung toward a looming hanok with a pearlescent tiled roof and shimmering blue wood trimmings. I haven't eaten since the Hangawi feast with Minju's parents. That feels like a lifetime ago, but it was only yesterday. They must be worried sick for their daughter.

"We're here." Jo Sanggung stops in front of the stone steps leading up to the audience hall and addresses the two royal guards standing watch. "I must speak with Gang Sanggung."

"The assembly is in session," one guard answers.

"And I have no intention of disrupting it." The court lady arches a sharp brow. "My guests and I will wait at the back of the room until an appropriate time."

The guards exchange a nervous glance and let us through, in the face of Jo Sanggung's imposing presence. She soundlessly opens the door to the audience hall and motions us through. We scurry to a dark corner in the back.

Even though morning light filters into the audience hall and light orbs dot the ceiling, the room remains dim and somber. Yet the Queen of Water is anything but. She is beautiful and radiant as she sits on a stunning throne made of fuchsia, blue, and purple coral, which undulates gently around her.

Her impish face holds a touch of mischief as she listens to the high officials drone on and on about one tedious topic after another. I shift on my feet, deathly bored and growing more impatient by the minute. But when a court lady steps down from the dais to accept a scroll from an official, Jo Sanggung makes a quick motion with her hand, signaling her.

The other court lady shows no outward sign of recognition. But after she presents the scroll to the queen, she takes a step back and seemingly fades into the shadows. Then she swiftly and silently makes her way toward us, hugging the side wall.

"Haesan, what is going on?" his aunt whispers, reaching for his hand. "Is something wrong?"

"We need an audience with the queen, Gomo." Haesan covers her hand with both of his. "The Realm of Four Kingdoms is in danger. Sunny will explain everything."

Troubled eyes flit toward me, then she says, "I will tell the queen. But do not approach the dais until you are summoned."

I'm awed by the implicit trust between Haesan and his aunt. She simply took him at his word. As Gang Sanggung hurries back to the dais, I shoot him a worried glance, wiping my clammy hands down my jeans. He nods at me in reassurance.

"I will take it into consideration," the Queen of Water says in a crystalline voice, dismissing the latest droning official.

But before the next official can vomit superfluous nonsense to sound self-important, Gang Sanggung approaches the throne and whispers in the queen's ear. Curiosity sharpens the queen's features before she nods her assent. Gang Sanggung bows low to the queen, then motions for us to approach the dais.

"Go," Jo Sanggung urges us. "Do not keep the queen waiting."

The audience hall is filled with rows and rows of high officials. I walk to the last row and clear my throat at their silk-cloaked backs. When nothing happens, I clear my throat louder. The officials turn around without moving an inch and look down their noses at me.

"Pardon us, my lords," Haesan says circumspectly, but his sheer size and strength warn the arrogant officials not to mess with him. "The queen wants us to approach the dais."

They shuffle half a step to make a narrow path down the middle for us, and Haesan and I walk toward the dais. But their mutterings soon grow sharp and shrill as they realize I'm a gumiho. I didn't dampen my magic—I can't make allies while lying about my identity.

I feel their rage and hatred prickle the back of my neck, but I stand before the Queen of Water and bow. "Your Majesty."

She offers me a cursory nod but addresses Haesan. "Have you grown even bigger since I last saw you?"

"I've reached the age of twenty-four, Your Majesty." He blushes. "I believe I am done growing any taller."

"I meant to the side." The queen waves her hand to encompass his humongous form. "You've definitely gotten broader."

"Perhaps." He coughs into his fist. "May I present Cho Mihwa to you. She is a trusted friend, and one of the most accomplished suhoshin cadets of this year. She wishes to bring a matter of great urgency to your attention, Your Majesty."

"Hmm," the Queen of Water says noncommittally, then narrows her eyes at me. "Nice clothespin. A gift from someone special?"

"Shit." I snatch it off my nose and hiss at Haesan, "Why didn't you tell me I still had this ridiculous thing on my face?"

"I thought you enjoyed wearing it," he answers without guile.

"You thought . . ." I exhale a long breath, fighting for patience. "Your Majesty, the Kingdom of Mountains needs your help. I have come to implore you to send troops to aid them against the Kingdom of Sky's invasion."

"That war is a travesty, especially when the new king brought such hope to those poor people." The queen purses her lips. "Their peace lasted mere days."

"Yes, Your Majesty." I take a small step closer. "The people of the Kingdom of Mountains and the new king did nothing to deserve this war."

"Hmm," she says again. I suppress the annoyance pinching my insides. "While I agree with your sentiment, it is a serious matter to risk the lives of my soldiers to defend another kingdom."

The high officials agree loudly with their queen. I can't stop my annoyance from flaring into full-fledged irritation. My instinct tells me that the Queen of Water is being difficult on purpose.

"The war in the Kingdom of Mountains affects all the kingdoms." I struggle to keep my tone appropriately deferential. "It affects every being in this realm."

"How so?" The queen arches her brow coolly, even though the corners of her eyes tighten slightly.

"The four kingdoms must unite in order to defend against the eternal darkness." I take a bracing breath. "Your Majesty, the Amheuk has breached the Realm of Four Kingdoms."

Chaos ensues, and of course, the loudest, shrillest voice is heard first. "The gumiho is spewing poisonous lies to our queen."

"Guards." Another shriek pierces through the outraged screams. "Capture the beast."

The palace guards come for me with their spears raised, and Haesan steps in front of me. "Do *not* touch her."

"Haesan, don't." I tug on his sleeve until he looks down at me. "I won't make you a criminal in your own kingdom."

I raise my hands in the air and allow the guards to push me to my knees, but I hold the queen's shocked gaze from the floor. "Your Majesty, I beg you to look past prejudices and hear the truth of my words. The fate of the realm depends on it. The King of Underworld has already agreed to send aid to the Kingdom of Mountains."

"I . . ." Her lashes flutter, then the distrust in her eyes finally melts away. "And he helped you get to the Kingdom of Wa—"

An earsplitting boom shakes the audience hall, and terrified screams rip through the air. Only two things can make such a huge impact. One is Godzilla. The other is the Amheuk. Since Godzilla isn't real, I'm going to assume it's the latter.

Shit.

We need more time, but the eternal darkness seems impatient to destroy the Realm of Four Kingdoms. I jump to my feet, tossing aside the two palace guards holding me down. They would never have been able to restrain me if I hadn't let them.

"Come on, Haesan." I sprint toward the doors with my friend at my side. From the sounds of it, more follow from behind.

We skid to a stop just outside the audience hall, with our eyes glued to the sky. Darkness crawls above the biodome like a kraken, destroying the illusion of daylight. Haesan reaches for my hand, and I grab it tight, anguish burning in my chest.

We're too late. The Kingdom of Water is lost.

CHAPTER TWENTY-THREE

Sunny

The Queen of Water runs out of the audience hall and stumbles to a stop at my side. The whiny high officials—who acted so brave and strong when they ordered the guards to arrest me—cower inside the hall.

"Are we too late?" the queen asks, her gaze intent on the dark tentacles above us.

"No." My voice is thready and unsure. I mark my palms with the crescents of my nails. "No, we are *not* too late."

The Amheuk cannot win.

"I will follow where the King Foretold leads." The queen meets my gaze. She is done playing whatever game she was playing with me. "The diviners said all will be right when the prophecies are fulfilled."

Again with the *prophecies*. Does the prophecy of the End of Days say that the King Foretold must kill the bearer of the Yeoiju? Do I want to know? *Nope.* Prophecies, fate, destiny . . . I don't care about any of that.

I only care about protecting the people I love. And that means finding a way to destroy the Amheuk. That means not giving up.

"All will be right?" I scoff. "What the hell does that even mean?"

"Sunny." Haesan grabs my arm from the other side, apparently alarmed by my lack of decorum.

But the queen just shrugs. "Beats me."

"How long do you think the dome will hold?" I ask.

"It is meant to be impenetrable . . . So, perhaps a day?" Ironically, the Queen of Water has a dry sense of humor.

"Then I guess we'll live to see another day." *My* sense of humor, as usual, borders on corny during times of extreme duress. Haesan groans beside me. I don't think he sees any kind of humor in the situation.

"First things first, I will send reinforcements to the Kingdom of Mountains," the queen declares, like that had been her plan all along.

"The Kingdom of Mountains doesn't have an impenetrable dome." Fear jolts through me. "Do you think the Amheuk already . . ."

"The Kingdom of Mountains lies above the Kingdom of Water." The queen stacks her hands as she explains. "The Amheuk won't be able to reach the Kingdom of Mountains without first going through the Kingdom of Water."

I nod, struggling to swallow. "What's above the Kingdom of Mountains?"

"The Kingdom of Sky lies at the top, farthest from the entrance to the Realm of Four Kingdoms," she answers.

"So the Kingdom of Underworld is closest to the entrance?" My heart pounds against my rib cage. Minju is still there—and my new friends. "Does that mean that the Amheuk already went through it? Is the Kingdom of Underworld g-gone?"

"Taeyoung is awfully clever." A nerve tics beneath the queen's right eye, and her voice trembles. "He wouldn't let something as silly as the Amheuk destroy his kingdom."

"You're right," I agree quickly. "I bet the King of Underworld devised a nerdy work-around to evade the Amheuk's invasion."

"At least, temporarily . . . But like I said, first things first." The Queen of Water raises one hand without glancing back. "General Dokgo."

"Yes, Your Majesty," a female says, stepping out in front of us.

"Assemble troops to deploy to the Kingdom of Mountains," the queen commands. "Without delay."

"At once, Your Majesty." General Dokgo executes a sharp bow, but she hesitates, glancing at the darkness thrashing above the dome. "But with this imminent threat, how many soldiers can we spare?"

"Half. We can spare half of our military force, General," the queen answers with steely determination. "No kingdom can last long against the Amheuk on its own. We must stop the war in the Kingdom of Mountains so we can unite the forces of all four kingdoms."

"Yes, Your Majesty." The general spins on her heels and marches away from the audience hall.

"General Jeong," the queen says, and a short, stout male steps up to bat. "Prepare to evacuate as many people as possible. I will send word to the Queen of Sky to request asylum for our people."

Of course. Everyone should evacuate to the kingdom farthest from the reaches of the Amheuk.

"Right away, Your Majesty." The general bows and takes his leave.

I want to go to Ethan so badly that pain claws at my chest. *But I can't.* I glance down at the mark of the blood oath on my palm, then curl my fingers over it. I have to focus on what I can do.

"Is there a way to contact someone in the Kingdom of Underworld?" I ask the queen. "I want to make sure my friend is okay."

"Whatever the King of Underworld did to evade the Amheuk"—she worries her lip as though she knows what that might be—"will probably prevent any typical means of communication."

"Gods." I tousle my hair aggressively. "What a shit show."

"There *is* one way." The queen blows out a long sigh. "I can call the King of Underworld."

"You can *call* him?" I gape at her, worried my eyeballs might pop out. "You have a *phone*?"

"A phone?" She snorts delicately. "Of course I don't have . . . Never mind. I'll show you."

"Sunny." Haesan places a hand on my arm. "I will go to the Suhoshin headquarters here. There must be something I can do to help."

"Be careful, Nephew." His aunt, who had been hovering beside the queen, pulls him into a teary hug.

"I will." He steps back from her.

I hug him as well. "See you soon, Haesan."

"Don't die, Stormy." He squeezes me a little too tight, then drops his arms. With a bow to the queen, he leaves us with long, determined steps.

Gang Sanggung turns to Jo Sanggung, who stands at the threshold of the audience hall. "What will you do?"

"I must prepare the queen's meals even if the world ends tomorrow," she replies staunchly. "I will do my duty."

"Stay safe." Gang Sanggung squeezes her friend's hand.

Jo Sanggung nods, pressing her trembling lips together. "You too."

"The rest of you"—the Queen of Water spins toward the audience hall and faces the cowering officials inside—"go make yourselves useful any way possible. Help keep the people calm and provide aid wherever it is needed. Understood?"

"Yes, Your Majesty." The officials bow low, quaking in their boots. The loudest ones, who wanted my head, eye the doors with shifty expressions. They are going to run the fastest to save their asses and only theirs.

Gods-damned cowards.

The queen shakes her head at them and glides away from the audience hall. Gang Sanggung motions for me to follow. With one last glance at the dark, undulating sky, I do as she bids, wondering how the hell the Queen of Water plans on *calling* the King of Underworld.

CHAPTER TWENTY-FOUR

Sunny

The Queen of Water and I walk side by side in silence, while Gang Sanggung follows close behind. The Amheuk's oppressive presence above the dome weighs heavier on us by the minute. And news of the chaos erupting throughout the Kingdom of Water—riots, stampedes, looting, and even disturbing rumors of planned suicides—dog our every step.

My chest pounds with two sets of heartbeats. At least, it feels that way. My Yeoiju is . . . reacting to the Amheuk. But I can't tell if it wants out or wants to hide deeper inside me. I envy people with inner compasses that always show them their true north.

I have no idea where to go—*Go to Ethan.* Or what to do—*Be with Ethan.* I rub my tired eyes. I obviously know what I want. *Ethan, Ethan, Ethan.* But with the whole realm at stake, what I want doesn't matter.

So . . . what? I should just go out there and throw down with the Amheuk?

Only fools pick fights they know they can't win. But I *did* defeat Daeseong. *Are you crying for me, daughter?* My empty stomach heaves, his dying words haunting me. How ironic is it that the only hope against the eternal darkness is the daughter of the dark mudang?

I can't change the past—and I can't change who I am. But I *can* look forward and try to do better. I have to do better so I might be worthy of Ethan. *What if I can never be worthy of him?* I ignore the scared little voice inside me. I know down to my bones that my place is at his side.

I will find my way back to you, Ethan.

But I have no idea what trying to do better looks like at the moment. I shake my head and pull my shoulders back. I'll figure it out. I've always been good at improvising. For now, I'll focus on putting one foot in front of another.

Panicked subjects stop the queen so often that we don't arrive at her inner chambers until late afternoon. Her jimil, though, is lovely, from the serene courtyard to the quiet hallways of the hanok.

Sliding latticed doors open up to a large rectangular room, adorned with exquisitely crafted wooden furniture. Plenty of hanji-pasted windows let in the soft, muted sunlight, adding to the warm ambience of the queen's chambers. And I glimpse a sleeping alcove tucked away in the back.

The silk room divider standing against the back wall snags my attention. It is beautiful. Not as beautiful as the one in the guest room at the Sunset Pavilion, but a close second. I walk to the room divider and run my fingers over the lily pads embroidered on it.

"When this is all over, I'm so getting one of these," I murmur.

The Queen of Water steps next to me and gives me a sidelong glance. "I did not peg you for someone who collects pretty things."

"I'm not." I drop my hand to my side. I don't understand my minor obsession with room dividers either. "At least, I wasn't."

My breath catches in my throat. *Home.* I want a beautiful room divider in my *home*. Not just a place I sleep in—with my figurative foot out the door—but a place I call home. A place *we* call home.

If Ethan doesn't want me after I tell him that I . . . that I'm . . . If he doesn't want me after I tell him everything, then he'll have to *make* me let him go. I will fight for his love.

I can't go to him in the Kingdom of Mountains, but I'll find a way for us to be together. I won't run from the only thing I've ever wanted.

Suddenly, I miss Ethan so much that I can't breathe. I dig the heel of my palm against the ache in my chest, taking in shallow sips of air. I steal an anxious glance at the queen, hoping she doesn't notice I'm *this* close to falling apart.

"I . . . I am afraid he won't answer," the Queen of Water says in a wavering whisper. Maybe she is just as close to falling apart.

"What?" I tilt my head, tucking my hair behind my ear so I can hear her better.

"What if I call Taeyoung and he doesn't answer?" She bites down on her bottom lip.

"Isn't *not* knowing worse, though?" I reach out and squeeze her hand. She seems to care deeply for the King of Underworld.

"You're right." With a firm nod, she heads toward the sleeping alcove. "Come with me."

With a sleeping mat, a low dresser, and an armoire, the small, tidy space feels cozy and inviting. But the nerves coming off the queen like buzzing bees, as she wrings her hands in the middle of the alcove, shatter any semblance of serenity.

"So where do you hide your phone?" I ask glibly to distract her.

"I told you it's not a phone," she chides, and I tuck my chin to hide my smile. Then she pulls open the armoire, revealing a full-length mirror attached to one door. "It's a mirror."

"You're going to call him on a *mirror*?" I don't know why I'm even surprised. It could've been a shiny stockpot, for all I knew. I will never understand this realm.

"You *have* moon shifted before, have you not?" She waits expectantly for my confirmation, and I nod. "So you must know that water has the power to open up pathways."

"Even without the moon?" I actually don't understand how any of it works. I just chalked it up as fancy high magic and left it at that.

"Water is the true conduit," she explains. "The moon merely amplifies its powers."

"That's interesting and all." I purse my lips. "But what does any of that have to do with calling the King of Underworld on your armoire mirror?"

With a mischievous smile, the Queen of Water waves her hand at the mirror, and it . . . ripples.

"This is a mirror of water." She flutters her fingers over the mirror, not quite touching it, but the surface undulates in response. "Water I created from my own gi and infused with my own magic."

I still don't get it, but I roll with it. "Can you call anyone you want on the magic mirror?"

"No." She sighs wistfully. "You can only reach the person connected to you by the threads of fate."

"A-are you connected to the King of Underworld in . . . that way?" My voice wavers. "Do you and the king share a love destined by the heavens?"

Ethan believes we are bound by the threads of fate. But I'm afraid that same fate might force him to sever the thread that binds us with his own hands.

"That is neither here nor now." The queen smooths her hands down her turquoise royal gown. *So, that's a yes.* "Shall we see if he answers?"

She arranges her expression into a serene mask, but her pulse flutters at her throat as she faces the mirror. I step back to give her space, but curiosity and . . . something else keep me from moving too far away.

"Taeyoung." Her hand hovers over the mirror. "It's Bora."

Nothing happens.

"It's me, Bora." A tremor weaves into her voice. "Answer me. Please, Taeyoung."

The mirror ripples and churns—glowing in pearlescent hues—then like a sheet pulled taut, the mirror stills with a ringing snap.

"Bora," the King of Underworld rasps from the other side, reaching an unsteady hand toward the mirror.

"Don't," the queen cries. "Remember, Taeyoung. You can't touch the mirror. Or else our connection will be lost until the next moonrise."

He swallows thickly and drops his arm.

"A-are you all right?" Her voice cracks on the last word. "The Amheuk . . . It reached the Kingdom of Water . . ."

"That is faster than I anticipated. Its strength must be fully restored. Are you okay? The dome is holding, right?" At the queen's nod, he sags, pushing his hair off his forehead. "We are also safe. For now. I moved the Kingdom of Underworld into purgatory."

"Thank gods," the queen breathes. "I suspected—"

"Purgatory?" I squawk, then clap a hand over my mouth.

"Don't worry. He can't hear you." She glances over her shoulder with a wan smile.

"Can't hear who?" The king squints past the queen's shoulder. "Who's with you?"

"It's Sunny. I heard you helped her get to the Kingdom of Water," the queen answers, turning back to the mirror. "She's very persuasive. General Dokgo is preparing to deploy our troops to the Kingdom of Mountains."

"Good. I'm glad to hear that." He clears his throat. "I-I'm glad to hear your voice."

"Me too." A sob escapes past her lips. "I thought . . . I couldn't . . . What if you were gone?"

"Bora." His voice deepens into a husky rumble. "You would have known if I was gone."

"Yes, I-I would have felt the threads of fate break." She nods rapidly, then covers another sob with her hand. "I've been so foolish, Taeyoung."

He stays silent, but his intense gaze bores into the queen.

"The Code of the Realm cannot dictate our love." She wipes away her tears and draws her shoulders back. "My crown does not rule my heart. If we survive this, I will leave the throne, if it means I can be with you."

"*When* we survive, I will do the same for you," he vows. "I love you, Bora."

"I love you too." The Queen of Water presses a palm over her heart, then takes a half step toward the mirror. "Taeyoung, I will appeal to the Queen of Sky to allow my people to receive asylum there. You should do the same for your people. You can't remain in purgatory for long."

"I will." The surface of the water shivers. And the king's eyes turn desperate as they dart over the queen's face.

"We don't have much time," she chokes out.

"I will see you soon, my love." He holds up a palm.

"And I you," she whispers, hovering her palm over his.

"I'm so sorry, Your Majesty." I hate to do this, but I interrupt their heartfelt moment anyway.

I can't pass up even the slimmest chance of seeing Ethan's face . . . of hearing his voice. I might not get another chance.

"Can you ask the king to relay a message to my friend, Captain Seo?" I speak in a rush. "If she and the generals haven't left for the Kingdom of Mountains yet."

"Of course," the queen says graciously, wiping the corners of her eyes with a delicate finger.

"I need her to tell the King of Mountains to listen for me in the mirrors." I can't hide my desperation. "Please."

"Taeyoung." When the mirror shivers again, she speaks so fast that her words tumble over each other. "Sunny has a message for Captain Seo. Ask her to tell the King of Mountains to listen for Sunny in the mirrors."

The King of Underworld moves his mouth, but no sound comes through. Then ripples spread across the surface of the mirror, severing the connection. The queen remains with her back turned toward me, her shoulders shaking gently. But with a sniff, she straightens to her full height and faces me.

"Is the King of Mountains your fated love?" she asks, a considering look in her gaze.

"I . . . I don't know . . ." I trail off and stare at my toes. "But I want to find out. More than anything, I want to see him. I miss him so much."

"Wouldn't you rather return to the Kingdom of Mountains with my troops?" She cocks her head to the side.

"I can't." Stupid tears fill my eyes, and I raise my left palm. "I was foolish enough to make a blood oath never to return to the Kingdom of Mountains. Not my finest moment."

The queen's eyes widen, but she leaves it at that. "You are welcome to use my mirror, but . . . the magic will not be restored until the next moonrise."

She and I both know the mirror and the rest of the Kingdom of Water might be gone by then. *No.* I won't let that happen. Not until I talk to Ethan. Even if it is to tell him that I love him for the last time.

"I will hold off the Amheuk with my bare hands if I have to." My nails dig into the soft flesh of my palms.

Wait for me, Ethan.

CHAPTER TWENTY-FIVE

Ethan

As soon as night falls, Jihun and I moon shift the Queen of Sky to the Shinsi Palace. We sent word to Captain Ha ahead of time so he could set out a bowl of water in front of the jimil for the shift. When we step into the inner courtyard, the captain receives us with the royal physician and the uinyeos at his side.

"Your Majesty." He executes a swift bow before reaching out to take the queen from Jihun's arms. "Please allow me, Lord Adviser."

"Thank you." Jihun carefully transfers her into Captain Ha's arms.

The captain carries the queen inside the opulent hanok with hurried steps, and the royal physician and the uinyeos follow closely behind him.

I run a weary hand across my eyes. I haven't been back to the jimil since I first infiltrated the Shinsi Palace to take down my father. It doesn't exactly bring back pleasant memories. But I have to stop thinking of it as *his* inner chambers.

"Let's go inside." Jihun claps me on the shoulder. "We might as well get some rest."

My chambers are pristine, with no signs of the damage we wreaked mere days ago. Magic makes quick work of both destruction and restoration in this realm. But even magic can't restore a life lost.

I shake away the morose thought and make my way deeper into the room. I sink onto the seat cushion in front of the silk folding screen and groan, long and loud. Everything hurts, but it also feels so fucking good to sit.

Jihun remains by the doors. "I will stand guard outside, Your Majesty."

"Like hell you will." I tilt my head left and right, stretching out my stiff neck. When the stubborn ass hesitates, I add, "Don't make your king waste his energy arguing with you."

With a quirk of his lips, Jihun comes and sits down on the cushion across from me, and he groans, half in pain and half in relief.

"Right?" I chuckle.

A comfortable silence settles between us as we enjoy the luxury of . . . sitting.

"Your Majesty," a court lady says from the other side of the hanji-pasted doors. "Captain Ha wishes to speak with you."

"Send him in," I answer, exchanging a glance with Jihun.

The captain of the royal guards enters the chambers and stands with his hands clasped in front of himself. I motion for him to have a seat on the last cushion, but he kneels on the hard floor across from me.

I hold back a sigh, but Jihun gives me the slightest shake of his head. Insisting the captain make himself comfortable will only make him *more* uncomfortable.

"How does the Queen of Sky fare?" I inquire instead.

"Even after initial treatment, the queen remains unconscious." Captain Ha drops his head.

"Will she be . . . Will she live?" Jihun's voice is rough with concern.

"The royal physician believes she will, Lord Adviser." The captain nods. "Her pulse and gi are stable, and the uinyeos are at her side to tend to her. For now, they said she needs time and rest."

Impatience vibrates in my chest. The sooner she regains consciousness, the sooner we can end this war. *If* that's what she wants. So far, all Jihun and I have is hope and conjectures.

"We should head back to our battalion." I push to my feet, and Jihun and the captain also stand. I'll lose my mind if I sit around for another second.

"You need more—" The commotion outside drowns out the rest of Jihun's sentence.

"There is no time to announce us," Hailey growls.

"Sorry, ladies. If you'll excuse us," Jaeseok says in a more cordial tone, then slides the doors open before the court ladies can object again. "We really are in a hurry."

Hailey makes a beeline toward us, leaving Jaeseok to catch up. "Jihun, we have to get the king to safety."

"What's happening?" I ask, my gaze jumping between Hailey and Jaeseok.

"The Kingdom of Sky is laying siege to Shinsi," he answers. "The battle battalion approaching from the east is almost at the walls. And the enemy's main forces have cut across the northeast quadrant and are rapidly razing through the southwest quadrant. They will soon reach the capital."

"Where is General Im?" Jihun says.

"He's at the front lines, fortifying the city walls." Jaeseok runs a weary hand down his face. "But no amount of magic can hold off an army that size for long."

I rake my fingers through my hair, then grab a fistful in a punishing grip. We can't seem to get a fucking break. We need to get back out there.

"I'm grateful for General Im's efforts." I release my hair from my fist and force myself to take a calming breath. I can't afford to lose my shit right now. "How are our forces in the northwest and southeast quadrants doing?"

"They are faring better than the northeastern division, but not by far," Hailey reports. "They don't have the numbers to overpower the enemy from behind. The best they can do is buy the capital some time."

"I will not sacrifice them to buy us time." I clench my jaw. "We need to tell General Jo and General Hong to retreat."

"I don't think they know the meaning of the word." Jihun meets my gaze. "The Queen of Sky is our only hope."

"The Queen of Sky?" Hailey's round eyes shoot toward him.

"You heard right." I quickly bring her and Jaeseok up to speed on our adventures this morning. "If General Bak indeed poisoned her, that means the queen opposed this war until the end."

Jaeseok's uncharacteristically grim face brightens by a fraction. "So once she wakes up, she can order the Kingdom of Sky's army to withdraw."

"*If* she wakes up," Jihun corrects.

"She *will*." I glare at my wet blanket of a royal adviser. "She has to."

"Maybe all she needs is a little encouragement from a former idol." Jaeseok puts on a brave smile and shifts his body in a casual half dance, subtle yet masterful.

I laugh under my breath. It's not hard to believe he used to be in a Korean boy band. He certainly has the looks and the moves.

"I thought your band broke up even before you debuted," Hailey teases.

"The hype about our debut already made us famous." The dokkaebi winks. "But the mystery behind our breakup made us legendary."

"I hope the breakup had something to do with you returning to your actual duties as a suhoshin." Jihun sounds as dry as the desert.

Even the crushing weight of my responsibilities—of my potential failure—feels lighter with the Sentinels by my side. They are the family I chose. The pain of my grandfather's betrayal pales in comparison to the strength each of them lends me.

"Let's head to the walls." I head out of my chambers. The Sentinels have never let me down, and I don't plan on letting them down.

"But Your Majesty—" Hailey begins.

"Don't bother." Jihun stops her mid-protest. "Have you ever known our king to put his safety first?"

With Jaeseok guiding us, we moon shift to a well at the edge of the capital. My eyes widen as we approach the chaos at the wall. Night has fallen, but the sky is lit an eerie orange from the fires burning outside the capital. Foot soldiers run to and from the wall, transporting cannons and catapults, and archers line the top of the fortification.

So this is what a war looks like.

The scene is horrifying yet surreal, like my mind took a step back to distance itself from the promise of violence.

"Have you heard from Captain Seo since the last message?" I ask in a low voice when Jihun comes to stand at my side.

"No." A muscle jumps in his jaw. "And not knowing where they are, it's impossible to send them even a short message from our end."

"Gods." I wipe a hand down my mouth. "We can't have them just walk into . . . this."

"Sunny and the others are smart and resourceful." Jihun squeezes my shoulder. "Being dropped into the middle of a raging war isn't ideal, but they can handle themselves."

"I can't argue with that." Even so, my hands twitch at my sides, ready to pull her into my arms—to keep her close, to keep her safe.

I raise my eyes to the orange sky. The soldiers of the Kingdom of Sky are seraphim. Although Shinsi stands at the top of a mountain, there are no trees tall enough to hide the walled city from the sky.

The enemy will attack from the air, but beings of Mountains are faster than our winged foes. We can shoot them down before they breach the wall—more often than not. This will be a bloody battle for both sides.

"Who are those soldiers behind the archers?" I ask Hailey.

"They are soldiers with elemental powers—mostly wind, fire, and lightning," she explains. "To counter the air attack."

"Whoa." Jaeseok rushes to help two soldiers, whose crate of cannonballs tips dangerously to one side. "Easy there."

"I should go join the archers." Hailey offers Jihun a solemn nod, then turns to me. "Your Majesty, please stay safe."

"I will." I hear Sunny's admonition. *Don't do anything stupid without me.* "I won't do anything stupid. I'll see you on the other side, Hailey."

With a quick bow, she sprints up the stairs to the top of the wall, but not before I see her bottom lip wobble. Sunny will kick my ass if I let Hailey get hurt—if I let any of the Sentinels get hurt.

My eyes scan the frantic scene before me. Even with the gi of the Mountains flowing through my veins, I can't take down the army heading toward us. I have to find another way to keep my people safe.

"I need to find General Im." I crane my neck, but I'll never spot him in this pandemonium.

Jihun stops a soldier rushing past us. "Where is General Im?"

"He doesn't stand in one spot." The soldier jerks an impatient thumb over his shoulder, not recognizing who we are. "But I last saw him somewhere over there."

"Thank you," I murmur and immediately head in the direction the soldier indicated.

But Jihun pushes me behind him as an uproar erupts from the wall. A seraph has taken to the sky. *It's too soon.* Did General Bak send someone ahead of his army? The archers scramble to nock their arrows, but the lone angel dives toward the capital much too fast for them to take aim.

"Halt," Jihun suddenly shouts, frantically waving his arms. "Hold your fire."

A second later, I recognize the seonnyeo in the air. "Captain Seo."

With wind stirring the dirt, she lands in a tight crouch, her hands and one knee braced against the ground. I frown down at her bowed head, then raise my confused eyes to the sky.

It's empty. My heart sinks. *She's alone.*

"Gods, Cheyun." Jihun reaches her first and helps her to her feet. "They could have shot you down."

"You think?" She cocks an eyebrow.

"Are you all right?" I rasp, blood pounding in my ears. I'm glad to have her back safely, but I barely manage to hold back my next question. *Where is Sunny?*

"Yes, Your Majesty." She bows, then her expression softens. "Sunny is safe."

The vise around my heart and lungs loosens for the first time in days, but my impatience only grows. "Then where is she?"

"She went to seek help from the Kingdom of Water," Cheyun says.

"The Kingdom of Water?" Jihun and I chorus.

"I have much to tell you, but it must wait." She plants her hands at her waist, hunching forward slightly. *Christ.* We didn't even give her a moment to catch her breath. "Before she went to the Kingdom of Water, Sunny convinced the King of Underworld to send reinforcements."

"The King of Underworld?" My royal adviser and I parrot her again.

"I led them through the portal above the Mirror Lake—the secret portal closest to the capital." After a deep inhale, she straightens to her full height. She is one tough seonnyeo. "The troops from the Kingdom of Underworld are standing by at the western edge of Shinsi."

"How many soldiers?" I gather my wits.

"Ten thousand," the captain answers with a sharp smile. Jihun and I meet each other's round eyes and barely refrain from repeating her words for the third time.

"We can protect Shinsi," Jihun breathes.

"We can do more than that." I grip his shoulder with a huff of incredulous laughter. "We can take down the Kingdom of Sky. We can end this war."

A part of me had believed that I might die without seeing Sunny again. I'd just refused to acknowledge it. But now, there's a real chance that we can win this war. I will fight with everything in me to see my love again. I will take down an entire army for a chance to hold her in my arms.

"Thank you for bringing the cavalry." Jihun sweeps Cheyun into his arms, and she emits a tiny squeak. He steps right back, but a rosy blush stains her cheeks.

"Like I said, Sunny is the one who convinced the King of Underworld." She tucks a loose strand of hair behind her ear, then clears her throat. "I just showed them the way."

"Then thank you for showing them the way." I tip my head. "As for Sunny, we'll thank her when she comes back."

"Yes." Captain Seo averts her eyes as a shadow mutes the quiet joy on her face. "You can thank her when you see her again."

My stomach dips, then ripples with nausea. Something is wrong, but I don't have the guts to question her about it. Instead, I tell Jihun, "We have to send for the generals."

"They won't get here in time," Jaeseok interjects, coming back to stand next to us. "General Im just ordered our soldiers to cover all the water surfaces inside Shinsi."

"Why?" My brows pull low. "I thought troops couldn't moon shift in mass numbers."

"No, but they *can* in small clusters." Jihun crosses his arms. "The longer we hold them off, the more likely General Bak is to risk moon shifting his soldiers into the capital. Even if he's sending them to their deaths."

"I'll go to the generals to bring them up to speed," Jaeseok offers without hesitation. "I'll shift from here using a bowl of water, then you can dump it out as soon as I'm through."

"You won't be able to come back here until the fighting stops." I don't like the idea of splitting up the Sentinels more than we already have.

"Then the generals and I will have to make quick work of it." The dokkaebi grins incorrigibly. "If I eavesdropped correctly, the Kingdom of Underworld's army will strike the enemy forces from the west. General Im will hold them off at the walls, here in the south. So

General Jo and General Hong will have to close in on them from the north and the east."

"They might not have enough forces to cover that much ground," Jihun points out.

"Then they should concentrate on hitting hard from the north." Captain Seo taps her finger to her chin. "Hopefully, the troops from the Kingdom of Water will be here in time to box in the enemy from the east."

"Sounds like a plan." Jaeseok turns to leave.

I stop him with a hand on his shoulder. "Be careful."

"You too." Then he meets Jihun and Cheyun's eyes. "All of you."

"Let's go find you that bowl of water." Jihun claps Jaeseok on the back, and they walk away together.

"Lieutenant Cha will be fine," Captain Seo says in a quiet voice. "He is more competent than he lets on."

"Yeah, I know." I rub my forehead with a half smile. "Are Minju and Draco with Sunny in the Kingdom of Water?"

"No." The captain stares at the ground and breathes a shuddering sigh. "Draco . . ."

When she doesn't go on, I wrap a hand around her arm and turn her to face me. "What is it, Cheyun?"

She finally meets my gaze, her eyes glassy with tears. "Th-they died."

"What?" My voice is barely above a whisper, but she flinches. I realize my fingers are digging into her arm, so I drop my hand to my side. "Sorry. But what . . . did you say?"

"Daeseong killed them," she rasps, her tears spilling over. "They died protecting Sunny."

"No." I stumble back a step, then another, like I can run away from her words. "Please no."

It doesn't seem possible. Draco dead? The surly teenager with a soft, kind heart? The magnificent azure dragon spirit? They had so much life. How could it have been snuffed out so early? They were just a kid. A good kid.

"I'm so sorry." She runs the back of her hand across her eyes. "Sunny and Minju laid them to rest at Heaven Lake."

They are really gone. I lock my knees so they don't buckle under me. They gave their life to protect Sunny.

Thank you for protecting her, kid.

"Draco will get a kick out of being remembered as the Cheonji Monster." My chuckle turns into a broken sob, but I press my fist against my mouth and clamp down on my grief. I can't fall apart in front of my soldiers. I need to lend them my strength, not burden them with my sorrow.

"Yes, they will enjoy that." Cheyun's voice breaks.

I clench my hands at my sides. "Sunny avenged the kid, right?"

"Right," the captain says grimly. "Daeseong is dead."

"Good." I take vicious comfort in knowing that the dark mudang will never hurt anyone again. "And Minju? Where is she?"

"She's at the Kingdom of Underworld, searching for ways to defeat the Amheuk . . ." Captain Seo trails off, her eyes going wide. "Your Majesty, I—"

"The Amheuk?" I feel ice run through my veins.

"Yes, Your Majesty." She bows her head. "The Amheuk has breached the Realm of Four Kingdoms."

My lungs seize, and my ears ring like someone struck a gong right next to me. *The Amheuk?* I widen my stance to maintain my balance. As the dizzying shock passes, my blood heats to a simmer. The eternal darkness is at our doors, and we're wasting our time and energy on this senseless war? All will be lost unless the four kingdoms unite.

A volley of arrows strikes the soldiers at the top of the wall before I can form a coherent response, and the night erupts into a hellscape of blood, fire, and screams. I summon my axes with a roar.

This ends now, Grandfather.

But when I take a step toward the wall, Cheyun stops me with a hand on my arm. "I have a message for you. Sunny said to listen for her in the mirrors."

"What?" I shake my head when more screams tear through the night. "Go alert the Kingdom of Underworld's troops. Press in from the west, and we'll hold the wall."

When Cheyun takes to the sky, I race up the stairs. I can't make sense of her message, but I know one thing for sure. I will subdue the Kingdom of Sky. I *will* see Sunny again. Not even the Amheuk can stand in my way.

We will be together in life. And I will love her till the end of days.

CHAPTER TWENTY-SIX

Sunny

As we stand outside the Queen of Water's inner chambers, the night deepens over the Dragon Palace, and the tentacles of darkness slither frantically against the curve of the dome—a few strands licking at the barrier like black, forked tongues. Something about the movement feels . . . obscene, like the Amheuk is aroused. Bile churns in my stomach as fear and disgust choke my throat.

"Has the Kingdom of Sky responded to your request?" I turn to the Queen of Water. "Will they offer asylum for your people?"

"I have heard nothing from them." Her gaze remains fixed on the Amheuk's frenzy. "While relations between the four kingdoms are often tense, the Queen of Sky and I have always remained cordial. This isn't like her."

The Kingdom of Water doesn't have time to wait patiently for an answer. Its people and the kingdom itself will be gone by tomorrow. I scrub a hand over my face. *Gods damn it.* I need to go there myself.

I have no idea how a lowly cadet will get an audience with the Queen of Sky, but I have to try. Or maybe I can sweet-talk that curmudgeon, Keeper Bae, into letting the people of the Kingdom of Water come through. I can get permission for them to stay once we get everyone to the Kingdom of Sky.

Too bad I don't speak "sweet talk" and Keeper Bae is persnickety about proper documentation. Now, if I were in the Mortal Realm, I knew a guy who knew a guy that was a master forger. For the last few decades, assuming a new identity in a new city became much smoother. But he might be retiring soon . . .

Shit. I'm really doing this.

I glance back at the Queen of Water's inner chambers, my mind's eye zeroing in on the mirror of water. I have to call Ethan tonight. This might be my last chance to see his face, to hear his voice.

What if he isn't my fated love?

I shake away my doubts. He believed we were, and I believe in him. I believe in *us*. I'll come back after I convince someone in the Kingdom of Sky to grant asylum to the people of the Kingdom of Water. I just have to make it back in time.

"I'll go to the Kingdom of Sky and talk to the queen . . . or to anybody who will listen," I say before I can change my mind.

"I'm afraid that's not possible." The Queen of Water finally looks away from the looming darkness and meets my eyes. "Keeper Ahn was standing post when the Amheuk came for the Kingdom of Water."

"Gods." I don't need her to tell me that the keeper is dead. The portal is in the water outside the protection of the dome. There is no other possible outcome. My heart constricts. Now Haesan will never get that drink with his childhood nemesis. "A-and the other keeper? Each kingdom has two, right?"

"Yes," she sighs, "but I had to deploy my army to the Kingdom of Mountains."

I struggle to swallow. I didn't have time to think about the ramifications of deploying the troops with the Amheuk in the water.

"That must've been a bloodbath," I whisper.

"Yes." The queen nods grimly. "And our remaining keeper died to get as many of our soldiers through as possible."

"None of us can leave," I murmur, my lips barely moving, "unless the Kingdom of Sky opens the portal from their end."

I spin away from the Queen of Water and pace the courtyard outside her jimil. How am I going to get into the Kingdom of Sky now? *Is there no hope?* Then I freeze on the spot. I forgot about the token Keeper Bae gave each of us that night Ethan, Jihun, and I infiltrated the Kingdom of Mountains to overthrow the tyrant.

"I have a . . . I have a token to . . . to the Kingdom of Sky," I stutter, hurriedly pulling out the small pouch hanging around my neck underneath my T-shirt.

The queen gasps and reaches for the pouch, but then she shakes her head sadly. "That is indeed a token to the Kingdom of Sky, but only via the Kingdom of Mountains. Did a keeper give that to you as a return passage?"

"Y-yes." Why does everything have to be so complicated in this fucking realm? "But this has to be better than nothing, right?"

"Perhaps." The queen does not sound at all convinced.

"Well, I have to try." I dig my heels in, trying to convince myself at the same time. "We can't just stand here and wait to die."

"If you do this, my people will forever be indebted to you, Sunny." She clutches my hands. "*I* will be indebted to you."

"No debts. We're all in this together." I clear my throat and quip, "Besides, there's a good chance I'll get myself killed for nothing."

"The fact that you are trying despite that risk means everything." The Queen of Water squeezes my hands, then lets them go. "I . . . I have the power to expand the dome to allow you to reach the portal without swimming through the Amheuk-infested water, but . . ."

"You need to save your gi for when you evacuate the entire kingdom," I finish for her, everything clicking into place. That's why she couldn't protect her troops. A trained soldier has better odds of surviving than a civilian, so she had to make an impossible choice. "Don't worry about me. I can take care of myself."

"Thank you," the Queen of Water says in a wavering voice before she regains her regal composure. "I can at least keep you dry. Will you let me do that much for you?"

"Hell yeah." The water is so freaking cold. "You definitely can."

"Well, then." With an elegant wave of her hand, she draws a loose outline of my body in the space between us.

I blink when nothing happens, but then, the air gently tightens around me, like I'm being vacuum sealed.

"Wow." I stare down at the shimmering blue gi coating my body. "Is this like an invisible wetsuit?"

"A wet what?" The queen squints.

"Never mind." I take a bracing breath. "I better get going."

"Let me escort you to the main gates." The Queen of Water looks as though she is on the verge of grateful tears.

"That's all right." I'm tired of saying goodbye. I'm tired *period.* "It'll be faster if I go on my own."

I step back from her and take my gumiho form. When she gasps and claps in delight, I huff—half in amusement, half in relief—and dash out of the courtyard, fast enough to be a white streak.

I'm in a hurry, but I mostly don't want to be seen. Unlike the Queen of Water, your typical shinbiin fears, or hates, animal spirits. And I don't have time to deal with a panicked stampede.

When I reach the main gates of the walled city, I hide behind a building and shift back to my human form. If the guards see me in my gumiho form, they're as likely to spear me as they are to open the gates for me. Plastering a bland smile onto my face, I casually approach them.

"Good evening." I nod politely at the two guards. They're not the same ones from this morning. "I need to leave the palace on an errand for the queen."

They gape at me in wordless shock. I don't blame them. I, too, think it's dumbfoundingly foolish of me to venture into the water with the Amheuk slithering around out there. But I don't have much choice, do I? Besides, doing incomprehensible, bonkers shit is so on brand for me these days.

"Please step aside." I pray they don't give me any trouble. I lack the patience to deal with pearl-clutching shinbiins at the moment.

The female guard does as I ask without hesitation, but her male counterpart sputters, holding his ground.

"She isn't lying," she says wryly. "Can't you see the queen's armor around her?"

Armor? I thought it was a wetsuit.

The male guard squints hard at me. "You're right."

"Then step *aside*." I'm a little less polite this time.

He complies with a scowl, making sure I know he isn't happy about it. I can't think why. *I* don't give a shit whether he's happy or not. The female guard's eyes nearly roll to the back of her head. She and I are in agreement.

The guards open the gates, revealing the dark water beyond. Yet not a single drop enters through the impenetrable dome.

"So how do I get out?" I pinch my nose with the King of Underworld's clothespin. "Do I have to push through it?"

"Going out doesn't take much effort at all," the female guard explains. "Just step out as though you are walking through."

"Thank you." I face the gates and inhale, ignoring how my breath seems to rattle. I shake out my arms, then mutter under my breath, "Stop stalling, Sunny."

I step out and plunge straight into the icy water. Swallowing my gasp, I kick toward the portal, not looking over my shoulder. I don't want to see the Amheuk's slithering tentacles, or its slimy tongue, branching out toward me.

I block out everything and swim. The queen's wetsuit, or armor, works wonders. The water feels cold against me, but it doesn't seep into my clothes and chill me to the bone. But I jerk to a stop with a watery scream when a tentacle grabs me by the ankle.

Gods damn it. Maybe I should've looked back.

It swiftly wraps itself around my calf, while several more serpentine strands flap toward me. I'm done for if I get snagged by the rest. I summon the Shin'gwangdo and slice off the tentacle climbing up my leg. The Amheuk roars in fury—I can't hear it, but the sound vibrates through me.

I swim toward the portal again, working my limbs so hard they burn. This time, a dark arm snakes around my waist and squeezes the breath out of me. I kick and thrash in panic as it slithers and tightens around my entire torso.

I hack at the tentacle until it loosens enough for me to swim free. The Amheuk must be distracted with its attack on the Kingdom of Water. If I had the privilege of its full focus, I would be dead by now. I'm sure of it.

"Fuck."

Four tentacles grab my arms and legs and wrap around them like corkscrews. Then they stretch my limbs out to the sides, holding me spread-eagle. I twist and thrash against their grip, but they only pull harder, and my left shoulder pops out of its socket. I groan, gritting my teeth.

They're going to tear me apart.

I swing the Shin'gwangdo in wild half arcs, only able to move my wrist, but I can't reach the Amheuk's serpentine arms at this angle. I need to switch my grip to point the blade down so I can slice upward toward my underarm. My vision swims with pain, and I take a huge gamble. I throw my sword in the water, nudging it so it tips and rotates while it sinks.

With my blood pounding in my ears, I force myself to wait until the blade floats past my reach. Then, I shoot my hand out, as far as I can, and grab for the hilt. My fingertips graze the handle. *So close.* But the sword slips and starts to spin away.

I scream and strain against the tentacle on my right arm. I barely gain an inch, but it's enough for me to snatch the hilt of the Shin'gwangdo, the blade pointing down.

Fuck, yeah.

I twist my wrist and slash the sword toward my armpit, hoping to cut the dark limb wrapped around my arm without hurting myself. I hack at it, but the water makes my movements sluggish. I have no choice but to keep going.

Then the tentacle slides limply off my arm, a furious roar vibrating through the water. With my sword arm free, I slash at the tentacles restraining the rest of me, scoring deep gashes into them. They finally drop away from me, and I kick toward the portal once more.

But the Amheuk's wrath reverberates around me, and I feel its focus shifting more fully onto me. I swim another yard, agonizingly slow with one arm out of commission. Then, a dozen strands of darkness shoot out from all directions and mummify me from ankles to shoulders, trapping my arms—and my sword—to my sides.

I thrash against the Amheuk's hold, panic overriding logic. The violence of my movement dislodges the clothespin from my nose and snaps the string tied around my neck. And the soil in the small pouch, my token to the Kingdom of Sky, spills into the water. It might not have opened the portal, but at least there was a chance.

Now . . . I'm dead.

My lungs burn as my oxygen supply depletes, and everything turns hazy. I want to inhale, even if it means sucking in a lungful of water. But my Yeoiju hums at my heart's center, reminding me that I am not alone.

I need your help, I speak to the nature around me.

I stop struggling and close my eyes, reaching out with my senses for the gi of nature. When I open my eyes again, only a pale-blue glow surrounds me. *I don't understand.* Nature's life force is so much more powerful than this.

What's making it so faint? Is it the Amheuk?

Even though it is diminished, the gi of Water trickles into me until the sword of light glows against my thigh. And after what feels like an eternity, white light shines through the dark tentacles, disintegrating them into specks of black ash.

The Shin'gwangdo dims in my hand, and I quickly sheath it. There isn't enough gi to light it again.

Air. I need air.

I swim toward the portal with the single intent of *breathing*. I don't know what I expect to happen when I get there, but I'm getting there. My head spins, and black edges into my vision, but I keep jackknifing my legs. The portal shimmers like a mirage in the water.

I'm so close.

But the Amheuk rises behind me like a gargantuan whale, and it swallows the bottom half of my body. Anguish twists through me until I can't feel my legs anymore. I can't hold my breath anymore. I can't . . . fight anymore.

I'm sorry, Ethan. I love you.

My last gulp of air spurts out of me, bubbling in the water, and my eyes slide closed. But two strong hands grab me by my armpits and haul me toward the portal. *Two disembodied hands.* I must be hallucinating.

Then I land on my back with a thump—*Is this a wooden floor?*—and the shock has me dragging in a heaving breath. *Shit.* But instead of the rush of salt water I expect, I breathe in sweet, sweet air.

Before I can sigh in relief, I flip onto my stomach and vomit a gallon of water, then I proceed to cough up my lungs.

"Stop that ruckus," a grumpy voice mutters, while a warm hand pats my back.

I inhale slowly through my nose to stifle my coughs before I crack a rib. Then I push my torso off the floor with one arm and struggle to my knees. The same hands—*They were real*—help me sit up, then lean my back against the wooden pillar.

"What in the world is going on?" Keeper Bae, the owner of the two lifesaving hands, barks at me. "What was that beast in the water? And why didn't one of the Kingdom of Water's keepers open the portal for you?"

I hold up a finger, asking for a minute, then scoot a little away from the pillar. I take a deep breath, then ram my left arm and shoulder against the pillar. My shoulder slides back into the socket with a pop. I grit my teeth against the pain, stars sparking behind my eyes.

When I can see straight again, I finally face the keeper.

Gods, do I have to say this again?

I almost wish I had another dislocated shoulder to reset. Anything to stave off the bomb I have to drop. But Keeper Bae—who just saved my ass—deserves an answer. I sigh past my raw throat.

"The Kingdom of Water lost both of its portal keepers to the Amheuk, Keeper Bae. The eternal darkness has breached the Realm of Four Kingdoms." No matter how many times I say it, the reality of the nightmare still jars me.

And the stunned keeper falls on his ass, his mouth opening and closing.

"It's attacking the Kingdom of Water, and their dome won't hold for much longer," I soldier on. "You have to allow their people to come through the portal. The Kingdom of Sky has to grant them asylum."

"Of course," Keeper Bae says without hesitation, making me do a double take. "While I don't have the authority to grant them asylum, I can at least help them through."

"You don't mind that they don't have proper documentation?" I gape at him.

"Do I look like a monster to you?" Keeper Bae scowls at me. "People's lives are at stake. Who cares about *documents* at a time like this?"

"I'm going to regret saying this"—I scowl right back at him—"but I like you."

The keeper blinks, then bites his cheeks. If I didn't know better, I would think he's holding back a smile. I tuck my chin to my chest to hide my own smile. *For fuck's sake.* With a sharp shake of my head, I clamber to my feet.

Keeper Bae rises with me, his arms loose at his sides. But I have a feeling those lifesaving hands are ready to catch me at the first sign of unsteadiness.

"I have to go back," I pant, winded from just getting off the floor.

"Go back?" He yells directly in my face, but I let it go, because now I know he's a softy deep down. "Back *there* with that *thing* trying to *swallow* you whole? That was the Amheuk, wasn't it?"

"Yes," I answer truthfully.

"And you want to go back to *that*?" He has an impressive falsetto.

"Yes." Another honest answer. I'll fight off the grabby darkness again—I'll do it a thousand times over—for a chance to hear Ethan's voice. We might never see each other again. I want this last moment with him. "Please. I have to get back. A-and you must need help keeping the portal open long enough to evacuate an entire kingdom, right? I-I can help with that from the other side. Just tell me what to do."

Without answering, Keeper Bae stomps down the wooden steps of the pavilion and walks over to the pond next to it. He kneels at the edge of the pond and sinks both hands into the water. Then he whisper screams at the poor pond in a seemingly endless tirade.

I slide down the pillar and wait as the keeper prepares the token to open the portal for the Kingdom of Water—and hopefully, my round-trip token as well.

I run my hands down my sides and the tops of my outstretched legs. I don't have a soggy spot on me. The Queen of Water's magic is still holding strong. It looks like I won't freeze to death in the water.

Unfortunately, I might drown since I lost the King of Underworld's clothespin. I shrug. I'll deal with that when I get there.

Besides, it's easier to survive without air than without Ethan.

CHAPTER TWENTY-SEVEN

Sunny

It's nearly dawn by the time Keeper Bae stomps back up the steps to the pavilion. I rub the fitful sleep out of my eyes and tilt my head back. He stands glaring down at me, holding a big jug of what I assume is pond water and two small vials, one on a looped thread.

"Are those vials for me?" I croak, pushing up to my feet.

"You are the most foolish child I've ever—"

"I am *not* a child." I stick up my pointer finger perilously close to his left nostril. "I haven't been one for over a century."

The keeper has the gall to scoff and turn up his nose at me. Or maybe he just wants to move it away from the range of my finger. "To someone over three hundred years old, such as myself, you are still very much a child, *especially* when you behave like one."

"I am not behaving like . . ." I blow out a sigh. "I have to go back. It's important. And like I said, I can help. Let me help."

"So be it." He shakes his head. "You were right about one thing. Keeping the portal open for such a prolonged period is going to take a substantial amount of magic. I have enchanted the entire pond and will project a steady stream to the portal from here. But it will help to have someone at the other end prop the door open, so to speak."

"How do you *prop* a magic portal open?"

"Find someone who can harness the power of the waves to funnel this jug of water to create a pathway through the portal. They have to keep churning the water to keep the tunnel open." Keeper Bae rubs his jaw. "In my two hundred years as a keeper, I have never had to hold the portal open for so many people."

"You let the Kingdom of Sky's army through to the Kingdom of Mountains," I say waspishly.

"That was not my proudest moment. But General Bak would not take no for an answer. With Keeper Choe behind bars, I had to maintain my post for the safety of the realm." His shoulders droop as though weary in body and spirit. I immediately regret lashing out at him. "Besides, an army is nowhere near as many as the people of an entire kingdom."

"Thank you for doing this," I mumble sheepishly.

"Anyone with an ounce of decency would do the same."

"I wouldn't be so sure about that." I cross my arms over my chest. "Some people would be busy building a wall to close off the portal."

"I said anyone *with an ounce* of decency." He grimaces as though he smells something foul. "Unfortunately for us, we are forced to share the world with those few who possess not a single ounce."

"Unfortunate, indeed." I shake away my deep-seated sadness. "Why did you prepare two vials?"

"You shouldn't need the second vial if you come back before the tunnel closes." Keeper Bae hides his hand behind his back when I reach for them. "But you seem to court danger, so . . ."

"I'll try my best to get back with the rest of the Kingdom of Water." I hold out my palm and flap my fingers. *Gimme.*

The keeper mutters something under his breath and places the vials in my hand.

"I would love to stay and chat, but . . ." I tug one threaded vial over my head, then take the jug from his other hand. "So much to do. So little time."

"When I sense the portal opening from the Kingdom of Water, I'll open this end and keep it open for as long as I can." His gaze bores into mine. "You must have the people move as quickly as they can. Even then . . . not everyone might make it through."

"I understand." I swallow with some difficulty. "All we can do is try our best, right?"

"Right." He dips his head in approval.

There are a lot of assholes in this realm, but I keep meeting the good guys. Maybe there is more good in the worlds than bad. The thought gives me much-needed hope and motivation. This realm might be worth saving.

With a determined nod, I throw my token at the pillar and squint at the flash of blue light. Then I run headlong toward it and splash into the other side. I ignore the icy shock of the cold water and swim like mad toward the underwater city.

I can't tell where it's coming from, but morning light streams into the water. And the frenzied flailing of the dark tentacles has grown slow and sinuous over the dome. If I wasn't already holding my breath, I would do so now, praying the Amheuk doesn't sense me right away.

I kick and swim, calling on the speed of my fox without shifting. The huge breath of air I took at the Kingdom of Sky depletes much too quickly, and my lungs catch fire. *Just a little longer.* I grit my teeth against the dizziness whirling through me and propel myself forward.

I clap my hand over my mouth when bubbles seep out of the corners. Hugging the jug against me with my free arm, I swim on with just my legs. More air slips past my lips, and I press my hand harder against my mouth.

All those people in the Kingdom of Water need my help. I have to get as many of them through the portal as possible. My mind grows foggy. I tighten my hold on the jug of enchanted water and fight to stay alert. But my lungs scream with pain, and my consciousness begins to slip away.

Ethan.

A muscular arm wraps around my waist as my eyes slide closed. My hand slips off my mouth, and my body grows limp. *I can't lose the jug.* Even as everything turns dark, I hug the jug tighter against me, curling my upper body around it.

Then, suddenly, the water pressing in on me from all sides disappears. My back arches as I draw in a heaving breath, coughing and convulsing. I should open my eyes, but I'm so weak I can hardly feel my body.

"Sunny." Someone shakes me hard enough to make my head loll and my limbs flap in the air. *The air?* The person shaking me is also carrying me in their arms. "Stormy."

Haesan. I don't want him to be worried, but my eyelids weigh a ton. Still, I force them open and focus my bleary gaze on him. Or at least, I *try*. But he's nearly nose to nose with me, making me go cross-eyed.

"Move back, you big oaf," I croak.

"Thank gods, you're okay." Haesan draws back, and I can finally see his smiling face.

"I wouldn't go so far as to say I'm *okay*." I choke on some residual water I swallowed and cough raucously. "Thank you for coming for me. Now, let me down."

He immediately sets me on my feet, but I sway and almost drop the precious jug of enchanted water. Haesan quickly takes the jug from my limp hold and props me upright with his free arm. I give myself some grace. Almost drowning twice in less than twelve hours would take a toll on anyone.

"I need to see the queen," I rasp. When the in'eo moves to pick me up again, I growl, "*Don't.* Just help me walk to the queen's chambers."

He basically ends up carrying me with one arm around my waist, my floppy feet barely touching the ground. The steady motion of being half carried is almost soothing. My eyelids grow heavy, and my head droops forward. *Jesus.* I'm nodding off like a granny.

"We need to find someone who can harness the power of the waves," I blurt too loudly, jerking awake. "There is no time."

"You don't need to scream." Haesan cringes, drawing his head back. "And you're in luck, because I have the power of the waves in my veins."

No. Not him.

"It can't be you." I shake my head and push away from him. Luckily, my legs don't give out. "We have to find someone else."

"But you just said there is no time." He scratches his head. "There are others, but not many. It is a rare power."

"The queen might know someone else," I say stubbornly.

Keeper Bae didn't need to explain to me that holding the portal open with the power of the waves would be dangerous. The keeper would draw from the pond to hold his end open, but the person here would have to draw from their own life force to harness the waves. With so many lives at stake, Haesan won't stop until he has nothing left to give. I can't . . . I can't lose another friend.

I walk on my own two feet the rest of the way, and the Queen of Water rushes down the steps of her inner chambers to meet me.

"Thank gods you're okay." She takes both my hands in her own. "Did . . . Will the Kingdom of Sky accept my people into their kingdom?"

"Yes." Keeper Bae and I actually have no way of knowing what the Queen of Sky will decide. But once we get everyone in, we can fight to have them stay. "Are they ready?"

"Nearly. I managed to evacuate many nearby cities," the queen says wearily. She must have worked all night. "Now I have to extend the dome to the more distant villages."

"Will you be okay?" I ask, noticing the queen's pallor.

"My remaining troops and the Suhoshin will assist with the evacuation." She evades my question, and unease flickers across my skin. "The young shinbiins under twenty-four will go first."

The ones who are as mortal as humans because they have yet to reach the peak of their powers. I wrap my arms around my midriff as dread churns in my stomach. They are so vulnerable.

"Do you . . ." I glance over my shoulder at Haesan and lower my voice. "Do you know anyone with the ability to harness the power of the waves?"

She looks past my shoulder and opens her mouth.

"Not him." I grit my teeth. "Someone else."

"Most of them have been deployed to the Kingdom of Mountains." She purses her lips in thought. "We can search for older shinbiins who remained behind . . ."

"Stop, Sunny." Haesan places a heavy hand on my shoulder. "It has to be me. Tell me what I have to do."

I hate that he is right.

"That jug holds the token to the Kingdom of Sky." I blink to clear my fuzzy vision. "But to keep the portal open for everyone to pass, you need to create a tunnel with the enchanted water."

"This isn't enough water to create a tunnel big enough for people to pass through." He bows his head in thought. After a moment, he raises his gaze back to me. "I have to go out of the dome and mix the token with our waters. That's the only way to generate a tunnel that big."

"And the bigger the better so we can get as many across at once," the queen murmurs, twin lines of worry between her brows. "I could lend you my strength . . ."

"No, Your Majesty. You are going to need every drop of your gi to grant our people safe passage to the portal," Haesan says. My lips part, ready to protest, but he lays a gentle hand over my mouth. "I can do this, Stormy. I am stronger than you think."

"When all hell breaks loose and the Kingdom of Water falls to the Amheuk," I say, pulling his hand off my mouth, "I need you to hightail it out of here. Get yourself through the portal. Go to the Kingdom of Sky. Promise me you won't die."

Haesan gives me a guileless smile, his cerulean gi pulsing around him. He *is* strong. If anyone can do this, he can. When he reaches out and ruffles my hair, I let him. I must be getting soft in my old age.

◆ ◆ ◆

"I miss cadet training." I plant my palms on my thighs, bent into an inverted *L*, and pant like a dehydrated puppy. I'll rest for just one minute, soaking in the warmth of the late-afternoon sun.

I glance at the long line of people waiting to cross through the portal, then look beyond the crowd to the shimmering tunnel of water connected to the dome. Haesan floats just outside, with his eyes burning blue, and he circles his hands in front of him like he's levitating a bowling ball. He must be freezing and exhausted. He's been at it for hours.

I'm so fucking proud of him.

But the indolent tentacles of darkness stir restlessly over the dome, signaling the setting of the sun. Soon, it will be night, and Haesan will be vulnerable. With one last glance at my friend and an apprehensive squint at the serpentine arms beyond the dome, I sprint toward the Queen of Water at the opposite end of the palace courtyard.

She stands with her palms outstretched, as her magic extends the dome to the last village. She sways lightly, but she widens her stance with grim determination.

"This way." I help the villagers coming through and point them toward the line to the portal. "Hurry."

Sweat drips down the queen's bloodless face as she takes labored breaths through her blue-tinged lips. She won't last much longer.

"Come on, people." I glance at the darkening sky. The sun is setting much too quickly. The vise around my heart tightens with each passing second. I practically push the villagers toward the portal. "Let's go."

"I . . . can't . . ." the queen whispers.

I reach her side before her knees buckle.

"Whoa." I wrap an arm around her waist and lean into her side to carry some of her weight. "You're almost there."

But her eyes roll back, and she collapses against me in a dead faint.

With an earsplitting crash, the dome extending to the village snaps back to the Dragon Palace. And the villagers . . . The dark tentacles snatch the shinbiins left flailing in the water, one by one, until no trace remains of them.

The Amheuk is awake . . . and hungry.

"Haesan." I crane my neck, trying to see if the dome extending to the portal is holding, but the orderly line of shinbiins has become a swarm of panicked people, blocking my line of sight.

Thunderous thwacks ring through the night as the tentacles whip violently against the dome. Thin fractures zigzag down the sides, and an icy drop of water hits my forehead. I hold the unconscious queen in my arms, not knowing what to do.

"Let me take the queen." Gang Sanggung stumbles in her rush to reach us and implores, "Please. Help my nephew."

"Get her through to the Kingdom of Sky," I shout to be heard, handing her the queen. "You have to go *now*."

Without waiting for her answer, I take off toward the portal, pumping my arms and legs to their limit. I'm halfway there when I slip and stumble in the torrential rain that hits the palace. *No.* It's not rain. It's the water from outside. The dome . . . is giving out.

I run faster. *Shit, shit, shit.*

My knees nearly buckle in relief when I see that the dome connected to the portal is still holding strong—as is the tunnel. And Haesan is unharmed, feeding the might of the waves into the water in a steady stream. The suhoshins calm the people the best they can and hurry them through the portal, urgency creeping into their stoic demeanor.

Carrying the Queen of Water on his back, a royal guard rushes to join the end of the line with Gang Sanggung next to him. But the good people of the Kingdom of Water stand aside, opening a path down the middle, and urge the guard to save their queen first. After a brief hesitation, the royal guard and Gang Sanggung share a nod of agreement and run through the tunnel of water and disappear through the portal.

I whip my head toward Haesan. *I can't believe I got distracted.* But he's still undisturbed.

Battering the dome in a frenzy, the Amheuk gives Haesan no notice. It's like an animal controlled by its basest needs to conquer, destroy, and consume. Fortunately, that means my friend is safe for the moment.

Unfortunately, while the ancient force of darkness could have ended this battle in one fell swoop by killing the in'eo and closing the portal, its Hulk-smash method is also getting the job done, albeit a smidgen slower.

I touch the vial around my neck and take in the chaos around me. We tried our best, but we won't be able to save everyone. The dome will collapse soon. *Too soon.* There's nothing more I can do for the Kingdom of Water.

I hesitate for a split second, then make a run for the queen's inner chambers. I need to get to the mirror of water. I don't have much time.

Please answer, Ethan. Please be my fated love.

CHAPTER TWENTY-EIGHT

Ethan

I stand back-to-back with Jihun at the gates of the capital, fighting the seraphim who make it over the wall. The forces of the Mountains and Underworld are pressing in, and the enemy troops are growing more and more reckless in their desperation.

Jihun grunts, jerking against me.

"Are you hurt?" I yell over my shoulder. "Answer me."

I hear his long sword slashing through the air, and a soldier groans before thumping to the ground. Jihun finally answers, "Just a scratch."

Gods damn it. He is hurt.

I cut across the chest of a seonnam with my golden axe, then cleave my silver axe into the stomach of another. I kick both of them away as they drop.

Blood. So much blood.

I spin out from behind Jihun and take on the soldiers coming at him. I don't let myself feel anything as I methodically chop them down. They are shinbiins. They are seraphim. Their silver gi also flows through me, entwined with the green gi of Mountains. But I can't let them hurt Jihun. I have to protect my brother.

My cheeks are wet. I swipe the back of my hand across my face. I expect to see blood, but my hand comes away clear. *Tears.* They're my tears.

With a wild roar, I ram my shoulder into an oncoming seonnam's unguarded midriff, knocking him to the ground. I whip around when I hear a choked gurgle at my back and come face-to-face with an enemy soldier, his sword raised high above his head. But instead of striking me down, his stunned eyes meet mine, then drop to the blade protruding from his solar plexus. He looks back up before his eyes roll back, and he crumples to the ground.

Jihun scowls at me as he pulls his long sword out of the soldier. "I told you it was just a scratch."

"Fuck you," I snap. Someone cut into his side, through his armor, deeply enough that the whites of his ribs peek through the gash. "Get your stubborn ass behind me. Give yourself time to heal."

"I just saved *your* ass," he growls.

Our argument falls to the wayside as we fight off another swarm of seraphim. More and more enemy soldiers are breaching the wall. Our troops at the top must be running out of steam. And no wonder. The sun is setting on the second day of battle, and we have fought without rest the entire time. This has to end.

Panicked screams roar from beyond the wall. Jihun and I catch each other's eyes and hurriedly fight past the remaining foe and race up the steps. I reach the top first and nearly collide into Captain Seo.

"Your Majesty," she pants. "Reinforcements from the Kingdom of Water have reached the capital. General Bak and his forces are surrounded."

"He cannot win this. He *knows* he cannot win this," I breathe, then say louder, "I have to tell the general to surrender."

"How?" Jihun steps in my way, a hand pressed against his wound. "The Kingdom of Sky has not stopped attacking the capital for over twenty-four hours. General Bak is unlikely to stop the battle to listen to reason."

"I have to try." I push past my royal adviser and approach the ledge of the wall.

"Ethan—"

I silence him with a look. "Clear some space for me, Lord Adviser."

"Yes, Your Majesty," he says, a muscle ticcing in his jaw.

A dozen soldiers move away from the ledge at Jihun's order, but the infuriatingly obstinate male stands at my side. "Move, Jihun. I don't want to hurt you."

"Come on." Captain Seo tugs him by the arm, and they back away from me, giving me a wide perimeter.

I take a deep breath and draw the life force of Mountains into my veins. The violence has taken a toll on this land as well as my body, and my gi pulses sluggishly through me. I cross my axes over my chest, brace myself, then push out my power with a strained shout.

The front line of enemy forces falls like dominoes before they can even scream in fear. I recall my power on a long gasp and stumble as it slams back into me. Captain Seo and Jihun catch me by my arms, one on each side. I drag in another breath.

I nod my thanks before gently freeing my arms and stepping up to the ledge again. I'm grateful when they stay close behind me.

"General Bak." I project my voice with my remaining magic. "You are completely surrounded by the forces of the Kingdom of Mountains, the Kingdom of Water, and the Kingdom of Underworld. Stop this madness and surrender."

"Not until one of us takes our last breath," the general answers, walking over his fallen soldiers to come closer to the wall.

"G-Grandfather." I shudder as grief runs through my body. "We must end the bloodshed. We have a bigger enemy to face. Together."

I can't broadcast the coming of the Amheuk to the tired soldiers. Once we end this war, we can rest and regroup as a united realm. But General Bak has other ideas.

"*Never*," he roars.

I realize with a jolt that my grandfather is . . . broken. My mother's death irrevocably shattered his mind.

"I will not surrender, even if it means the death of every last one of us." He waves his fist in the air. "Attack!"

His soldiers run out from behind him but falter at the sight of their unconscious comrades on the ground.

"Attack, you worthless cowards," the general screams, spittle flying from his lips.

They take to the air en masse with no one to cover them. The general is treating the lives of his soldiers like disposable utensils. Even as our soldiers take down seraph after seraph, more follow and cross over the walls.

"Oh gods." I look down the length of the wall—on the outside and the inside. The soldiers, fellow shinbiins, cut one another down. What a senseless waste of precious lives—all to satisfy one male's twisted hate. "He won't stop. He's going to let them all die."

I have to awaken the Queen of Sky. Only she can stop this war without more bloodshed.

"Protect Shinsi while I'm gone," I say to Jihun.

"You won't make it to the palace," he warns, knowing what I plan to do. "Too many enemy soldiers have breached the capital."

"If you must go, then allow me to accompany you," Captain Seo implores. "I will protect you with my life, Your Majesty."

"I have to do this on my own." I give them a ghost of a smile. "I only have enough strength left to cloak myself."

Then I make myself invisible, and the captain gasps, taking half a step back.

"Show-off." Jihun huffs a tired laugh. "I'd forgotten you can do that."

"I'll be back before you can miss me," I grouse.

Not bothering with the stairs, I jump down from the top of the wall, landing in a half crouch, then sprint for the Shinsi Palace. I can fly, but I am faster on the ground with the gi of Mountains propelling me.

"Captain Ha." My sudden appearance startles the captain of the royal guards, who stands sentry outside my jimil. I hold out my hand. "Easy there. Has the Queen of Sky regained consciousness?"

I know the answer before the captain shakes his head. "Regretfully, no, Your Majesty."

"I must see her." I march up the stone steps to my inner chambers.

"If I may, Your Majesty." Captain Ha follows me inside, and I nod at him to continue. "The uinyeos are administrating acupuncture on the queen. May I escort you to your chambers? I will bring word as soon as they are finished."

"Very well." Impatience sparks against my skin, but the acupuncture might push the last of the poison out and help her wake up. "There's no need for you to escort me. I know my way."

"Of course, Your Majesty." The captain bows. "I will take my leave."

I walk into my chambers with weary steps, then slide down the nearest wall. I press a hand over my eyes, which sting with fatigue.

"Ethan."

I jump to a stand, my head whipping left and right. I heard Sunny calling my name. *Am I losing my mind?*

"Ethan, can you hear me?" Her voice cracks at the end.

Listen for her in the mirrors.

I stumble through my chambers in a frantic search for a mirror . . . any mirror. The jimil is mine in name alone. I haven't spent enough time in it to know where anything is.

"Fuck." I grab my head with both hands.

"Ethan. Please." I hear a muffled sob. "Tell me you can hear me."

I race to my sleeping alcove and turn over the room. I feel like a fool when I fling open the armoire to find a full-length mirror on the inside of the door. I'm pissed I checked the most obvious place last, but I'm not in my right mind.

"I can hear you, Sunny," I say, my heart bruising my ribs. "I'm here, baby. I'm here."

For a moment, all I see is my reflection, my wild eyes skittering across every surface of the mirror. The wooden armoire protests under my punishing grip, but the mirror ripples like silvery water, and . . .

I *see* her.

"Sunny." My hoarse growl is a prayer of gratitude—*She is safe*—and a vow of possession. *Mine.*

"E-Ethan?" Sunny raises her hand toward the mirror, then drops it, giving her head a sharp shake. "Don't touch the mirror, okay? Our connection will be lost if we touch the mirror."

She is wearing a black T-shirt and nearly black jeans—her favorite color palette—and her long hair falls down her shoulders. I want to run my hand through its silky strands. I want to cup her face, kiss those lips, run my hands over her body. I want to *touch* her. But not if it means I lose even a second of seeing her . . . of hearing her warm, husky voice.

"I . . . I won't." I struggle to swallow as I stare at her like a man starved. I *am* starved. I don't know how long we have, but it won't be nearly enough. "Are you safe? You're not injured?"

She spreads her arms and looks down at herself, then meets my eyes with a cocky smile. I immediately want to kiss it off her mouth. I want to hoard her every smile, every laugh. Even her tears. If they are hers, I want them . . . to hold and to cherish.

"As you can see, I'm still in one piece." Her smile and her bravado falter as her gaze skitters over my face and body. "H-how about you? Are you okay?"

"Yes." A corner of my mouth kicks up. "Still in one piece."

We stare at each other for two heartbeats, grinning like the lovesick fools we are.

"I miss you, Ethan." She clutches her shirt over her heart. "It hurts *so much* that I can't be with you. It's tearing me apart."

"It nearly broke me when you left." I reach out for her without thinking, then snatch my hand away from the mirror. "Not knowing where you were. Not knowing whether you were safe. I thought I was losing my mind. Y-you *are* okay, right?"

"I am." She juts that pretty chin of hers. "And nothing will stop me from finding my way back to you."

"To where you belong." My voice drops a register. "You *belong* to me."

"But . . ." She glances away, her throat working. "I've done things . . . I'm not the same person you fell in love with, Ethan."

"No matter what you've done, you will always be Sunny Cho." I search her face and see heartbreak there. *What happened, Sunny?* "You will always be my prickly, beautiful, perfectly imperfect Sunny."

She sniffs and swipes the back of a hand across her eyes. "Still cheesy as ever."

"Only for you, baby." I grin at her as my gaze devours her.

A lovely pink steals into her cheeks, and she tucks a strand of hair behind her ear, so shy and endearing. I grow painfully hard and bite my lip to hold back a groan.

"Whoa. Your pupils just swallowed your irises." Sunny smirks, even though her blush deepens. "Having naughty thoughts, are we?"

"You have no idea." I chuckle, low and dark. "You might go running if you could see the things that I want to do to you."

"It can't be as bad as everything I want to do to you," she says in a breathless whisper. But she suddenly whips her head to the side with a sharp gasp.

I can't see anything beyond her. Everything is a silvery blur except for her. I was more than fine with that—she is the only thing I want to see—but now fear clutches my heart.

"Sunny, what's going on?" I step closer to the mirror. "Where the hell are you?"

"We don't have much time, Ethan," she whispers. "Once you defeat General Bak, you have to come to the Kingdom of Sky. I'll wait for you there."

"The Kingdom of Sky?"

"It is the kingdom farthest from the reaches of the Amheuk. We can prepare for the war there. Together." She glances to the side again. "I love you, Ethan. I'm so happy you are my fated lo—"

A coil of darkness pierces the silvery haze and wraps around her throat. Her hands claw at the darkness as her eyes widen in fear.

"Sunny," I scream. "Don't touch her!"

The hilts of my axes press against my palms. I have no recollection of summoning them, but I grip them tight, my blood rushing in my ears. She is mine to love and protect. I will not let anything touch her.

With a roar, I lunge for her. But I hear the crack of wood and glass, then the door of the armoire crashes to the floor. The mirror is just a mirror again—shattered from the impact—and Sunny is gone. I fall to my knees with a hard thud, barely noticing the dig of the glass shards.

I would have gone mad . . . if I hadn't seen white fire burst in her eyes before I lost sight of her. *My fierce, glorious warrior.* She harnessed the power of the Yeoiju.

Give the Amheuk hell, Sunny.

CHAPTER TWENTY-NINE

Sunny

I kick my legs, struggling to breathe, as the creepy tentacle does its best to strangle me. Desperation fueling me, I claw at the strand of the Amheuk until my nails crack and bleed. With a tug at my heart's center, my hands flare with white fire and burn the tentacle to ashes.

Sucking in a heaving lungful of air, I sprint out of the Queen of Water's inner chambers. I have to get to the portal before the dome collapses. I put my head down and pump my legs harder. Then I stumble to a halt just outside the gates of the inner courtyard.

All hell has broken loose.

Countless tentacles have crashed through the dome, and they whip and slash at the shinbiins remaining in the palace. Anguished screams tear through the night, and blood and water swirl on the ground, rising higher by the second.

"No." I summon the Shin'gwangdo and slash at the closest tentacle. I help a guard up from the ground and shove her in what I hope is the direction of the portal. "Run. Don't look back. Get to the portal."

Drawing from the strength and speed of the gumiho, I stab and cut as many tentacles as I can, helping as many people as I can. But soon, my arms, legs, abs, and chest burn, and I taste iron in the back of my throat. Still, I fight on until my swings grow sluggish and ineffective.

There are too many of them. I will never cut enough tentacles to save everyone. I need to attack the source of these monstrosities. I trace the snakelike cords of darkness to the top of the dome, wiping away the water raining down on my face. I almost expect to see the body of a kraken up there, but the Amheuk has no bloated, misshapen body or scary bulging eyes.

It is a vast darkness.

But when I peer closer, I see a concentration of it—from where the tentacles stem. That is where I need to attack. I reach for my Yeoiju, and it hums quietly at the center of my soul. I can't count on nature's life force in the Kingdom of Water, and the Yeoiju might siphon my gi to fuel itself, but it's a risk I have to take.

"Let's do th—"

My words—my body—are swept away by a tidal wave. The force of the water flooding the dome twists me around in disorienting circles, and my back strains painfully as I fight against the current. But as suddenly as it sucked me in, the vortex spits me out into the dark water.

I calm my pounding heart and struggle to get my bearings. But once I do, I get the sinking feeling that I'm drowning. *He-he.* I choke on my morbid humor as I take in the carnage around me.

So many bodies . . .

They float in the water, their life forces sucked dry by the parasitic tentacles of the Amheuk. Then even the bodies disappear into the darkness. I should've done more. They're dead because I couldn't save them. My body sinks deeper as desolation drags me under.

The light shimmering from the open portal is gone. Even if I had the air and strength left to swim, I wouldn't know the way out of here. I try to think—I shouldn't give up—but shock and exhaustion shroud my mind like a dense fog.

Then something as thick as a tree trunk wraps around my waist, and I'm dragged through the water. *Did the Amheuk find me again?* But it doesn't feel like a tentacle, but a warm, strong arm. I blearily focus my gaze on the owner of said arm, and an enraged screech escapes from my mouth in a blast of bubbles.

What are you doing? I yell telepathically at Haesan. *Why didn't you go through the portal? I told you to leave when all hell breaks loose.*

Of course, he doesn't answer. The big oaf won't even meet my eyes. *No, no, no.* His life is more valuable than mine. He is so kind and unpolluted. My scarred, battered soul is not worth his life.

I have one vial, the token to the Kingdom of Sky, around my neck. Haesan has to use it. I have to force him to use it. I clench my jaw to stay conscious. I tilt my head and see the portal ahead of us. With black edging into my vision, I tug the vial free from around my neck and tie it around Haesan's arm, hoping he doesn't notice.

I'm so sorry, Ethan. Grief wrings my heart until it burns. *I can't watch another friend die.*

It's okay. It'll be okay. Ethan is my fated love. If I can't be with him in this life, then I will be with him in the next.

I will always find you, Ethan.

When we reach the portal, I'll rip myself away from Haesan and push him through. He's strong, but I'm a gumiho—I am stronger. I just . . . have to stay . . . conscious. My head lolls back and forth.

Gods damn it, Sunny. Hang on. A few more . . . seconds.

But I'm fading away. I lose time, and we're already at the portal. I try to pull Haesan's arm away from my waist, but I'm too weak. I can't . . . The in'eo rips off the token I tied to his arm and meets my eyes at last.

No, Haesan. Please, I beg telepathically, my body too limp to move. *Don't do this.*

"Bye, Sunny." He smiles sweetly.

Then he throws the vial against the portal and propels me through with the power of the waves. I want to claw my way back out, but my body won't . . . listen.

Everything fades.

CHAPTER THIRTY

Ethan

As far as I'm concerned, the Queen of Sky is done sleeping. I will make her wake up and end this fucking war, even if it kills me.

I stalk down the halls to where she rests, clenching and unclenching my hands. I feel strength returning to my body as the Mountains restore my gi. Or it might be adrenaline raging through my veins at how the Amheuk dared to touch Sunny.

Whatever the case, I am waking up the queen, ending this war, and going to the Kingdom of Sky. The blood-soaked screams of the Shinbiin soldiers ring in my ears. I will stop the senseless massacre, then I will hold Sunny in my arms again. Nothing will stand in my way.

When he sees me marching down the hallway, Captain Ha comes to attention in front of my study, where they settled the Queen of Sky. "Your Majesty, the queen is not—"

"Are the uinyeos finished with the acupuncture?" I ask, my voice sharp with impatience.

As soon as the last word leaves my mouth, the study door slides open from the inside. An uinyeo jumps, her hand flying to her mouth.

"Your M-Majesty. We are f-finished administering acupuncture on the queen." She wrings her hands. "Her gi is much improved, b-but she has not regained consciousness."

"I must see her." I step toward the door, and the uinyeo scrambles away to let me through.

My reckless anger falters when I see the Queen of Sky lying on the sleeping mat, pale and still. I've seen my mother's face reflected on the mirror of her memories, and my aunt looks so much like her that yearning twists in my chest.

"Your Majesty." I sit down next to her. "My name is Ethan. I . . . I am your sister's son. She didn't leave me many memories of you, but I know she loved you very much."

I stare expectantly at her, hoping for a reaction—even a twitch of her finger—but she remains absolutely still. What if she doesn't wake up?

No, she has to.

"General Bak waged war against her people, and he refuses to surrender, even though the Kingdom of Water and the Kingdom of Underworld fight at our side." I keep talking. "He would rather see all his soldiers die, and die himself, than admit defeat to the Kingdom of Mountains. And he plans on taking as many people as possible with them."

Please wake up.

"More than anything, he . . ." My voice breaks, and I cover my eyes with my hand. "He wants to see *me* dead. And I can't watch more people die because of me. You're the only one who can stop this war. Please."

"Is it truly you?" a reedy voice rasps.

"Your Majesty." I drop my hand from my face and scramble closer to her. "Are you awake?"

Her eyes remain closed, and I hold my breath. *Did I imagine it?*

"Hyeok." She calls me by the name my mother gave me—a name I only learned of when I broke the stone of tears. No one has ever called me that before, and it warms my heart.

"Y-yes, Imo." My eyes round at my own slip, but calling her *aunt* feels so natural.

She opens her eyes, and I suck in a sharp breath. Wordlessly, we stare at each other for a long moment. Then she shifts onto her side, and I rush to help her sit up.

"Hello, Nephew." She offers me a soft smile. "I am so happy to finally meet you."

"Me too," I say with an answering smile, but it fades abruptly. "I-I need your help. You have to order the arrest of General Bak and stop this war. We have to stop this bloodshed. Too many have died already."

"War?" She looks around my study in confusion. "Where are we?"

"We're at the Shinsi Palace. Jihun and I found you on the battlegrounds, being held prisoner under General Gim's watch," I belatedly explain. "Grandfather poisoned you, then launched an attack on the Kingdom of Mountains. Then he brought you with him to hide what he'd done."

"So it has come to that," she sighs, her shoulders falling.

General Bak betrayed and hurt her too. "I'm sorry."

"There will be time for that later. Help me up, Hyeok." The queen holds on to my arm and rises to her feet. She sways and leans heavily against me, but her voice is implacable. "Take me to my father. There is no time to waste."

By the time we reach the courtyard, her breath is already labored. She's in no condition to make the trek to the wall. She was poisoned and unconscious for days. It's a miracle she is standing on her own two feet. She needs more rest, but so much is at stake.

I glance over my shoulder at Captain Ha, who followed us from the study. "Please assist the queen."

"Yes, my king." He rushes to the queen's side, then pauses. "With your leave, Your Majesty."

The queen nods, and he takes her arm. The captain towers over her, but her regal posture lends her a more imposing presence. The knot in my stomach loosens slightly. She is more formidable than she appears.

"I must go ahead of you to the fortress wall," I tell my aunt. "I will prepare a bowl of water for you to moon shift there."

"I understand." She squeezes my hand. "How long do you need to reach the wall?"

"Minutes." With my gi partially restored, I should be able to get there in ten minutes, but I can't risk stranding the Queen of Sky in the abyss. "Captain, wait thirty minutes, then fill a bowl with water for the queen."

"Of course, Your Majesty." He bows with his head, holding my aunt steady.

"You must not try to cross until after thirty minutes, Imo," I warn sternly.

"Do not worry, child," she says with a gentle smile, not at all intimidated. "Everything will be all right."

"I know." My lips wobble at the corners. It has been a long time since someone told me that. "I'll see you soon."

I cloak myself in invisibility and run. But I stagger to a sickened halt when I reach the wall.

The Kingdom of Sky has taken to the sky in a last-ditch effort to storm Shinsi. The archers at the wall volley flaming arrow after arrow at them, while the soldiers with fire magic hurl fiery balls, fed by the wind of other elemental soldiers.

The night sky glows red, orange, and yellow from the countless seraphim writhing in flames, and their dead plummet to the ground like shooting stars. But as quickly as they fall, more winged soldiers rise to fill the violent skies.

Those who make it out of the fire and over the wall strike out, their eyes wild, felling as many of our soldiers as they can, until their charred bodies give out. The ground on this side of the wall is black with the fallen seraphim.

They are General Bak's sacrifices—good soldiers giving their lives for their kingdom. But they have been lied to. They are dying for one male's perverse vengeance. My rage rises like a tidal wave.

No more.

"Your Majesty." Jihun flies down from the top of the wall and grabs me by the arm. "It is not safe here."

"Jihun." I dig my heels in. "The queen is awake. We need a bowl of water for her to moon shift here from the palace."

"Is she well enough?" My royal adviser glances at the burning sky with a grim frown. "I guess she has to be. This madness has gone on for long enough. While a bowl is easy enough to procure, water is another matter."

An arrow whooshes past Jihun's ear and over my shoulder before either of us can react. Then I hear the heavy thud of a body hitting the ground behind me.

"Are you all right, Your Majesty?" Hailey bounds up to me, nocking another arrow to her crossbow.

"Yes, thanks to you," I say through the pounding of my heart. I meet Jihun's eyes just as they widen with realization.

"Hailey." He spins his wrist and summons a small, earthenware bowl to his hand. "We need water."

His lieutenant fills the bowl without question, her trust in Jihun implicit.

I nod my thanks at them and take the bowl of water. We place the bowl on the ground, close to the wall, so the Queen of Sky will be less exposed. Then we stand on the other side of the bowl, leaving just enough room for the queen to step through.

"We might have a few—" I begin, but I'm interrupted by the queen's arrival.

"I asked you to wait thirty minutes," I protest.

"I knew you were underestimating yourself." She smiles serenely. She has more color on her face and stands strong and steady in front of us. The speed of her recovery astounds me.

The Queen of Sky is truly a powerful shinbiin, as I assume all the kings and queens of this realm are. *Will they truly bend the knee to me?* I shake away the intrusive uncertainty. We have a long way to go before we get to that part.

"Your Majesty, I am glad to see you awake," Jihun says, with Hailey standing quietly by his side.

"It's good to see you, Captain." The queen looks to the sky, then shudders. "Though I wish it was under better circumstances."

"We have to go. I will shield the wall so you may speak to your army." I guide her up the steps with a gentle hold on her elbow. "General Bak has lost his mind. He is using the soldiers as cannon fodder."

"Yes, I can see that." She steps to the edge of the wall, anger and hurt bracketing the corners of her mouth. "Whenever you are ready, Hyeok."

Jihun and Hailey flank me as I spread my arms wide, calling to my magic. I have never covered an expanse this large before, but there is no room for doubt. The gi of Mountains rushes into me—fluid, vibrant, and powerful.

Thank you, Mountains.

When my body practically vibrates with power, I thrust my hands up to the sky and unleash my magic across the wall. I grunt as the shield snaps into place. I close my eyes and reach out my senses, pushing gingerly at the boundaries. It holds strong. With a relieved exhale, I nod at the Queen of Sky.

"Hear me, my people." Her voice carries far into the night. "I am the Queen of Sky. And I command you to stop fighting."

Eerie silence falls over the army of the Kingdom of Sky.

"This is not your fight, but my father's," she continues. "General Bak waged war on the Kingdom of Mountains against my opposition. He silenced me by poisoning me and keeping me prisoner. The King of Mountains, my nephew, rescued me and saved my life."

One by one, the soldiers on the ground lower their weapons, and the seraphim in the sky descend toward their brethren. Confused murmurs break through the shocked silence, then their voices grow until pure outrage roars through the air. I can't imagine the shock, horror, and betrayal they must be feeling.

Maybe I can a little.

"The people around you are not your enemy. The Kingdom of Underworld and the Kingdom of Water came to aid the Kingdom of Mountains to stop this misguided war." She pauses. "General Bak is your enemy. He is *my* enemy."

The soldiers of the Kingdom of Sky shout and stomp their feet.

"But as his daughter, I will give him one last chance to surrender." Grief leaks into her words. "Father, you can still choose to end this war. We . . . Hyeok and I . . . are your *family*."

My stomach dips when my grandfather steps away from his troops and looks up at the queen. Will he finally listen to reason?

"That *mongrel's* father killed the last of my family," he spits, his words landing like arrows in my heart. "And you, as always, are nothing but a disappointment. Your sister will be ashamed of you."

My aunt and I share twin gasps of pain. She recovers first.

"No, you are the one breaking her heart. My sister gave her life for Hyeok, who she believed carried the hope of the entire realm. And he is everything she wished for and more. I am as proud to call him my nephew as I am ashamed to call *you* my father." She pulls back her shoulders and stands tall, every bit a powerful queen. "Soldiers, arrest General Bak. He is a traitor to his queen and his people. I want him imprisoned until the time of his trial."

With a shrill laugh, the general unsheathes his broadsword and takes to the sky.

"*You.*" He bares his teeth at me, hovering in the air. "Did you think I would not find your father if you hid him in the dungeon?"

I shake my head slowly, stunned into silence. My grandfather thinks I was trying to protect my father?

"My assassin said he begged for his life before she killed him." He cackles, hovering in the air. "My only regret is that I did not have the pleasure of killing him with my own hands. But I had this war to win, didn't I?"

I feel nothing more than a twinge of surprise at the news of my father's death, but I am horrified by the general's glee.

"You are pathetic. Just like your father," General Bak spits. "I was merciful to let him die quickly. I'm not inclined to show you the same mercy."

"Stop this, Father," the Queen of Sky shouts. "What has this child done to deserve your wrath?"

"My daughter would not have died if he had never been born." Gripping his sword with both hands, the general points it straight down at me. "You will pay for her death with your life."

"No," I scream as he plunges toward me. If he hits my shield, he will die from the impact. But I can't take down the shield and put everyone on the wall in danger. "Grandfather, stop. Do *not* do this. *Please stop.*"

General Bak does not stop. He doesn't slow. He slams full force into the dome of gi.

I . . . I don't even feel the collision—my powers are too far beyond his. *Why, Grandfather? Why?* The impact flings him back, disintegrating his body into fine specks of blood. And the only thing that hits the ground is his broadsword.

I withdraw the dome and lean over the ledge of the wall, shaking from head to toe. My aunt wraps her arms around my waist and presses her cheek against my back.

"Hush, Hyeok," she whispers. I didn't realize I was sobbing. "We must be strong for our people. We can grieve later."

I take a heaving breath and dry my eyes with a rough swipe of my arm. I give my aunt a nod over my shoulder, and she drops her arms from around me. What I'm about to tell the people will alarm her as well, but she is the Queen of Sky. She will rally and add her strength and wisdom to our fight.

"People of the Realm of Four Kingdoms." I spin in a slow circle so every shinbiin, inside and outside the walls, can hear me. "We are weary, not merely from this war, but from the years of strife between the four kingdoms. Somewhere along the way, we forgot that we are all born of the Cheon'gwang. We are beings of the four life sources, and the four life sources stem from the true force of light. It is past time we remembered that we are *one* people.

"I wish I could give you time to rest and heal, but our realm is in peril. Every one of us must unite and stand as one to face our true enemy." I pause to swallow. *Am I making the wrong decision?*

Will telling the truth to these battle-worn soldiers crush them? "The Amheuk has breached the Realm of Four Kingdoms. The people of the Kingdom of Water have been evacuated to the Kingdom of Sky, but the eternal darkness has already destroyed the Kingdom of Water."

The distraught cries of the Kingdom of Water's troops rise above the panicked clamor from the rest of the soldiers. They must have known about the Amheuk, but they still came to fight at our side. And I can't even give them time to digest the horrible news about their kingdom. But keeping them alive must come first.

We have to move now.

"And the Amheuk is coming for the Kingdom of Mountains next." I raise my voice to be heard over the soldiers' shock and distress. "There is no time to waste. We, too, must go to the Kingdom of Sky and prepare to take a stance against the eternal darkness."

The shouting gradually softens into quiet murmurs. They raise their gazes toward me, waiting for their orders. I am humbled by their trust and emboldened by their courage. They are trained soldiers, and they will focus their fear and distress into achieving the new objective set before them.

"Generals of the Realm of Four Kingdoms," I boom. "Lead your troops to the Mirror Lake. There is a portal to the Kingdom of Sky above it. Those of you who can fly, carry those who cannot through the portal."

"For the realm." Jihun's voice rings with strength.

"For the realm." Determined shouts rend the air, and the masses beneath the wall converge into smaller groups, moving with purpose.

First, I will see my people to safety, then . . .

I'm coming, Sunny.

OF LOVE AND GREED

Ungnyeo and her husband, Hwanung, watched over the Mortal Realm, and life, harmony, and balance flourished amongst all beings. With the birth of Dangun, their beloved son, the god of Earth believed his happiness complete.

As the days, months, and years passed, he grew afraid of his wife's mortality. Even if she lived a hundred years, it would be but a moment for a god, and Hwanung could not bear to lose her so quickly. More and more, he longed to take Ungnyeo to a place that would imbue her with near immortality.

The Realm of Four Kingdoms understood greed and selfishness. Rather than using their disproportionate powers for good, the Shinbiin used it to sequester the Realm of Four Kingdoms and hoard the magic for themselves. They chose to forget they were all beings of the Cheon'gwang and looked down on everyone less powerful than them.

Hwanung had always shunned their ways, but in his fear and desperation, he convinced Ungnyeo to live as a shinbiin—as someone who didn't know illness or endure injuries. For his sake. The god of Earth did not tell his wife that the Shinbiin's powers were begotten from theft of the worst kind.

Ungnyeo believed mortality to be a gift, and injury and illness to be a part of life. Its fleeting, fragile nature was what made life so unbearably beautiful, so precious. But she loved her husband and followed him to the Realm of Four Kingdoms to ease his suffering.

True love was selfless, and too late would Hwanung realize that his manipulations came from greed, not love.

CHAPTER THIRTY-ONE

Sunny

I come to with a gasp and bolt upright. I woozily glance around the familiar pagoda in the woods, except the pond next to it is drained dry.

The nightmare in the Kingdom of Water crashes into me with my next breath, and I scream, "Haesan!"

"Easy, Stormy. I'm right here." The in'eo crouches next to me, one forearm resting on his raised knee. "Did you enjoy your na—"

My fist connects with his jaw before he can finish his sentence. The bastard doesn't even teeter, and—*fuck*—I might have broken my pinky finger. I don't get a chance to be infuriated, because profound relief crashes over me, and I throw my arms around his neck with a choked sob.

"You steaming pile of putrid shit," I wail. "How dare you sacrifice yourself for me?"

"Do you have to paint such a vivid picture? Besides, I only *tried* to sacrifice myself for you. That scary keeper over there?" He peeks at the scowling keeper on the opposite side of the pagoda. "He somehow dragged me over along with you."

I shove Haesan away like he's the one who's been clinging on to me. "Did everyone make it over?"

"No." The in'eo thumps onto his ass and scrubs his face with both hands.

Of course everyone didn't make it over.

I saw it with my own eyes. Lifeless bodies floating in the water, then disintegrating into darkness. I don't know how many. *Too many.* I'd repressed the horrifying image for a cowardly second.

"I'm so sorry, Haesan," I whisper. "I should've done more. I could've—"

"Don't." He reaches out and squeezes my shoulder. "Stop beating yourself up. You helped save so many lives."

I nod, but I still wish I'd done more—done better.

"Where have they all gone?" I push up to my feet.

There is no time for regrets. I'll do better next time. I won't give up.

"The people of the Kingdom of Sky really came through for us." Haesan's face lights up. "They are working nonstop to feed and house everyone from the Kingdom of Water."

"I'm so glad to hear that." It took an apocalypse to smack the bigotry out of these shinbiins, but at least they stepped up when it counted. "How long was I out?"

"A couple of hours," he says. "I think you needed the rest."

"You should've woken me up," I grumble, but he's probably right. I feel more alert after the nap. I jerk a thumb toward the cranky keeper. "I should go talk to him."

"Sure thing." Haesan grins, and I stare blankly at him for a moment too long. I still can't believe he's alive.

I spin away from the in'eo before I do something foolish, and I skulk up to Keeper Bae. I cough into my fist and wait for him to turn around. "I, um, thank you for saving my friend."

The male turns a mottled red, but he manages a curt nod. It seems we're on our way to becoming best buds.

But in a sudden panic, I step closer to him, and his eyes widen in alarm. He must think I'm trying to hug him or something. Instead, I just grip his sleeves, my knuckles turning white. "Has anyone come through from the Kingdom of Mountains?"

"No, not yet." Keeper Bae looks relieved not to be hauled into my arms.

"Well, they'll come over soon." I don't like the slight waver in my voice. They are coming. *He'll be here.* "When they're ready, we need to keep the portal open for everyone to come through. Do you think the portal keepers from the Kingdom of Mountains will help from their end? It will make the evacuation much easier."

"I'm afraid not." The keeper's mouth twists in distaste. "Before they went through, I heard General Bak order the troops to kill the keepers to stop them from trying to close the portal."

"*Gods.* Those keepers aren't soldiers. The general just ordered them to be *murdered*?" I shudder at the male's callous cruelty. "D-do you think they succeeded?"

"I can't say for sure." Keeper Bae's voice is grim. "But I was able to keep the portal open for the army without resistance from the other side."

"Maybe you're just *way* better at your job than they are," I quip, tired of all the ugliness. "Do we need to send someone over there to twirl dirt around like Haesan did with the water?"

"Twirl?" The in'eo scoffs from behind me. "You mean *generate a massive vortex*."

I smirk at him over my shoulder. *Serves him right.* I'm still mad at him for trying to sacrifice his life for me.

Keeper Bae first nods at Haesan, acknowledging his great feat, then answers my question, "No, the portal to the Kingdom of Mountains can be propped open from our end."

"With what?" I crinkle my nose. "With like a tree?"

"A tree will suffice." He confirms my wild guess. "A very *large* tree."

"Someone has to wedge a giant tree in the portal?" I massage my forehead, my fingers digging into my skin. "How the hell do we do that?"

"I am somewhat restored from enchanting the pond, but my magic will be drained after I prepare the tree," the keeper says grimly. "I won't be able to move it."

"I can help carry the tree." Haesan raises his hand, volunteering for the job.

"But you expended so much life force generating that massive vortex," I protest, inadvertently borrowing his earlier words. What he did was really incredible, though.

"I did." He crosses his arms over his chest with a proud, boyish smile. "This time, I'm merely offering brute strength for the job. I still have plenty of that left."

"Then I will prepare the token." Keeper Bae clomps down the stairs to the pagoda and walks over to a stand of trees across from it. He places his palms against the biggest of the bunch and, wearing a bad-tempered scowl, commences berating the tree.

"I like him," the in'eo says.

"You like everybody," I scoff, even though I like the grumpy keeper too.

I throw my hand over my eyes when a brilliant green light bursts from one of the wooden pillars of the pagoda, and a beautiful seonnyeo flies out of the portal and lands gracefully on the floor.

"Who—" Before I can finish my question, Jihun flies through the pulsating green portal with Captain Seo in his arms.

A tornado of questions and emotions slams into me at once, and I don't know what to do. *Thank gods, Jihun is okay. Is Cheyun hurt? Where is Ethan?* But everything quiets in a heartbeat. *My friends need me.* I rush to their side.

"Is she okay?" I squeeze Jihun's arm in silent greeting, even though I want to give him a rib-cracking hug. I scan him from head to toe to make sure he's unhurt, then sag in relief.

"She was injured during battle, but she will be fine once she gets some rest." His eyes roam my face, like he's imprinting it into his memory.

Oh, Jihun. My heart cracks, dreading the moment I have to hurt him. But Ethan *heard* my voice. He answered me through the mirror of water. I don't know why I'd been afraid to accept the truth till now. Ethan is my love destined by the heavens. We are bound by the threads of fate. It will *always* be him.

I drop my hand from Jihun's arm.

"*She* is already fine." Captain Seo squirms to be put down, but Jihun doesn't budge.

"Sorry for talking about you like you aren't here, Cheyun." I smile sheepishly at her. "But I'm glad you'll be okay."

"It's good to see you, Sunny." She grins back. "Good job getting the Queen of Water to send her troops."

"Thank you for leading the Kingdom of Underworld's troops to Shinsi," I counter to deflect her praise. Then it suddenly hits me—*really hits me*—that Jihun and Cheyun are here, standing in front of me. "D-did we win? I-is Ethan . . . safe?"

"Yes, we defeated General Bak." Jihun holds my gaze. "And the king is safe."

"Oh thank gods." I clap a hand over my mouth. *I can't fall apart. Not until Ethan is back at my side.* I sniff loudly and clear my throat. Then I jerk my chin toward the unidentified seonnyeo who came through the portal first. "Who is that?"

"She is the Queen of Sky," Jihun answers.

"The one who gave General Bak the green flag to attack the Kingdom of Mountains?" I spin around and bare my teeth at her. "Against her own nephew? What kind of fucked-up aunt does that?"

"That would be fucked up." An amused half smile curves the female's lips. "But I did no such thing."

"No, she did not." Jihun sighs, squeezing the bridge of his nose. *What?* Did I embarrass him or something? "To truncate, the general poisoned and kidnapped the queen so he could steal her army. But as soon as she regained consciousness, she ordered the soldiers to lay down their arms and stopped the bloodshed."

"Oh." I tuck my lips between my teeth as heat rushes to my cheeks. I should be thanking her, not snarling at her like an angry gumiho. "My apologies, Your Majesty. For the accusation . . . and the cursing."

"We will deal with such pleasantries—starting with a proper introduction—at a better time." The queen seems to grow in stature as steel enters her eyes. "For now, we have a kingdom to evacuate. Where is Keeper Bae?"

"He's preparing the token for the Kingdom of Mountains." I point toward the keeper, where he stands yelling at the tree. His scowl is fainter, and his lips move slower. "But he is exhausted from enchanting the entire pond for the Kingdom of Water."

"Put me down, Jihun. I'm serious. I hurt my wing, not my legs." Cheyun pushes against the stubborn male's chest. "Keeper Choe can help. I threw him in jail at the Suhoshin headquarters. I can bring him here."

My fists tremble at my sides, my nails digging into the flesh of my palms. My sweet roommate, Hana, gave her life to protect her twin, Duna, who framed her for her own crimes. And Keeper Choe helped the murderous spy escape. He was deceived like everyone else, but I still don't like the arrogant prick.

"I . . . You're right." Jihun sets the captain down with a hand hovering behind her back. When she stays steady on her feet, he reluctantly steps away. "And I must go back to the Kingdom of Mountains."

"Are Hailey and Jaeseok okay?" I grab his forearm, not ready to let him go. When Jihun nods, I force myself to drop my hand. "Did they stay behind with Ethan to help everyone through the portal first?"

"Of course they did." An affectionate smile curls one corner of his mouth before disappearing. "And I must return now. Ethan promised not to do anything reckless, but I need to make sure he keeps his promise."

I nod, struggling to swallow. I hate how Ethan has to be noble and brave all the time. But that's one of the many reasons why I love that stubborn ass.

"Please be—" I jump out of the way when a suhoshin flies through the green portal with an in'eo in his arms. Then another suhoshin follows, carrying a dokkaebi.

Oh, it's a buddy system.

"Come." The Queen of Sky motions at the incoming suhoshins, taking charge of the situation. "This way. Quickly."

"The keeper on the other side is injured and will not be able to keep the portal open for long," Jihun says, looking at the people streaming into the Kingdom of Sky. "Keeper Bae and Keeper Choe must be ready to take over soon."

"They'll be ready," I assure him, relieved that at least one keeper from the Kingdom of Mountains survived.

"I should be on my way. Be safe, Jihun." Captain Seo opens her mouth as if to say something more, but she turns to me instead. "As for you, please remember to think before you act."

"Don't I always?" I give her a cheeky grin. "*Fine.* I will use my head if and when the situation calls for it."

After a two-fingered salute, the captain sprints toward the Suhoshin headquarters to spring Keeper Choe from prison. I'm not too keen on the idea, but Keeper Bae definitely needs a hand. I glance at the exhausted keeper, then at the people pouring through the portal. That sniveling prick better pull his weight.

Jihun turns to go, and I blurt, "Try not to die."

"I'm not that easy to kill." His lips curve in a ghost of a smile before he jumps through the portal.

Please stay safe. All of you.

"Wow," Haesan breathes. My head swivels toward him. I'd forgotten he was here. "You never told me you were close to Captain Song. And to Captain Seo, for that matter. You are so lucky."

"You are such a fanboy," I grouse. "You should have asked Jihun for his autograph."

"I apologize for interrupting the fun," the Queen of Sky says wryly, "but is the Queen of Water in the Kingdom of Sky?"

Haesan turns a touch green around his gills and stammers, "Y-yes, Your Majesty."

"Do you know where she is?" She takes a step closer to him.

"Her Majesty is at a nearby village, helping our people settle in." He stands at attention.

"Take me to her." Without waiting for the in'eo to respond, the queen glides down the pagoda steps.

"S-see you, Stormy." He hurries after the queen. "I will be back to move the tree."

After I wave him on, I'm tempted to slide down to the ground—to sit and be scared. But there is no time for such indulgences. I cast a worried glance at the flickering portal.

The green light grows dimmer with each passage. The keeper in the Kingdom of Mountains will not be able to hold it open for much longer. It is up to the portal keepers of the Kingdom of Sky. But Keeper Bae sways on his feet, his lips barely moving as he continues to chant.

The fate of the Realm of Four Kingdoms feels as precarious as a house of cards. A gust of wind is all it'll take to bring everything crumbling down. But this has to work—it *will* work—because I can't live with the alternative.

Come home to me, Ethan.

Someone behind me cries out in alarm, and I spin back toward the portal. A being of Mountains falls onto the pagoda, and the suhoshin, who got her through, lies sprawled on his stomach, his arms still outstretched. But . . . the bottom half of his body is still on the other side of the shrinking portal.

The portal is closing.

"Hold on," I yell and grab on to his forearms, and he wraps his hands around mine. Calling on the might of my gumiho, I drag him out from the portal, inch by precarious inch. "Come. *On.*"

I haul the suhoshin into the Kingdom of Sky with one last mighty heave, and the green light blinks out, a hair's width away from the soles of his shoes.

I fall onto my ass and stare at the wooden pillar where the portal used to be—horrible images of the suhoshin cut in half or embedded in the pillar flashing through my mind. With my chest heaving, I groan and flop onto my back.

Fuck my life.

CHAPTER THIRTY-TWO

Sunny

I silently inch closer to Keeper Bae and press into his side. He leans on me without acknowledgment, other than to grunt in relief. He looks ready to keel over as he shouts instructions to Haesan and Keeper Choe as they carry the enchanted tree toward the portal opening.

"No, not there." He leaves the *you idiots* unsaid, but it's heard as clear as a bell. "Position the token vertically at the left corner. The portal will be more stable that way. You should know this, Choe."

"I do know," the younger keeper wheezes, readjusting his grip on his end of the token. "Why don't *I* stand over there and scream at *you* on how to properly maneuver a *giant* tree?"

Keeper Choe proved himself useful when he took over enchanting the tree from an exhausted Keeper Bae. Even so, he is in no position to mouth off at anyone.

"Shut up and work, *Inmate* Choe," I warn. "The moment you step out of line, Captain Seo will throw your ass back in prison so fast you won't even get a chance to pout before the door slams on your face."

"You mean *in* my face," he grumbles, shuffling to the left as instructed.

"Nope." I shake my head. "I meant *on* your face."

Morning has dawned without my permission, and I'm *this* close to crawling out of my skin. Jihun left hours ago. If I have to wait another minute for the portal to be opened, I might lose my mind.

"Keep an eye on that one, Haesan." I push away from the pagoda railing, too restless to stand still. "If he so much as sneezes funny, knock him out. I'm not saying you should break his nose." I narrow my eyes at Keeper Choe. "But I'm not saying you shouldn't."

"Break his nose if he sneezes." The in'eo nods earnestly, adjusting his hold on his end of the tree. "Got it."

"I . . . You . . ." The keeper sputters, his legs shaking under the weight of the gigantic token.

Haesan speaks over the whiny male. "Right here, Keeper Bae?"

"Yes." The older keeper gestures with his hands. "Vertically."

Haesan picks up the giant tree and shakes off Keeper Choe from the other end. Then, with a strained grunt, he heaves and props the token up at the left corner of the opening.

I stop breathing, and Keeper Bae tenses at my side. As we watch, the small green light expands, encompassing the giant tree, then the portal . . . flares wide open. I shield my eyes with my hand.

After a few seconds, suhoshins and seraphim fly through the portal, carrying shinbiins in their arms. One by one, they drop off their passengers and jump back through the portal.

Finally.

"Everyone coming into the Kingdom of Sky," Keeper Bae booms, "proceed through the left side. Everyone leaving, proceed through the right side. Tell those at the other end. We need order for this to work."

I break free from my paralysis and run to the portal. I help the people coming through—even though they aren't the ones I'm waiting for—because every life is precious. And to somebody, these people are the ones they are waiting for.

◆ ◆ ◆

I wipe my damp forehead on my shoulder and glance at the sky. The sunlight fades into a burnt orange as the moon makes its slow ascent. I continue passing out water to the exhausted shinbiins and seraphim evacuating the Kingdom of Mountains.

"Thank you." A seraph soldier accepts a cup of water from me and throws it back in one gulp. The teacup immediately refills with water, and she drinks all of that too.

When she turns back toward the portal, I stop her with a hesitant hand on her arm. "H-have you seen the King of Mountains?"

"His Majesty is hard to miss since he seems to be everywhere, all at once." A tired smile tugs at her lips. "The Kingdom of Mountains is fortunate to have such a dedicated king."

"So he . . . he's okay?" I clutch a fistful of her sleeve. Catching myself, I relax my grip and drop my arm to my side. "He isn't hurt?"

"He seems exhausted but otherwise unharmed," the seonnyeo says kindly. "I must return."

"Of course. Sorry for delaying you. Th-thank you," I stutter, my knees weak with relief.

I keep my head down and provide much needed water to the people coming through. I am grateful for something to do. And soon, the seraphim and suhoshins collapse onto the ground instead of leaping back through the portal.

It's almost done. Ethan is coming.

When Jaeseok comes through the portal, I run up the pagoda steps with an undignified squeak.

"There's my favorite gumiho." He pulls me into his arms, laughing and ruffling my hair.

"I'm the only gumiho you know," I mumble, too happy to slap his hand away.

"Like I said, my favorite." The dokkaebi sets me away from him and flashes a grin I can't help returning.

"Sunny!" Hailey literally flies into my arms, straight out of the portal.

"Whoa." I stumble back a step before I regain my balance. Then I hug her so tight that she might not be able to breathe.

She doesn't seem to mind and squeezes me equally hard. "You're here, Sunny."

"I am." I laugh. "I guess that means you missed me."

"Like crazy." And the smile she offers me is indeed a bit off kilter. "It's been a long week."

"I know." I drop my arms from around her. "I'm sorry I wasn't there for you. For everyone."

"Uh, you were kind of busy, destroying the dark mudang and all." Then her beautiful face crumples. "I heard about Draco. I can't believe they're gone."

"They were good and brave till the very end." I offer her a tight smile, because if I let a single tear fall, I might never stop crying. "You would've been so proud of them."

"Damn it all to hell," Jihun shouts, flying through the portal. "That male is too proud for his own good, *not to mention* my sanity."

My heart drops to my toes then bounces straight into my throat, choking off my breath.

"I'm guessing he forced you to go ahead of him?" I drawl to hide my dread. "Because, of course he—Watch out!"

I tackle Jihun away from the portal as a black tentacle snaps toward him. The Shin'gwangdo is in my hand before I even realize I summoned it, and I slash clean through the swinging arm of darkness.

"Oh gods," Hailey breathes. "The Amheuk reached the Kingdom of Mountains."

I stumble back from the portal with a hand to my forehead, my sword arm hanging limply at my side. "E-Ethan."

"Get everyone off this pagoda," Jihun barks.

"We have to close the portal." Keeper Bae rushes toward it. "Haesan, help me remove the tree."

"No!" I step in front of the glowing green portal and spread out my arms. "Not yet. Ethan hasn't come through."

"We are all dead if the Amheuk reaches the Kingdom of Sky," the keeper says, regret in the lines of his grumpy face.

My fist tightens around the hilt of my sword. *I'll take down anyone who tries to*—I blink in shock. Keeper Bae is not the enemy. I deliberately sheathe the Shin'gwangdo.

"You're right. You have to close the portal," I say as a calm settles over me. "I'll go to the Kingdom of Mountains and bring him back."

"You will need a token." Keeper Bae breaks off a small branch from the giant tree and hands it to me.

Jihun looms in front of me. "You are not going anywhere."

"I'll stave off the Amheuk and bring Ethan back before you can say, *Damn it, Sunny.*"

"Damn it—" Jihun doesn't get a chance to finish yelling.

"Close the portal, Keeper Bae," I shout and leap for the green light.

I fall through the portal and keep falling. I swallow the scream building in my chest. Too late, I remember this particular portal opens up to the middle of the sky, and . . . I can't fly. My body hurtles through the sky, tumbling out of control.

I have to slow my descent.

Focusing on the pull of gravity and the rush of air against me, I figure out which way is up and which way is down. I press my flailing arms against my sides and press my legs together. Then I reposition my body so my stomach faces the ground, goal posting my arms above my head and bending my legs toward the sky.

Now what?

I'm still falling. Not at the same dizzying speed, but the end result will remain in the *splat* category.

"Cocksucker," I seethe through clenched teeth.

"I love that foul mouth of yours." Ethan's warm breath brushes my ear as he scoops me out of the air. "I love everything about you."

Ethan.

There are no words to describe how I feel, seeing him at last. *At. Fucking. Last.* With a heartfelt moan, I crush my mouth against his.

He holds me in his arms, hovering in the sky, and returns my bruising kiss, groaning deep in his throat. He dips his tongue into my mouth in a rough sweep and claims me. I claim him right back, licking, biting, and suckling.

I can't get enough. The taste of him . . . the smell of him . . . the feel of him.

Home. I'm home.

"Sunny," he whispers before pressing another kiss to my lips, nibbling my bottom lip, then sucking it into his mouth. "Don't ever leave me again." He punctuates his plea with more kisses. "It nearly destroyed me. I don't want to exist another second without you by my side."

"You won't have to, Ethan. I lov—" My backs arches as pain lances through every cell in my body, and a tortured scream erupts from my mouth.

"What's happening?" Ethan cups my face and scans every inch of my body with frantic eyes. "Tell me, baby. What can I do?"

"Blood . . . oath . . ." I hold out my left palm, blood gushing from the mark of the oath, then cry out as agony slashes through me, my body jerking in his arms.

"That motherfucker," he hisses through gritted teeth, understanding immediately. "My father made you vow never to return to me?"

"K-Kingdom of Mountains. Never r-return." I writhe as pain threatens to shatter my mind.

"I'm getting you out of here." He streaks through the sky toward the portal. "I have a token. You go back first."

Miraculously, I haven't dropped the tree branch that Keeper Bae handed me. I wave it in front of Ethan's nose. "Me too. T-together."

"Thank gods," he breathes.

Unfortunately, his relief was premature. A black tentacle shoots up from the ground like a giant beanstalk with deadly intent.

"Look out!" I shout.

Muttering a curse, Ethan grips me tightly against his chest and dives straight for the dark limb.

"Wh-what are you doing?" I shout, digging my nails into his shoulder.

At the last possible millisecond, he swerves sharply to the right, and the tentacle shoots past us, carried by its momentum. Ethan hovers in the sky, whipping his head left and right, but another serpentine limb punches through the sky from directly above us.

"Eth—" The blood oath sears my insides, and a shriek tears past my throat, preventing me from warning him.

Not like this.

But the darkness doesn't rip through us. A second passes, then two. And I pat his chest, then mine to make sure there are no gaping holes in either of us. My whole existence is pain at the moment, but we're both unhurt.

How?

I glance around, struggling to focus my gaze through the torture of the blood oath. Then I blearily make out the tight dome of green and silver gi above us. Ethan threw a shield around us in the nick of time.

"H-handy that," I croak.

"I don't know how long I can hold—" Ethan grunts, lurching forward as though someone punched him in the stomach. His arms loosen from my body for a terrifying heartbeat before he tightens his grip again.

"What's wrong?" I cry. "Are you hurt? What's going on, Ethan?"

"Gods." His eyes grow distant, then fill with horror. "The Amheuk is destroying the Kingdom of Mountains. Its life force is . . . weeping."

"I'm so sorry, Ethan." I raise a shaking hand, even as I whimper in pain, and cup his cheek.

"I . . . I can't breathe." He sounds faint, as though he's fading away. "My kingdom . . ."

"Ethan, look at me." Strangely enough, the agony shredding me apart eases by a fraction, and I manage to suck in short little breaths. *"Look at me."*

He shakes his head, his gaze darting around as more and more black tentacles tear through the Kingdom of Mountains. A tear slides down his cheek as he sways in the sky, and he says brokenly, "I'm sorry, Mother."

"No, Ethan." I grasp the nape of his neck, forcing him to meet my eyes. "Your mother loved the Kingdom of Mountains, but she loved you more. You did everything you can. This isn't your fault."

My spine tightens with a shattering ache. Yet . . . it doesn't hurt enough to make me scream at the top of my lungs anymore. With a soft whimper, I curl against Ethan's chest, and his attention snaps back to me.

"Let's get you out of here." He tightens his arms around me, determination bracketing his lips.

I sag with relief. We need go. I wish I could fight for his kingdom, but I'm useless in this state. I can't even protect him.

Ethan flies toward the portal, straining to hold the shield around us. My pain eases by another notch, allowing the exhaustion to roll in. *Hurting is hard work.* My eyelids grow heavy, but I force my eyes open.

My vision gradually clears, and a part of me wishes it hadn't. Ethan's face is haggard with grief. The Amheuk is smashing his beautiful kingdom to pieces, and he's suffering to the depth of his soul. My heart clenches in my chest.

I wish I could make it stop.

I take a deep breath, then stop with a frown. I can breathe normally again. I exhale as though to prove my point. And the pauses between the bouts of pain are growing longer. *What is going on?* I stare down at my palm, and the rough circle barely seeps blood now. I gasp softly as understanding dawns on me.

My blood oath is fading.

"Wait, Ethan."

The eternal darkness is hurting him, and I want to hurt it right back. With the curse waning, I can finally do something about it. I won't let him lose his kingdom without a fight.

"What is it?" He peers into my face with frantic eyes. "Are you hurting?"

"I-I can manage the pain. The blood oath is weakening because . . . the Kingdom of Mountains is dying," I say in a husky rasp. "I'm so sorry."

Relief and devastation vie for dominance on Ethan's face. "You're okay. That's all that matters."

"Well, I'm not going to watch the Amheuk destroy your kingdom lying down. I'll—" I hiss as the curse digs into my skin like a knife scoring a thousand cuts in my body.

"We're getting out of here," Ethan growls. "You're still in pain, whether the blood oath is weakening or not."

"Please listen. I'm not being bullheaded for no reason." I grip his arm. *Yes, I want to hurt the Amheuk for hurting Ethan, but that's not all.* "I can buy everyone in the Kingdom of Sky some time so they can prepare for a last stand against the Amheuk."

"How will you buy them time?" Ethan narrows his eyes on me.

"Will the dome keep me from falling?" He nods warily, and I push against his chest. "Put me down."

When he reluctantly complies—and I don't plummet to my death—I summon the Yeoiju to my heart's center.

"Whoa." His face slackens with wonder. "Your eyes are on fire—white fire."

"Are they?" I smirk, then summon the Shin'gwangdo with a snap of my wrist.

"Show-off." A crooked grin curves his lips.

I'm distracted for a second, but I'll have to kiss the hell out of him later. "That wasn't showing off . . . This is."

Spinning away from him, I reach out to the nature around me. *We need your help.* I spread my arms wide as the gi of the trees, of the lakes, of the earth flows into me. *I know you're hurting, but we have to fight.*

The life force of nature flows through my veins, powerful and verdant. Even as the Kingdom of Mountains dies, its gi is stronger than the faint life force I felt in the Kingdom of Water. It still isn't as formidable as nature's life force in the Mortal Realm—perhaps because it's the gi of a single life source—but it's more than enough to infuse my Yeoiju with power.

I grip the Shin'gwangdo with both hands until it gleams with white light, as bright as the sun. Another black tentacle shoots toward us from below but bounces off Ethan's protective dome. Then another and another charge at us, and Ethan grunts behind me. The dome holds, but his labored breaths tell me it won't for much longer.

Adrenaline pumping through my veins, I search the ground below. I freeze when I find what I'm looking for—a swirling black mass with countless tentacles branching from it.

"Ethan." I glance over my shoulder and point toward the core of the Amheuk. "Can you get us closer to that?"

"I can try," he rasps.

He picks me up in his arms and dives toward the ground. My heart lodges in my throat as my toes squirm in my shoes. He slows down as we approach the dark mound, and I pull away from him.

"Stay here. Don't come out of the dome." I pray that he listens for once.

Taking a deep breath, I push through the dome and free-fall toward the ground. The wind rushes past my ears and stings my eyes, a scream building in my chest. Maybe I should have thought this through.

Shit, shit, shit.

Closing in on my target, I shift into a diving form with my sword pointed down. There is no turning back now. With a battle cry, I bury the Shin'gwangdo into the Amheuk, momentum pushing my blade in deep.

An earsplitting screech shakes the entire kingdom, and one by one, the squirming tentacles fall to the ground with dull thuds. The eerie scream finally quiets, and a heavy silence descends around me.

Did I kill it?

I pull my sword out with a weak grunt and stumble back from the black blob. I spin in a slow circle, taking in the devastation the Amheuk wreaked on the Kingdom of Mountains. I feel sadness seep past my dull stupor.

"Sunny!"

Before I can turn toward Ethan's voice, the Amheuk swallows me whole and muffles his desperate cry.

CHAPTER THIRTY-THREE

Sunny

Darkness is the absence of light. The absence of life.

I can't exist in the dark. *I am no more.*

But my heart . . . aches. It bleeds.

How can I feel this piercing sadness if I don't exist?

My Yeoiju hums inside me.

I can't see, but I can feel . . . my hands, my feet, my face.

I am alive. *I am still me.*

But I am surrounded by the darkness. Ensconced in it.

There is only one way out.

I have to blow up the eternal darkness with the Cheon'gwang. I did it once in Santorini when Daeseong enveloped me in darkness, but I had the help of nature's gi. Inside the core of the Amheuk, there is only me.

Gods, I hope I have enough life force left in me.

The gi of nature lingers in my veins, and I concentrate to pool that into the Yeoiju. But it's not enough. I have to draw from my own life force. Will I be able to control my powers? Or will the Yeoiju siphon the life out of me?

I have no other choice. I take a deep breath, but suddenly, the life force of Mountains rushes into me.

No, it isn't the gi of Mountains.

Ethan is pouring his silver-and-green life force into me. I don't understand. *How?* But his powerful gi chases away the cold numbness drowning my senses and warms me to my toes. It's almost too much. Yet his life force keeps flowing into me in powerful torrents.

Stop, Ethan.

He will deplete himself. I have to get out of here. I have to stop him before he kills himself.

I call to all the life force flowing through me—mine, nature's, and Ethan's—until my Yeoiju expands and glows impossibly bright. My chest pushes out, and my back arches as it fills every corner of my body.

With a scream, I release the pulsating power, my arms and legs spreading open like a star. The light of the Yeoiju shatters the darkness until I see the sky and mountains surrounding me once more.

I slip and fall as I climb out from the cavernous black cocoon, then I stumble away until the dark mass lies behind me, bubbling and steaming like cooling lava. I plant my hands on my thighs and catch my breath. When the burning in my lungs becomes bearable, I straighten my back and rub my eyes to clear them.

My gaze flits left and right, hardly registering the gaping black wounds that tear through the dying mountains.

Where is he? Did I take too long?

"Ethan." Dread crawls down my spine. I run to the other side of the revolting blob, whipping my head around. "Ethan!"

Then I see a prone body on the ground a few feet ahead.

"No." I fall to my knees next to him. "No, Ethan. What have you done?"

I don't know how he poured his life force into me through the Amheuk. Ethan is a powerful shinbiin. He figured it out. *Gods damn it.* I shake him hard, but his limp body just flops beneath my hands.

I drop my ear close to his nose and mouth. I can't tell if he's breathing. *What am I doing?* I narrow my eyes and zero in on his body. He's alive. His gi is weak, but it flows steadily through him. I expel a shuddering breath.

"You fucking asshole." I collapse next to him. "I'll kill you if you don't wake up."

Then I sit up with a gasp. The tentacles on the ground undulate, like a boat bobbing on a calm lake—the movement so slow and subtle that I nearly missed it. *What the fuck?* I blew up the Amheuk's core from the inside out.

I don't want to believe it, but the eternal darkness is beginning to recover. I have to get us out of here.

"Shit, shit, shit." I throw Ethan over my shoulder in a fireman's carry and take off into the sky.

I can fly. I don't know if it's the Yeoiju or the remnants of Ethan's life force that's giving me the power. Frankly, I don't give a shit. I need to get this foolish, stubborn, generous, and brave male out of here before the Amheuk truly awakens.

I wobble precariously in the sky, and Ethan slips down my shoulder. With a scream, I gather him in my arms, bending backward to bear his weight. Just because I *can* fly doesn't mean I know *how*.

The portal appears light-years away, and I push myself to fly faster, grappling with Ethan's limp, heavy body.

Almost there.

Muttering curses under my breath, I reach back and awkwardly tug his token free from his neck. Then I summon my tree branch and fling both our tokens at the portal. Bright, silver light flares in the sky, and I fly us toward it, dipping and swerving.

"No, no, no." Ethan slips out of my arms just as the pagoda comes into view on the other side. I scramble to hold on to him, and my feet tangle on the floor. "Fuck."

"Whoa." Jihun somehow catches me and Ethan, one in each arm. But he quickly sets me down to grab his unconscious king with both arms. "Your Majesty."

I glance around the pagoda, my heart rate refusing to slow. We made it out of the Kingdom of Mountains. *We're alive.* Only the Sentinels remain at the pagoda in the woods. *We're safe.*

"Why isn't he responding?" Captain Seo asks, helping Jihun lower Ethan to the ground.

"The asshole poured his gi into me." I wrap my arms around my stomach, willing my body to stop trembling. "It's all my fault. I thought I could buy us some time from the Amheuk by attacking it at its core. I stabbed it with the Shin'gwangdo. I thought I did some damage to it, but it swallowed me whole the next second."

"The Amheuk swallowed you whole?" Jaeseok's jaw drops. "And you're still alive?"

"I wouldn't be if Ethan hadn't shared his gi with me," I confess in a small voice, my teeth chattering. Hailey rushes to my side and puts her arm around my shoulders. I lean my head against her, grateful for her warmth and support. "I charged the Yeoiju with his life force and blew up the Amheuk from the inside out."

"Is it gone?" Hope and disbelief war on Hailey's face.

"No." I shake my head. "I hurt it badly, but it's already starting to recover."

"But you bought us much-needed time," Jihun says gently.

"What about Ethan?" I cry. "What if he d-doesn't wake up? I wish Minju was here to heal him."

"I am." Minju walks up the steps to the pagoda. She's traded in her white bodycon dress for a lovely pink hanbok. *Gods.* She's a sight for sore eyes.

"Minju." I rise to my feet and stumble to her side. "How did you get here? I thought the King of Underworld moved his kingdom to purgatory?"

"I did not have the privilege of asking the King of Underworld how he transported everyone to the Kingdom of Sky. Or how he'd moved the Kingdom of Underworld to purgatory in the first place." A small frown mars her forehead as she puzzles out the mystery. Then she gives her head a sharp shake. "But never mind that for now. I must attend to our king."

I wring my hands, standing behind the historian, as she examines Ethan. "Will . . . will he be okay?"

Minju glances over her shoulder and smiles at me. "See for yourself."

Worried out of my mind, it takes me a second to realize that she's talking about my magic gi goggles. I shake my head and swallow the tears gathering in the back of my throat. His gi was so weak when I found him unconscious.

Blowing out a long breath, I focus my gaze over Ethan. His life force glows an exquisite silver green and flows over his prone body, growing stronger with each heartbeat. I clap a hand over my mouth as my legs give out from under me.

"Ethan, can you hear me?" I crawl to his side. "Wake up. Please."

"Sunny." Jihun crouches next to me and squeezes my shoulder. "Give him time. Even without expending his gi on you, he has not rested in days. Let him sleep and recuperate."

"And you should rest as well," Minju says.

I think I nod, and Jihun helps me to my feet and leads me down the pagoda steps. I look over my shoulder at Ethan the entire time. In a sudden intake of breath, my gaze flies to Jihun's profile. As usual, I can't read his stoic expression.

I displayed my feelings for Ethan in plain sight just now. I had no room for anyone else in that moment. *Even so, how could I be so callous?* Jihun might've already known that my heart belongs to Ethan, but I haven't told him that we decided to be together.

"Jihun, I—"

"Don't make this any harder," he interjects, looking straight ahead. "I know. I knew it the moment I returned to the cave with the palanquins, the day we infiltrated the Shinsi Palace. Both of you were . . . glowing."

"I still should have told you," I whisper. "I'm sorry, Jihun."

"I asked you not to make this harder for me." He sighs and turns to me with heartbreak and tenderness in his eyes. "You and Ethan deserve to be happy. As for me . . . I'll survive."

"You'll do better than survive. You will thrive." I glance back toward the pagoda, where Captain Seo stands guard over Ethan. "Because you'll find someone who loves you with her whole heart."

"Don't," he rasps. "I don't want nor need your pity. And I sure as hell don't need you to play matchmaker. Like I said before, I will do with my heart as I see fit."

"But—"

"Go to the Sunset Pavilion. Miok will take care of you." He stops at the edge of the woods, a muscle ticcing in his jaw. "Get some rest, and I'll send word when His Majesty awakens."

"Wh-where will Ethan be?" I can't breathe at the thought of being separated from him.

"The Queen of Sky has asked him to stay at the Celestial Palace." The lines bracketing his lips soften. "The King of Underworld and the Queen of Water are also there. They are preparing for our fight against the Amheuk. When he regains consciousness, Ethan must lead the four kingdoms."

"Yes, of course," I say numbly.

The Realm of Four Kingdoms needs the King Foretold. Ethan's place is with them. I always knew that.

Then where's my place?

"Sunny—" Jihun begins.

I cut him off. "I'll see you later."

I shift into my gumiho and streak through the woods. I've fought too hard and come too far to lose Ethan. But I don't know how to hold on to him without holding him back, especially with my dark secrets hanging over me.

CHAPTER THIRTY-FOUR

Ethan

My eyes shoot open, my heart pounding in my chest. "Sunny."

"Sunny is fine," Jihun says. "She got both of you back to the Kingdom of Sky in one piece."

My warrior saved both of us.

"But you need to recuperate, Your Majesty." My royal adviser presses a hand against my shoulder when I try to sit up.

"Do *not* tell me what I need." I push his hand away and struggle to a seat. *I need Sunny.* "Where is she?"

"She is resting at the Sunset Pavilion." His nostrils flare as he fights for patience. "If you are well enough to sit up, then you need to meet with—"

"Later." I cut him off and push to my feet. I'm already at the doors when I turn to ask, "Where am *I*?"

"You are at the Celestial Palace." Jihun pinches his nose. "Go, Ethan. I will stall for you. It's not like the fate of the realm is at stake."

"Thank you," I say, softening my tone. "I won't be long. I just need to see with my own eyes that she's okay."

My royal adviser flaps his hand, shooing me away like an annoying gnat. I'll take that. I flash him a grateful smile before dashing out the doors and into the sunlight. I squint up at the sky.

How long was I out?

Sunny must be dying with worry. *Shit.* I ignore the startled eyes of the people in the courtyard and run like hell to Jihun's estate.

I stop at the steps to the Sunset Pavilion, huffing like an angry bull. I try to even out my breathing, but my heart ping-pongs in my chest at the thought of seeing Sunny, and my breaths only grow shorter.

"Your Majesty?" Miok, Sunny's lady-in-waiting, starts when she sees me from the main hall but quickly regains her composure and bows low from her waist. "How may I assist you?"

"I want Sunny." My voice comes out an impatient, possessive growl. I clear my throat and try again. "I am here to see Sunny."

"She is not here, Your Majesty."

"What?" I sound more like a gawky teenager than a formidable king. "Where is she?"

"She said she was going out for a walk," Miok answers evenly.

"Out . . . for a walk?" Disappointment crushes down on me. "She could be anywhere."

"True." The lady-in-waiting lowers her gaze, but not before I see the amusement sparkling in them. "But she did mention a lovely garden she once had a picnic . . ."

I don't hear the rest of her sentence as I sprint toward the gates. Sunny is at my mother's garden. She is so close. Even as I run fast enough to make my lungs burn, a cheek-cramping grin spreads across my face.

I'll see her soon. Not when she's falling out of the sky, or being swallowed by the Amheuk. I stumble, clutching at my chest. *She's okay,* I remind myself. *She's here.* I take off again.

I'm finally going to see Sunny, on solid ground, in relative safety. I won't have long with her—I haven't forgotten my duties—but even a minute alone with her will be a gift from the heavens.

My mother's garden lies ahead of me, and I push myself faster. I burst through a stand of trees and skid to a stop at the clearing.

Sunny.

She stands in the pavilion, as exquisite as a statue, and stares out at the pond with her hand on a pillar. She's wearing a silk hanbok with a sky blue jeogori and a lush lavender chima, and her hair hangs in a sweet braid down her back.

Mine.

She looks like a Joseon maiden out of a historical K-drama, delicate and unapproachable. And I feel an irrepressible urge to dishevel her. I want to kiss her lips raw. I want to tease her until temper sparks in her eyes. I want to tug her hair free. I want her to come undone in my arms. I want *her*.

Mine.

I reach her in a heartbeat. Forgetting my strength, I grab her too fast, too hard, and crush my lips against hers with a rumbling groan. *I have waited for an eternity.* I swallow her startled gasp and deepen my kiss, hanging on to my control by a thread. She stumbles back half a step but holds her ground. She is no delicate maiden. She is my beautiful, powerful Sunny.

I push her up against the pillar and growl against her lips, "Mine."

"Yours," she whispers, pushing up to her toes. "I'm yours, Ethan."

My teetering control shatters. Tearing her shirt open, I bury my face in the soft mounds of her breasts, overflowing from the bodice of her chima, and breathe her scent, both sweet and crisp, into my lungs. I drag my lips over her silken skin, and she pushes her chest into my face.

With a rough tug, I pull the bodice down and reveal the dusky peaks of her breasts, and suck one tip none too gently into my mouth. I swirl my tongue around the areola and pull away, scraping my teeth along her pebbled nipple.

"Ethan," she moans.

I'm famished, and I feel as though I will never get my fill. I lather her other breast with equal attention. I fall to my knees and bunch the hem of her skirt in my fist. I pause and look up through my lashes at her flushed face.

"I need to taste you." I hardly recognize my own voice.

She nods without hesitation. *Gods, she's magnificent.*

I push up her full, floor-length skirt, already cursing the layers of undergarments I'll have to get through. But my breath seizes in my chest.

"Sunny?" I wheeze in a strangled voice.

"I told Miok life is too short for six layers of undergarments," she says pertly, even though she is breathless. "The worlds as we know them might end in a matter of days."

"You are as wise as you are beautiful." I stare at the dark triangle between her legs.

"Did you just figure that—ahh." Her head falls back on the wooden pillar as I push her folds open and . . . lick.

"Gods," I moan against her clit, and her hips jerk against my mouth. "Hold still, baby. I'm trying to eat."

And I feast. I worship her with my mouth and tongue, her pleasure my reward. My cock strains against my pants, and I'm afraid I'll come just like this if that breathless whimper slips past her lips one more time.

"Ethan, please." Her husky plea sets my body on fire.

"I'm right here. I got you." I swirl the tip of my finger around her slick entrance and plunge in, deep and hard. "Gods, you're wet."

Her teeth sink into her bottom lip, and her head thrashes against the pillar. I add a second finger and work them in and out of her. My fingers squelch against her desire. It's fucking obscene. And it is mind-blowingly hot.

I lap at her, pumping my hand faster, and when she's close—so close—I suck her into my mouth.

"Ethan," Sunny screams and clenches around my fingers.

"There's my good girl." I murmur against her mound, gradually slowing the movement of my hand—bringing her down gently.

"Don't *good girl* me." Her small, strong fingers fist in my hair, and she jerks my head back and looks down at me. "I want you to defile me, Ethan. Fuck me like you mean it."

I surge to my feet and wrap her legs around my waist in one motion. I free myself with an impatient tug at my pants, and I tilt her hips and plunge inside her. We still for a second, reveling in the perfection of the moment—of coming home.

"Hold tight," I growl, my entire body taut with feral desire.

When I feel her fingernails digging into my shoulders, I plant a palm on the pillar above her head, and I *claim* her. My hips piston as I plunge in and out of her, going faster, deeper, and harder with each thrust. Her cries catch and break in her throat as I drive into her again and again.

I need to get closer. I need to meld with her. Even as I take her, I already miss this closeness because I know it's going to end. It will never be enough. I will want her—I will love her—for a thousand years. She is my obsession. She is my everything.

"E-Ethan," she pants. "I'm close . . . I'm so close . . . Come . . . come with me."

"Always." I crush my lips against hers. "I am yours, Sunny. Take me any way you want."

She buries her fingers in my hair and deepens our kiss, bruising and demanding. She is claiming me, and I am humbled, honored. I don't know if I deserve her, but I am never letting her go. I thrust myself inside her, and our mingled shout fills the garden.

My body goes limp, and my weight presses her into the pillar. But I can't make myself move away from her—pull out of her. We lean against the wooden pillar, still connected, and catch our breaths until our hearts beat in sync.

"Hi." She wiggles her adorable bottom, asking to be put down.

I reluctantly pull out of her, feeling bereft, and she drops her legs from around my hips. I hold on to her waist until her feet touch the ground and her skirt falls between us. I hate her skirt. I hate everything that separates us. Even so, I close her shirt, then right my own clothes.

"Hi." I tuck a loose strand of hair behind her ear as my other hand roams up and down her back. I love her so much, I can hardly stand it. I feel like I'll combust into flames and burn to ashes in my next breath. I stare into her eyes, hoping to convey all my love and longing through my gaze. And like the cool, suave male that I am, I croak, "Hi."

A shadow passes over her expression. Sunny gently pushes on my chest, and I step back from her. She walks over to the railing and looks out at the lily pond. I stay back by the pillar, fighting the urge to crowd in on her. She grips the wooden railing and worries her bottom lip raw, her throat working to swallow.

"There are . . . things I need to tell you," she says in a flat voice, and my stomach lurches.

"You can tell me anything, Sunny." As long as it isn't to tell me we can't be together.

"Before I killed Daeseong, h-he told me that he was my . . . father." Her gaze stays on the pond.

I huff a relieved laugh. "That bastard was lying to mess with your head till the very end."

"I have the power to bewitch people, Ethan," she whispers, and I would've laughed again if she didn't look dead serious. She takes a shuddering breath. "I swore to my mother to never use that dark power, but when Daeseong called me *daughter*, I lost my mind. I compelled him to tell me the truth. I took away his free will a moment before he died. I violated him in a way a person should never be violated."

My mouth opens and closes. The truth of her words drops like an anvil on my head. Sunny is Daeseong's daughter? She can compel people to do her bidding? *And she actually used that power on a dying man?* That is the hardest part to believe.

Behind the irreverent, brash demeanor, Sunny is the most honorable person I know. I can't imagine her robbing someone of their free will. But if she says it happened, it happened. My chest constricts as I gaze at her profile, noticing the harsh line of her lips and the tightness around her eyes. She is hurting.

How hard has she been punishing herself?

"I-I don't know what I'm more ashamed of." She tucks her chin into her chest. She looks so small, so vulnerable. My heart cracks in jagged lines. "That I am that monster's daughter. Or that I used that perverse power on him. I'm afraid that makes me a worse monster than him. Y-you must be disgusted with me."

That snaps me out of my stupor. I march up to her and spin her around by the shoulders. "I am in love with you. I will *always* love you. I can never be disgusted with you, Sunny. You are here, alive and by my side. That is all that matters to me. Do you understand?"

Her chin trembles, her gaze still averted. She says nothing.

"Do you understand, Sunny?" I shake her lightly, afraid I won't get through to her.

Baby, please. Look at me.

"I don't care who your father is. I understand why you bewitched him." Pleading enters my voice. *Why won't she look at me?* "And you're disappointed in yourself—even if that bastard deserved everything he got—because you're a *good person*. A monster would feel no remorse, but your guilt is eating you alive."

"I want to be someone who deserves you." Her voice breaks. "I want to be worthy of your love."

"Someone who deserves *me*? I worship the ground you walk on." A breathless laugh leaves me. "*You* want to be worthy of my love? It is *my honor* to love you. In case I'm not being clear, I love you, Sunny."

"Can you say that last part again?" She sniffs. "I'm not sure if I heard you."

"I love you, Sunny Cho, with everything in me." I pinch her chin and turn her to face me. A tear trails down her cheek, and I wipe it away with the pad of my thumb.

"Please look at me, baby." I duck my head to catch her eyes. "I will love you, in this life and the next."

She finally meets my gaze, and her lips part on a soft gasp. She sees the truth in my eyes. I love her, and nothing can ever change that.

"I tried to do the honorable thing. I tried to give you a way out," she says haltingly, then a sinful smile curves her lips. "Now I will never let you go. You are mine for all eternity."

With a low growl, I crush my lips against hers and kiss the hell out of her. I'm so hard for her, I can't think straight. I frantically grab her skirt in my fists with every intent to have her again. But she spins out of my reach with a tinkling laugh.

"Down boy." She wags her finger at me. "We are in an open pavilion."

"Within a private garden." I flash her a rakish grin. "Where I already had you once."

"Let's call that a lapse in judgment." She blushes.

"That was quite a long lapse." I stalk toward her. "One I'm sure I can replicate for you."

"Don't you have a fancy meeting with the other monarchs at the Celestial Palace?" She lets me catch her this time and rises to the tips of her toes with her hands on my shoulders. She kisses me with sweet tenderness and whispers, "Later, Ethan."

A shudder runs through me, and I gather her in my arms. "Promise?"

Her arms tighten around my waist, and she buries her face in my chest.

"Sunny?" I try to lean back, but she holds me even tighter.

"I don't want to make promises I can't keep." She looks up at me. "Let's save the Realm of Four Kingdoms from the Amheuk first. I'll promise you all kinds of things afterwards."

"What kinds of things?" I tease, even though the weight of my responsibilities presses down on my shoulders.

Sunny takes my hand and leads me down the steps of the pavilion, then glances sidelong at me. "Filthy, filthy things."

I lunge for her, but she jumps back with a squeal and takes her gumiho form. I go utterly still. The graceful length of her body, the regal flare of her nine tails, and the brilliance of her snow-white coat steal my breath. She is so glorious that I can only stare at her.

"I'll race you to the palace," she says telepathically.

I snap out of my trance and give her a cocky grin. "If I beat you there, you have to tell me *one* filthy thing you plan to do with me."

"I'll tell you a hundred of them . . . but you'll never beat me."

In this moment, I don't care that the worlds might end tomorrow. I'm just thankful for every minute I get to spend with her. "Oh, it's on."

She takes off in a white blur before the last word leaves my mouth. With a carefree laugh, I sprint after her.

CHAPTER THIRTY-FIVE

Sunny

I run toward the Celestial Palace, Ethan's impassioned words playing on repeat in my head.

I don't care who your father is. I understand why you bewitched him.

I want to believe Ethan.

And you're disappointed in yourself—even if that bastard deserved everything he got—because you're a good person.

I *do* believe him—even if the male *is* a little biased since he's head over heels in love with me. I huff smugly, but guilt pinches my insides. *Am I taking advantage of his love?*

I put my head down and run faster, the wind brushing against my coat. Even if I don't deserve him, I love him too much to let him go. I have to *do better* to be worthy of his love. I will never stop choosing to do better. *For us.*

I skid to a stop in front of the main palace gates and shift back to my human form. The two males standing guard jump a foot in the air. I ignore them and take a heaving breath. Then I pretend to buff my nails against my jeogori, just as Ethan reaches the palace, mere seconds after me.

"I was wondering when you'd get here." I manage a shit-eating grin while pretending not to be out of breath.

"I was right behind you," he wheezes, with his hands planted on his thighs, and squints up at me. "I could've reached out and grabbed one of your tails anytime I wanted."

"Shoulda, woulda, coulda." I stick my tongue out at him.

"Brat." He tugs on my braid in a lightning-fast move and drops a kiss on my lips.

"Ethan." I hop away from him, glancing over my shoulder at the palace guards. The shinbiins distrust and dislike animal spirits. He won't garner their trust by kissing a gumiho, and he needs their trust more than ever. "People will talk."

I haven't exactly flaunted my gumiho form in front of the shinbiins. When I've had no choice but to shift, the shinbiins would shriek and scramble to get away, both scared and disgusted. Whereas when I'm in my human form, they're just disgusted.

"Since when do you care about what people think?" He crosses his arms over his chest, double grooves forming between his brows.

I never let on that I cared, but it hurt. It always hurt. But this isn't about me. Why can't he see that?

"Since my fated love stood at the cusp of his destiny," I snap, throwing my hands up. *I can't believe I have to* explain *this to him.* But Ethan's face suddenly goes slack, and my stomach drops. I step close and grab his arms. "What's wrong . . ."

Shit. I squeeze my eyes shut. *Did I really blurt that out like that?*

"Your fated love?" Ethan pinches my chin between his fingers, and I open my eyes to meet his. "I thought you didn't believe in that."

"I guess we're having this talk now," I mutter under my breath, my face heating for some reason. Tugging him by his shirtsleeve, I drag him behind a tree, a few steps away from the guards. "Remember how I called for you through the mirror from the Kingdom of Water?" When he nods, I suck in a big breath. "Only those bound by the threads of fate have a strong enough connection to talk through the mirror of water."

"I heard you through the mirror. I *felt* you." An intense, possessive light enters his eyes. "Because I am your fated love."

"As I am yours." My throat tightens with overwhelming love and gratitude. My timing sucks, but I am so happy to be his.

Ethan gathers me in his arms and kisses me so thoroughly that I forget we're trying to avoid the palace guards' prying eyes.

Come on, Sunny.

I break off the kiss and push against his chest. He immediately stops and drops his arms but obstinately remains toe-to-toe with me. So I take a step back, trying—and failing—to check my libido. I am embarrassingly out of breath from just one kiss.

"I'm serious, Ethan," I say in a *be reasonable* tone. "You can't . . . we can't . . ."

"I can, and we will." A muscle clenches in his jaw even as his chest heaves from our kiss. *At least I'm not the only one.* "I don't care what anyone thinks. I will not hide my love for you."

"Will you stop being so stubborn?" My pulse flutters in my throat at his words, but I double down. I want what's best for Ethan. I don't want to stir up trouble and make things harder for him. We can still be together, just not out in the open. "You have to unite the four kingdoms and lead the people of this realm. I'm not saying I can't be with you, but we don't need to announce it to the worlds."

"I won't have you hide in the shadows." Steel lines his words, but his touch is tender as he tucks a loose strand of hair behind my ear. "You belong at my side for all the worlds to see. Either they accept us or they reject us both. I will not—*cannot*—compromise on this."

"What would I stand at your side as? Your girlfriend? Or your pet?" I ask bitterly, remembering his father's scathing words.

He draws back as though I slapped him, and I immediately regret lashing out at him. I open my mouth to apologize.

"No, Sunny," he says, his voice raw. "I want you to stand at my side as my queen."

I gasp, my blood rushing in my ears. *His queen?* He can't mean that. But my eyes trace the lines of his face, open and vulnerable, and I know he means it. Every word.

Doesn't he understand I'll only make things harder for him? Panic builds in my chest. The Shinbiin will never accept a gumiho as their queen.

I can't do this. I'll ruin everything. I'll ruin *him*. I—

"Be my wife, Sunny." Ethan cups my cheek and holds my gaze.

His wife.

I know nothing about being a queen, but loving Ethan comes as naturally as breathing to me. I can't *not* love him. I will always be his, body and soul. Isn't that what being someone's wife means? A promise to always stand by their side and love them no matter what happens—to love them even if the worlds end?

The love shining from his eyes silences the last of my insecurities, and everything in me stills with absolute certainty. "I can do that."

"Yes, you can," he says huskily. "You can do anything."

"But that would make you my husband," I whisper and bite my bottom lip.

Aching tenderness fills his expression, and he traces my cheekbone with unsteady fingers. "Yeah, it would."

I trap his hand against my cheek and turn my face to kiss his palm. Then I look at him with a tremulous smile. "Weird."

The corners of his eyes crinkle as laughter rumbles in his chest. *Gods, he is so beautiful.* And he is all mine. My husband. My family. I won't be alone anymore. Euphoria, pure and bright, pulses through me.

Home. I am home.

With a squeal of unadulterated joy, I jump into his arms and wrap my legs around his waist, dropping kisses all over his handsome face. He laughs and spins me around.

"Your Majesty," Jihun rasps.

Oh gods.

I squirm to be put down, but Ethan doesn't budge for a long second. Then he sets my feet on the ground and drops his arms, but he links his fingers through mine and pulls me close to his side. When I tug on my hand, he tightens his grip, and I stop fighting him.

Jihun is our closest friend, and he deserves our honesty. Besides, if we can't express our love in front of him, how will we face the people of the Realm of Four Kingdoms as their king and queen?

Their queen . . .

I want to be Ethan's wife more than anything. But the queen part will take some getting used to . . . for everyone. Will the Shinbiin hate me less as their queen? Or more?

More importantly, can I forget their past wrongs and forgive them? Will I be able to look past their flaws and see the best in them? See their potential to do better?

I sure as hell hope so.

A queen is meant to love her people, and I have to try for Ethan. And no matter what, I will give everything in me to save them from the Amheuk.

"I gather you have good news to share." Jihun's gaze drops to our hands, and a melancholy smile curves his lips. "But I'm afraid we can delay no longer. Everyone awaits your presence at the audience hall."

"Ethan, you should go—" I begin.

"*Both* of you," Jihun interrupts. "The Sentinels are also there, since what Minju discovered pertains to all of us."

"What did she discover?" I ask even as we hurry toward the palace gates.

"It will be best if she explains." Jihun glances around. "In private."

When we arrive at the audience hall, Captain Ha stands guard on his own. All the other guards seem to have been sent away.

What the hell did Minju find out?

The captain bows and opens the door for us, and we walk inside in grim silence. The Queen of Sky, the King of Underworld, and the

Queen of Water stand near the dais, and the Sentinels huddle near the back of the audience hall.

Hailey catches my eyes and offers me a somber nod. *What? No tackle hug?* I sigh in resignation. Whatever they're preparing to tell us must be worse than I imagined.

Ethan, Jihun, and I, along with the rest of the Sentinels, join the monarchs in front of the dais. For a moment, no one says a word, and tension threads through the audience hall. I belatedly remember that the kings and queens of the four kingdoms are not known to get along.

The King of Underworld stands next to the Queen of Water, closer than strictly necessary. The two of them don't look at each other, but every time one of them shifts, the backs of their hands brush. I bite my cheeks not to smile, but lose the battle when the back of Ethan's hand brushes mine.

"Hi, I'm Ethan. The, uh, King of Mountains." He awkwardly sticks his hand out to the rumpled male across from him. "You must be the King of Underworld."

"Call me Taeyoung," the King of Underworld mumbles equally awkwardly, shaking Ethan's hand.

"I'm Bora, the Queen of Water." She inclines her head at Ethan, who nods back in acknowledgment. "And I think we all know the Queen of Sky already."

"It should not have taken us this long to put aside the old grudges, which never belonged to us in the first place." The Queen of Sky glances at Bora and Taeyoung. "The strife between our kingdoms should have ended with the passing of our predecessors."

"The shinbiins live for more than a thousand years. We were lulled into thinking we had plenty of time to put things right." Taeyoung sets his riotous curls bouncing with a shake of his head. "But better late than never, and no time like the present . . . and all that."

"What he means to say is"—Bora directs a chiding look at Taeyoung, but the hearts in her eyes ruin the effect—"the Kingdom of Water and the Kingdom of Underworld will accept the hand that the fates have dealt us." She bows formally to Ethan. "For the sake of the Realm of Four Kingdoms, I swear allegiance to the King Foretold."

Ethan sucks in a sharp breath and stiffens at my side.

"I swear allegiance to the King Foretold," Taeyoung repeats, stamping his fist over his heart.

All eyes turn to the Queen of Sky, and she recites the prophecy of the King Foretold in a resonant voice.

Cruelty bends the heart of kindness,
Melds a union that should not be.

From the depth of twisted fate,
Born is hope to free the realm.

Beings of light shall not divide,
The will of good, the will of life.

Brave is the King who discerns,
Path of truth from path of shame.

"I swear allegiance to the King Foretold," the Queen of Sky says and takes Ethan's hand. "We will fight at your side to save the Realm of Four Kingdoms."

When he doesn't reply to her for three long seconds, I glance at Ethan. He stands as still as a marble statue. He might have stopped breathing. *Shit.* He is freaking the hell out. Who wouldn't freak out, seeing your destiny unfold in front of you? It is absolutely understandable, but I don't know how to help him.

Jihun leans close to Ethan from his other side and whispers something I can't make out. Ethan snaps out of his stupor with a long gasp, then gives his royal adviser a solemn nod. Then he takes a step closer to the monarchs.

"I swear to uphold the trust you have placed in me." Ethan presses his fist against his heart. "I will protect and lead the Realm of Four Kingdoms as the fates have willed it."

As the fates have willed it.

His words echo in my head, and my knees nearly buckle beneath me. How could I have forgotten? I avoided learning about the prophecy of the End of Days, but I have long guessed what it says. The fates have willed the King Foretold to kill me. And no amount of avoidance can change that fact.

What if that prophecy comes to pass as well?

But I refuse to withhold my love from Ethan because of a future that neither of us might live to see. Odds are much higher that I'll die fighting the Amheuk before Ethan has to kill me. I suppose I should take comfort in that depressing reassurance.

"Shall I perform a song to celebrate this auspicious moment?" Jaeseok quips into the heavy silence. "I can do a K-pop medley."

Minju claps a hand over her mouth to smother a snort, and the dokkaebi beams as though she just plucked a star from the heavens and handed it to him.

"Your Majesty?" Hailey says, pinching the bridge of her nose.

"Yes," the four majesties respond at once.

"Eeek." Hailey turns into a tomato. "I-I meant Ethan."

"We really have to dispose of the whole 'Your Majesty' thing." One corner of Ethan's mouth quirks up. "What is it, Hailey?"

"I just wanted to ask you to write it into law that Jaeseok can't perform K-pop songs at random moments," she mumbles. When laughter fills the room, she turns even redder and elbows the dokkaebi at her side. "Gods, I'm turning into *you*. I can't believe I'm making ridiculous jokes at a time like this."

"Turning into me is a *marvelous* thing." Jaeseok pats the top of Hailey's head, and she slaps his hand away with an affectionate scowl.

"Besides, it's called comic *relief* for a reason," Captain Seo says with a soft chuckle. "We all needed a good laugh."

"Well said," Jihun murmurs, and the captain's surprised gaze shoots toward him. "The darker the times, the more we should cherish every moment of joy and laughter."

Ethan takes my hand and meets my eyes, and I know what he is asking. I nod, my bottom lip quivering.

Yes, and yes again. Yes always and forever.

"Which is why Sunny and I would like to be wed as soon as possible," Ethan says with a smile that lights up his whole face—his whole body. Even the life force around him shimmers like glitter raining down on him.

I did that. I made him happy.

"But Hyeok, my dear child." The Queen of Sky's eyes tighten with worry. "The prophecy of the End of Days—"

My heart turns to stone and drops to my feet. To hear my fears spoken out loud makes it all the more real.

"Is but one *possible* future." Ethan cuts her off sharply. "A future I have no intention of realizing."

My breath leaves me in a whoosh, and I squeeze his hand. Neither of us has forgotten that dark prophecy, but we are determined to love each other in spite of it.

"Sunny and Ethan share a love destined by the heavens." The Queen of Water presses her hand against her chest. "The fates cannot be so cruel . . ."

"Yes, and prophecies are notoriously obscure," the King of Underworld adds. "We might be completely misinterpreting it."

"And the present is more important than an uncertain future," Jihun says with absolute conviction. "Sunny and Ethan fought so hard to be together. They *deserve* this."

Like mine, Ethan's eyes shine with unshed tears. We both owe Jihun so much. *Well, I have no choice now.* I have to kick the Amheuk's ass into oblivion so our friend can have a chance to find his happily ever after. Because *he* deserves it.

"Very well then," the Queen of Sky sighs.

"If I may add . . ." Ever proper, Captain Seo waits for the four monarchs to nod before she continues, "Their union is also best for the people. Everyone is afraid, but we have to lift their spirits and give them a reason to fight. They have to believe that we can win."

"Yes, Sunny and the Yeoiju can be that reason." Minju nods, starting to pace in a tight back-and-forth. "Especially since she is our best chance of defeating the Amheuk."

"Is that a fact?" I croak.

"A theory," the historian murmurs earnestly. "Based on my research, I found one possible way of destroying the Amheuk, and it involves you and the Yeoiju."

"Lucky me," I mutter weakly. Ethan squeezes my hand, and I put on a brave smile. "So . . . what? I have to put on a little light show for the people of the Realm of Four Kingdoms?"

"That's entirely up to you and your muse," Captain Seo says dryly.

"Sunny and Ethan need to speak to the people as soon as possible," Jihun says with a decisive nod. "But first, they must wed."

My heart does an awkward somersault and lodges itself in my throat. *I'm getting married?*

"We should elope to Vegas," I mutter to hide my nerves.

"When this is all over, we'll have the tackiest Vegas wedding you can think of." Ethan lifts my hand and places a lingering kiss on my knuckles. "But for now, we'll stick to something simple. Something we can do right now."

"Right *now* now?" I blink, my pulse fluttering.

"*Now* now." He gives me a crooked smile and boops my nose. I tamp down on the instinct to bite his finger off. I love him to death, but come on. The nose boop?

Then why are you grinning like a dingus?

I ignore the voice of my conscience and ask with faux chill, "So what do we do? Wait, it *is* something we can do in front of our friends, right?"

Not that I would mind something that requires privacy. I blush, revealing my naughty thoughts.

"I'm afraid so." Ethan's smile turns devilish. "But I can try to arrange something private for later."

Yes, the world is about to end. But I'm also about to be Ethan's bride, and I can't help but feel incandescently happy. Literally.

My Yeoiju hums and glows in my chest, and my joy fills the entire audience hall with beautiful white light.

I wish this moment could last forever.

CHAPTER THIRTY-SIX

Sunny

"Wait right here." Ethan kisses my forehead—and I melt just a tiny bit—then he walks to the back of the audience hall, motioning for Jihun to follow him.

"I will see if they need my assistance," Taeyoung murmurs with a secret smile at Bora.

"Well, I guess all the boys are on that side. Ladies," Jaeseok drawls and winks rakishly at us, before sauntering after Taeyoung. Minju's head slowly tilts to the side as she studies the dokkaebi's retreating ass, like she has a final exam on the topic tomorrow.

"Come on." Hailey grabs my wrist and drags me to an alcove. "Let's get you ready."

"Ready?" I protest weakly as my friends, both new and old, grab me, tug me, and spin me around. "Ethan said it'll be something simple."

"The ceremony itself might be simple, but that does not mean you can't look the part," Captain Seo says.

I wrinkle my nose at the no-nonsense warrior. "Et tu Brute?"

"Who can resist a makeover?" She shrugs sheepishly.

"We can work with the attire I wore for my wedding." The Queen of Sky holds out an old-fashioned hanbok that looks like it belongs in Goguryeo, ancient Korea.

"Where did that come from?" I squawk.

"I summoned it from my chambers." She arches a regal brow.

"Right." I sigh and resign myself to my fate. "Magic."

I make myself supple and pliant—practically boneless—as I'm *helped* out of the hanbok Miok put on me this morning. I move my limbs into the layers of undergarments—*Ethan is not going to be happy about these*—then into a full, pleated chima in the color of pale jade.

I swallow my protest and slip my arms into the ivory jeogori, which is closer to a long coat than a shirt. It hangs well past my knees, with wide bell sleeves that swallow my hands.

Bora holds out a plain silk belt and asks, "What's your favorite color?"

"Black."

She sighs, her shoulders drooping. "What about your second favorite color?"

I have a feeling she won't be happy with dark gray either, so I give her my *third* favorite color. "Purple."

"That'll do." With a small smile, she flutters the silk in her hands until it turns a rich aubergine. Then she wraps it around my waist and ties it at the small of my back.

I glance down at my dress. The dark purple of the belt is striking against the cream of the jeogori and the cool green of the chima.

"Her hair," Hailey gasps as though my simple braid is no better than a beehive, and I wince as multiple hands free my hair from the offending braid.

I endure the rest of my glow-up in meek silence until the fussing blessedly ceases and everyone takes three steps back.

"You are missing one thing." The Queen of Sky holds up a jade hair ornament, shaped like the silhouette of a mountain. "My sister, Ethan's mother, gave this to me before she left for the Kingdom of Mountains. I want you to have something from her."

"Th-thank you, Your Majesty," I whisper, my chest constricting.

"Come closer." She gently pushes the two-pronged hair ornament into my half updo, then tilts my face up with a finger under my chin. "And call me *imo*."

"Thank you, Imo." *Oh my gods.* I have an aunt.

She opens her arms, and I walk into them without hesitation. I let the cocoon of warmth and safety surround me. I have an elder I can turn to and lean on—someone who will pick me up and dust me off if I fall.

"Minju, can I speak with y . . ." Jaeseok stumbles to a stop after rounding the corner and gapes at me with a goofy smile. "So pretty."

"Speak to me about what?" Minju yanks at his sleeve.

"We need something for the ceremony." He leads her off to the side. "I told the boys you might be able to help us since you know everything."

I can't make out the rest of his words as they walk farther away. Then I'm distracted by the sight of Hailey and Captain Seo, who stand in their battle armor.

"Speaking of looking the part . . ." I arch a brow.

Hailey and Captain Seo glance at each other, and the captain shrugs. "At least we cleaned the blood off the armor."

"I want to forget about the war and the Amheuk," I say quietly, "at least for the ceremony."

"Of course, Sunny." Hailey tugs the captain by her elbow toward the room divider. "We'll change."

Minju returns to the alcove and says, "He's ready for you, Sunny."

My stomach dips, and a tremor spreads down my limbs. *Why am I so nervous?* It's Ethan. I want this—I want him—more than anything. I clasp my shaking hands and nod at Minju.

The Queen of Sky gives me a kind smile before she walks out of the alcove, followed by Bora, who flutters her fingers at me in a small wave.

Cheyun squeezes my shoulder as she passes, then Minju and Hailey pull me into a quick three-way hug before bustling into the audience hall.

"I guess it's my turn." I take a wavering breath. "It's now or never."

On knees like water, I step out of the alcove to a chorus of gasps from the "boys." But I'm only interested in one boy, who stands closest to the dais, with the other males lined up behind him.

Love, tenderness, and desire burn in the silver-green flames of his eyes. And I know mine reflect those same emotions as I drink in the sight of him in an ancient Korean hanbok in emerald green. He looks impossibly tall and broad in his long, resplendent robe, with his crown of gold and jade nestled snugly on his overgrown hair.

Cheyun, Minju, Bora, and Hailey stand opposite Jihun, Jaeseok, Taeyoung, and . . . the Judge of Tenth Hell? He grins at me from behind his dark sunglasses. *What in the world?* But I set aside the question. That can wait.

Everything can wait but Ethan.

I join him at the head of the line and offer him a tremulous smile. He doesn't return it at first, gaping at me, his eyes wide. Then one corner of his mouth kicks up in a crooked grin. He takes my hand in his and presses a kiss on my knuckles. I laugh under my breath at his boyish eagerness.

But when he glances up at me through his lashes, the dark promise in his eyes makes my toes curl. *I'm not mad.* They can curl, as tight as they want. It's a foregone conclusion that I'm head over heels for this guy anyway.

The Queen of Sky stands at the edge of the dais. It seems fitting that she is our officiant. I already feel close to her. But when she offers me an encouraging nod, I gulp, my nerves kicking into overdrive.

I have no idea how impromptu wedding ceremonies work in the Realm of Four Kingdoms. I've actually never been to a wedding—impromptu or not—even in the Mortal Realm. I shift my gaze to Ethan when he squeezes my hand.

I got you, he mouths.

I smile and speak into his mind, *I know you do.*

Just like that, my nerves unknot with a sigh, and I feel calmer and more present than ever before. This moment, right now, means everything to me, and every fiber of my being is here for it—here for him. Hand in hand, we turn to face the Queen of Sky.

"A love destined by the heavens," she says, "is a blessing not often bestowed by the fates. Yours is a love that completes your souls. You will make each other whole and strong, and bring each other joy beyond measure. But your love is also a great responsibility, because once united by your vows, your bond can never be broken, even by death.

"Sunny and Ethan," the Queen of Sky continues, "love each other fearlessly. Hold nothing back, because your love is more powerful than any challenge you will encounter. A love like yours can change the course of destiny."

My heart pounds in my chest, my throat, and the tips of my fingers. My life force beats in every corner of my body. The cynic in me wants to laugh off the queen's words as flowery exaggeration for her nephew's wedding, but they ring true in the depth of my soul.

I glance sideways at Ethan, and his heated gaze collides with mine. My chest tightens to the point of pain, because I love him so much. Our love is bigger than the two of us. We are not only meant to be together. We *have* to be together. There is no truer path.

"Now for the vows." The Queen of Sky waves one hand, and a bowl of water with tiny white petals appears in her other hand. "You may kneel."

Ethan bends his knees, and I follow him to the ground. The queen holds out the bowl, and he accepts it with both hands. He shifts on his knees to face me, and I do the same.

He takes a sip from the bowl, silver-and-green fire flickering in his eyes. Then in a voice that echoes with timeless truth, he says, "Ours is a love destined by the heavens. I will love you until my dying breath."

I accept the bowl he hands me with a rush of panic. I don't know the words to the vow. Do I just repeat what he said? It would be true, right? Before I can spiral, Ethan nods at me to drink.

With more headstrong determination than courage, I sip from the bowl, and I squint in confusion. I taste the salt of tears and the mineral of earth, laced with the lovely scent of flowers. *Cloud blossoms.* I don't know how I know, but I do.

The audience hall and everyone in it fades away, and Ethan and I stand at the foot of a mountain with sunlight streaming down on us. His face shines with love brighter than the sun, and I know what I am meant to say.

"And I will love you in this life and the next," I vow in a voice that is both mine and not mine—repeating the words spoken by the first fated lovers in a union blessed by the heavens. I blink and the eerie overlay of thoughts and feelings dissipates. Then we're back in the audience hall, and I find my own simple words. "I'll love you forever, Ethan."

"Even when I die and turn to dust, my love for you will endure for all eternity." Ethan takes the bowl from my limp grasp and hands it to the Queen of Sky.

"From this day forward, you no longer live for yourselves but for each other," she says. "Your joy is not yours alone but each other's. Your pain is no longer yours but each other's. Every choice you make must be for the two of you, because you are now one."

Ethan stands and helps me to my feet. "May I kiss you?"

"Please," I whisper.

His eyes hold mine until his face blurs, and his lips brush against mine with sweet tenderness. But when he tries to draw back, I growl and tug him back with a fist in his hair. His restraint shatters, and he plunges his tongue into my open mouth. I nip and suckle his lips, and kiss him until I have no air left in my lungs.

Ethan lifts his head. His pupils are blown wide and his chest heaves, but he smiles at me with such undiluted joy that I beam up at him. I have never been so happy in my long, hard life. With a laugh, I jump into his arms, and he spins me around and around.

My life is perfect. I regret nothing. I fear nothing.

CHAPTER THIRTY-SEVEN

Sunny

Hugs are had. Backs are clapped. Laughter is shared.

Ethan, Ethan, Ethan.

I *am* happy to share this moment with my friends, but I have no room in my mind, or in my heart, for anything other than Ethan. I think he feels the same way, because he hasn't let go of my hand, lacing our fingers tightly together, since we spoke our vows.

Death looms outside, but we have this moment—our moment. I glance at him from beneath my lashes.

My husband.

Laughter bubbles in my chest, and tears blur my vision and sting my nose. I am a flaming mess, but I'm okay with that.

Today is my wedding day.

But Minju coughs quietly, her hands clasped in front of her. Immediate silence falls across the audience hall, as though we were all waiting for this moment—were dreading it.

"It's so soon." Bora's eyes are full of sympathy as she looks between Ethan and me. "I wish you two could have had more time."

"Yes." The Queen of Sky sighs. "But we have delayed too long already."

Everyone slowly shuffles toward the dais, but I can't get my feet to move.

Just one more second.

Ethan catches me around my waist and pulls me into his arms. "The Amheuk is totally killing the vibe."

"You are a mega dingus." I muffle my laugh against his shoulder, and he kisses the crown of my head.

"'You are a mega dingus, *Yeobo*,'" he corrects, his warm breath ruffling my hair.

"Dude," I choke, heat climbing up my cheeks. The term of endearment is used only between married couples. It's so intimate. "I am not calling you that."

"Why not, Yeobo?" He tips my chin up with the crook of his finger. Sweet tenderness and steely possessiveness war for dominance in his eyes. "Am I not your husband?"

"You are my husband." I trap his face between my hands and kiss him soundly on the lips. "And I will consider calling you . . . that, but we should reserve it for when we're alone."

"Why is that?" He brushes the tip of his nose down the side of my cheek, and I shiver.

"Because I want to avoid climbing you like a tree in front of unsuspecting victims," I whisper.

Ethan groans against the side of my neck. "You can have me anytime, anywhere, any way you want."

"I'll keep that in mind." I reluctantly draw away from him and tug him toward the dais. Because another second of these sweet, sultry whispers would make me take him right now.

"I think it'd be best if we all sat down for this." Hailey hurriedly sets out seat cushions in a circle.

"Thank you," the Judge of Tenth Hell murmurs to her in that dark, sexy baritone of his.

I can't make out his expression behind those black sunglasses, but color floods Hailey's cheeks before she spins away from him.

Ethan and I sit down, and he slides my seat cushion—with me on it—so close that I might as well be sitting on his lap. I roll my eyes but press up against him. He brushes his lips against my cheek with a low chuckle, and I get hot all over.

Gods, it doesn't take much, does it?

While I lust after my husband over a peck on the cheek, everyone takes a seat in the circle. Jihun sits to Ethan's left and nods at the two of us, and my chest constricts. I was so drunk on happiness I didn't once think about how Jihun must feel. He seems . . . fine, but this can't be easy on him. He just has his poker face mastered.

I don't know what to do—how to make him hurt less—so I offer him a sorry excuse of a smile. And he awards my awkward olive branch with a fleeting quirk of his lips. I swallow, tasting salt in the back of my throat. He is such a good friend.

"I believe we're as ready as we will ever be." Ethan nods at Minju, who sits across from us, with Jaeseok and the Queen of Sky on either side of her. "Tell us. How do we defeat the Amheuk?"

"With the Cheon'gwang." Minju stares down at her rumpled skirt.

"Which is impossible." Ethan frowns. "It sacrificed itself to stop the Amheuk during the Endless War."

"The Yeoiju is a remnant of the Cheon'gwang . . ." Minju's soft voice dwindles into silence.

"Exactly." I have no idea where this is headed, but I don't like it. "The Yeoiju is *only* a remnant of it."

"A remnant"—the historian aims an apologetic grimace at me—"with the potential to become *the* Cheon'gwang, the true force of light powerful enough to subdue the Amheuk."

"Become the true force of light?" Ethan asks, his voice dangerously soft. "Have you forgotten that Sunny and the Yeoiju are inseparable?"

"Of . . . of course not," Minju stutters.

"Your Majesty." Jihun puts a hand on Ethan's arm. "Please allow her to explain."

From their expressions, everyone in the circle, except me and Ethan, already knows what she has to say, and none of them likes it. Dread creeps down my spine, and Ethan plants a protective hand on my back.

"I . . ." Minju wrings her hands until they turn bright pink.

"It's okay." Jaeseok covers them with his own. "Take your time."

She nods and takes a big breath. "In Santorini, Sunny defeated the dark mudang by absorbing the life force of nature."

"But th-that doesn't work in this realm," I protest, interrupting her again. "I could barely draw any gi from the Kingdom of Water. The Kingdom of Mountains was a little better, but nature's life force in this realm does not compare to that of the Mortal Realm."

"There's a reason for that, Sunny." The King of Underworld rubs his forehead. "It's because nature's life force has been sucked dry in the Realm of Four Kingdoms."

"Taeyoung," Bora gasps.

"We are asking her to risk everything to save this realm," he persists. "She has a right to know the truth."

"I agree. We must tell her." The Queen of Sky holds Bora's gaze until the younger female nods haltingly. "Magic is the foundation of the Realm of Four Kingdoms, and we need more gi than we can produce to fuel our magic. For generations, we have been siphoning nature's life force for our own consumption."

My blood pounds in my ears, and I barely register Ethan stiffening next to me.

"That can't be true. The Kingdom of Mountains would not have stood for it." Ethan shakes his head slowly. "We respect nature. Nurturing it is the only way to foster life for *all* beings."

"The Kingdom of Mountains capitulated when your father took the throne." The Queen of Sky sighs. "He wanted more power, and he was a male used to taking whatever he wanted. That is why Dangun, the god of Mountains, abandoned the Realm of Four Kingdoms."

My breath comes in short pants. First, the Gray Void, and now, *this*? Is there anything not tainted in this fucking realm?

"How could I not have known?" Ethan frowns down at his hands. "I would have seen this in my mother's memories."

"She could only share the memories you needed to remember who you are and to fulfill your destiny," his aunt explains. "Your mother was over two hundred fifty years old when she had you. As powerful as she was, there was only so much she could imbue into the stone of tears."

"W-wait. Is this why the shinbiins are nearly immortal?" My voice breaks as the horrifying realization dawns on me. I glare at every shinbiin in the room. "And all of you are okay with this? Bleeding nature dry for your own gain?"

"Our predecessors who chose this path are long gone, but we were complicit in it," Taeyoung owns. "Your friends, on the other hand, only learned of this mere hours before you. Do not blame them—or the people of the Realm of Four Kingdoms—for the sins of their rulers."

"You're right." Ethan narrows his eyes at the three monarchs. "The blame lies solely on you, and those who came before you. How could—"

"Please stop fighting. All of you," Minju interjects, raising her voice. "We can't change the past, and we are running out of time to protect our future. Besides, it would not have been enough. Even if the realm hadn't stolen nature's life force, it would not have been enough to defeat the Amheuk."

"Then . . . what?" I am so fucking tired. "How am I supposed to *become* the Cheon'gwang?"

Because Ethan is right. My Yeoiju and I cannot be separated. If the Yeoiju becomes the true force of light, I become the light too.

"You have to . . ." Minju fists her hands on her lap. "You have to absorb the gi of the sleeping gods."

I burst into unhinged laughter. "How the fuck am I supposed to do that?"

"Shhh. It's okay, Sunny." Ethan pulls my head onto his shoulder and kisses my forehead. "We'll figure it out together."

My laugh sputters, and I swallow the sob that follows it. *What use is falling apart?* It's not like I can stand back and watch the Amheuk destroy the Realm of Four Kingdoms. I'll never stop fighting for Ethan and my friends.

"We know the locations of three of the gods—Hwanin, the god of Heavens, Yongwang, the god of Water, and Yeomla, the god of Underworld." Taeyoung clears his throat, guilt still shadowing his face. "However, no one knows where Dangun, the god of Mountains, has gone."

"We'll cross that bridge when we get there." I sigh and raise my head from Ethan's shoulder. Minju is right. We're running out of time. "So how do we get to Hwanin, Yongwang, and Yeomla?"

There has to be more to it than just finding the gods—I doubt they'll just hand over their life forces—but one step at a time.

"That's where I come in," the Judge of Tenth Hell says. "I can teleport you there."

Twin grooves form between my brows. "The gods are in hell?"

"No." Gyun chuckles. "They're not in the Ten Hells."

"They are in purgatory," Taeyoung supplies unhelpfully.

"Uh-huh." I nod and keep nodding. "That makes much more sense."

"It doesn't matter where they are." Ethan's voice dares anyone to disagree with him. "I'm going with her."

"Aww." My wonky sense of humor kicks in full throttle. "I guess we're honeymooning in purgatory."

"I am coming as well," Jihun adds, crossing his arms.

"On our honeymoon?" Ethan digs a playful elbow into the seonnam's side, and the stoic male deigns to roll his eyes.

The hysterical edge of my laugh smooths out, and genuine amusement takes its place. This is the only way we'll get through this—by giving one another shit. But more importantly, with shared laughter.

"I'm afraid I cannot carry a third," Gyun says to Jihun, raising his arms as though demonstrating he only has two.

“Then I’ll come. I’m a jeoseungsaja.” Hailey juts her chin. “I can travel to purgatory without anyone carrying me.”

“Very well.” The judge tips his head at Hailey, his expression appraising. “I have a feeling you will have no trouble keeping up.”

We all get to our feet as though everything is set. I don’t ask when we need to leave. *One step at a time.* Ethan helps me up, then he immediately gets pulled into a conversation with the Queen of Sky, Taeyoung, and Bora. And I sigh wistfully.

Our wedding day is officially over.

CHAPTER THIRTY-EIGHT

Sunny

Pale-pink blossoms swirl in a cyclone of wind, creating a pathway that rises above the rooftops of the Celestial Palace. And the Queen of Sky glides up the airy path to stand before the people of the Realm of Four Kingdoms.

"In a union destined by the heavens, the King of the Mountains wed Cho Mihwa today." Her voice rings out to reach everyone gathered in front of the palace, and disgruntled muttering rises from the crowd. "This is a blessing for every one of us because the Queen of Mountains bears the Yeoiju, the gift of the Cheon'gwang. She is our only hope against the Amheuk."

Right. No pressure.

The people are not happy with their gumiho queen. And they sure as hell don't want me to be their "only hope."

Well, it's me or nothing, assholes.

I sigh. That was not a very queenly thought.

Ethan's worried gaze scans my face, and I squeeze his hand with a reassuring smile. His brows furrow, not buying it for a second. I look away first and give a jerky nod to the Queen of Water and the King of Underworld.

"We're ready," I say. *I am so not ready.*

Bora and Taeyoung hold their palms out toward us, and dark smoke and water swirl beneath our feet. I can't hold back my gasp when the smoke and water sprout into a tall, striped column, lifting us above the palace.

Ethan instinctively pulls me close to his side but slowly releases me once we reach the top. The people can't see me huddled against him. We must stand before the people as partners.

With a respectful bow toward us—both genuine and for show—the Queen of Sky descends to the ground, scattering the pathway of wind and flowers into the air. The people ooh and ahh at the beautiful display.

We agreed the kings and queens of each kingdom will participate in this pep rally. The people of this realm need to know that we all stand with Ethan, ready to fight against the eternal darkness. And we need them to fight with us.

The Amheuk is stirring, impatient to strike the Kingdom of Sky. I made it angry by blowing it up, and I can sense its growing malice. Our people must hold it at bay while we find the four gods.

"The Queen of Sky, the King of Underworld, and the Queen of Water have bestowed their trust in me to lead this realm. The four kingdoms and their rulers are each formidable in their own right, but we are stronger united," Ethan proclaims. "We are beings of Mountains, Sky, Water, and Underworld. Each life source is different, but no one source is greater than the other. We must stand as equals. We must stand united."

That's my cue.

"Only when we combine each life source does it become something extraordinary." I speak to the people before me—the same people who shunned me because I am a gumiho. But they can change for the better when they open their hearts and minds. I have to believe that. "I am not a shinbiin, but I *am* a being of the Shingae, just like you. At the core, we are all beings of the Cheon'gwang."

The muttering below us sounds generally displeased, which is no surprise. They are too tired and scared to trust pretty words, especially from me. That's why we came prepared with an extraspecial light show.

I take a step forward on the water-and-smoke platform holding me aloft, five stories above the ground. Since no one else can see the colors of the gi, we decided that the queens and kings will contribute their gi through a symbol of their life source. I open my arms wide, and the Yeoiju hums in my chest.

"Mountains," I rasp in an unsteady voice.

Ethan sends a flurry of emerald green leaves toward me. I collect the leaves into a ball between my hands. With an inhale that pushes my chest out, I absorb it into my heart's center as the life force of Mountains. The crowd gasps below me, and I bite my cheek to hold back my smirk.

"Water," I say with more confidence.

Bora shoots a gentle stream of water from the ground, and I gather it in my hands then let it flow into my chest as the gi of Water.

"Underworld."

Taeyoung, the show-off, hovers a ball of smoking fire in front of me. I have to admit that performing in front of an enraptured audience is kind of fun. So I hold the fireball between my hands—it doesn't burn because I've deconstructed the magic already—and spin it in the air. I wait for the applause to die down before I absorb the gi of Underworld.

"Sky." I nod at our auntie.

The Queen of Sky blows swirling pink blossoms toward me, fluttering in the wind. The flowers dance to the roar of the giddy audience, then melt straight into my chest as the life force of Sky.

I feel the familiar pulse of the Yeoiju inside me, churning and growing with the green, blue, red, and silver life forces. It pounds against my chest, wanting to be released.

"Together, we become the Cheon'gwang," I intone and let the white light burst free, my head and arms thrown back.

Everyone is far away enough not to be affected by the light. It is only a small surge, but it is true and brilliant. Even so, anyone close might be swept away . . . except Ethan. I risk a sideways glance at him, and he stands in place with one hand shielding his eyes. I knew he was powerful enough to withstand the light.

The light fades away, and the gi returns to the four life sources. I straighten, lowering my arms to my sides. There is no gasping, cheering, or clapping from the people. It seems I have awed the Realm of Four Kingdoms into silence.

But when the sea of people falls to their knees, *I* gasp, pressing my hand against my chest. I shoot a startled look at Ethan, and he reaches for my free hand.

"Long live the King and Queen of the Realm of Four Kingdoms," someone shouts as the people rise to their feet. Soon, it becomes a booming chant.

I know they are euphoric with hope that the world might not end tomorrow. I know they haven't truly accepted me. Even so, tears of gratitude sting my eyes. Maybe—someday—they *will* accept me, and I can stop worrying that I'll hold Ethan back.

"You're a star, baby." His smile crinkles the corners of his eyes.

"Shut up." I stick my tongue out at him. He kisses me, flicking the tip of his tongue against mine. I squeak and push him away. "*Ethan*, everyone can see us."

"And you think someone will object to me kissing my wife?" He arches his brow.

I want to both combust and melt into a puddle. "Think? I?"

Ethan chuckles under his breath and cups my face, the tenderness in his eyes my undoing. "What am I going to do with you?"

I guess I am his undoing too.

"This," I whisper. "This is exactly what you should do with me."

He kisses me again, and I don't push him away this time. I wrap my arms around his neck and deepen the kiss, pushing up to my toes. With a groan, he crushes me against him, and the world narrows until there is only us.

I don't even bother opening my eyes when my feet hit the ground. Bora and Taeyoung must have brought us back down to the palace courtyard. I don't want this kiss to end, and Ethan obliges enthusiastically.

"Your Majesties," Jihun murmurs close to us. "There isn't much time."

We finally break apart. But even then, we can't look away from each other.

"I know." Ethan blows out a rough breath and steps away from me. "We're ready to lea—"

"Not yet," Cheyun says, as the rest of the Sentinels surround us in a half circle. "We bought you a couple of hours."

"What?" I blink.

"Yes, we have prepared your honeymoon suite," Minju explains with a shy blush.

"Consider it our wedding present." Jaeseok grins.

"Oh my gods." I clap a hand over my mouth, tears stinging my eyes. "Why are you guys so good to me?"

"Because we love you, silly," Hailey says as though it's the most obvious thing. But I want to shake her by the shoulders and demand that she say it again. I barely control my manic gratitude.

How am I so lucky?

"Now, come with us." She tucks her arm into mine. "We have to get you ready for your wedding night."

I glance at Ethan, and he grins crookedly at me, looking shy and boyish.

"A quick word, Your Majesty." Jihun pulls Ethan off to the side and gives me an encouraging nod.

Waving inanely at Bora and Taeyoung, I let Hailey, Minju, and Cheyun whisk me away. But I'm too overcome to notice where we're going until I'm standing in front of a hanok, tucked away behind a picturesque courtyard.

"This way." Cheyun leads us into the hanok and opens the double sliding doors. "Your honeymoon suite, Your Majesty."

"Don't call me that," I grumble half-heartedly, hesitating outside the room.

My cheeks heat as I take in the "honeymoon suite." Floating light orbs and soft candlelight cast a warm, muted glow across the room. And a sizable sleeping mat—with a white, silk comforter and two pillow blocks—lies toward the back of the room. Pale-pink rose petals are scattered across the comforter, filling the room with their perfume.

"Well, don't just stand there." Hailey practically shoves me inside, and Minju giggles next to her.

I consider bolting back outside.

"Your Majesty." My lady-in-waiting steps forward and bows with her hands folded neatly in front of her. "I am honored to help you get ready for your wedding night."

"Miok." I smile, her presence calming my frazzled nerves a tiny bit. "I'm so glad you're here."

The doors slide closed behind me, and my friends' soft laughter quickly fades away. For a split second, I want to yell at them to come back.

"The king will be here for his bride soon," Miok says gently, but I startle anyway. "Allow me to get you ready."

I gulp as my eyes dart around the honeymoon suite. It really is lovely, but all I can think is that I'll be sharing the room with Ethan. I press my hand against my fluttering heart. *What is the matter with me?* It's not like we've never made love before.

But this will be our first time as husband and wife.

Ethan and I are bound by the threads of fate, but once we consummate our marriage, we will be *choosing* each other for all time. When we make love this time, it will be a vow to love and cherish each other forever.

Blowing out a shaky breath, I follow Miok to the bathing chamber and step into the warm bath she prepared. She washes me with gentle care and guides me back to the honeymoon suite. I sit where she indicates, while she carefully brushes my hair until it gleams. Then I offer her my pulse points to dot with fragrant oil.

Miok helps me to my feet, then leads me to the armoire. She pauses and clears her throat, and I blink out of my daze. I've never seen her discomfited before. "Your friends have left strict instructions to dress you in this . . ."

She reaches inside the armoire and holds up a tiny, off-white thong. The lace triangle in the front is minuscule. A nervous giggle bubbles up my throat, but I take the panties from her and slip them on under my robe. The scrap of satin feels ridiculously soft and surprisingly comfortable.

"I am not sure what this is," my lady-in-waiting continues, frowning down at the next piece of lingerie, "but the fabric is exquisite."

"It's called lace, and I think you're holding a garter belt," I hedge. "I don't know how that works, either, so we'll have to figure it out together. Let me see the rest."

The remainder of my wedding-night ensemble consists of a matching white lace bra and sheer, thigh-high stockings in the softest beige, edged with more delicate lace. I sigh in relief when I find a relatively simple, off-white nightgown, cut low in a deep V with delicate spaghetti straps.

Miok dresses me efficiently, despite her unfamiliarity with the mortal undergarments. It doesn't occur to me to look at the label until she holds the nightgown out to me.

"La Perla?" I gasp. Even I know the luxury lingerie brand. I must be wearing thousands of dollars in satin and lace right now. "Fuck me."

Well, you only live once.

Secretly happy, I raise my arms in the air for Miok to slide the nightgown over my head. The silky fabric falls down my body, all the way to the floor, and I almost groan from the decadence of it all.

"You look beautiful, Your Majesty." My lady-in-waiting turns me toward the mirror.

My lips part on a soft gasp, and I run the tips of my fingers over the lace lining the V of my neckline. I look both angelic and sexy as sin, and I turn away blushing. Then a wicked smile slowly lights my face.

I might bring Ethan to his knees, looking like this.

"I will take my leave now." Miok bows.

"Thank you." I take her hand in mine. "For everything."

"You are most welcome." She squeezes my hand. "Be happy, Your Majesty."

I nod wordlessly, not wanting to make any promises, and my lady-in-waiting leaves the room with another bow. But I stare after her with unseeing eyes.

Maybe . . . I *can* be happy. *In this moment.* Ethan and I might not have long, but I can still be happy in every moment I share with him. Even if we only have today. Even if this is the last time.

We can be happy together.

With one last look in the mirror, I close the armoire and stand beside it. Suddenly, my nervousness returns full throttle, and I don't know what to do with myself. *I still have time to run before Ethan gets here.* I'm being ridiculous, but my heart disagrees, beating out a bruising ruckus in my chest.

What happened to cherishing every moment together?

Before I can climb out of my skin, a firm knock sounds at the door, and I jump a foot in the air. *Get a grip, Sunny.*

"C-come in," I wheezc.

Ethan steps inside and slides the doors closed behind him with more care than necessary. I take the time to study him while he has his back turned to me. His simple green robe, cinched around his narrow waist, accentuates his broad shoulders. My eyes drop past the hem to the muscled contours of his bare calves. Moisture gathers between my thighs, because he is definitely naked under his robe.

His hair is wet, like he's just taken a bath. He obviously brushed it, but it's already starting to curl every which way in thick unruly waves. His shoulders rise and fall as though he's preparing himself, then he turns around and takes a good look at me.

He goes very still, like someone hit pause on him. He definitely stopped breathing. But his eyes . . . they run wildly over me.

"Breathe, Ethan," I say softly, feeling more powerful than I've ever felt before. This beautiful male is my husband, and he wants me as much as I want him.

With a heaving gasp, he finally resumes breathing. I beckon him, and he stalks toward me, his eyes frantic. He takes my hand in his trembling one and drops a reverent kiss on my knuckles. Biting my bottom lip, I run my fingers through his damp strands.

"Sunny," he whispers, his head still bowed over my hand. When he raises his eyes to meet mine, my knees turn to water at the hunger burning in them.

"Oh you poor, poor male." A sultry smile curves my lips. "At this rate, you won't survive what I'm wearing under this."

A low growl my only warning, he pulls me into his arms with a rough tug, and I melt against him. My smile widens, even as tears prickle behind my lids.

I am home.

CHAPTER THIRTY-NINE

Ethan

"Sunny." I belong to her so completely that I don't know if I can exist without her, much less live or breathe.

She consumes me.

I drop featherlight kisses on the corners of her mouth, on the delicate lids of her closed eyes, on the smooth planes of her cheeks. I breathe in the scent of her, both bright and warm like a sunny autumn day in Los Angeles. I really should consider ripping that silky nightgown off her and consummating our marriage, but I could kiss her like this for an eternity.

To be honest, I'm a little nervous. This is my first time making love to her as her husband—first time making love to my *wife*.

"Ethan?"

"Hmm?" I slide my lips down the length of her neck. I can't resist licking the pulse fluttering at the base of her throat. She moans, and smug satisfaction spreads through me.

"Why aren't you kissing me?" She tilts her head to the side, offering me more of her neck. "Why aren't you touching me?"

A part of me still can't believe I can kiss her and touch her. She is mine. We are married in the eyes of the people, in a union blessed by the fates. But when I kiss and touch her now, it would be *my* vow to her that I am hers—body and soul.

I want it to be good for her—*so good*—but a part of me snarls like a beast, urging me to claim her, to mark her as mine. The ferocity of my desire unsettles me, warring with my instinct to protect her . . . even from me.

I have to get this right. This might be our last time. I have to show her what she means to me.

"I *am* kissing you." I plant a line of kisses on her jawline until I reach her stubborn, perfect chin and move up the other side. And I slide my hands down her back, the cool silk of her gown warming under my hot palms. "I *am* touching you."

She squirms at my teasing touch and presses her body harder against mine. I groan, burning for her. I am a nervous, snarling mess, but I need to have her.

Please gods, let me get this right.

Heart thumping with nerves and anticipation, I kiss my way up her jaw and hover my lips a breath away from hers. "I love you, Sunny."

"I love you, Ethan." Her sweet breath tickles my lips, and my mouth waters, wanting to taste her. "Are you going to kiss me? Or do I have to do everything around here?"

I pull her flush against me and kiss her like a man starved. I greedily lick the curve of her smile. *Mine.* Her smile, her lips, her eager fingers digging into my shoulders . . . *All mine.*

She pushes up to her toes with a whimper, and I all but lose my mind. I fist my hand in her hair and tilt her head to the side, so I can plunge my tongue deeper into her mouth to taste her properly. A groan rumbles in my chest when her tongue tangles with mine and her teeth scrape against it.

I grab her by the waist and hoist her up, and she clamps her strong legs around my torso, her nightgown pooling around her hips. More by instinct than sight, I stumble to the nearest wall and push her up against it. Our kiss turns rough and desperate, and I grind against her core.

I slip a hand under her gown and slide it over her thigh until her round ass fills my palm. Then every muscle in my body clenches, and my mind goes electric white with shock. I was already painfully hard, but my cock hardens even more, and I get lightheaded enough to sway slightly.

"What . . . are you wearing?" I choke out, leaning back to meet her eyes.

She offers me a slow, sinful smile. "I think it's time you unwrap your present, husband."

CHAPTER FORTY

Sunny

Despite my bravado, nerves knot my stomach when Ethan eases my legs down to the floor. Thank gods there's a wall behind me, because I'm not quite steady on my feet. But some of my timidity melts away when Ethan extends a shaking hand toward me.

He's nervous too.

Ethan catches the spaghetti strap of my nightgown with one finger and tugs it past my shoulder. I exhale a shaky breath, and his eyes jump to meet mine. His pupils are blown wide with good old-fashioned lust, but he still searches my face to make sure I'm okay.

"Go on," I murmur, stepping away from the wall.

His intent gaze returns to the task at hand, and he slides down the other strap. Impatience seeps into his movement as he grips the front of my bodice and pulls it down, the satin slipping to my waist without resistance.

A choked gurgle sounds in his throat, and I worry that he might have swallowed his tongue. *That would be a shame.* I have plans for that talented tongue of his. His blatant desire infuses confidence into my veins, and I lift my breasts with my hands, offering them to him.

"Do they meet your approval?" I tease in a husky whisper. He practically slaps my hands away and continues to stare open mouthed at my lace-covered boobs. "Ethan?"

"I like." He nods jerkily.

"Oh my gods." Laughter bubbles out of me. "I didn't mean to break you."

"Break good," he slurs. "Look more."

He hooks his thumbs into the nightgown bunched at my waist and pushes it down, but the fabric has no stretch and gets stuck at my hips—just low enough for the lacy top of my garter belt to peep through.

He tugs on it a bit harder, dragging the gown down an inch lower. With a desperate growl, he bunches the luxurious fabric between his hands and tears the gown straight down the middle. We both gasp at the same time.

"My La Perla," I cry.

"Fuck me." He gawks at my garter belt and thigh-highs, gripping the halves of my poor, ruined nightgown in each of his fists. "What the *hell* are you wearing?"

I can't stay upset with him when he looks at me like that—with feral hunger and a tinge of fear, as though I'm a mirage that could disappear any moment.

"What? This old thing?" I slide my hands down my waist and over my hips, the lace of the garter belt tickling my palms.

"Take it off." His voice turns dark and silky, and a shiver runs down my spine. "Take it *all* off."

I clench my thighs at his rough command. I want to obey him . . . please him. With trembling hands, I unclasp my bra after two tries and shrug out of it. Then I dangle the lacy garment on my index finger before dropping it lightly on the floor.

A breath hisses through his teeth, but he doesn't touch me. Instead, he crosses his arms over his chest.

"Slower," he says, a muscle jumping in his jaw.

Bending at the waist, I trail my hands down one thigh and *slowly* free one dainty clip from my stocking. Spurred on by an unfamiliar instinct, I arch my back and raise my ass in the air as I free another one.

When I reach the last clip, I look at him from beneath my lashes before I unlatch it from my thigh-high. And holding his wild gaze, I roll the stocking down my leg, inch by agonizing inch, and step out of it.

"Shall I go on?" I sound like a siren, my voice husky and inviting.

Ethan gulps, then nods. I repeat with my other leg and stocking. *Gods, this is so hot.* Impatient for his touch, I straighten my back and reach for the clasp behind my garter belt.

"No." He finds his voice. "Leave that on."

"Okay." I drop my hands and stand before him in nothing but my lacy thong and garter belt.

For a moment, he clenches and unclenches his hands at his sides, like he's fighting an inner battle, and makes no move toward me. Then with careful, measured steps, he closes the distance between us until I can feel the heat coming off his towering frame.

He gently folds me into his arms and just holds me. A nice, innocent hug. I would think he wasn't affected by my striptease, if it weren't for the frantic beating of his heart and the press of his hard length against my stomach.

I melt against him and wait patiently. *Well, not quite patiently.* Our friends bought us time, but the world is about to end. We might actually not have time. I expect a knock at the door any minute now. But I need us to consummate this marriage. I want it fucking official that we are husband and wife. I want there to be no doubt that this male is mine.

"I'm going to make you feel good." His lips brush against the shell of my ear, and a trill runs down my spine. "Then I'm going to take you hard until you come around my cock, screaming my name."

"S-sounds like a plan," I stutter, aching with need, and gasp when Ethan lifts me into his arms.

He carries me to the sleeping mat and lowers me to the comforter. The cool silk feels decadent against my bare back, my senses heightened by my arousal, and the scent of roses fills my nostrils as they crush beneath me. I reach for him, greedy to touch him. But he evades my hand with a dark chuckle, grabbing me by the ankles instead.

"My turn first." He spreads my legs apart and settles his head between them. Before I can draw breath to argue, his hot mouth is on me, my thong pulled roughly to one side.

What was I going to argue about?

My body writhes as my orgasm builds low in my stomach. His wicked words had already gotten me halfway there, and it only takes a lick and a suckle for me to start falling apart. He lifts his head, his lips glistening with my desire, and he has the audacity to smirk at me.

"What? Don't stop." *Pride? What pride?* "Ethan, please."

He obliges with relish, only to pull back again when I'm at the precipice of release.

"What the fuck, Ethan?" I whimper, clutching the silk comforter in my fists. "You're asking for an ass kick—"

Oh gods.

His mouth finds me again, and I come undone. My hips arch off the mat, a silent scream hissing past my throat. As the aftershock of my climax rolls through me, Ethan plunges a long finger inside me, sliding in and out in an even tempo. I clench around him again and again in a slow descent. But before I can catch my breath, he adds another finger in me and sucks my clit into the warmth of his mouth.

"Ethan," I scream, the second orgasm plowing into me so hard that I see stars behind my eyes.

This time he eases me down, his thumbs drawing soothing circles on the inside of my thighs, and his smile is tender as he looks up at me. I lie limp on the bedding, my chest rising and falling like I've run a marathon. I release my punishing grip on his hair and haphazardly drop my arms by my head, like a wonky goal post.

Ethan lies on his side next to me and brushes my hair away from my face. "I should let you rest."

"Only if you have a death wish." I scowl at him despite my euphoric state. *This might be our last time.* "Stick to the plan, Lee. I don't need you taking it easy on me."

He chuckles and drops a kiss on my forehead. With a ferocious growl, I clamp my hand behind his neck and push off the sleeping mat to crush my lips against his. He smells like the earth and the wind, and I forget my ire and lose myself in the kiss.

I might mewl like a fucking kitten. Ethan either doesn't hear me or he chooses to ignore it. *Wise choice.* Besides, he's too busy devouring my mouth to care about anything else at the moment.

I put my hands on his chest but pout when I feel silk, not skin, beneath my palms. "Why are you still dressed?"

"Patience, wife," he murmurs against my lips, and I shiver beneath him. I will never tire of him calling me his wife.

"Fuck patience." I bite down on his lower lip, then lick it better. "Strip, husband."

"Bossy." Ethan leans back, his half-hooded eyes crinkling with amusement.

But he rises to a seat and shrugs his robe off, the muscles on his chest and shoulders working. I watch with blatant lust, my mouth watering. When he throws the robe halfway across the room and sits naked before me like a feast, I sit up and push him down onto the mat. I run my hands over the breadth of his chest and let my fingers bob over the contours of his abs.

"Beautiful," I whisper. Walking on my knees, I step between his legs. "And you're all mine."

I never dared dream of us getting married. It seemed too perfect, too impossible. But it happened. Now, I intend to claim him as my husband in every sense of the word.

"Sunny . . ."

"Shh. Let me look at you." I cock my head to the side and trace a finger down a purple vein on his jutting erection. "On second thought, I want you in my mouth."

"You don't have to—" he rasps.

Gripping his cock at the base, I wrap my mouth around him. *Gods, the head is so soft.* I drag my lips back and forth across the tip, and his legs jerk at my sides. I frown at the interruption and continue with my exploration.

I take him deep into my mouth, and his back arches off the mat. I instinctively rise and fall over him, letting my lips and tongue do what feels good to me. A mix of praise and profanity tumbles from his mouth. It must feel good for him too.

Then I become fixated with that silky head again. I suckle it and pop my lips over it like a sweet lollipop, then swirl my tongue on it. With a low growl, Ethan catapults upright and hauls me onto him, straddling my legs over his lap.

"Enough." He crushes his mouth against mine.

I hear the sound of my thong ripping off, but I'm too busy kissing him back to lament the loss. Then, gripping me by the hips, he lifts me up and brings me down on his hard length, pivoting his hips to bury himself inside me. I take him with ease, soft and wet from my orgasms and my playtime with his cock.

"Fuck me." He groans long and deep.

"I already am." I laugh, giddy with happiness. I love how well we fit together, how he stretches and fills me.

But after a heartbeat, I crave friction, and I ride him like a cowgirl subduing a bucking bull. I dig one hand into his slick shoulder and rake the other through my hair, down my neck, and over my aching breast. Ethan urges me to take him faster with his hands and hips until I whimper with pleasure bordering on pain.

"That's it." He drags his mouth over my jaw and suckles my sensitive earlobe. I pivot my hips, trying to relieve the pressure building in my clit. Knowing exactly what I need, he pushes the pad of his thumb against my throbbing nub and draws rough circles over it. "I got you, Sunny."

With a staccato of high-pitched screams, I clench around him as wave after wave of my orgasm crashes through me. When I finally float back down, I sag limply against him, my head flopping onto his shoulder. But he doesn't let me rest. He rises to his knees and spins me around so I'm standing on my knees as well.

"I need you to come for me again." He pants roughly in my ear.

"I can't." I'd slide down to the mat if he wasn't holding me up with a hard arm around my midriff.

"You can." He nudges my legs wider with his knee. "Come for me, Sunny."

"Okay," I breathe.

Ethan drives into me again. The change in position somehow lets me take him in deeper, and I feel another orgasm fluttering at the base of my spine and down to my core. His free hand comes to cup my breast, squeezing and kneading it, as he pistons in and out of me, setting an unrelenting pace.

"Harder," I moan. "Ethan, harder."

"Fuck," he growls and pushes me down until I'm on my hands and knees. His fingers dig into my waist. "Hang on."

"Yes." I arch my back and take him greedily. He pounds into me even faster and harder, and the room echoes with the sound of our skin slapping against each other. *"Yes."*

A part of me never wants our primal coupling to end, but the greedy part of me chases after another orgasm. Then, suddenly, I'm lying on my back. His hips still pumping, he wraps my legs around his waist and plants his hands on either side of my head, arms locked straight.

"Look at me," he says, both a command and a plea.

"Ethan." I meet his eyes and see silver-and-green fire flickering in them.

"You're mine." His dark voice rumbles in his chest, his hips jerking erratically. "Mine."

"As you are mine." White light flares in my chest, and I know my eyes are on fire. "I love you, Ethan."

"I love you." He kisses me with aching tenderness even as he continues taking me with wild hunger. "So much."

We climax together with twin cries of fulfillment, each of our gazes never leaving the other's. The threads of fate tighten around my heart, and I know I will never be untethered again. Even in death.

THE AMHEUK STIRS

Centuries after the Endless War, Hwanin, the god of Heavens; Yeomla, the god of Underworld; and Yongwang, the god of Water grew complacent in their duties, enjoying their decadent lives too much for moderation. And Hwanung, the god of Earth, poured all his love and attention into his family, neglecting to look after his people.

The gods, every one of them, convinced themselves that the shinbiins of the Realm of Four Kingdoms were powerful beings in their own right and did not need the gods' constant protection.

Then, on a fine day like any other, each god stilled in their kingdom, gripped by fear. Because they all felt it. The Amheuk was stirring beyond the abyss.

The four gods understood that combining their divine gi had the force of the Cheon'gwang—the only force strong enough to defeat the Amheuk—but it required a sacrifice none of them were willing to make.

The gods were not evil, but they were flawed with selfishness, greed, and cowardice. And when Hwanin devised a plan that required little sacrifice from them, Yongwang and Yeomla compromised their souls to cling on to the status quo that suited them so well.

CHAPTER FORTY-ONE

Sunny

Ethan spoons me from behind and pulls the comforter over us when the dreaded knock comes. He groans and buries his face against my neck. He doesn't seem surprised, though. Like me, he expected this to happen.

At least I got to make him officially and irrevocably mine.

"I am so sorry," Hailey yelps from outside. "But we couldn't buy you as much time as we wanted."

"That's okay." I speak loudly enough to be heard through the hanji-pasted doors. "We'll be right out."

"I-I'll go wait in the audience hall," she says. "I'm leaving some clothes out here for both of you. Just . . . hurry."

Ethan and I dress in the mortal clothes that Hailey left for us—me in my favorite all-black ensemble of a fitted top and jeans, and him in a white T-shirt and blue jeans. But even with the Shin'gwangdo strapped low on my waist, I feel far from prepared for an audience with the gods.

We rush into the audience hall, only to be greeted by stifling silence. And the gravity of the situation slams back into me with the force of a wrecking ball.

What did it cost our friends to buy us that hour?

Taeyoung, Gyun, Hailey, and Jihun stand in one cluster, and the rest of our group stands in another. Everyone looks weary and exhausted. I narrow my eyes in suspicion and turn my magic gi goggles on them.

Their life forces . . .

"What have you done?" I breathe.

"We reinforced the boundaries of the Kingdom of Sky," Jihun says matter-of-factly, as though they didn't nearly deplete their gi doing it.

I bite my cheeks to stop myself from berating every one of them, because . . . a small part of me knew what it meant for them to buy us time. I didn't realize they would sacrifice so much, but I knew there would be sacrifice. I glance at Ethan, who stands silently at my side, his expression grim.

Both of us knew.

Still, we let them do it. We couldn't refuse their heartfelt gift, so selflessly given. And we selfishly wanted that one moment to carry with us, no matter what lies ahead.

I will make it up to them. I will protect them with my life.

"What happened while we were . . . gone?" I ask, even as guilt twists my stomach. Something must've happened to cut our time short.

"The Amheuk is stirring," Taeyoung answers. "It is still daylight, but darkness is seeping into the Kingdom of Sky."

"Shit." I grab my forehead, and Ethan smooths his hand down my back. I meet his gaze and nod. "That's okay. We got this."

I turn to the Judge of Tenth Hell, the only one with his gi intact. The rest of our friends must have stopped him from contributing his life force—he wouldn't have sat out by choice—because he needs his full strength to teleport us on our . . . quest.

Our quest to find the sleeping gods so I can absorb their gi. I swallow the urge to laugh, as trepidation tightens my scalp. My instinct screams at me to run, but Minju said this was the only way. I can't let my friends down.

"So what's the weather like in purgatory?" I quip with false bravado. "I want to make sure I pack the right stuff."

The tension breaks in the room when Hailey bursts into laughter. And Gyun's gaze shoots toward her and stays there. She looks gorgeous in a pair of black yoga pants and a pale-pink T-shirt, so sheer that it hints at the black sports bra she's wearing underneath.

"You will feel neither too cold nor too hot," the judge says, reluctantly glancing away from Hailey. "You won't *feel* much at all. Purgatory is governed by its own unsettling rules."

"That sounds fun." I scowl at him for tanking the morale in the room an extra notch. "Not sinister at all."

"It is not particularly sinister either." Gyun shrugs his big shoulders, his tailored suit jacket shifting fluidly with his motion. "You will see when we get there."

While I mutter grumpily under my breath where the judge can shove his enigmatic reply, the Queen of Sky, Bora, Minju, Jaeseok, and Cheyun join us.

"When do we leave?" Ethan asks.

"Soon," Jihun says grimly, even for him. "Every shinbiin willing and ready to fight has been dispatched to protect the perimeter of the Kingdom of Sky. But once the Amheuk forces its way inside, we won't be able to hold it off for long."

"We'll be back in time," I assure him—a bold statement, considering I have no idea what awaits us in purgatory. *But in for a penny, in for a pound, and all that.* "With reinforcements."

"Sunny." Minju steps hesitantly to my side and whispers, "There is more you need to know."

"Of course there is." I force a wry chuckle. "I don't suppose this can wait . . ."

"No, I must tell you before you leave," she insists, then turns to the others. "I need to borrow Sunny for five minutes. We will not be long."

Too many pairs of eyes turn toward us, and I'm suddenly desperate for air.

"I guess we're doing this now." With a resigned sigh, I tuck her hand in the crook of my elbow and head toward the doors. "Let's talk outside."

Ethan raises his head from his conversation with Taeyoung, and I mouth, *Be right back.*

We stroll to the pond in the courtyard in subdued silence. I stare out at the water, trying to give Minju time to work up the courage to tell me whatever it is she needs to tell me. But my heart trips and stumbles in my chest, and my stomach wraps itself into an anxious knot.

"Let me guess," I blurt. *How bad can it be?* "If I absorb the life force of the gods, I might die?"

"Yes." Minju flaps her hand like that's a foregone conclusion. "But it can be so much worse."

"So much . . . worse?" I gulp. *Worse than dying?*

"No mortal being, even one nearly immortal, can absorb the gi of a god and survive." The historian taps her chin in full nerd mode. She doesn't realize she's telling me—her dear friend—that I'm *for sure* going to die. "Never mind the gi of all *four* gods."

"Interesting." I copy her chin tapping, but she doesn't even catch my teasing. *Well, that's no fun.* I can't even rely on my snark to distract me from the blood-draining sense of doom. "But that just means I'll die, like we already discussed. What do you mean *it can be so much worse*?"

"The thing is you might *not* die," she continues, making that sound like a bad thing. "At least, not until you destroy the worlds."

"Until I do *what*?" My knees go weak.

"Because of the Yeoiju, you might be the one mortal being in all the worlds who can absorb the gi of the four gods." She paces back and forth, gesturing with her hands. "But controlling such power is an entirely different matter. And if you lose control . . ."

My breath comes in rough pants. *Oh gods.* I need to know, but I don't want to know.

Minju stops pacing and meets my eyes, finally seeing me. "Oh, Sunny."

"Tell me." I dig my nails into my palms, clenching my back teeth.

"You might burn down the Realm of Four Kingdoms," she whispers, "*and* the Mortal Realm. You will be . . . unstoppable."

Now I understand what can be worse than dying. *That.* Stopping the Amheuk will be meaningless if *I* bring about the end of the worlds.

And everything comes full circle.

"I want to hear the prophecy of the End of Days," I rasp.

"Prophecies don't have to come true—"

"*What* does it say?" She backs away at my tone, and I bite my lip. *Get your shit together, Sunny.* "I'm sorry, Minju. Please tell me. I need to know."

My friend takes a shuddering breath and recites:

Darkness takes its final breath,
Double dragons reunite.

Fierce shall jade and silver burn,
The truth of tears and blood unchained.

Blinding sorrow extinguish dreams,
Hope shines forth, the unveiled pearl.

The true heart of the righteous shall
Shatter the light that reveals all paths.

Ethan and I are the double dragons. We were both born in the year of the dragon—one hundred and eight years apart. And by breaking his jade necklace, he unchained the truth of his mother's blood and tears, along with his silver-and-green magic.

The Yeoiju, of course, is the unveiled pearl. I bitched and moaned about being the last hope to save the worlds, but a secret part of me was

. . . proud. I always feared that I was the bad guy, but the Yeoiju gave me hope that I *could* be the good guy after all—the good guy who saved the whole freaking world.

But I had it all wrong, didn't I?

"And I presume 'the righteous' in the final verse refers to Ethan?" I ask woodenly, even though I already know the answer.

"I-I believe so." Minju's chin trembles as tears rain down her cheeks.

I know so because I remember the last verse of the prophecy of the King Foretold:

Brave is the King who discerns,
Path of truth from path of shame.

When Ethan broke the stone of tears, his mother's memory revealed the prophecy of the End of Days to him. That's why he told me at Heaven Lake that he is the one destined to kill me. Even then, he understood who he was—the righteous king who discerns the path of truth. But he didn't understand *why* he has to kill me.

I do, though.

When the time comes, he and his true heart will know what to do. He will kill me before I burn down the Realm of Four Kingdoms and the Mortal Realm. He will understand that I would rather die than become the destroyer of the worlds—the death of everyone I love.

"Stop being a crybaby, Minju." I wipe away her tears with the pads of my thumbs. "I know what must be done. Everything will be okay."

Because I understand now.

My destiny is to become the End of Days. And Ethan is meant to be my salvation.

CHAPTER FORTY-TWO

Sunny

Ethan catches my gaze when Minju and I return to the audience hall, raising his brows in question. I widen my eyes innocently and offer him a closed-mouth smile.

I'll tell him everything when it's time. No matter what, he will be by my side through it all. I will not be alone, even in death. Especially in death.

Forgive me, Ethan.

"Is everyone ready then?" Gyun asks.

"I'm ready." Hailey nods, calm and determined.

"My king." Jihun bows formally to Ethan, then raises his head with a wry quirk of his lips. "Try not to die."

"I'll do my best." Ethan claps him on the shoulder, grinning back at him.

I honestly can't get enough of the bromance between these two. I'm so happy they have each other.

Then Jihun turns to me and bows, a fist over his heart. "My queen."

I had his loyalty before I became the queen, but now he has sworn his allegiance to me. I was grateful then, and I am grateful now.

"Thank you." My chest aches, and I hold my breath without realizing it. Jihun clicks his tongue and wraps his arms around me. I exhale and say in a tremulous voice, "For everything."

"Be safe." He gently sets me away from him.

Cheyun and Minju take turns hugging me and Hailey. Even Bora hugs me. I hate goodbyes, but I linger over this one. I am definitely stalling.

Fuck this.

I have a long way to go till the finish line. I can only jump one hurdle at a time.

"Let's get on with it." I work my features into a bad-tempered scowl, but Ethan looks at me like I'm the cutest thing and kisses the tip of my nose. And I further undermine my badassery by making heart eyes at him. I catch myself and clear my throat. "How far is purgatory, Gyun?"

"I wouldn't say it's far at all," he says enigmatically, then turns to Hailey. "Are you all right?"

She's chugging water straight from the teapot, hydrating in preparation for expending her jeoseungsaja powers. Generating all that creepy fog around her really wrings her dry.

"Mm-hmm." She pulls the spout out of her mouth. "Why do you ask?"

"No reason." The judge looks so bemused that I have to bite my lips not to cackle. With a sharp shake of his head, he holds his arms out to me and Ethan. "Your Majesties."

My husband obliges without hesitation and seems perfectly at ease when Gyun wraps a beefy arm around his waist. Ethan has never been prone to masculine posturing—males with true confidence generally don't bother with that nonsense.

I have no idea why, but I salute the Queen of Sky and the King of Underworld—probably because I didn't get to hug them goodbye—then step into Gyun's free arm. From the judge's other side, Ethan catches my gaze and mouths, *I love you.* And like a sap, I mouth back, *I love you too.*

Ignoring our admittedly cringy exchange, Gyun nods at Hailey, and she promptly switches to her grim reaper mode.

Her skin leaches of color, her eyes glow red, and her hair floats around her like sinister shadows. Then she rises off the floor on a cloud of icy fog. Her transformation is so fast and so sudden that I can't hold back my horror-queen scream. I clap a hand over my mouth and squeeze my eyes shut.

"Here we go," the Judge of Tenth Hell says.

We levitate into the air, then that eerie sensation of not existing shrouds me. I would shudder if I could feel my body.

"We're here." Gyun drops his arm from my waist.

"How?" I open my eyes and take in my surroundings. "Even moving through the Kingdom of Underworld took longer than this. And if we're really here, then why do I still feel . . . unreal?"

We *are* somewhere, though, because I'm standing on wood floors . . . in a large room . . . I stumble back half a step. It's the audience hall at the Celestial Palace.

But everything looks faded and washed out—nearly transparent. And there isn't anyone here but us. Our friends, who had just been surrounding us, are gone.

I don't like this.

"*This* is purgatory?" Ethan spins in a slow circle. "And I agree with Sunny. I still feel like I'm fading away. My consciousness is intact, and I'm still me, but I don't feel . . . alive."

"That's because purgatory is the in-between place dividing life and death," Hailey explains, back to her beautiful self. I breathe a sigh of relief. *At least there's that.* "This is where souls who lose their way come."

"Like the stranded?" I flip my hands back and forth to make sure I'm not as see-through as I feel.

"No." Gyun motions for us to follow him out of the audience hall. "The stranded are truly dead. Their han merely holds them back from moving on to their next life. Whereas the souls here are neither dead nor alive."

"How does that happen?" Ethan asks.

"When someone is severely injured in a traumatic incident—like car accidents, natural disasters, wars—their souls sometimes get lost in purgatory, while their bodies lie in a coma." Hailey shakes her head. "They have to find the courage to wake up and continue living or let go and move on to their next life. Until they make their choice, they remain in limbo here."

"Poor souls." I shiver.

"And the longer they stay," Gyun picks up, "the harder it becomes to choose—to remember—because there is no time in purgatory."

"No . . . time?" I follow him into the phantom streets of the Kingdom of Sky.

"There can be no passage of time without life or death," the judge says as we round a corner.

"Whoa." I stumble to a stop. "Are we in the Kingdom of Underworld?"

"Yes, the capital." Gyun glances around him as though he, too, is surprised by the sudden shift. "As you can see, space becomes jumbled here as well."

"Then how do you know where we're going?" Ethan's brows dip as he takes in the faded metropolis.

"I am the Judge of Tenth Hell. I know the Ten Hells and purgatory like the back of my hand." Gyun then concedes, "Even so, finding my way here is not easy."

We trudge through the deserted streets in grim silence. After five minutes or three hours—I can't tell for the life of me—the modern city abruptly shifts into a wide open field. Hailey gasps at my side, and I grab her hand as my pulse spikes. Purgatory is a creepy-ass place.

"That's going to take some getting used to," Ethan mutters.

"It is rather jarring." Gyun scans the field, then does an about-face. He squints into the distance, then nods in satisfaction. "This way."

"If you say so." I follow our guide, tugging Ethan close. I do not want to get lost here. "How did you find the gods anyway?"

"When the gods of Underworld, Water, and Heavens arrived in purgatory, they put themselves into a deep sleep to hide their presence," the judge answers without slowing down. My short legs work double time to keep up with his long ones. "But even in slumber, a trace of their magic leaked through. I didn't understand what I was sensing for a long time—this place distorted their magic beyond recognition—until I came upon the first sleeping god."

I nod, out of breath from marching across the desolate field that stretches on endlessly. "Are we even going in the right—"

"Whoa." Ethan skids to a stop, shooting an arm out in front of me. A sheer cliff had appeared out of nowhere.

Gyun points toward the horizon. "Yeomla, the god of Underworld, sleeps there."

"There's nothing there." I squint, following the trajectory of his finger. But as soon as the words leave my mouth, I see a long, dry river snaking through a rocky landscape. And a lone, thatch-roofed hanok stands along the curving path. "What is that place?"

"It's the Tea Shop," the judge murmurs. "Or the shadow of it, at least."

"*The* Tea Shop?" Ethan arches an eyebrow. "The one where they serve the tea of forgetfulness?"

"It sure looks like it. In a creepy, washed-out way. The real Tea Shop is quite charming." Hailey rises to the tips of her toes for a better look. "But why would Yeomla choose to sleep there?"

Gyun reaches toward her but catches himself and drops his hands back to his sides. "Maybe he was being sentimental."

"Or maybe he did something he wanted to forget," I murmur. "If that's the case, it must be something truly awful. If an immortal god messes up, they gotta mess up big time."

"Do you think it wise to awaken such a remorseful god?" an echoing voice whispers in my ear.

I spin around with a gasp . . . but there's no one there.

"Sunny." Ethan grasps my arm. "What is it?"

"I . . ." I shake my head. "I thought I heard someone . . ."

"What did they say?" Worry pinches his brows.

"They wanted to know if it was wise to awaken a remorseful god," I whisper, wondering if I'm losing my mind.

"Well," the voice drawls, "do you?"

This time all four of us whip around to face the most terribly beautiful being, floating naked in the air. I throw a hand up to shield my eyes from his brilliance but squint to peek through my fingers.

Liquid ribbons of vibrant red fabric whip through the air, draping over his shoulders and wrapping around his torso and legs. By the time his feet touch the ground, he is dressed in a resplendent, ruby-red robe.

"Because personally"—he brushes imaginary dirt off his shoulder and walks toward us—"I think it would be a bad idea."

Gyun drops to his knees and presses his forehead against the ground, his dark, powerful voice unsteady as he says, "Lord Yeomla."

The god of Underworld.

CHAPTER FORTY-THREE

Sunny

I drop to my knees, tugging frantically on Ethan's sleeve. Even after absorbing his mother's memories to learn the ways of the Shingae, he still lacks the healthy dose of fear and respect the rest of us bear toward the gods. At my continued urging, he places one knee on the ground, then the next, but he does not bow his head.

"The King Foretold, I presume." Lord Yeomla directs a mildly interested gaze toward Ethan. "I suppose it is useful for the long-awaited king to have backbone."

The god flicks his fingers in the air, as though chasing away a fruit fly, and Ethan falls to his hands with a grunt. His neck muscles straining, Ethan struggles to raise his head far enough to glare at Yeomla.

"And strong too." The god of Underworld purses his lips with reluctant respect. "You are rather impressive, but I must teach you some manners."

Ethan growls, but I cover his hand with mine and whisper, "This is not a fight you can win."

"Yes, listen to your . . ." Lord Yeomla pauses to consider me. "She is so many things to you, isn't she? Your friend, your fated love, your queen, your . . . ruination."

"Enough." I glare at the god, forgetting my own advice. "We are not here to play your games."

"No." He forces my head back down by crooking his pinky. "I suppose you are not."

"Lord Yeomla," Gyun intercedes. "The Realm of Four Kingdoms is in great peril. The Amheuk—"

"The one thing I do not understand is . . ." the god of Underworld interrupts, tapping his chin with a long, elegant finger. "How did the Amheuk breach the Realm of Four Kingdoms? No dark magic, including the eternal darkness, could have withstood the Gray Void. We fueled its magic with the han of the stranded—a force that grows even more powerful through suffering."

"We?" I jerk my head up, the Yeoiju flaring in my chest. "You had a part in entrapping those countless stranded souls in there?"

Yeomla's eyes widen with surprise, either over the glimpse of my power or over my insolence. Then, for the first time since his appearance, a hint of solemnity infuses the god's expression.

"We four gods do not have the luxury of playing the hero," he says. "It is our duty to protect the realms, and the Gray Void was the only way to stop the return of the Amheuk."

"At the expense of all those souls?" I persist. *There must have been another way.*

"We did what we had to do." He motions for us to rise, and our bodies obey before our minds can catch up. "Which brings me back to my question, how did our foolproof plan fail?"

"I destroyed the Gray Void." Satisfaction flashes through me at the shock on Yeomla's mind-bogglingly perfect face.

"*You* destroyed the only defense against the Amheuk?" He narrows his eyes on me, and terror floods my veins. "And what? You came here to ask for my help? To fix *your* mistake?"

"It was not a mistake," I declare, even though I'm far from certain I mean that.

If I had known my survival meant the destruction of the Gray Void, would I have chosen to die? Would I have left the stranded imprisoned in their endless suffering?

I'll never know.

But what is done is done. The past cannot be changed. I can only move forward.

"Lord Yeomla." I aim for a more respectful tone. "We do need your help."

"I already did everything I can to help." Disdain twists his beautiful lips.

"Is it not your duty *still* to protect the realms?" Ethan steps closer to me, laying a protective hand on my back.

"There is nothing more I can do." The god of Underworld shrugs, turning up his nose. I am sorely tempted to break that pretty nose.

"Lord Yeomla." Gyun bows with due deference, then straightens to his full, considerable height and breadth. "We know you can do more."

"Do you, now? Let me rephrase my answer," Yeomla drawls. "There is nothing more I am *willing* to do."

"But are we not your people?" Hailey blurts. "How can you be so selfish?"

"I am a god." His voice thunders, making the ground shake beneath us. "I can be whatever I want, my pretty saja."

"Do not speak to her that way," the Judge of Tenth Hell warns in a dangerously soft voice.

"Or what?" Yeomla cocks his head. "I grow tired of this nonsense."

"We are not asking you to fight with us." I rush to explain before he disappears to take another century-long nap. "We only need a part of your gi—"

"A *part* of my gi?" The god scoffs, something like fear flickering in his expression. "You do not know what you ask. Now, be *gone*."

"I'm not going—" My objection gets lodged in my throat as I'm sucked in through a straw. Or at least, it feels that way. Then, before I can scream, I'm spat back out.

"Wh-what happened?" I stumble, and Ethan catches me by the elbow.

Even when I regain my balance, he doesn't let go. Instead, he slides his palm down my arm and laces our fingers together. And I need the reassuring warmth of his touch because . . . we are in a barren desert, made bleaker by the nearly colorless world surrounding us.

Shit.

The god of Underworld didn't disappear. He *disappeared* us.

"I have never felt so ashamed to be a being of Underworld," Hailey huffs. "Are you guys okay?"

"Yeah, I think so." I nod. "Where the hell are we anyway? Which kingdom has a desert?"

"We are not in a desert," Gyun answers. "We are in the Kingdom of Water."

"Where?" Ethan spins in a circle. "There isn't a drop of water here, much less a kingdom of it."

"That river in the Kingdom of Underworld was bone dry as well," Hailey murmurs, pursing her lips.

"Maybe Yongwang, the god of Water, is using purgatory's water as his blanky," I joke.

"Something like that." Gyun walks out to the cracked earth that used to be the ocean. "I believe Lord Yongwang went to sleep in his dragon form, in the only body of water left in purgatory."

"What body of water?" I ask.

"You will see," he says in a deep voice.

I scowl at his enigmatic back as we follow the Judge of Tenth Hell out to the dry ocean and trek on for what feels like hours. Our landscape changes back and forth between the four kingdoms, but we unfailingly end up back here, with nothing but the salted earth as far as the eye can see.

"Are we there yet?" I whine for the eleventh time.

Gyun mutters unintelligibly under his breath, and Hailey giggles at his side.

"Are you getting tired?" Ethan says close to my ear. "I can carry you."

"We should've brought a palanquin," I grumble crossly, then I blush like a beet, recalling a *particular* palanquin ride.

With a knowing grin, Ethan runs his hand down my back and slides his thumb beneath the hem of my shirt. "I can always go for a palanquin ride."

I lose my chance at a sexy comeback when his thumb finds the shallow valley dissecting my back, drawing lazy circles right above the waist of my jeans. A shiver runs through me, and his eyes darken.

Distracted by the desire singing between us, we walk straight into a wall of . . . water. We stumble back before steadying each other. Then our gazes trace the length of the dark-blue wall from the bottom to the top, until it disappears into the sky.

"Holy Moses." I glance down at myself, expecting to find my clothes soaking wet. But I don't have a single drop of water on me.

My gaze returns to the wall in front of us. Its surface isn't smooth like glass but churns tumultuously. It is a living, breathing vertical ocean. A shaky breath leaks out of me. I'm terrified the unforgiving sea might swallow us whole if we so much as blink wrong.

But does my Ethan blink wrong? *Nooo.* He just reaches out and fucking *touches* the wall of water.

"Why the hell would you do that?" I slap his hand away.

"I . . ."

Before he can defend himself, the ocean comes crashing down from the sky with a furious roar.

CHAPTER FORTY-FOUR

Ethan

I pull Sunny into my arms and curve my body around her, even as her thunderstruck question rings in my head. *Why the hell would you do that?* That is a valid question, but I don't have a good answer to it.

It makes no sense, but the wall of water reminded me of Draco, and I reached toward it before I realized what I was doing.

Fucking hell.

If Sunny gets hurt because of me, I'm going to kick my own ass. This must be the most brainless, impulsive thing I've ever done.

Even as I berate myself, I brace for impact. But . . . the ocean doesn't crash down on us. I don't even feel a spray of water. And after another nerve-racking second, I peek out with one eye, then the other one shoots open.

The wall . . . It's gone.

After another beat of taut silence, Sunny squirms in my arms, and I gingerly release her. I stay alert, scanning the dry, cracked ocean around us. The hair stands on the back of my neck. The churning ocean might be gone, but the danger isn't. *Far from it.*

"Can you put me down?" Hailey asks in a muffled voice. The Judge of Tenth Hell holds her aloft in his arms, his head bent protectively over hers.

"Guh." He drops her to the ground so abruptly that Hailey stumbles. With a sharp yelp, he reaches out and steadies her by the waist, then he drops his hands as though she burned him. Fumbling to straighten his sunglasses, he mutters, "My apologies. I do not know what came over me."

I turn to Sunny to share a knowing smile, but something else holds her attention. She's gaping at the sky with her head tipped back. Her parted lips wobble and tears leak from the corners of her eyes. Trepidation shortening my breath, I follow her line of sight.

Draco.

Sharp, searing grief slams into my chest, and my throat tightens with unshed tears. The serpentine dragon undulating above us is far larger than Draco, and several shades darker, but I can't help but see the kid in the god of Water.

Sunny must see it too.

Not trusting my voice, I take her hand and squeeze it tight. Her fingers feel like ice. She stares at Yongwang for a second longer, then she buries her face in my chest with a broken sob.

"I'm so sorry, Sunny." I wrap my arms around her and kiss the top of her head. "Gods, I'm sorry. I know how much they meant to you."

She cries as though a dam broke inside her. I gather her close so she can grieve for the kid. She's held her heartbreak at bay for long enough. Both she and Draco deserve this moment before she lets them go.

With a mournful sigh, I tuck her head under my chin and rub her back. Even in grief, I want her to know she is not alone. My chest constricts so tightly that I can hardly breathe. I wouldn't be holding Sunny in my arms if it wasn't for Draco.

But why did it have to be them? They were just a kid. A good kid.

Gratitude, guilt, and sorrow claw at my throat, and I tighten my arms around Sunny. It hurts, but we'll hurt together.

"Your Majesty," the Judge of Tenth Hell murmurs. "The god of Water—"

"Can wait a moment longer," I cut him off.

"I have an eternity at my disposal," a voice like the roar of waves rumbles above us, "but you do not have a moment to spare."

I glare up at the dragon, holding Sunny closer.

"Ethan, it's all right." She pushes against my chest and runs the back of her hand across her eyes. "I'll be okay."

I keep my gaze trained on Yongwang as I reluctantly drop my arms from around her. Then she faces the god of Water—with me standing at her back.

"Lord Yongwang, do you know why we seek you?" Sunny rasps, her throat raw from tears.

"Yes." The god descends in a cyclone of water to stand before us in his human form, wearing a long, flowing gown of darkest blue.

"But you won't help us." Sunny sighs, rubbing her forehead wearily. "Why?"

"Perhaps I lack your futile courage." Condescension warps his handsome face. "Or your unrelenting hope."

"What are we without hope? You must see that daunting odds are better than certain death. Please, Lord Yongwang." She drops to her knees, and I follow her to the ground. Hailey and Gyun kneel as well, adding their own silent pleas. "If I must die, I want to go down fighting for life rather than waiting docilely for death. I want to fight it with hopeful desperation, rather than surrender to it with helpless fear. Death comes for everyone, but I will decide how I meet it."

"You are"—the god cocks his head, interest sparking in his eyes—"wholly unexpected."

"My wife *is* extraordinary." I manage to keep my tone civil, even as my jaw clenches. In his human form, the god of Water looks nothing like Draco. I would feel no compunction punching his freakishly handsome face, if he doesn't stop ogling Sunny. "But she speaks for all of us in the Realm of Four Kingdoms. We will not go down without a fight."

"*All* of you?" Yongwang deigns to address me.

"Yes, Lord Yongwang," Gyun responds in my stead, with a nervous glance my way. "His Majesty has united the four kingdoms. We, all of us, will follow our king and queen wherever they lead us."

"This indeed intrigues me." The god of Water resumes watching Sunny, and a warning growl slips past my lips. "I cannot share my life force with you, but I will fight at your side."

"That won't be enough to save the realm," I object from the ground, my hands fisting on my bent knees.

"It's okay, Ethan." She gives Yongwang a flat stare. "It's gotta be better than nothing."

The Judge of Tenth Hell makes a choking sound, kneeling next to us.

"Thank you, Lord Yongwang," Hailey rushes to say. "We are grateful for your generosity."

"I have never seen such disrespect." The god of Water gives a bemused shake of his head. "Perhaps the gods have slumbered for too long. The people need to be reminded of our might. Isn't that right, Yeomla?"

"I suppose," a disembodied voice answers before the god of Underworld materializes at Yongwang's side, his red robe flowing artfully in the air. "But it is unlike you to be swayed by a pretty face, old friend."

"It isn't her beauty that compels me, but the strength of her spirit," the god of Water murmurs, his gaze roaming over Sunny. "I have never seen anyone more vibrant—more full of life—than this gumiho."

"And she may have met her equal in her fated mate," Yeomla says with a meaningful glance my way.

"I merely strive to deserve her." I bow my head to the god of Underworld, grateful for his unexpected support.

"It will serve you well to remember, Yongwang," he continues as though I haven't spoken. *So much for support.* "Even a god cannot separate lovers bound by the threads of fate."

"I have not forgotten." The god of Water shrugs with careless grace, and I narrow my eyes at him. "But you must admit it is exciting to find someone unique and surprising after all our years."

"Indeed." Yeomla studies Sunny too closely for my comfort. *These fucking gods.* "Even so, it will be best to employ the *look but don't touch* policy with this one."

I try very hard to remember that I cannot take on a god, much less two, and walk away with my life intact. The problem is I'm starting not to care.

"*This one*"—Sunny raises a finger then points it at her ear—"can hear you."

Yongwang and Yeomla exchange startled glances, as though asking each other, *Did she really just say that to us?* I cover my triumphant laugh with a hacking cough. I might not be able to take on two gods, but my wife certainly can.

"You may all rise," Yongwang says with as much dignity as he can muster. Then he gazes into the horizon, striving for godly gravitas. "We have a long way to go."

"We?" Gyun asks, rising to his feet with the rest of us.

"You do know where Hwanin slumbers, do you not?" Yeomla manages to look down his nose at the taller male.

Before the Judge of Tenth Hell can respond, Yongwang sweeps his long blue sleeve through the air and transports us without warning. I hold Sunny's hand in an iron grip as we shrink and expand, dissipate and solidify, all at once.

"Hwanin has hidden so deeply that even we cannot sense him," Yeomla murmurs when the four of us land on solid ground, fighting for our balance. "We will rely on your guidance, Judge of Tenth Hell."

The gods brought us to a faded version of the Kingdom of Sky, where everything is muted and blurry, like June Gloom settled over purgatory.

"I will do my best." Gyun bows to the two gods before leading the way. Then he nods at us over his shoulder. "It will be another taxing search."

"Where exactly is the god of Heavens?" Hailey asks, falling into step next to the judge.

"There is no particular landmark to indicate Lord Hwanin's sanctuary." He pauses to glance down at her. "But we will know when we get there."

"Must you always be so enigmatic?" Hailey side-eyes him.

"No, not always," Gyun answers enigmatically.

I plant my hand on Sunny's hip and pull her close to my side. She rolls her eyes at me, but her mouth curls into a pleased smile. I grin back at her like a lovesick fool, and we set out to play hide-and-seek with yet another god.

Too bad we're always *It*.

CHAPTER FORTY-FIVE

Sunny

How long have we been walking?

We have long since grown silent, too exhausted to talk. I trudge on, staring down at the ground, sick of purgatory's jarring changes of scenery—one minute in the Kingdom of Sky and the next minute in another kingdom.

I am both impatient and afraid to find Hwanin, the god of Heavens. If he agrees to share his gi with me, I will be one step closer to my death. But if he refuses, we are all doomed. My life in exchange for the lives of every other being in the worlds is more than a fair trade.

Then why does it feel so unfair?

The watery daylight shuts off without warning. We stumble to a halt and stand in the pitch black of a moonless night. Ethan's hand tightens around my waist, and my heart melts at his protectiveness.

I can only see the silvery-green light of his beautiful life force, but I don't need to see his face to know that I am cherished. As unfair as it seems, I am truly blessed. When it comes time for him to save me from becoming the End of Days, I will die knowing I am loved beyond anything.

"We are here," Gyun announces.

"This is rather dramatic of Hwanin," the god of Water murmurs.

"And a wall of churning ocean isn't?" Yeomla shoots back at him.

I'm beginning to like the god of Underworld. He's an asshole, to be sure, but at least he owns it.

"Why is nothing happening?" Hailey whispers. "This is usually when the gods make their grand entrance."

"I know, right?" I hover a grapefruit-sized ball of light over my palm. "Maybe this will wake him up."

Ethan gasps when my light orb illuminates purgatory's version of his mother's garden. "Why would Hwanin choose to sleep here?"

"It reminds me of Mountains." A lone figure with long silver hair stands, facing the waterless pond. "It reminds me of my son. Of my grandson."

I disperse the light as the unrelenting night fades into a colorless day. When the god of Heavens turns to face us, his face is unlined and ageless—eerily beautiful like the other gods. But the desolation in his eyes almost makes me regret waking him up from the oblivion of sleep.

"Lord Hwanin." I hesitate. "W-we come to plead for your help."

"You do not know what you ask, child." He holds my gaze with an intensity that dries out my mouth. "Absorbing my life force might kill you."

Ethan tenses at my side. *I'm so sorry.* I can't bear to look at him, because my next words will hurt him even more.

"But it's the only way," I plead.

"You . . . knew?" Ethan drops his hand from my waist, then steps back from me.

"Ethan—"

"Don't." He cuts me off, a muscle working in his jaw.

"If I don't try, it means certain death. For *all* of us," I explain anyway. "This is our only chance at a different outcome."

I can't tell him that it means certain death for me either way. *Not yet.* At least, if this works, Ethan will live. My friends will live. The Realm of Four Kingdoms will survive.

My life for the life of everyone.

It really is more than fair, but he won't see it that way. I know because I wouldn't trade him for all the worlds.

"I will not lose you." His voice breaks, and a fissure runs down my heart. "I can't. I won't—"

I crush my lips against his, holding his face between my hands. For a heartbeat, he stands as still as stone before he kisses me back with desperation . . . and devastation. He understands. He knows I have to try.

My kind, noble Ethan.

"You won't lose me," I whisper against his lips. "You will never lose me because I am your heart. As long as it beats, I will be with you."

After another hard kiss, he raises his head. "Better yet. Just fucking live, Sunny. Promise me you'll live."

"I promise."

I'm not full of shit. I know I can absorb Hwanin's life force without dying—I can absorb the gi of all four gods and live. *You know how I know?* Because fate is a sick motherfucker. I'll survive so I can die at the hands of my fated love.

My blood thunders in my ears, and light tremors skate down my limbs. I am terrified of the gods, but I'm getting tired of all their hemming and hawing. And honestly? I have zero fucks to give at this point.

I address the god of Heavens. "I know exactly what I'm asking for. Will you share your gi with me if I'm willing to risk dying for it, Lord Hwanin? Or is your *concern* just an excuse to hoard your mighty powers?"

"I will share my gi with you," the silver-haired god answers.

"You . . ." I did not expect that.

"Hwanin," Yeomla interjects, alarm skittering across his face. "Are you certain?"

"Of course he is not certain," Yongwang hisses. The god of Water narrows his eyes into angry slits, his dragon looking out from within. "Hwanin, you will do no such thing."

"The atrocity we have committed . . ." The god of Heavens slowly shakes his head. "We must right our wrongs. We must try."

What atrocity? What wrongs? What the hell are they talking about?

"We did what had to be done to protect the—" Yongwang blusters.

"We were *not* trying to protect anyone but ourselves," Hwanin roars, and lightning flickers in the gray sky. He breathes through his nose and continues in a subdued voice, "In the end, even a god is but one soul. The same as every being we must protect."

"Then let us wait until we find Dangun," the god of Water says in a placating tone, trying a different tactic. "We all four must do this in order for it to work."

"We do not need to find my grandson." Hwanin raises his chin. "I already know where the god of Mountains dwells."

"We did not part in the best of ways," Yongwang mutters darkly. "He might not want to have anything to do with us."

"That is why I must share my gi with this child. Only she can go to Dangun." The god of Heavens steps close to me. "He will listen to her. He *must* listen to her and help us right our wrongs."

There they go with the *wrongs* again. *What wrongs?* I open my mouth to ask, but the gods aren't done yapping yet.

"*Can* we right our wrongs?" Anguish lines Yeomla's words. "Can we be . . . forgiven?"

"No, we cannot be forgiven." Hwanin deflates before our eyes. "But I grow weary of running from the guilt. Do you not? This time, we can choose to do the right thing."

"There will be consequences." Yongwang runs an unsteady hand through his hair. "Consequences that cannot be undone."

"And those consequences will be our salvation," Hwanin says.

What consequences?

"With all due respect," I snap, my nerves stretched taut, "what the fuck are you guys talking about?"

Silence descends on us like a soaked blanket. When every shocked gaze zeroes in on me, the blood drains from my face.

I might have gone too far.

"You know," Yeomla observes wryly, flicking invisible dirt off his red robe, "saying 'with all due respect' does not make what you just said respectful."

My breath wheezes out of me.

"Yes, quite." Yongwang's lips quirk in a ghost of a smile. "We would smite you on the spot if you weren't so essential."

"Uh, thank you?" I *think* he's joking. It's a tiny bit reassuring that the gods have a sense of humor. "Wh-what happens now?"

"Are you ready to receive my life force?" the god of Heavens asks almost kindly.

"I . . ." My terrified gaze shoots to Ethan. He squeezes my hand, nodding once, and I take a steadying breath. "I am ready, Lord Hwanin."

"Stand back." The god of Underworld flaps his flowing red sleeve at Hailey, Gyun, and Ethan. "The power they generate will burn you alive, starting with your eyes. Keep them closed. You cannot look at them until this is over. Is that understood?"

"Yes, Lord Yeomla," Gyun answers.

Hailey sends a worried glance my way before consenting. "Yes."

"And you?" Yeomla arches a perfect brow at Ethan.

"I will do as instructed"—Ethan narrows his eyes at the god of Underworld—"unless Sunny needs me. Then, I will do whatever is necessary to protect her."

"Ethan—" I croak, preparing to beg him to stop.

"Are you asking me to do nothing even if you're in danger?" He cuts me off, his voice as rough as gravel. "You cannot be so cruel."

It would be cruel of me. I press my lips together to keep them from trembling. I can't ask him to do something that I would never be able to do.

"I'll stand back and keep my eyes shut." He closes the distance between us. "But if you need me, you have to promise to ask for me. Please, Sunny."

"I promise." I nod, my heart bleeding for both of us.

"Thank you." Ethan presses his forehead against mine, cradling the back of my head with his big, warm hand.

His unsteady sigh brushes against my lips, and I shift my weight to my toes. But before I can kiss him, he spins on his heels and joins Hailey and Gyun off to the side. It's probably for the best because three somber-faced gods stand waiting for me.

I walk toward them, and the god of Heavens meets me halfway. "Are you able to summon the Yeoiju at will, child?"

"You mean like this?" I hold out my palm and float a plum-sized white orb above it.

"Not externally." He shakes his head with a frown. "We cannot pool my life force outside of your body. It is much too dangerous. You need to collect it *inside* you before you fully absorb it."

"Oh." I curl my fingers over my palm and extinguish the white orb. Then I close my eyes and listen, until warmth gathers in my chest and my Yeoiju hums inside me. I meet his gaze again. "You mean like this."

"Yes." Something close to wonder replaces his frown. "Just like that."

"W-will it hurt?" I whisper.

"More than you can imagine. But once I begin, I cannot stop until I have transferred all of my divine gi to you," he says gravely. "If the transfer is interrupted, it will kill us both. If you die during the transfer, I will die as well. The only way for us to survive is to complete the transfer."

"Well, we better complete it then," I grit out.

He reaches toward me, but when I flinch, he snatches his hand back.

"No, please." I shake my head and fist my hands. "I'm ready now."

Hwanin gingerly presses his palm against the flat of my chest, right below my collarbones. My torso jerks at the light touch, as though I've been shocked by a defibrillator.

Still, I don't pull away. I clench my back teeth and prepare myself. I've survived unspeakable pain before. I can handle this.

I was wrong.

Hwanin's gi is both ice and fire, and I . . . burn. Torrential power floods my body, bringing unimaginable pain with it. It shreds me, piece by piece. It melts my skin off of my bones. But when I look down at myself, I remain unscathed on the outside.

It hurts.

My mouth opens on a gasp, but no sound escapes. My eyes widen until the skin around them tightens with strain, and tears fall soundlessly down my cheeks. I want to pull away from Hwanin's hand. I want to die to make the pain stop.

But I can't move.

"Uh . . . uh . . ." I can only whimper when I want to scream.

My hands twitch as Hwanin's life force pulses through me, then my arms jerk against my sides. I can't control my body, and my limbs flail against my will. I don't know how I stay upright as my whole body starts convulsing, and my head whips back and forth.

"E-Ethan." His name is a reedy whisper that clings to my lips. There is no way he heard me, but it's the best I can manage.

"Stop," Ethan cries at my side. "She's hurting."

What have I done?

I've sentenced him to certain death. Hwanin's divine gi is too powerful, horrible in its beauty. It will burn Ethan alive.

"Please stop," he says again.

He's still alive? How?

"They will both die if he stops," Yongwang answers, not unsympathetically. "Step away from her. Or the light will burn you to cinders."

"I don't give a fuck what happens to me," Ethan growls.

"N-no," I stutter. *Ethan, go back,* I want to tell him, but neither my voice nor my telepathy cooperates.

"Please tell me what to do," he pleads. "Wh-what can I do to help her?"

"You can hold her." Yeomla relents. "You can help anchor her, but you might not survive the contact."

"Thank you," Ethan says with genuine gratitude, completely uncaring about the part where he *dies* if he touches me.

Stop, you foolish, stubborn male!

I feel him step close behind me.

No, Ethan. No.

And he gingerly wraps his arms around my waist. With a sharp inhale, he pulls me flush against him. He groans quietly, like he's holding in his pain. *He's hurting.* But his arms don't slacken their hold.

An exhale bursts past my lips, and I can breathe again. My arms fall limply to my sides, and my flailing legs still beneath me. And my head stops thrashing and drops against his shoulder.

"E . . . than . . ." I manage to mumble past my numb lips.

"I'm here, baby." He kisses my temple. "You're okay now. I'm right here."

"Ass . . . hole . . ." I rasp. "I'll kill . . . you if . . . you die."

"Sure, sweetheart." He squeezes me tighter against him. "Survive this, and you can do whatever you'd like with me."

I feel his heart beating against my back, strong and steady. My heart slows its frantic thumping and mimics his solid rhythm until they beat as one. *I'm home.* I don't have to be scared anymore.

Hwanin's gi continues pouring into me with devastating force, but my Yeoiju grows and shines—powerful and unwavering. I no longer feel stretched too tight, like a balloon about to pop.

The divine life force is not too much for me. My Yeoiju and I can contain it. We can absorb it. It almost feels natural now.

Then as suddenly as we began, Hwanin drops his hand from my chest and stumbles back with a grunt. And I go limp against Ethan.

My breathing steadies as my strength returns to my body. I straighten away from Ethan, and he drops his arms without hesitation. I look over my shoulder at my beautiful husband.

"No," I scream, my shaking hands hovering over his ruined body. The skin on his arms and chest has been burned clean off, down to his muscles. "N-no, no."

"Look away, Sunny." I hear the strain in his voice. He's in agony. Of course, he is. "I'm going to be fine. I'm already healing. But I need you to look away, baby."

"You're *hurting*," I wail.

"Not for long," he rasps, then he turns to Hailey. "Please take her away. Just until I heal."

"Come with me, Sunny." Hailey wraps her arm around my shoulders and leads me away from Ethan.

I let her because I'm a coward. I can't watch Ethan suffer a moment longer. So I turn my back on him and bury my face in Hailey's neck. I don't know how long I stand like that, shivering uncontrollably.

"I can take her now." Ethan gently gathers me against his bare, unmarred chest. "I told you I'd be okay."

I can't stop shaking. He's better now, but my horror is too raw.

"I'm so sorry I h-hurt you," I force past my tight throat.

"Shh." He runs his hand down my hair. "It hurt more to watch you suffer. It's better this way."

"B-better for who?" I fist my hand and pound weakly on his chest.

"For us." His hand engulfs mine, and my fingers unfurl beneath it. "We're both alive, aren't we?"

If I wasn't already in love with him, this would have done the job. And impossible as it seems, I fall even more in love with him.

"Thank you for being my anchor." I press my cheek against his smooth, taut chest to reassure myself that he's okay.

"It's an honor," he says with absolute sincerity.

"Who says things like that?" I scoff and push away from him, but I would never tire of all the corny nonsense that spews from his pretty lips.

"Me." His guileless smile warms me like the sun in the dreary emptiness of purgatory. "But only to you."

I dig my teeth into my bottom lip and drop my gaze to my toes. If I look at him for a second longer, I will pounce on him. And now is not the time nor the place for that. With a wistful sigh, I turn just in time to catch Yeomla and Yongwang gaping at me, their divine mouths hanging to the ground.

"Thought I'd drop dead, did you?" I drawl archly.

Yeomla, the god of Underworld, gulps. "Absolutely."

"I had no doubt in the matter." Yongwang nods in agreement. "Only a being with divine blood could survive absorbing a god's life force. Or so I thought."

But their gazes soon drift to a point past my shoulder, and all hint of humor leaches out of their expressions. *Hwanin.* I remember Yongwang's grim warning. *There will be consequences.*

I warily face the god of Heavens, but Hwanin isn't . . . a god anymore. He is still very handsome, his youthful face striking against his silver hair, but not so unbearably beautiful that I want to run away screaming. And his gi . . .

Hwanin doesn't seem to notice the stares directed his way as he studies his hands, like he's never seen them before. Then he pats down his body and bounces on his feet a couple of times. When he finally raises his head, the devastation darkening his eyes has faded ever so slightly.

"You . . . you're mortal," I accuse to the shocked gasps of my friends. "Your gi almost looks as faint as a human's."

"You are right." A ghost of a smile flickers over Hwanin's lips. "I am still a being of the Shingae, but I am as mortal as a human."

"H-how is that possible?" I shake my head, dread creeping across my scalp.

I cannot stop until I have transferred all of my divine gi to you.

He transferred his *divine* gi to me. Why did it not occur to me sooner? How did I not realize that the "consequences" would also apply to *me*?

I thought I was only absorbing a part of his mighty powers. But he already told me the truth. He transferred *all* of his divine gi to me.

"I am mortal now because you absorbed my divinity," he answers evenly. "You are now the goddess of Heavens."

CHAPTER FORTY-SIX

SUNNY

"No." I don't recognize my voice, distorted by fury.

I don't want to be a fucking immortal goddess. I want to be me, Sunny Cho. A bad-tempered gumiho with wonderful friends I don't deserve. I want a chance to grow old with my husband. I don't want to live an eternity alone when he moves on to the next life.

What is the point of all this effort *if I can't have the things that matter most?*

"Undo this." My lip pulls back in a snarl as I turn on the former god of Heavens. I stalk toward him but stumble when the Yeoiju flares in my chest.

No, I don't need you right now. Stop.

Not heeding my command, the fire spreads inside me, wild and fast. I go dead still, recognizing the sensation.

This can't be happening.

Only it is. I can feel it. The burn of the white fire. The scream of its reckless violence.

If I lose control of the Yeoiju, it will siphon my gi to feed the white light. I nearly died facing off against Daeseong until I learned how to wield the Yeoiju by borrowing nature's life force.

But there is another way to fuel its power.

I glance toward Gyun. I don't want to acknowledge what happened in the depth of hell, but I think I already knew the truth deep down. I siphoned the life force of the Judges of Ten Hells to save my friends from the demons.

Desperation makes my powers dangerous.

The Yeoiju will take whatever life force it needs to fuel the white light and destroy without reason or thought. And there is no life in purgatory, except for the seven of us here. If I don't calm the fuck down, the Yeoiju will suck the life out of Ethan and my friends.

I am the only thing standing between the Yeoiju and them. *I* have to be its reason and thought. I need to regain control.

"I'm here, Sunny. Don't be scared." Ethan envelops me in his arms, one hand cradling the back of my head. "You are still you. You are still mine. Everything will be okay."

The fire, on the brink of combusting in my chest, simply . . . shuts off. I sag against him, wrapping my arms around his waist. I breathe him in until my heart stops racing and a calm determination settles over me.

He's here. We're together.

I will worry about the unknown future later. And the future *is* still unwritten, prophecies or not. *Goddess or not.* I huff a humorless laugh. I can only try to do good, one choice at a time. And right now, I choose not to lose my shit and risk hurting Ethan and my friends.

"Thank you." I step out of his arms but hold on to his hand. He's my anchor *and* my fail-safe. I need to keep him close. "I'm okay now."

He searches my face until he's convinced that I'm all right. Then a slow, crooked grin curves his lips. "It really isn't a big deal, though. You've always been a goddess in my eyes."

"Right?" I wink at him and flip my hair over my shoulder, wanting to make him laugh. I sigh when I succeed. Then I turn to Hwanin, with less murder in my heart. "Where is Dangun? And why did I need to absorb your life force to go to him?"

"He is at Shinsan in the Mortal Realm," the former god replies. "With the Amheuk surrounding the Realm of Four Kingdoms, you cannot traverse between the realms unless you are a deity. Since Dangun would want nothing to do with the three of us, *you* needed to become a goddess."

"What makes you think he will help me?" I narrow my eyes at him.

"Because my grandson is decent to the core." Hwanin takes a deep breath. "He will always choose to do the right thing."

"And if he agrees to share his life force with me"—I pin Yeomla and Yongwang with my steely gaze—"will you two do the same? I need the gi of all four gods to stop the Amheuk."

"Yes," Yeomla says, his face haggard.

I can understand his turmoil. While I would choose to become mortal in a heartbeat, it can't be easy for a god to give up his immortality, when that is all he has ever known.

"I will do the same." Yongwang smooths out his impeccable blue robe, not meeting my eyes. I hope he doesn't give me any trouble when the time comes.

"I have to go," I tell Ethan.

He nods. "I'll come with you."

"Of course you will." I laugh through my nose, half-exasperated, half-relieved. I need him by my side. At least going to the Mortal Realm to meet Dangun shouldn't be dangerous. *Right?*

"We're coming too." Hailey steps toward me, tugging Gyun by his sleeve.

"No." I shake my head, grimacing in apology. "We've been gone for too long. Our friends at the Kingdom of Sky need you."

"As I mentioned, time works differently in purgatory. For those in the Kingdom of Sky, we've only been gone for a few minutes." Gyun crosses his arms over his massive chest. "But I agree that Hailey and I can do more good back at the Realm of Four Kingdoms, especially when we bring two gods"—he glances at Hwanin—"and a former god to fight alongside us."

Hailey sighs in resignation. "Be safe, Sunny."

"I will." I squeeze her hand. "You too."

"When you travel to the Mortal Realm, time will flow as it should again," Gyun adds. "Every minute of your journey will be felt in the Kingdom of Sky."

"That doesn't sound ominous at all." I gulp.

"Nah." He flashes a row of perfect white teeth. "It could just mean the end of the worlds if you are too late."

"I won't be too late." I jut my chin. "The Amheuk better be ready to rumble when I come back."

The god of Underworld snorts. "We have definitely been missing out on the fun, Yongwang."

"You may be right, Yeomla. Someone should have woken us up sooner," the god of Water drawls, as dry as the desert. "Who knew we had a comedic gumiho in our midst?"

I roll my eyes at them. As an immortal goddess—and a *comedic gumiho*—I should be free to give them as much sass as I want. Even so, Yongwang glowers in disapproval, and I resist the urge to stick my tongue out at the god of Water.

My loopiness, in the face of imminent danger, has become my whole personality.

"You go first." I look at Hailey and Gyun. "We'll see you soon."

"Godspeed," Hailey says, then the assortment of gods and ungods disappears in a blink.

And suddenly, it's just me and Ethan in the shadowy echo of his mother's garden. "Are you—"

Ethan crushes his lips against mine and absolutely plunders my mouth. I don't pause to process my surprise. I scrabble to climb onto him, and he hoists me up by my ass so I can wrap my legs around his waist. I moan against the slick heat of his tongue and draw a groan from him with my teeth. He kisses me until I'm breathless and lightheaded.

"I don't know when we'll be alone again." He punctuates every word with a kiss, then draws back to look at me. "We should take advantage of purgatory's strange flow of time before we go to the Mortal Realm."

I fist my hand in his hair and tug him down for another hard kiss. "You are a smart, smart male."

Our mouths fuse again, and I tear at his clothes as he maneuvers us to the pavilion. We don't get much further than the stairs. I squirm until he sets me down on the top step, and I push him onto his ass.

Ethan rips off his T-shirt, and I squirm out of my jeans and panties along with my shoes. I plant my knees on either side of his slim hips and unzip his jeans to free his hard length. Without pause, I sink down on him, taking him inside me to the hilt.

I don't feel the dig of the wooden floor against my bare knees as I ride him, full throttle. Ethan pivots his hips to meet me, every time I bear down on him. This isn't tender lovemaking. We fuck hard and fast with the jagged edge of fear and uncertainty dogging our every thrust.

"Sunny," he growls, gripping my hips to move me up and down even more frantically.

He's close, and so am I. When he tilts my hips and pushes his cock against a secret spot deep inside me, I unravel with a throaty scream. He holds me still as he rams into me, once, then twice, and finds his own release.

Ethan collapses onto his back, with me on top of him, his legs stretching down the steps of the pavilion. My head rises and falls with his chest as he fights to catch his breath, and I lie limply against him.

"Best honeymoon ever," I murmur, my words a little slurred.

"You need to set your bar higher, sweetheart." He chuckles. "I will take you on a proper honeymoon when this is all over."

"Somewhere more romantic than purgatory?" I gasp. "How ever will you manage?"

"I'll have to find a way." He cups my ass with his big hands and squeezes.

"Hey," I protest and squirm, embarrassingly turned on.

"Sorry." He loosens his grip, then pats one cheek in apology. "I love your round ass. I couldn't resist."

"'My irresistible ass' and I forgive you." I rest my chin on his bare chest and look up at him. "We should go."

"Yeah." He raises his head a fraction to meet my gaze. "We should."

Neither of us move for a full minute, then with a long, reluctant sigh, Ethan sits us both up and sets me down next to him. I retrieve my underwear and jeans and pull them on with far less enthusiasm than when I practically tore them off. I pout when Ethan zips up his jeans and tugs on his T-shirt.

Much too soon, we're ready to leave.

"Crap." I cup my forehead. "I forgot to ask the gods to teach me how to get to the Mortal Realm."

"You don't need them to teach you anything. Not anymore." He dips his head to catch my eyes. "Think like a goddess. How would *you* get us to Shinsan?"

"Well, I liked how the god of Water swooshed his long sleeve like a magician when he transported us to the Kingdom of Sky." I pinch my lips to the side. "But I'm not wearing anything swooshable."

"I know exactly what you can swoosh." Ethan's lips spread into a gleeful grin. "You were actually *made* for this."

Laughter bubbles up my throat when I catch on to his meaning. I shift without hesitation and proudly raise my nine tails toward the sky.

"Whoa." Ethan steps close and runs his hand down my snout. "You are . . . brilliant."

"I know," I say telepathically before looking down at myself. *Whoa.* My coat sparkles like I've been glitter bombed. "Oh I get it. I am literally brilliant."

"Cool, right?" He chuckles. "Well, Goddess? Swoosh away."

I flare my tails wide and swoosh them with dramatic abandon. I'm not worried about how to get us to Shinsan anymore. I think like a goddess and simply . . . will it so.

CHAPTER FORTY-SEVEN

Sunny

Ethan steadies himself with a hand on my back when the verdant hills and forests of Shinsan materialize around us. I shift back to my human form and link my fingers through his.

Holy fuckaroni.

Knowing I could do it, and *actually* transporting us to a different realm with a single thought, are two completely different things.

"Do we look under every rock on this entire mountain to find this elusive god?" Ethan muses with worry tugging down his lips.

Every minute counts. The Kingdom of Sky might already be under attack.

"No." I scan the trees around us, determination coursing through me. "I can sense him. This god isn't asleep."

I lead us down a hill and deeper into the forest until we reach a cave, nearly hidden from view. The towering trees barely let needles of light touch the ground, but vegetation flourishes around the cave.

"Do you think Dangun is in there?" Ethan whispers close to my ear.

"He is," a soft, resonant voice answers from the cave.

"Lord Dangun," I project my voice without raising it. A neat goddess trick. "We come to seek your help."

The god of Mountains comes to the mouth of the cave with his hands clasped behind his back. He wears a simple hanbok of unbleached cloth, with a thick, long vest on top. He is ruggedly handsome, with shoulder-length waves that fall haphazardly over his broad shoulders and a dark beard that can't hide his strong jawline. If it weren't for his kind eyes, he could be mistaken for a sanjeok, a mountain bandit.

He tilts his head for us to follow him inside, and we do as we're bid. I glance around the cave, which is surprisingly bright and warm, then settle my gaze on the god of Mountains. Dangun exudes a soothing calm that steadies my frazzled nerves.

But when he does a double take on me, his jaw dropping in shock, I promptly freak out. *What?* I glance down at myself. Is he not a fan of all-black attire?

"Hwanin," he chokes out. "My grandfather gave you his divine life force?"

"Y-yes." I can't tell if he's mad about it, so I prattle on. "I bear the Yeoiju, the last of the Cheon'gwang. I'm pretty sure I was able to absorb Hwanin's gi without dying because of that."

"Among other reasons." The hard lines of Dangun's face soften, and he releases a long, resigned breath. "I am glad Hwanin did his part. Did Yongwang and Yeomla also agree to transfer their gi to you?"

Wait. What other reasons? Never mind. There is no time to waste.

"They did." Then I feel obliged to add, "That is, *if* you give me your divine life force first."

His lips press into a stern line. "They likely believed you will not survive receiving my gi."

"Why is that?" Ethan wraps his arm around my shoulders and pulls me close to his side. "Why would your life force affect her any differently than Hwanin's?"

"The King Foretold." Dangun angles his head to study Ethan. "You truly love her."

"With all my heart," Ethan confirms, and my knees grow weak. I will never tire of hearing that he loves me, no matter the circumstance . . . even when he's mouthing off at the god of Mountains. "But you haven't answered my question."

I resist the urge to pinch his arm. Since he is now the husband of a goddess, he should be able to get away with *some* disrespect toward the gods. Even so, my stomach instinctively clenches.

"Each god is the embodiment of a distinct source of life," Dangun explains evenly, instead of smiting Ethan. "Yeomla and Yongwang must believe that no god is able to embody more than one divine life source. It is too much power—conflicting power at that—for even a god to survive. Or so they think."

Ethan's gaze snaps toward me.

"Don't worry. *I* can survive." I place my fingertips on his mouth before he can speak. "The Yeoiju burns the brightest when all four life forces are combined within me. When the blue of Water, the green of Mountains, the red of Underworld, and the silver of Sky merge, the Yeoiju shines white—the combination of all colors. That white light *is* the Cheon'gwang."

"You are right." Dangun nods. "The Yeoiju will allow you to absorb all four divine life forces."

Ethan kisses my fingertips before gently tugging them off his lips. Then he asks, "How can you know that for sure?"

"Because the Yeoiju showed me the truth a long time ago," the god of Mountains says with a faraway look. "Sunny was always meant to be the one to vanquish the eternal darkness. She was always meant to be the light."

"How d-do you know my name?" Icy fingers of trepidation scrape down my spine.

"A god knows many things," he hedges, then plows forward after a jagged pause, "but I know your name because I am your father. The blood of the gods runs through you. That is how you survived absorbing Hwanin's gi."

Vertigo spins the cave in dizzying circles, and I sway on my feet. My laugh starts as a quiet giggle, then gradually snowballs into a shrill cackle. I wrap my arms around my aching ribs as tears rain down my face.

I keep laughing. I can't seem to stop. Then, suddenly, I do stop with jarring abruptness, because despair rides through me in a merciless tidal wave of self-loathing.

"Daeseong is my father," I say flatly. "He wasn't lying—he couldn't lie—because I stole his free will. I *bewitched* him to tell me the truth."

"The dark mudang believed that you were his daughter." Dangun's shoulders slump as though he feels the weight of the world on it. "Your *mother* believed that you were his daughter. It was the only way."

It's too much. I would give anything to be *anyone's* daughter but Daeseong's. And to be Dangun's daughter? I realize a part of me badly wants this kind-eyed god to be my father, but what if it's not true?

"Stop talking in riddles," I snap, my shoulders rising and falling. "Just tell me what you *think* you know. You're wasting time we don't have, Dangun."

"Sunny, you should listen to him." Ethan rubs my back in soothing circles.

Normally, that would have worked wonders. But right now, no amount of comfort, even from my fated love, will calm my nerves. I want the truth. Yet finding out the truth terrifies me.

Then Ethan goes deathly still next to me, and the sounds of the mountain shut off in an instant.

"Wh-what's going on? Ethan? *Ethan.*" When he doesn't respond, I frantically run my hands over him. His body is warm, but he isn't breathing. I spin on Dangun and rage, "What did you do to him?"

"Do not worry. Ethan is unharmed, merely frozen in time," the god of Mountains reassures me. "But I can't stop time for very long, so you must listen, Sunny."

Ethan is okay. I focus on that and not on the time-stopping shit, lest my brain blow up.

"Fine." I duck my head and dry my cheeks on my shoulder. "I'm listening."

"I loved your mother. More than life." Dangun's voice breaks. "But I had to let her go when she became pregnant with you."

"Why?" I don't believe he's my father—I don't know what to believe—but this hurts anyway. *This* is why I shouldn't get my hopes up. "Did you not want me?"

"You are everything I have ever wanted in a child." Love shines from his eyes, and I look away. "The moment you were conceived, you already bore the Yeoiju in your soul, and it showed me your destiny."

My brows knit above my eyes. What is he telling me?

"I don't know why the Yeoiju chose to show *me*—perhaps because I was meant to be the first flap of the butterfly's wings—but it showed me *everything*. Far more than even a god could foresee."

I stagger back as his words finally sink in. He has seen my destiny. The *whole* of it. Does he know how it ends?

"In order for you to fulfill your destiny, your mother had to leave me before she realized she was pregnant with you." He wipes a hand down his mouth. "That very night, I told her that the novelty of toying with a gumiho had worn off, which made her run into Daeseong's arms, wishing she could be human."

"How could you?" I gasp, my hand fluttering to my mouth. *Oh, Mother.*

Instead of making excuses, Dangun takes a bracing breath and continues, "I broke your mother's heart because Daeseong had to believe that you were his daughter. He had to believe he had every right to the Yeoiju so that he would hunt you, even after death, by becoming the dark mudang."

"You could have stopped everything before any of it happened," I seethe. "It's because of you . . . Everything is because of you."

If the god of Mountains had stayed with us, my mother would not have died at Daeseong's hands. I wouldn't have left Korea. I would never have met . . . Ethan.

I grab my head in my hands, my breaths coming shallow and fast.

Would I trade my time with Ethan to avoid all the loss, grief, and loneliness I've endured for over a century? To avoid the pain and devastation that is yet to come?

I don't know what to think—how to feel. I drag my fingers down my face, then my arms fall limply to my sides. It's . . . too much.

"In time, you will understand." Dangun brushes the hair off my face and cups my cheek. I am too exhausted to push him away. "When the Yeoiju reveals your true destiny to you, you will know that this was the only way."

"Even if you really are my father, you abandoned me," I accuse past numb lips. "You let Mother die. You left me all *alone*."

He draws away, his face crumpling, and I see the broken male behind the god. This hasn't been easy for him. He didn't want to push his family away. He had no choice but to break our hearts, as his own broke with ours.

For the first time since it sang for me, I hate the Yeoiju.

"I am so sorry, child. But believe me when I tell you that you were *never* alone." He holds my chin and doesn't let me look away. "I was always with you. Every step of the way. Sometimes as my various manifestations. Most times in my heart."

My eyes drop down to the arm that hangs down by his side—the arm that stops at the elbow. Why hadn't I seen the half-empty sleeve before? My gaze shoots back to his.

"Halmeoni?" I ask in a small, childlike voice.

Samshin Halmeom was my family. My favorite storyteller and fellow adventurer in the mountains of my childhood.

"For a few precious years, I was." Dangun's eyes are wet, even though his lips are curved into a soft smile. "You were such a precocious child, and I loved you so much."

Halmeoni loved me. My . . . father loved me? A faint tremor spreads through me—a spark of timid hope.

Then my lungs seize, and icy fingers grip the back of my head. Did he say . . .

"Loved?" This is exactly what I feared. He must not love me anymore.

"I loved the carefree little girl that you were." His hand feels warm and heavy on my shoulder, grounding me in the moment. My pulse flutters in my throat, and I hold my breath for his next words. "But I love you more than ever as you are now—scarred and conflicted, strong and loyal."

This is real. He has no reason to lie to me. *This must be real . . . right?*

"I am so proud of you, Sunny," he says in a voice rough with emotion. "You are *good* through and through. Even through the heartache of losing the love of my life and the torture of keeping myself away from my only daughter, I never resented my fate. It is a privilege to be your father. I would not trade it for anything."

I think I see . . . love, deep and tender, in his gaze, but his face blurs in front of me. I swallow the salt in the back of my throat and drag my forearm across my eyes.

Can it be true?

"May I?" He raises his hand and hovers his palm over my head.

"Wh-what are you doing?" I shrink back from him.

"Nothing, unless you want me to." He ducks his head to catch my eyes. "I . . . want to share my memories with you. May I show you? Can I ask you to trust me?"

Don't think, Sunny. My intuition has saved my ass, time and time again. *Trust your gut.*

"Y-yes," I pant. "I want you to show me."

"This will not hurt," he says, laying a gentle hand on the crown of my head. "Just . . . absorb it. See what I've seen. Feel what I've felt."

Memories, comfortably faded like old photographs, flow into my mind. I see what my father—yes, my father—has seen. And emotions, the edges rounded not to hurt me, swirl into my heart. I feel what my father has felt—his love, his joy, his heartbreak.

I am not Daeseong's daughter. *Thank gods.* The horror clawing my insides loosens its hold on me. I am Dangun's daughter.

He slides his hand off my head and squeezes my shoulder. The corners of my lips wobble as they curve into a watery smile.

He loves me. He has always loved me.

My father bled when I fell and wept when I hurt. I was never alone.

And he believes I am good. He is . . . proud of me.

"Father," I breathe.

I could stay angry with him for all the pain he put me through, but we have both hurt enough already. I want to skip to the good part—the part where I am the beloved daughter of a proud father.

"Will you . . . come back to the Realm of Four Kingdoms with me?" I ask haltingly.

"I cannot." He turns his head away. "If I come with you, I would not be able to stop myself from trying to protect you. No matter how hard I try not to, I would get in the way of your destiny. I cannot do that." He digs the heel of his hand into his chest. "Not after everything we've been through—you, your mother, and I."

"Is my destiny so important?" I ask with lingering bitterness, even though I understand him. "Then why did Mother tell me to run?"

"While she was pregnant, the Yeoiju showed her the prophecy of the End of Days," he says, and I stiffen and step back from him. "She wanted you to run from your destiny because she couldn't bear the thought of you dying at the hands of your fated love. Your mother thought she could protect you by hiding you."

"W-was she wrong?" I force myself to ask him. "Does the prophecy of the End of Days c-come true?"

Will I become the End of Days? Do I have to die at Ethan's hands?

"Yes, the prophecy comes true." Anguish and tenderness war on his face. "I cannot say any more. I fear I might influence your decisions. But be brave, Daughter. Face your destiny head-on."

"I wish . . ." I stare sightlessly down at my hands, then shake my head.

What do I wish?

I don't wish for *me* to live, but I desperately wish for Ethan to live. For my friends to live. For the people of the Realm of Four Kingdoms to live. And if I fulfill my destiny, then I get my wish, right?

So that's what I'll do.

"I will embrace my destiny, rather than succumb to it." I pull my shoulders back and glance up at my father. "And I will fulfill it on my own terms."

"You are so strong." He squeezes my arms. "I am proud of you."

The mountain seems to take a shuddering breath, and the chirping of birds and the rustling of leaves flit through the cave again.

"Sunny?" Ethan stares back and forth between me and Dangun. "How are you standing over there?"

I meet my father's gaze. "Is it time?"

"Yes, Daughter." His smile is gentle and sad. "You're going to need your husband for this."

"I need him for everything." I hold my hand out, and Ethan takes it without hesitation.

He raises his brows in question.

I shrug. "Yes, Dangun is my father. And we . . . worked things out."

"In the time it took for me to blink?" Ethan asks wryly, accepting my explanation without question. He turns to his father-in-law and says in a much more respectful tone, "Are you sure she will be able to absorb your gi safely?"

"Yes, I am sure." Dangun nods.

"But . . . you won't be a god anymore if you do this." I worry my bottom lip.

"You say that like it is a bad thing." My father cocks his head as though he truly does not understand the downside of being mortal.

I know there is no other way, but I don't want him to become mortal. Mortals die—that's kind of the deal—and the thought of losing another parent wrings my insides raw. If I had my way, everyone I love would never die—at least not until I die first.

I know that's selfish of me, but it hurts too much. I don't want to live through that pain again. I . . . can't. *You know what?* I'll just have to add Dangun to the list of people I need to protect with my life.

I must defeat the Amheuk.

If I fail, both realms fall—first the Realm of Four Kingdoms, then the Mortal Realm—and everyone dies. *We can't have that.* I will succeed, then Ethan will save me. We will fulfill the prophecy of the End of Days together.

"Okay, then." I smile at my husband and my father, feeling rich beyond imagination. "Let's do this."

CHAPTER FORTY-EIGHT

Sunny

My father transfers his life force to me in much the same way as Hwanin—my great-grandfather?—did.

And this time, I don't let the divine life force touch a hair on my husband's head. I use Hwanin's gi to create a barrier between us as I absorb my father's life force. As an added bonus, focusing on protecting Ethan from harm is a great distraction from the pain of the process.

The light from Dangun's gi and the Yeoiju fade as they settle inside me, and my father withdraws his hand from my heaving chest. Ethan lets go of my waist and spins me around.

"Are you okay?" Cradling my cheek, he searches every inch of my face, eyes dark with concern. Even so, his worry barely penetrates the numb place where I had to go to get through it.

"I'm fine," I say automatically, even though I'm not really sure.

"You did well, Daughter." Dangun's smile shines with unbridled pride.

"Thank you." I peer at him in the dimness of the cave. "How do *you* feel?"

"Fragile." He tips his head to the side in thought. "It is wonderful."

"It is?" I crinkle my nose.

"Mortality is a . . . gift." He smiles wistfully.

"If you say so." I don't bother hiding my skepticism.

"Are you sure you're okay?" Ethan's gaze hasn't left my face.

"Yes," I reassure him with a too-bright smile, but this time I know I'm lying.

Absorbing Dangun's life force went as well as it could have. But *containing* his gi within me is another question. The gi of Mountains and the gi of Sky clash inside me like mortal enemies, each life force fighting for dominance. The Yeoiju strains to hold on to them, but I feel like I'm being ripped down the middle.

How can I absorb two more divine gi? It's already too much. I take a shuddering breath, panic sharpening the struggle of the divine life forces inside me. I can't do this. I can't . . .

"Try not to hold on too tight." My father lays a heavy hand on my shoulder. "Expand your Yeoiju, like spreading your arms to invite an embrace."

I give him a grateful nod and exhale slowly through my mouth. I concentrate on opening the Yeoiju, imagining a lotus flower blooming wide. The two divine life forces, swirling at opposite ends, calm once they flow through the white light at my heart's center. And strand by strand, they begin to intertwine.

"Phew." I huff an unsteady laugh. "That's much better."

"You said you were fine." Ethan narrows his eyes at me.

"*Fine* is such a broad, fluid word," I hedge, wincing with guilt. "Sorry. I didn't want you to worry."

Rather than responding, Ethan turns to Dangun, a muscle working in his jaw. "Will the next two be even harder on her?"

I open my eyes wide and silently *beg* my father not to make him worry even more.

"Uh." My father glances between me and Ethan. "Nothing she cannot handle."

"So that's a yes." Ethan's voice is flat and hard.

"Yes." Dangun sighs. "Stay by her side and help her through it. Anchor her with all your heart."

Ethan gives him a curt nod. Then, not quite meeting my eyes, he says, "I'll give you two a moment to say goodbye."

He spins on his heel and walks out of the cave, and my heart sinks. He's so angry with me.

"He is worried more than anything," Dangun says quietly.

"I know, but I shouldn't have lied to him." I kick at the pebbles on the ground. "He sensed something was wrong, and hiding it from him only made him worry more."

"Then that is a good lesson learned." My father chuckles. "My parents always told me that marriage is a lot of work, even though theirs was a love destined by the heavens like yours. But they also said that it was worth every bit of effort they put into it."

"Your . . . parents?" I blink. "Hwanung and Ungnyeo?"

"Yes." He smiles. "Your grandparents."

"Wow." It's strange that my grandparents are characters from old stories. I can't wrap my head around it.

"You would have liked them," he continues. "Your grandmother was the first animal spirit."

"But the folklore says she became human . . ."

"And you believe everything in human folklore?" Dangun arches his brow. "To be fair, your grandfather granted her wish to become human first. But later in their marriage, he saw that she missed the freedom and power of being a bear, so he gave her the ability to shift—to be both a human and a bear."

"It sounds like he loved her very much," I murmur.

"Yes, every part of her," he says softly. "He loved her so much that he cut ties with his father, Hwanin."

"Cut ties?" My stomach sinks. "Why?"

"Hwanin did not approve of his only child marrying an animal spirit." His lips twist with bitter memory. "But his prejudices cost him his beloved son."

Come to think of it, where *is* Hwanung? Other than in Korean folklore, I have never heard of the god of Earth. As far as I know, there are only the four gods of each life source.

"Wh-what happened?" I ask.

"When I was still a young boy, my mother moved on to the next life, and my father's heart became untethered, setting his soul adrift. He could not go on without his fated love." Dangun takes a pained breath. "I was not born a god. I was a being of the Shingae with the blood of the gods running through me. Like you, I stopped aging at eighteen and was *nearly* immortal."

"That's why," I gasp as relief courses through me. I can't believe I finally got an answer to that mystery. A part of me had been afraid that I'd been subconsciously stealing nature's life force, like the Shinbiin. I shake my head and ask, "Then how did you become a god?"

"Soon after I turned eighteen, my father asked me to absorb his divine gi so he could be with my mother. I couldn't bear to watch him hurt for an eternity, so I agreed." His eyes take on a faraway look. "I became the god of Mountains, and my father . . . A bond destined by the heavens is unbreakable. Once he became mortal, he simply faded away."

My heart breaks for Hwanung. "How did Ungnyeo die?"

"My father never told me." He rakes his fingers through his hair, the old frustration unforgotten. "I assumed she died from old age or illness, because she was mortal. But as the years passed, I began to have doubts, and those doubts kept growing. Living in the Realm of Four Kingdoms should have granted my mother near immortality. She should have lived for hundreds of more years." Then fury ripples across his face. "I believe Hwanin and the other gods had something to do with her death."

"What?" I gasp. *Is this the atrocity those gods spoke of? The wrongs they were trying to right?* "How?"

"I do not know." Dangun wipes a weary hand down his face. "With my father gone, I couldn't prove anything. Then I left the Realm of Four Kingdoms and that selfish lot behind."

"I'm so sorry you had to lose your parents like that," I whisper. *I need to find out what happened.* What did those arrogant gods *do* to my grandmother? "The grief never fades, does it? Time only makes it hurt less often."

"Your grandmother was strong, noble, and brave." My father cups his hands around my shoulders. "You remind me so much of her."

I glance away from him with an embarrassed snort. "Why? Do I look like her?"

"You are her mirror image, but your strength, courage, and capacity to love also come from your grandmother." He grasps my chin and turns me to face him. "Do not be afraid, Daughter. Trust yourself as I trust you. You will choose correctly."

"You speak in riddles, Father," I say softly, even though I understand him. Whatever happens next, I will choose to do good—regardless of the price I have to pay. "I hated it when the Seonangshin, the ancient cypress trees, did that."

Daeseong's undead assassins would probably have gotten Ethan and me if the lone cypress tree hadn't told me about the dark mudang's return. The Seonangshin helped me face my destiny when all I wanted to do was run from it. That . . . was my father too. He was never far.

"Even a god cannot speak the secrets of the Shingae, but I did my best to help you figure it out on your own." Dangun smiles, looking every bit the proud father, but he swiftly sobers. "I wish I could hurt *for* you, Daughter. But the best I can do is hurt *with* you from afar."

"I wish you wouldn't have to hurt at all." I wrap my arms around him and bury my face in his chest. I wish I had more time so I could make him happy, but . . . I don't. The best I can do is give him time to find his own happiness.

"Go now." He leads me toward the cave opening. "Ethan is waiting."

I don't want to leave. I've only just found him. What if this was my one and only chance to be with my father?

"Just five more min—" I begin, turning toward him.

But he's gone.

"Father." My throat clogs with emotion. He left first so I wouldn't have to walk away from him. He knew how hard that would be for me. "Thank you. I will make you proud."

I run out of the empty cave without looking back. I won't cry—I bite my lip until I taste salt and iron on my tongue—it would break my father's heart.

Ethan pushes away from the tree he was leaning against and watches me approach with a hooded gaze. But the moment he sees my face, he rushes toward me and gathers me in his arms, his anger forgotten.

"It's okay, Sunny." His warm breath ruffles my hair. "You'll see him again. I promise."

I cling to him for a heartbeat, then step back with a bracing breath.

Every minute counts.

"Our friends are waiting." I hold out my hand. "Are you ready?"

"Define *ready*." He offers me a crooked grin before linking his fingers through mine. "Let's do this."

CHAPTER FORTY-NINE

Ethan

I don't know what I expected to find when we returned to the Kingdom of Sky, but it certainly wasn't this. We weren't gone for much longer than an hour.

I guess it doesn't take long for all hell to break loose.

Jihun, General Jo, Haesan, and Jaeseok stand shoulder to shoulder, summoning their magic to hold off a writhing tentacle. Not too far from them, Minju, Yeomla, Bora, and Captain Ha attack the base of a long black arm until they tear it off, leaving behind a useless stump.

"This way." Sunny tugs my hand and runs headlong into the war zone.

The dark tentacles are attached to the body of the Amheuk, still concealed beyond the boundaries of the Kingdom of Sky. *Thank gods.* The bulk of the ancient darkness hasn't penetrated the kingdom, yet.

More clusters of four shinbiins fight off thick strands of dark terror, and I belatedly understand that beings from each of the four kingdoms have been united to form units. It is their combined magic—the power of all four life sources—that has been keeping the Amheuk at bay. Unfortunately, they are slowly losing ground.

Sunny roars at my side, and before I can react, she leaps into the sky with the Shin'gwangdo raised above her head and slashes down on the tentacle inching closer to Jihun's unit. The dark arm disintegrates into black dust before her feet touch the ground again.

Jihun and his unit barely have time to thank Sunny as another arm of the Amheuk attacks them, but they manage to subdue the flapping tentacle quickly.

"Is everyone okay?" I ask, running to their side.

"Those of us in the capital have only endured a few casualties," General Jo from the Kingdom of Mountains answers. "But I'm afraid not every region has been as fortunate."

"Haesan, thank gods you're okay." Sunny hugs the in'eo, then shoves the boulder-sized male out of the way. "Watch out."

A tentacle three times the size of the earlier ones whips toward us, knocking General Jo off his feet and sending him skidding across the field. There is no time for Sunny to draw the sword of light, so she grapples the darkness with her bare hands.

"Sunny." I hack at the black arm with my axes.

"I'm okay," she grits out.

I glance over at the general, who pushes his torso off the ground, and I release a sigh of relief. But when Sunny's feet skid back, I renew my attack on the tentacle.

"We need your magic, Ethan," Jihun shouts, summoning the wind.

"Welcome back, Your Majesties." Jaeseok joins us with his hands on fire. "Sorry about the poor reception."

"You're funny, Lieutenant." A wall of water builds behind Haesan. "I like you."

"Aww, thank you," the dokkaebi gushes, stretching out the fire into a long stream. "Hey, Sunny. Where did you find this giant marshmallow? He's so sweet, I can't even give him a hard time."

Understanding the assignment at last, I gather the gi of Mountains in my hands to contribute to the collective attack. But before we can launch our magic, Sunny rips the tentacle in two, white light bursting from her hands.

"Embrace . . . the challenge . . . Jaeseok," she pants, bent at the waist, her hands gripping her thighs. "You'll find his inner . . . asshole if you dig deep . . . enough."

"Are you okay?" I push her hair back from her clammy forehead.

"She needs the rest of our divine life forces," Yeomla says, joining us. "Summoning the white light with just Sky and Mountains will deplete her. She needs all four life forces."

"I c-can't leave them now." Sunny glances behind her as another dark arm bursts into the Kingdom of Sky, and Taeyoung joins Minju's unit to make up for the loss of Yeomla and the gi of Underworld.

"More will fall to the Amheuk the longer we wait," the god of Underworld says implacably.

"Go." Jihun squeezes her arm. "We will hold it off until you come back."

"You better not die." Sunny pokes my royal adviser in the chest, then turns toward me. "We have to go, Ethan."

"Where to?" I ask, even as I run at her side.

"We will be safe for the time being at the Suhoshin headquarters." Yeomla leads us away from the battleground. "Sunny and I will be entirely vulnerable during the transfer of power. We cannot afford *any* interference. Neither of us will survive if the transfer is interrupted before it's complete."

When the three of us stand apart from the rest, the god of Underworld flaps his long, scarlet robe and teleports us to the front of the Suhoshin headquarters. I find my balance quickly, which is fortunate, because Yeomla bursts through the first set of gates without pause and steps into a large, spartan courtyard.

"Ugh," Sunny moans. "The cadet training yard? I don't have fond memories of this place."

"*That* is your worry right now?" Yeomla gapes at her. "I am about to become mortal at the worst possible time to be killable. Please focus on staying alive so you can save my fragile life once the transfer is complete."

She grunts in bad-tempered acquiescence.

Gods, she's adorable.

She's also terrified to absorb Yeomla's life force. I know my wife. Her shoulders are slouched, and she keeps picking at her nails. I slide the wooden bar closed to lock the gates and come stand behind her.

"Don't worry, Sunny." I drop a kiss on her temple. "I won't let anything happen to you."

She releases a rough breath and glances back at me. "Promise?"

"I promise." I squeeze her shoulder, then take a step back.

"I'm ready, Lord Yeomla," she says, her small hands curling into fists.

"Remember, I cannot stop once I begin." Yeomla holds her gaze.

"I know. I'm ready," she assures him, jutting her stubborn chin.

"Very well." He comes to stand in front of her and nods once. "Summon the Yeoiju."

Her chest glows with white light, and the god of Underworld presses his hand against it. He gasps, his forehead creased with pain or concentration. And Sunny jerks violently, flailing her arms and legs. She's done this twice before, but it still scares me shitless to see her like this.

But I know what to do. Stepping up to her back, I wrap my arms around her and press her against my front. Taking a deep breath, I close my eyes and anchor her with my body and soul.

I'm here, Sunny. Stay with me.

The light of Yeomla's life force pierces through my eyelids. I bury my face in the crook of Sunny's neck, even though her skin burns like smoldering coal. She is protecting me from Yeomla's divine gi so it doesn't burn me. But she doesn't know that I can still feel the searing heat down to my bones.

I grit my teeth against the pain and hold her as though my life depends on it. Because it does. She is my life—my beating heart.

"Shh," I murmur when she whimpers quietly. "You are so strong, Sunny. I am in awe of you. You can do this."

"Ethan . . ." Her head thrashes weakly against my chest.

"I'm right here." I tighten my arms and curve my whole body around her. "And I'm not going anywhere. Lean on me, baby. I got you."

I don't know how long I hold her like that, but it's almost over. I can tell by the way the tremors jolting through her body gradually calm. But my eyes spring open at the twin cries of agony, my heart thumping wildly.

Yeomla's shocked gaze meets mine before dropping to his chest . . . and the sword tip protruding from it.

What the fuck is happening?

"S-Sunny?" I stutter when she moans and grows limp against me.

"Wh-what have . . . you done, Yongwang?" Blood dribbles down the god of Underworld's chin.

"It would not have worked." The god of Water stumbles back from his old friend, staring down at his bloody hands. "It would never have worked."

"Why?" I shout as I hike Sunny up by the waist, arching my back to bear more of her weight. "Why, you fucking coward?"

"I had to stop this madness once and for all." Yongwang's voice rings shrilly. "I will never give up my divinity."

"Sunny, listen to me." Yeomla's reedy voice resonates with divine power as he places a trembling hand on her shoulder. "You can still absorb my gi. Let your Yeoiju take what it needs. I will hang on until it is done."

But the light of her Yeoiju dims little by little until there's . . . nothing. And her head flops forward.

"No, Sunny," I cry, frantically holding her upright in my arms.

The god of Underworld crumples to the ground at her feet. "You m-must live, child."

"Stay. Please." I rock our bodies back and forth. "Please, stay with me. I love you, Sunny. I love you so much."

At first, I don't hear it past my rough, panicked breaths. But a low hum vibrates in the air, growing louder and louder still.

She's fighting.

"That's it, sweetheart." I crush my lips against her temple. "Fight, Sunny. Come back to me."

"Ethan." It's more air than sound, but I hear her loud and clear.

"I'm here, Sunny." *Please gods.* "I'm here."

A sound like the buzz of a thousand bees fills the air. I grind my teeth together and hold on to Sunny. Then . . . a crystal clear chime disperses the buzzing. *The song of the Yeoiju.* A sob slips past my lips when I feel Sunny's body vibrate with its power.

Her chest expands on a heaving breath, and white light spreads through her, even to the tips of her fingers. *Gods, the heat.* My body writhes against the burn, and my eyes roll back from the pain, but I don't let her go. *Never.*

Then she growls deep in her throat, and white light flares from her eyes. Yeomla's mouth opens on a silent gasp, and his body seizes on the ground.

"Y-yes, ch-child," the god of Underworld says in a wet gurgle, blood leaking from the corner of his mouth. "Take it all."

"Impossible," Yongwang whispers. "This is not possible."

"Ethan, you can let me go." Sunny's voice resonates through the air, as soft as a breeze and as strong as a mountain. When I reluctantly drop my arms to my sides, she addresses the god of Underworld. "I hope you find peace, Lord Yeomla."

She thrusts her chest forward, her head tipping back, and his body levitates off the ground until he is suspended in the air.

"What are you doing?" Yongwang screeches and lurches toward Sunny with his hands curled into claws.

"*You,*" I snarl as I summon my golden axe and silver axe and stand in the way of the enraged god of Water. "You stay where you are."

"You think you can stop me." Yongwang cackles, hysteria dripping from the sound. "I am a *god.*"

"And *I* am the King Foretold." This is not a fight I can win, but I'll buy her as much time as I can. "Fate stands with me."

I gather my magic inside me, praying it will be enough for what I'm about to do. Infusing all of my life force into a single stream, I blast it at Yongwang, hitting him in the chest.

The god of Water grunts and stumbles back two steps, the whites around his eyes a testament to his shock. But it is only shock—even all of my magic didn't do substantial damage to the powerful god—and it will wear off all too soon.

I have to buy her more time.

With the last dregs of my life force, I shoot out my hand and project a protective shield over Sunny and Yeomla. I fall to my knees. The dome barely covers them, and I don't know how long it will hold. But they won't survive another interruption.

They need more time.

My chest heaves for air, but I keep the dome over them. I groan and plant one hand on the ground, my raised arm shaking. Still, I shield them.

Roaring with murderous rage, Yongwang shifts into his dragon form. Before I can react, he wraps his serpentine body around me. How could I have thought he looked anything like Draco? The god of Water's merciless eyes narrow into slits as he squeezes the life out of me.

Fuck. The shield is down.

"Did I make you angry, Dragon King?" I goad to hold his attention. "Did my magic hurt you? You should've seen the look on your face. I had a feeling you were the weakest god."

"I will teach you to respect the gods, little king," he hisses and coils his body tighter around me.

My ribs crack under the pressure, but I don't make a sound.

That's right, fucker. Look right at me. Don't turn around.

"Don't trouble yourself," Sunny murmurs, and my gaze shoots toward her. "My husband already respects me, and I am the only god he needs to respect."

Even as the dragon crushes the life out of me, I fight to focus on Sunny. Her long black hair falls like silk down her back as she lays Yeomla gently on the ground. When she rises to her feet, palpable power shimmers around her.

My wife. She is glorious.

I'm running out of air fast. My head swims, and my eyelids droop. At least she will be the last thing I see.

"You should be dead, gumiho." The dragon's voice rumbles with menace. "I stopped Yeomla before he gave all his life force to you."

"I thought you knew." Sunny cocks her hip to one side and holds her palm out toward Yongwang. "I don't need any of you to *give* me your life force. I can *take* what I want."

White fire flares in her eyes, and the dragon screeches and writhes in the air. Yongwang loses his grip on me, and I crash to the ground with a thump. I wheeze, the wind knocked out of me. I fight for much-needed air, my feet kicking in the dirt. After a long second, I suck in a heaving breath, past the pain in my ribs, then another. My vision finally clears, and I struggle to my knees.

Sunny is pointing both palms toward the god of Water, a growl wrenching past her gritted teeth. Her entire body glows with white light. I raise my hand to shield my eyes.

Color leaches out of the dragon until he looks as faint as a pencil sketch. Then his serpentine body jolts and stiffens.

A vicious smile curves her lips as she wrings the dragon until his keening cry rends the air. Still, she doesn't stop. The dragon spasms and curls in on himself, and Yongwang shifts back to his human form—his face twisted into a mask of pain.

Sunny closes her fists and lowers her arms at last. And the god of Water crumples to the ground in a heap of broken limbs.

Yet, she continues to . . . burn.

Her hair floats around her head like white flames, and the shadow of her nine tails flickers behind her.

"S-Sunny?" I rise unsteadily to my feet, wrapping an arm around my battered ribs, and stumble toward her. "You absorbed Yongwang's gi. He is mortal now. Y-you can stop now."

She doesn't respond and levitates high off the ground, her eyes burning a fathomless white.

Shit.

She's losing control of the Yeoiju and the four life forces. They are going to tear her apart unless she absorbs them. *What do I do?* Panic wipes my mind clean. *How do I help her?*

"Fuck." I fist a hand in my hair.

Then, Dangun's words reverberate through me. *Stay by her side and help her through it. Anchor her with all your heart.*

Sunny will be okay. A stoic calm spreads through me. I will anchor her. I will *become* her anchor.

No matter what it takes.

I retreat a few steps, then take a running leap into the air and grab her by her hips. Every part of me that comes into contact with her burns, but I ignore everything but saving her.

I let gravity do its job and pull us down. Before we hit the ground, I pivot to take the brunt of the impact. Then I immediately roll over and pin her down with my body.

"Sunny." My voice breaks, seeing her white, unseeing eyes. "Remember not to hold on too tight."

Her head thrashes on the ground, and her back arches even with my weight on top of her.

"Please, Sunny." I cup her pale cheek. "Expand your Yeoiju."

Why is she cold? Her skin doesn't burn me anymore. Something's wrong. *Very wrong.*

"Open your heart." I don't know if she can hear me. "Embrace the divine gi of Underworld and Water like you did with Sky and Mountains. Make them a part of you."

Her lips move, but no sound comes out, and spit dribbles down from the corner of her mouth.

"Listen to me," I yell in a ravaged voice. I stop and take a shuddering breath. "Listen, Sunny. Let the divine life forces flow through you and the Yeoiju. Just like your father taught you. You can do this. Please."

"It . . . hurts . . ." Her eyes finally meet mine, white fire glowing like amber in her irises.

"I know, baby. Just hang on a little longer." I drop a kiss on her forehead. "You're so strong. You're already starting to control it. I can see it in your eyes."

She moans, shuddering beneath me. I want to scream and wail. I hate seeing her hurt, but I can only hold her—anchor her. After an eternity, her body goes soft, and her head lolls to the side with a sigh of relief.

With a wavering breath, I push up onto my arms and struggle to a seat. Then I get Sunny off the hard ground and lift her onto my lap. She wordlessly burrows against me, her breath warming my collarbone.

"Hey there," I croak.

"Hi," she whispers.

"You did good, baby." I struggle to swallow. "You did real good."

Hwanin bursts into the courtyard and stumbles to a stop. "Yongwang, what have you done?"

The former god of Water curls into a ball on the ground, sobbing pathetically. After a disappointed glance at Yongwang, Hwanin rushes over to Yeomla.

"It's good to see you one last time, old friend." Yeomla smiles wanly, his teeth coated with blood.

"Is this truly goodbye then?" Hwanin whispers.

"I believe so. Then again, I am not familiar with mortality." His chuckle turns into a sputtering cough. "But I am at peace at last. I don't know if I deserve it, though."

"Do not worry." Determination hardens Hwanin's face. "I will set everything right."

"Can you?" the dying god of Underworld asks, a tear seeping out the corner of one eye.

"I will die trying," Hwanin vows.

"Ethan." Sunny buries her head against my chest. "I'm so tired. So much death, so much loss. I want it all to end. *I* want to end it all."

"And you will." I run my hand down her hair, as Hwanin closes Yeomla's lifeless eyes. "Is Sunny ready to face the Amheuk, Lord Hwanin?"

He opens and closes his mouth, then tries again. "Perhaps she—"

The screams of countless people rise in an earsplitting roar, drowning out Hwanin's words.

We are out of time.

CHAPTER FIFTY

Sunny

I don't remember getting up from Ethan's lap, but I'm already running out to the street. The screams grow impossibly loud as a swarm of terrified shinbiins form a dam in front of me.

We have to get to our friends.

"This way." Ethan snatches my hand and runs into a narrow alleyway.

"Where are we going?" I ask, keeping pace with him. "We need to find them."

"There." He points at the sky with his free hand.

An incomprehensible wall of black hovers in the distance, but vibrant beams of red, blue, green, and silver light up the sky. It's not enough to drive back the Amheuk, but the magic of the four life sources is slowing the darkness down.

"They're okay," I breathe. I *know* our friends are okay. I *know* they're the ones giving the Amheuk a run for its money.

"We have to hurry, though." Ethan picks up his pace.

As I run next to him, something niggles at the back of my mind. In our rush to reach our friends, I forgot that I'm a fucking goddess. With an irritated click of my tongue, I tighten my grip on Ethan's hand.

"Hang on," I warn, then teleport us to our friends.

Unfortunately, we materialize in front of a black tentacle mid-swing. Ethan shoves me behind him—he *really* has to stop doing that—and takes the hit in his stomach. We are flung back, but I stop our fall midair and float us down to the ground.

"Ethan." I catch him when his knees buckle.

"I'm okay." He groans as he regains his balance and waves me away.

"We can't hold them off for much longer," Jihun rasps, limping over, and points toward the Queen of Sky, Bora, and Taeyoung, pushing back a monstrous arm of darkness at the other end of the field.

"Right," I say grimly.

Absorbing two divine gi at once should have flattened me, but strangely enough, everything is quiet within me. The four life forces flow through my Yeoiju without hesitation—as though they've been a part of me all along—braiding together into one force.

"Now that I've absorbed all four divine life forces," I tell my friends, "let's see if all the fuss was worth it."

I teleport to where the monarchs fight. To their credit, none of them so much as yelp when I appear out of nowhere.

"Imo," I shout in alarm as the Queen of Sky staggers back, her lightning flickering weakly from her fingers.

Bora and Taeyoung aren't in much better shape.

"Step aside," I yell.

I form a ball of white light between my cupped hands as easily as taking a breath, and I fling the light at the dark monstrosity. With a keening screech, the tentacle disintegrates into dust.

Before I can even register the small victory, four more tentacles attack from all directions. I push out streams of white light with both hands, drawing a wide arc in the sky, and black dust rains down around us.

I glance behind at the three monarchs, and they gasp in unison. I guess my eyes are lit with white fire.

"Get to the Sentinels," I order. "I got this."

"We're not going anywhere." Taeyoung juts his jaw. "Besides, the Sentinels are coming to us."

"They're what?" I groan when I see the cluster of shinbiins sprinting toward us, dodging the Amheuk's tentacles drilling down at them.

Ethan reaches my side in the next second, and my heart can't decide whether to jump or fall. "Sunny."

While I'm distracted, a tentacle sneaks up on us, and I barely have time to shove Ethan out of the way before I blast it with a pulse of light. He spins around to stand with his back against mine and jets silver and green gi at the next one that lashes toward us.

"Shit." I pissed off the Amheuk, burning off its arms, and now we have its full attention.

The Sentinels and the monarchs join us, and we form a tight circle, magic flaring in our eyes. A dozen black arms attack at once, whipping and slashing past the bursts of our collective powers. Cheyun grunts next to me, taking a hit to her side. She growls and renews her attack.

I will not lose another friend.

"Stand back." My voice rings through the chaos. *"Stand back."*

The Yeoiju churns inside me like a tornado gaining momentum. I fist my hands to hold on to the magic impatient to burst from my chest. I am finally powerful enough to fuel the Yeoiju on my own without depleting my life force—without borrowing gi from any other source.

"Everyone, go!" Ethan yells.

They try to retreat, but they have to stop every two steps to fight off the tentacles slashing down on us.

This won't do.

I shape a strand of my power into a long white whip and strike at the swirling darkness to corral it toward me.

"Shield them, Ethan," I shout, my entire body vibrating with the need to unleash my power.

I don't check to see if he got the protective dome over them. I trust him. Plus, I can't hang on another second. With a guttural cry, I let it rip.

My back arches as power, pure and brilliant, bursts through my chest, my eyes, and my mouth. *The Cheon'gwang.* My arms and legs spread wide as white light floods out of me.

I'm breathless with fear and exhilaration, but my power doesn't falter. I burn on and on, and I don't relent.

The Amheuk shudders as the light scorches through its coiled tentacles. *Try and run, motherfucker.* I growl and push out another pulse of light.

The darkness tugs desperately at its bound arms and rips them free from my whip in ragged stumps. Vicious satisfaction sizzles through me. With a thundering cry, the Amheuk retreats into the sky.

But I am not done.

I ignore the faint tremors running through my body and burn through the tentacles remaining in my grasp. Black dust rains down from the sky, atmospheric in the white light.

It's so beautiful.

"Sunny," Ethan shouts hoarsely. "They're gone."

I come to with a jolt. He's right. The sky brightens as the eternal darkness recedes beyond the boundaries of the Kingdom of Sky. But shutting off my power proves more challenging than unleashing it.

I wrap my arms around my midriff and listen for my Yeoiju. It whirs sharply in my ears, rather than singing its usual gentle hum.

Hush now. I clench every muscle in my body. *We did it.*

The Yeoiju pauses at my words, and I curl myself tightly around my heart's center. *It is done. Hush now.* I don't know how long I stand like that, but the frantic whirring slowly quiets.

When at last the song of the Yeoiju becomes a gentle hum again, I fall to one knee and swipe my arm across my forehead. I'm surprised Ethan didn't rush up to catch me before I fell. After a heaving breath, I push up to a stand. There is no time to rest.

"Ethan," Jihun shouts in alarm, and I whip around to face them.

"I got you." Taeyoung wraps an arm around Ethan's shoulders before his knees buckle.

Oh gods.

"Thank you," Ethan murmurs, leaning heavily against the King of Underworld.

I run to him and take one of his hands in mine. He's shaking. "I'm so sorry."

"For what?" He smiles wanly. "For saving us all?"

"I should have stemmed my power sooner." I can't return his smile as guilt rams into me. "I made you hold the shield up for too long."

"I'm fine." His eyes search my face. "How are you? Did that deplete you?"

"No." I shake my head. "It was actually a . . . relief."

"You guys?" Hailey croaks. "Something's wrong."

I look over my shoulder, and blood drains from my face.

Fuck.

I slowly pivot on my feet and confront what I hope isn't our doom.

The leviathan tentacles are gone, but the bodies of the shinbiin strewn across the field twitch and jerk as they rise up from the ground. Then fist-sized black holes appear in the air by each reanimated corpse.

With the unnerving sound of bones snapping, the shadowy portals suck in the bodies like powerful vacuums.

"What in the worlds . . ." Minju whispers. If she doesn't know what's going on, then we are definitely in trouble.

Darkness spreads across the Kingdom of Sky once more. Not as slashing black arms, but as torn, twisted bodies with misshapen limbs hanging off at wrong angles. I recognize the white of their pupilless eyes and the red slash of their screaming mouths.

The Amheuk is consuming the dead and regurgitating them as nightmare monsters.

CHAPTER FIFTY-ONE

Sunny

Ethan cuts down the horrific creatures coming at me, his axes flashing. I stand paralyzed, trapped in a waking nightmare, and the Shin'gwangdo shakes in my hands. The trauma of Heaven Lake still haunts me—these monsters still haunt me.

Cheyun slashes at the dark beasts, her eyes growing wider and wider with disbelief. Every time she cuts them down, they stitch themselves back together. She wasn't with us at Heaven Lake. There is only one vulnerable point in their twisted bodies.

I open my mouth to warn her, but no sound comes out. Then my panicked gaze shoots to Minju when she cries out. The nightmares are slicing her arm ragged.

Get it together, Sunny.

"Do not touch her," Jaeseok roars.

Leaping into the air, he spears a dark monster in its red mouth—its Achilles' heel—and it blinks out of existence. The dokkaebi fights the rest of the monsters around Minju with deadly precision, his handsome, playful face distorted into a furious mask.

But the historian is no shrinking flower. With her lips pressed into a determined line, she heals her ruined arm with silvery light from her other hand. Then she draws a vicious-looking dagger—I recognize it as the one she stabbed me with once upon a time—and hacks at the unending stream of monsters coming at them.

I snap out of my paralysis with a furious growl.

I head toward Minju and Jaeseok—I don't know if I'm running or flying, but my surroundings become blurred from my speed—and I slash the dark creatures in their red, screeching mouths. But as soon as one blinks out of existence, two more take its place.

"Watch out," Minju screams.

I spin and barely manage to evade a misshapen maw, then I stab the monster in the eye, too startled to aim for its mouth. But it blinks out—sucked into a black pinprick in the air, then gone.

"Your sword of light." Minju points at it. "It kills the monsters anywhere you cut them."

"Sweet." I offer her a smile of vicious delight and go to town on the terrifying motherfuckers. And even as adrenaline rushes through my blood and roars in my ears, the blurry outline of a plan forms in my mind.

"Jaeseok, you have her?" I yell over my shoulder.

"I think my violent little historian has herself," he shouts back.

I risk a look behind me, and Minju is airborne, swooshing down like the angel of death to stab away at the bloody red mouths of the monsters. Her heart-shaped face scrunches into a scowl, and growly screams burst past her Cupid's-bow lips.

"Fuck yeah." I hoot, then I fly to my darling, stabby friend. "Minju, let me try something."

I place my hand over hers, gripping the hilt of her dagger, and push the Yeoiju's light into her weapon.

Once her dagger glows white like my Shin'gwangdo, my nerdy friend whispers fervently, "That is brilliant."

"Now try." I smile.

With a high-pitched squeal, Minju ferociously slashes the closest monster at hand, and it winks out obligingly.

"It works, Sunny," she says with a gleeful smile. "Now go do everyone else's."

"You got it." I whoosh away with a wink. I fly—not like an airplane, but more like a UFO—popping in and out of view.

To think, Draco made fun of me for being the only Sentinel who couldn't fly. *Look at me now, kid.* And I'm going to save the worlds like I promised them.

I grab the handle of Jaeseok's spear and infuse my power into it. Then I do the same for Hailey's crossbow, Cheyun's twin swords, and Jihun's long sword.

"Thank you, Goddess," Jihun says with a shit-eating grin before thrusting his sword backward to kill a monster behind him.

"Shut up." I stick my tongue out at him and fly away to find my husband.

A horde of nightmare beasts rushes him from all sides, and he chops them all down with ice-cold accuracy. "Ethan."

I realize my mistake the moment his name leaves my mouth—the only sound that could penetrate his razor-sharp concentration. He glances up at me, and a monster takes advantage of his distraction to slash him down the back. Ethan grimaces, arching his back against the pain, then he cuts the hateful thing down with a growl.

"I'm so sorry." I land by his side. "Are you okay?"

He shifts his shoulders with a wince. "I'll live. How are you?"

"Just swell." I swing my sword of light to keep the nightmares at bay and crush a swift kiss on his mouth. "Here, I can help."

"Yes," he groans and tugs me toward him. "More."

"No, not like that," I chide. "This."

I grab the handles of his axes until the blades shine with white light.

He smirks, testing them out on the beasts leaping toward us. "This will come in handy."

We flatten the nightmare beasts with the help of the supercharged weapons, but they keep coming.

Will it ever end?

I don't know how long we've been fighting when I raise the Shin'gwangdo and stab the last monster. It blinks out of existence, and silence descends around us. I scan our surroundings, fighting for my breath.

The monsters are gone.

Cheyun falls gracefully to her ass, her twin blades still gripped in her hands, and Jihun plants his long sword in the ground to prop himself up.

I weave on my feet, and Ethan appears at my side. He wraps an arm around my waist, and I press a grateful kiss on his cheek.

He smiles down at me, then cranes his neck to check on our friends. "Is everyone okay?"

"Define *okay*," Taeyoung says, limping toward us. He didn't have a weapon for me to juice up, but he battled brilliantly with his nerdy magic.

"Don't be a baby." Bora elbows him gently in the side. "You'll be fine."

The Queen of Sky floats down from above, lightning retreating into her fingertips. "I could use a moment to catch my breath, but I am otherwise unharmed."

"Please forgive me, Your Majesty," Minju says, "but we might not have a mo—"

An enormous dark hand rips past the barrier to the Kingdom of Sky and grabs the historian, cutting off her words. The fist of darkness tightens around her, and she screams in pain.

"Minju!" Jaeseok races toward her.

Her eyes flare red and silver, drawing on the magic of both her life sources, and her lips move with a silent incantation. Her small body burns with silver-and-red fire, and she raises her dagger and brings it down on a dark finger. The hand twitches and drops her, and Jaeseok catches her in the air.

I fly over the hand of the Amheuk and strike its wrist with the Shin'gwangdo. I hear a keening scream from beyond the kingdom, and the darkness swallows my sword and creeps up my arms.

Ethan leaps from the ground and slashes his axes across the black hand. The darkness suddenly releases me, and I'm flung into the air. He doesn't reach me in time to catch me, but he maneuvers himself beneath me and takes the brunt of the impact.

His skull hits the ground with a crack, and his body goes limp. I scramble off him and cup his face in my hands. The fall knocked him unconscious, but his gi pulses with power and strength.

I raise my head as a shadow passes over us. The hand of darkness mends itself and rises to the sky. Then it falls to the ground so swiftly that I only have time to flinch.

Jaeseok's scream of anguish rends the air.

"No, no, no," I breathe. Ethan moans next to me, his eyelids flickering. "You'll be okay, Ethan. Let me check on Minju. I'll be right back."

I push up to my hands and knees, but my legs give out when I try to stand. I have to get to Minju. Gritting my teeth, I stagger to a stand and run toward her. When I get closer, I see her lying limply in Jaeseok's arms as he rocks her back and forth.

No. Please, no.

"Minju." I stumble the last few feet and fall at her side. "Please open your eyes."

To my utter relief, her eyes flutter open, but her gaze is faraway. And when she speaks, her voice is faint as a soft breeze. "I need . . ."

"What is it? What do you need?" I swallow my sob. She'll be okay. There's no reason to cry. "Anything, Minju. I'll do anything."

"I need to tell you . . . The true heart of the r-righteous . . ." She finally looks at me. "Sunny, the prophecy . . . You have it all . . ."

"I don't care about the prophecy." I angrily swipe a hand over my eyes. *Don't fucking cry.* She will be okay. "Just tell me how to help you."

"You have it all wrong . . ." she breathes.

"Don't talk, my love." Jaeseok tenderly smooths her hair off her forehead. "Save your strength."

"You're so handsome and kind. And terribly funny." She cups his cheek with a shaky hand and smiles up at him. "Did I ever tell you that, Jaeseok?"

"You haven't, as a matter of fact," he says, his Adam's apple bobbing. "Now you have to tell me that every day to make up for lost time. And don't forget about what a great dancer I am."

"I love you, Jaeseok." A single tear rolls down her temple. "I will find you in the next life."

"No. Please, Minju," he cries, anguish twisting his face. "I love you so much."

"I know," she says sweetly, and her arm falls limply to the ground. "You made me so happy . . ."

"That's all I ever wanted. To love you and make you happy." Jaeseok takes a deep breath, and steely determination cements over his sorrow. Then he places a featherlight kiss on her forehead. "Don't be scared, my love. I'll see you soon."

With a serene smile, she closes her eyes.

"M-Minju?" My teeth chatter. "O-open your eyes. I can't lose you too."

"Don't hold her back, Sunny. Let her go on to her next life in peace." Jaeseok hands me her body with precious care. "Here. Keep her company while her soul leaves her body. She'll feel safe with you."

I numbly take my beautiful friend from him and cradle her head against my chest. Then ugly animal sobs erupt from me. Her body is still warm. *Why her?* She was the smartest, sweetest person I ever knew. *Oh gods.* Her parents are waiting for her in the Mortal Realm.

"Why?" I ask in a plaintive whisper.

"Everything will be okay." The dokkaebi ruffles my hair. "You will set all things right. Minju believed that, so it has to be true."

"Jaeseok." I raise my grief-filled eyes to peer at his face.

He taps my nose and gets to his feet.

Something isn't right.

"Wh-where are you going?" I follow his gaze and see the Amheuk's arm rise slowly to the sky. Ethan is out of harm's way, but our battered friends stand in the shadow of darkness as the dark hand clenches into a violent fist.

"Run," Jihun shouts. "Everybody, run!"

They might not make it. I have to buy them time—a few seconds is all they need—but my grief has me in chains. My ears ring, and I can't stop shaking.

"Goodbye, Little Sister." Before I can respond, Jaeseok saunters toward the shadowy fist, swirling his spear lazily above his head. Then he takes off in a dead sprint and leaps into the air, his entire body bursting into scorching dokkaebi fire. "Get away from my friends, motherfucker."

As the dark fist falls toward our friends, Jaeseok slams into it in a blaze of red flames. The Amheuk falters while Jaeseok's fire burns against it.

Then . . . he's gone.

"Noooo," Hailey screams.

Jihun drags her away as they all run out from under the murderous shadow. She flails her limbs, screeching bloodcurdling screams. But the monarchs and the Sentinels, or what remains of them, stumble away seconds before the fist falls onto the ground where they stood.

"It's okay, Minju." I carefully lay her on the ground. "Jaeseok will find you soon."

Ethan reaches me at the same time as our friends and falls to his knees next to me. He squeezes my hand, and I bite down on my lips.

I would've lost him too. I would've lost everyone.

An ominous rumble shakes the ground beneath us, and my Yeoiju emits a sharp chime. Yelping in pain, I press my palms against my ears, even though the sound came from within me.

"What is happening?" Bora widens her stance when the ground shakes beneath us.

The sky is literally falling around us. The hand of the Amheuk tears at the barrier to the Kingdom of Sky, and its other hand pushes through. More cracks split open in the sky, zigzagging down to the field of clouds.

I rise to my feet as my power flares with horrifying violence.

I will not allow Minju and Jaeseok's sacrifices to be in vain.

"Do not follow me," I order the others in a voice I hardly recognize. "The Amheuk is *mine.*"

"Wait," someone rasps behind me.

My feet falter at the desperation in the single word, and I turn to face Hwanin. He steps out from under Gyun's arm, which was around his shoulders, and stumbles toward me.

"You must come with me." Something of his former power returns when he intones, "*Now.*"

"I'm rather busy at the moment." I shoot an impatient scowl at my great-grandfather, the male who disapproved of my bear-spirit grandmother. I'm not inclined to listen to a single thing he says.

"It will not be enough. Your power . . ." He swallows. "Your power is not complete. You cannot stop the Amheuk yet."

"Sunny." The Judge of Tenth Hell squeezes my upper arm to get my attention. "You have to go with him. He is telling the truth. He told me everything."

My lips part with surprise. No one can lie to the Judges of Ten Hells.

"Go with him." Gyun nods when he sees the realization in my eyes. "He will explain everything on the way."

Ethan stands. "I'm coming with her."

"No, Your Majesty." The judge holds up a hand. "No one can follow where she goes. Not there. She needs to focus on keeping herself safe—not on keeping *you* safe."

I glance at Gyun, his face tight with fear and worry, then at Hwanin, his eyes wide and wild.

"Ethan." I turn to him and cup his cheek. "Hwanin is telling the truth. I need to do this. *Alone.*"

"We do this together," he growls. "Or not at all."

"This is how we do this together. Please let me go, my love," I plead, knowing how much I am asking of him. "Minju, Jaeseok, and Draco cannot have died in vain. I can't let that happen. I need to stop the Amheuk. Please, Ethan. I will come back to you. I promise."

Ethan exhales a shuddering breath, heartbreak in his eyes. "I will hold you to that promise, wife."

I crush my lips against his but draw away before he can pull me close. Then I grab Hwanin's arm and yank him away from the field of clouds. "Where to?"

"The Suhoshin headquarters." He huffs as he struggles to keep up with me.

The damn fool will slow us down, but I don't have enough strength to teleport us yet. "Why? What's there?"

"You have only absorbed three-quarters of each of the gods' gi." Hwanin ages before my eyes, stooped and ancient. "The rest of our divine life forces is in the . . . Donggul."

"The place of the Suhoshin trials?" My brows pull together.

"Yes." The old man begins to weep. "The monster within holds the remainder of the four gods' gi."

Then he tells me the horrifying story.

A FATE WORSE THAN DEATH

Hwanin, the god of Heavens, told himself it was for his son. Besides, he had every right to do as he wished. He was a god. He mattered more than a mere mortal. And so did Hwanung.

"Ungnyeo's heart is strong and pure," Hwanin said to his son. "If we do this, she will become immortal, and she will be able to keep the Amheuk at bay. She will be a hero—a goddess. She will be at your side for all eternity."

"My wife is perfect as she is," Hwanung, the god of Earth, insisted, but there was doubt in his voice—there was greed. "I will speak to her. This must be her decision."

Hwanung wanted to hold on to his wife. He wanted her to say yes. His greed blinded him to his father's shadowed heart. That night, Hwanung asked Ungnyeo to become an immortal goddess in order to protect the realms.

"Do it for Dangun, beloved." Hwanung clutched his wife's hand. "You can keep our son safe."

Ungnyeo did not wish to become an immortal goddess—not even to spend all eternity with her fated love and their son—but she could not turn her back on the realms. "I will do as you ask."

Hwanin was right. Ungnyeo's heart was strong and pure. Her mortal soul should have shattered from the force of the divine gi she absorbed, but her strong and pure heart preserved a speck of her true self.

Even as she became a monster too horrific to behold.

Even as the monster killed countless suhoshin cadets to satiate its gnawing hunger for blood and death.

Even as the monster gave birth to the Gray Void.

CHAPTER FIFTY-TWO

Sunny

"You selfish, evil motherfucker." I shove Hwanin to the ground. "She was my grandmother. I am Ungnyeo's granddaughter."

His shoulders shake, not with tears, but laughter, as though his sanity is slipping through the sieve of his tattered mind. Or maybe he feels relieved—it must be positively *freeing*—now that he has unburdened himself of the horrifying truth he and the other gods kept secret for so long.

"Fuck this," I snarl.

Where even are we?

I was so consumed by his chilling confession that I stopped paying attention to the road. It doesn't matter. I already know where we need to go. The sooner we get this over with, the sooner I can be rid of Hwanin. He disgusts me to the depth of my soul.

At least the last few minutes with him allowed me to restore my magic.

I grab him by the collar of his robe and pull him up to his feet. Then I teleport us to the entrance to the Donggul and fling him away from me.

I remember my father's face as he spoke of my grandfather's soul-shattering grief. *And my poor grandmother.* I clench my fists and scream toward the sky, as impotent sorrow and rage pummel my insides. I spin on the male responsible for all that pain.

"Hwanung lost his fated love. Dangun lost both his parents. Ungnyeo lost *herself*. All because of you," I spit at him, shaking from head to toe. "How *could* you?"

"I have no excuse." The piece of trash drops his head. "I am a monster."

"Damn right you are." I remember the pain of the stranded in the Gray Void. All those suhoshin cadets—young, hopeful, and noble—deceived into sacrificing their lives to preserve the immortality of the selfish, unworthy gods. "You make me *sick*."

"As I should," he says and opens the gates to the Donggul. "But I will do what I can to atone for what I have done."

A chill runs down my spine, and terror wraps around my body. I am immortal, but what I have to face in this place is far worse than any manner of death. The monster in the Donggul is no longer the kind, strong bear spirit my father described.

From what Hwanin told me, I am about to face a monster so dark and depraved that anyone who dies at its hands becomes a stranded—their life force twisted and corrupted into han.

But the former god of Heavens steps inside without fear—as though he wishes to suffer all the horrors the Donggul promises.

As I follow him into its eerie depth, I understand why the unassuming hanok was given that name by the Suhoshin. The darkness inside the "cave" feels fathomless and expands all around us.

In a few steps, the light from the gates disappears, and we stand in the pitch black of the space. But it's different from the Amheuk's darkness—which is the absence of light, desolate and empty. The darkness here feels *alive*, like it's slithering with malice and violence.

Even though I listened to Hwanin's confession, I didn't understand the extent of the evil the former gods have created.

"What have you *done*?" I snarl.

"This way." Hwanin sounds stronger than before, in a stoic, hopeless kind of way.

I float a ball of white light above us and follow him, only because I have no other choice. I glance around the cavernous space, where the Suhoshin trials are held every Lunar New Year. I always imagined there would be endless obstacle courses that grew ever more harrowing.

But the Donggul is completely empty. No walls. No rooms. Not even pillars—much less a gauntlet. Because it was never an obstacle course that killed the suhoshin cadets.

I want this horror to end. I want to end Ungnyeo's suffering, even for the speck of herself that remains. And I want to end the Amheuk so that it never haunts us again. I just want everything to fucking end.

Maybe not *everything*. I don't think I'm ready for my life to end . . .

Fuck.

Panic grips me by the throat. I am *immortal.* How do you kill a god? I stumble over my own feet, my breath coming in sharp pants. Is it inevitable then? Must I become the End of Days? I cup my clammy forehead with a trembling hand.

Ethan will save me.

He loves me more than anything. He will find a way to kill me. I bring my hand down to cover my mouth.

My poor Ethan.

I drop my hand and drag air into my constricted lungs. I can only take one step at a time. I have to focus on the harrowing step ahead of me.

"Where is she?" I growl at Hwanin.

"She will come for us," he says with absolute certainty. "She was created to inflict suffering. To *crave* your blood, your pain, your screams."

I raise my head and pierce Hwanin with my enraged gaze. "*You* deserve to suffer."

"Yes." He turns and resumes walking.

I trail after him, deeper into the darkness. My white orb only lights a few steps ahead of us, and I trip over a long, pale bone—a femur. My stomach heaves.

Every faltering step reveals more bones and skulls—the remains of the suhoshin cadets who died at the monster's hands. Soon the bones cover every surface of the floor, and we have to march atop the mass grave.

Hwanin shoots out a hand, and I bump into his outstretched arm before I come to a stop. "She is here."

Then I hear it.

A low, feral growl that tapers into a manic clicking. The beat of silence as the monster inhales. Then another clicking growl. Goose bumps spread across my arms, and the hair on the back of my neck rises to a stand.

"I will distract her." Hwanin meets my eyes. "You must absorb the four life forces inside her, like you absorbed Yongwang's. Let your Yeoiju take what it needs."

I almost lost control after I absorbed the treacherous god of Water's gi. I forgot in the chaotic aftermath, but if it wasn't for Ethan, I don't know what would've happened. Without him as my anchor, I don't know if I can do this.

What if I lose control?

"Ungnyeo," Hwanin booms, stepping out of the halo of the white light. "It is I, Hwanin. Take your vengeance. Be free of your han."

The growling and clicking grow louder as heavy, limping steps approach us. I don't want to see what stands across from him, but I expand the light of the Yeoiju.

"Oh gods." I gag and vomit on the floor.

The Donggul Monster stands three stories tall, and . . . I scrunch my eyes shut against the grotesque sight. But I force them back open.

The monster is nearly torn up beyond recognition, but the faintest hint of a bear remains in it. Half of its skull is missing, along with one ear, and its brain pulses in its exposed head. One of its eyeballs dangles from its socket, hanging on by a single strand of muscle. And a long, black tongue flicks restlessly inside a mangled snout, jagged teeth flashing in the maw.

Its arms hang down its sides at gruesome, broken angles—one with patches of fur and skin missing, the other almost chewed down to the bone. *Oh gods* . . . its stomach . . . I gag, but there is nothing left to throw up. Its stomach is ripped to shreds, and its intestines dangle from the open wounds. And its legs and feet are almost burned to stubs. I don't know how it stands and walks.

I shrink away from the thought that a speck of my grandmother remains in the monster—that someone so good has been rendered to this.

"Ungnyeo." Hwanin pounds his chest. "I am here, the one who trapped you in this hell. Come at me, you hideous monster. I am the one responsible for your suffering."

"Hwan . . ." Its malformed mouth moves, a guttural voice emerging. "Hwan . . . in?"

Before a shudder finishes running through me, the monster launches itself at Hwanin with an earsplitting howl.

"Now, child," he yells at me before he hits the ground. *"Now."*

I watch paralyzed. The Donggul Monster works almost delicately, piercing one of his eyes, then ripping off one of his ears. Hwanin's screams sound inhuman. I hear the snap of bones as it breaks his arm. It pauses as if to listen to his tortured cries, then tears off the useless arm. Then it bites off the side of his head.

The monster is inflicting on Hwanin the same injuries it endured.

"No," I say without sound. When the monster draws a jagged nail down Hwanin's torso, opening up his stomach, I finally find my voice. "Stop it."

"N . . . no," Hwanin wheezes. "Do . . . it. P-please. Save us both."

"Grandmother, stop," I shout.

The monster's hand pauses, and it tilts its head toward me. The growling and clicking return, and it rises to its feet with surprising fluidity. Then . . . it's upon me before I can blink. My head hits the floor with a thwack, and pain rings through my skull.

Its jaw unhinges, the smell of rot and death bathing my face, and it bites down on my shoulder. I scream as its teeth drill down to my bones. I thrash my legs against the pain, and consciousness becomes too much to bear. My eyes roll back, and darkness edges into my vision, but my survival instinct belatedly kicks in.

I punch the monster's head, and I knee its ruined stomach. Yet the Donggul Monster doesn't budge. It only clamps down harder into my shoulder, and I hear the crunch of bones.

I cry out in agony, and my Yeoiju cries with me. *Help.* I feel my Yeoiju unfurl, and the four life forces spin and expand inside me. The shivers running down my body become violent until I flop around on the ground like a fish out of water.

Then, at last, the light of the Yeoiju explodes out of my chest, my back arching from the force.

But the monster remains on top of me, unaffected by the white light. My vision wavers. *Of course.* This monster has the power of the gods, but it isn't the Amheuk. The white light can't kill it.

I . . . I have to remember something. It's important.

I can't . . . kill the monster. Not until I absorb its gi. Everything will be ruined if I don't absorb the divine life forces inside it.

Draco. Minju. Jaeseok.

I push weakly against the Donggul Monster as it tugs on one of my arms, like it's toying with it before it tears it off.

"Ungnyeo," Hwanin roars and jumps onto the monster's back. "I know you are in there, somewhere deep and dark. Find yourself, one last time. I know it hurts. I know you are scared. But you have to come out of hiding. Fight the madness."

The monster slaps at its own back, trying to dislodge Hwanin, but the old man hangs on tenaciously.

"Look down, Ungnyeo." He shakes the monster by its hackles. "That is your *granddaughter*. She is Dangun's daughter."

The Donggul Monster finally lands a hit on Hwanin and throws him to the ground. Then it lumbers to its feet and steps on Hwanin's head, crushing it into a red pulp. I watch, lying on my back, and sob brokenly.

I don't know if I'm crying because of the agony in my ruined shoulder or from the shock of seeing my great-grandfather's head smeared on the ground. What he did to my grandmother and the countless suhoshin cadets is unforgivable. But he tried to do the right thing in the end. He tried to save me.

The monster seems . . . confused as it stares down at the limp, headless body of the former god. I force my limbs to move, and flip over to my stomach. When my shoulder begins to heal and the pain passes enough for me to see straight, I crawl up to my knees.

I have to do this—not only for Ethan and my friends—but for my grandmother. Hwanin said she's still in there somewhere. Only I can help her. I don't resent the lonely power of the Yeoiju anymore. Because of it, I can untangle the curse that broke her mind. I can free her from her tortured existence.

"Grandmother," I whisper, pressing my hands against my chest. I summon my Yeoiju. *We have to help her.* "Grandmother, hear my voice."

The Donggul Monster growls and clicks, then she slowly hobbles toward me, leaving bloody paw prints on the floor.

"Help me, Grandmother." My husky voice breaks on the last word. "I need to absorb your gi to stop the Amheuk from destroying the Realm of Four Kingdoms. If I don't stop it, it will destroy your beloved Mortal Realm next. That's my home too. So please. Help me, Grandmother."

The monster pauses halfway, as though she hears me.

I rise to my feet and reach my power toward her, expanding the light of my Yeoiju. And she allows my magic near her. But as soon as I come into contact with her psyche, I flinch and draw back my power.

She is hurting so much.

The four strands of divine life forces struggle inside her, fighting each other. Their strife is tearing her apart—her soul, her mind, her body—but the immortality of the divine gi mends her, only to rip her to shreds all over again in a torturous cycle.

I harden my resolve and delve my magic deeper inside her, cold sweat breaking out on my forehead. The four life forces are frantic—their discord too jarring. I have to unravel the knot of divine gi before I can absorb them. But they are tangled so badly that I don't know where to start.

What do I do?

Panic unfurls in my stomach, and indecision threatens to paralyze me all over again. My gaze jumps frantically over the monster. She cocks her head at me, like she's trying to decide whether to keep cooperating or to just kill me.

Fuck this.

I have always been an intuitive person. There's no reason to stop listening to my gut just because the fate of the worlds hangs in the balance. Led by pure instinct, my magic pulls at the silver thread first. It is Hwanin's gi, and it unravels from the knot without resistance. I had a feeling it would be cooperative.

I tug on the red thread next. Even though he was one of the assholes who entrapped my grandmother to preserve his divinity, Yeomla died honorably. Little by little, his red gi comes loose, and some of my anger loosens too.

When I pull on the blue thread, I'm not surprised that Yongwang's gi resists. Gritting my teeth, I yank it harder, but it clings to life as its cowardly owner had done.

Across from me, the monster lowers herself to the ground with huffs of tired breath, then curls herself into a ball.

My grandmother is helping me.

I push on, swallowing past my tight throat. At last, I unknot the stubborn blue gi and wrench it free. But when my magic reaches for the green gi, the monster jerks and recoils. It is Hwanung's life force—her husband and fated mate's gi.

"Grandmother." I speak into her mind. "You have to let him go. He waits for you in the next life."

A keening cry—not quite human, not quite animal—slips past the monster's lips.

"When he lost you, Hwanung transferred his divine gi to Dangun and became mortal. He couldn't live on without you," I continue. "Now you have to release the last of his gi so you can join him in the next life."

The monster moans plaintively. I don't know if she'll let go, but I have to try. Trembling from head to toe, I gently tug on the green gi, and it . . . slips loose. The evil gripping the Donggul loosens its hold, and the darkness becomes just . . . darkness.

I withdraw my powers from her, then look at the Donggul Monster, searching for her gi. I gasp, pressing my hand against my chest.

All four divine life forces flow in harmony inside her.

The monster lies so still that I stop breathing. *Did I . . . fail?* Then, with a sigh that echoes through the cavernous room, she uncurls her body and slides onto her back.

I release a rough breath and drop my head toward my chest. My lips wobble, but I press them together.

Please let my grandmother be finally free.

"My dear child," a serene voice says.

I jerk my head up.

A beautiful apparition floats above the monster, glowing white.

"G-Grandmother?"

"Yes, Sunny." She has the kindest smile. "Come closer. Let me get a better look at my granddaughter."

I stumble toward her, exhausted from unraveling the divine gi inside the monster. I stop less than an arm's length away and reach my hand toward her. My fingertips brush against the glowing specter, and it . . . flickers.

I can *touch* her. Ungnyeo isn't a ghost. She is manifesting her true self through the divine gi of the gods—through the four life forces that I need to absorb.

But once I do, she will be gone.

"Are you afraid, child?" Her ghostly hand cups my cheek. Her touch feels warm.

"Y-yes." I lean into her hand.

"Good. Only a fool would not be afraid." She tilts her head to the side. "But you know what you have to do, right?"

"I do." I bite my lower lip.

"My brave child." She smooths her hand down my hair.

"But I don't know if I can do it without my fated love anchoring me," I whisper.

"Your fated love?" She presses her hands to her chest. "I am so happy the gods have blessed you as they blessed your grandfather and me. Even if he is not with you, his love will anchor you. And I will help. I will not let you lose your way, my dear child."

"Thank you, Grandmother." I swallow thickly. We don't have time. "A-are you ready?"

"Is your father well?" The words tumble out of her. "Is my son . . . well?"

"Yes, he's well." I smile. "My father is kind, strong, and loving. He reminds me of you."

"And you remind me of him." She returns my smile. "Dangun has always been a good son."

"I think . . . I think he is a good father as well."

"I am glad." She sighs. "Very well. I am ready to leave you now. I long to see Hwanung."

I nod, my throat working to swallow. I take a deep breath and call on the Yeoiju. Calm spreads through me, and my chest glows white. My grandmother places her pale hand against it. Then we close our eyes, our hearts aligned.

The four divine life forces flow into me like a gentle stream. There is no hesitation, no conflict. Only harmony. I absorb the last of my grandmother's gi and fall to my knees.

"Goodbye, Granddaughter."

I open my eyes in time to see her fade away. "Goodbye, Grandmother."

The green gi of Mountains, the silver gi of Sky, the red gi of Underworld, and the blue gi of Water coalesce inside me until the white gi of the Cheon'gwang flows through my veins and pulses around me. And it is done.

I am the goddess of Light.

CHAPTER FIFTY-THREE

Sunny

With a groan, I rise to my feet and look around the Donggul. The darkness is gone, but death still lingers in the graveyard of bones and skulls. The stranded souls have already been freed from the Gray Void, but their remains also deserve proper respect.

I float out of the Donggul to avoid stepping on the dead, then I set the entire structure on fire with a flick of my hand. Unease threads through me, even though I contained the white fire to the Donggul.

I shake off my worry. The fire will burn off once the remains are gone.

But as I turn away from the burning hanok, I sense Ethan's life force rise with the force of a tsunami.

"What in the . . ."

Then, with a sonic boom, a protective dome closes around an enormous perimeter, including the Suhoshin headquarters—including *me.*

Shit.

Something must have happened to put his protective instinct into overdrive. He's in danger. They all are.

Ethan will die if he keeps the shield up for much longer—and the stubborn male *will* keep it up until I am at his side. I take off in a dead run, searching for the epicenter of his magic. Once I locate him in my mind's eye, I command time and space to do my bidding and take me to him.

I feel a slight tug, and I am there.

Ethan, the Sentinels, and the other three monarchs have retreated further into the Kingdom of Sky, and they stand just outside the walls of the capital. I quickly appraise the situation as I hover high above them.

The hands of Amheuk, along with the rest of its monstrous, humanoid form, have broken past the boundaries of the Kingdom of Sky. Its head is half-hidden beyond the clouds, but its vast body spans the horizon. The surface of its shadowy form churns and whips, coiled with serpentine strands of darkness.

Our friends surround Ethan in a semicircle, pouring their life forces into him. His protective dome—powered by the gi of all four life sources—is the only thing standing between the Amheuk and what remains of the Kingdom of Sky.

"I'm here, Ethan." Love infuses the whispered words, carried to him by the winds. "You can rest now."

He doesn't look up—he can't—but his shoulders sag with relief. He heard me. He knows I am safe.

"Taper off your life forces," I say to the rest of my friends. And with a thought, I stand before them. "I'll take it from here."

Our friends withdraw their gi, one by one, but my stubborn husband maintains his shield.

"Sunny," Ethan rasps past his clenched jaw.

"I know." I glance over my shoulder. "I'll be careful."

"Liar." He gives me a strained smile. "Besides, I was about to say, 'Go kick ass.'"

"That's a given." I give him a saucy wink, then turn back to face the Amheuk. "Now, withdraw your shield like a good husband. I'll buy you guys time to retreat behind the wall."

I throw a glimmering white shield over Ethan and our friends, drawing the Amheuk's attention to me. But I flinch when it leans down and pushes its face through the clouds.

Its glowing red eyes exude pure malice—an evil so elemental that a scream lodges in my throat. *Get it together, Sunny. That thing killed Minju and Jaeseok.* I swallow my fear and meet its violent gaze with one of my own.

It will never take another life. I will not allow it.

Ethan finally withdraws his protective dome and staggers back, his knees buckling. Jihun and Cheyun each catch hold of his arms to support him, but they aren't much better off. The exhausted group stumbles toward the gates to the capital, leaning on one another.

Once they are inside, I give the Amheuk my full, undivided attention.

"I am the goddess of Light." I push forward the shield of light until the Amheuk squints against the glare. "Otherwise known as *your demise*."

I call to my Yeoiju, and the Cheon'gwang swells within it. The white light grows fast—too fast—making my entire body vibrate with unleashed energy. Before it can overwhelm me, I launch balls of light at the Amheuk, punching gaping holes across its body.

Its furious roar is the sound of nightmares—the sound of unimaginable pain and boundless fear. It resonates inside me, and I scream, gripping my head. I sink my teeth into my lip to stem my cry.

The Amheuk's soul-rending howl morphs into an insidious laugh. I watch in horror as the holes mend themselves.

A strand of darkness unrolls from its stomach and whips down on me with incomprehensible speed. I feel the burn of ice across my chest, and my pained shout gurgles in my throat.

Gagging on my own blood, I glance down at the flayed gash on my chest, deep enough to show the whites of my upper rib cage. Shock shudders down my spine and my limbs, and I lock my knees to stop them from buckling.

"Mother . . . fucker." I grit my teeth until the gaping wound begins to heal—flesh, muscle, and skin knitting back together.

"Goddess of Light." The Amheuk sketches a mocking bow. "Have you learned that a mere god is no match for the ancient force of darkness? Or do you need another lesson?"

"Oh goody. You can talk." I spit a mouthful of blood on the ground. "That will make kicking your ass much less boring."

The evil incarnate narrows its scary eyes into even more terrifying slits.

"Now, use your words and tell me." I launch a volley of white cannonballs, making certain I get the fucker's chest. *Payback is a bitch.* "On a scale of one to ten, how much does that hurt?"

The Amheuk resorts to more roaring and lashes down at me with four dark tentacles. I am ready this time and evade most of them, but one pierces through my thigh, wrenching a scream out of me.

"I . . . told you . . ." I growl, my hand already glowing with white light, "to use your words."

I aim at the darkness and propel the light at its face. The Amheuk spins away, but not before the light burns a gash across his cheek. It groans, the grating sound rumbling through the sky.

I smirk, but ten more tentacles reach for me, wiping the smile off my face. "Shit."

I fly headlong toward them, but at the last minute, I spin toward the left, evading all of them. Carried by their momentum, they crash into the ground where I stood mere seconds ago.

The choreography of violence stretches on without pause until I forget what it's like not to be exhausted.

When will this end?

The Amheuk sprouts endless arms and whips them toward me again and again. And I launch my attacks of light, giving him hell right back. I want to teach the darkness to feel fear. I want it to fear pain—to fear death—before I *end* it.

I flit through the air, weaving between the tentacles, but my luck runs out and one finally punches through my shoulder.

"Fuck me." I groan.

A good thing about adrenaline is that I don't feel the pain as much as I should. So I draw the power of my divine gi from my chest and hurl it at the Amheuk before it can gloat. The ball of white light tears off its massive arm.

I land on the ground and stumble for balance. I hope I bought myself some time. It should take a while for the darkness to heal itself from that injury. I plant my hands on my thighs and drag air into my burning lungs.

Unfortunately, the Amheuk doesn't even pause for its arm to grow back. It brings down its other fist, and I take a flying leap before I'm creamed. I roll to a stand, but I'm so turned around that my next attack barely skims the Amheuk's pinky.

I fall, and I fall again. And every time, I get up like an obstinate teeter-totter. Like this, the relentless battle rages on until night descends on the Kingdom of Sky.

Too tired to strike first, I sway on my feet and brace for the next attack. But . . . it doesn't come.

What is the Amheuk waiting for?

"Has hope blossomed in your heart, Goddess?" Its red mouth stretches into a condescending sneer. "Have you begun to think maybe you can defeat me?"

"I *can* defeat you," I pant. My T-shirt and jeans are in tatters, but the copious amount of blood that I have spilled doesn't show through. *Black is always a good choice.* "I will end you and wipe that nasty smile off your hideous mug."

"Ah, yes," it drawls. "You feel more than hope. You have *faith*. It would be satisfying to crush your pathetic hope. But crushing your faith will be transcendent."

Fuck.

Dread spreads through me as I glance at the dark sky, and realization dawns on me. The Amheuk has been stalling this whole time because it is most powerful after nightfall.

"I changed my mind," I snarl. "You talk way too much. Stop using your words."

"Did you truly believe that you, the *goddess* of Light, can defeat *me*?" Rage spills past the red slash of its mouth. "I am no mere god. I *am* Darkness. I existed even before time itself."

The Amheuk explodes and blankets the sky. Soon, the darkness will encompass the Kingdom of Sky—the last of the Realm of Four Kingdoms—and all will be lost. I have to stop it. My panicked eyes skip left and right, searching for an answer.

I have to become the Cheon'gwang.

I hug my arms around my stomach. *This body.* A sob tears through my throat. *This mind.* I have to stop being . . . me. I can't become the Cheon'gwang until I cease to exist. My teeth chatter as I curl in on myself.

I'm scared, Ethan.

I can't be me. I can't be yours. Not anymore.

But I hear his voice as though he's standing right next to me. *You are still you. You are still mine.*

I dig my nails into my palms and hiss a shaky breath. I straighten to my full height and glare at the dark sky. *Everything will be okay, Ethan.* I will make sure of it.

The Yeoiju spins at my heart's center and calls to my life force. My gi, turned white from the union of the four divine gi, answers the call and flows into the Yeoiju.

The orb grows and expands, beating to the rhythm of my heart, until my chest gleams white. Then the white light spreads to every corner of my body, down to my toes and to the tips of my fingers.

I let go.

Light bursts from my chest, my mouth, my eyes. My arms crack like porcelain, and my fingers split apart. Agony rips through me, but I no longer have a throat to form a scream, a mouth to release the sound.

My human form shifts into my gumiho as I seek relief from the pain. My gumiho is strong. She can hold me together. But the light of the Yeoiju tears through her body, and we shatter.

I become the Cheon'gwang and fill the Kingdom of Sky, expanding to the farthest reaches of the night. I meet a wall of darkness, and the Amheuk trembles in fear, clinging on to its existence. Silent laughter flickers through me. It is hanging on to false hope.

I am Light.

I shine on the darkness, and the Amheuk dissipates with a terrible shriek until . . . there is only light.

I am Life.

But for there to be life, there must be death. This balance is immutable—a fundamental truth.

I am Death.

CHAPTER FIFTY-FOUR

Ethan

The brilliant flare of white light explodes in the skies, and I throw my arms up to shield my eyes.

I don't know how long it takes before the light fades enough for me to squint my eyes open, but I sprint toward it the instant I can.

"Sunny!" I shout as I run out of the city gates.

It took all of them—every single one of my friends—to hold me back when the Amheuk hurt Sunny . . . again and again. I roared at them to let me go until my voice turned hoarse, but I couldn't break free without hurting them.

With my sanity back, I am grateful to them for saving me from a futile death. I would've only gotten in her way.

Now, I have to go to her. Even if it's not . . . her anymore.

I push myself until I become a blur. My heart pounds—more from fear than exertion—because I don't see her anywhere. The Cheon'gwang shines brightly enough to chase away even the hint of a shadow.

But I can't see Sunny.

I know she became the light to defeat the darkness, but she is still her. She has to be. Because she's mine.

"Sunny!"

As I keep running, the white light fades away, and it's night again in the Kingdom of Sky. I whip my head left and right, screaming her name until the tang of blood coats my throat.

Then in the shadowy darkness, I finally find her. Her small body, glowing with white light, lies limply on the ground.

"Sunny." I fall to my knees next to her. "I'm here. I'm here, baby."

I gather her into my arms and rock her back and forth. I hear the keening wail of mourners rising from the field—but there is only me. My grief tears through my throat, threatening to unravel my mind.

"Fuck." I shake her. "Come back to me, Sunny. Gods damn it, you stubborn fool. Open your eyes. *Come back to me.*"

Her eyelids flicker, and I stop breathing. Then miraculously, she blinks open her eyes. "Ethan?"

"Yes." I laugh, blinking my eyes to clear them. "Yes, Sunny. It's me."

She raises a trembling hand and cups my face. Her palm scalds my cheek. I flinch and nearly draw away from her, but there is no way I will ever avoid her touch—not even if I burn to cinders.

"What happened?" She lifts her head to look around, and I help her sit up. "Is it . . . over?"

"You don't remember?" I keep an arm around her shoulders to steady her, but I tuck her hair behind her ear with my free hand. "You did it, baby. You stopped the Amheuk. The darkness . . . it's gone."

I laugh again. She did it. She fucking did it.

Sunny blinks at me, a frown tugging at her brows. I smooth out the two grooves with the pad of my thumb. Then her eyes widen, and she scrambles away from me. I am too shocked and confused to stop her.

"Sunny?" My blood pounds in my ears, and a premonition sends a shiver down my spine. "What's wrong?"

"You have to get everyone out of here." She crawls back even farther from me.

"Sunny, stop." I gingerly raise my hands in the air. She stops moving, but her eyes flit left and right as though looking for escape. "Out of where?"

"They have to leave the Realm of Four Kingdoms," she whispers. "They have to go to the Mortal Realm. *Everyone.*"

"Everyone?" I scowl, ready to argue I am not going *anywhere* without her.

"Except you," she says, and I deflate with relief. "But you have to get everyone to leave *now*. The Amheuk is gone. The Gray Void is gone. They just need to leave. Make sure the seraphim and the suhoshins carry the ones who can't fly. Just do it now. Please."

"They're going to want a little more expla—"

"Hurry." She screams, her body jerking and writhing.

"What's happening, Sunny?" I jump to my feet. "Are you hurt—"

"You have to go, Ethan." She opens her eyes, and her pupils are engulfed in white flames. And her voice booms like the roar of fire when she says, "*Go now.*"

I don't want to leave her, but her desperation breaks my heart. She is *terrified*, and I can't refuse her.

"I'll come back," I vow. "Wait for me, Sunny. I'll come back to you."

For a split second, the brown of her eyes flickers through the white. "I know."

I take off in a run, back toward the capital.

The dream.

My recurring dream about the fiery ruination of the worlds rockets back into my consciousness. The female in my dreams—the one engulfed in white flames—is Sunny. I see her face clearly now, as well as the destruction that lies around her.

Everything burns.

I run faster, my heart thumping in my throat. My lungs burn, but I push myself harder. I have to hurry. I need to get everyone out. She will never forgive herself if even a single person gets hurt because of her. Everyone has to leave.

Now.

I burst through the gates of the walled capital and run straight into Jihun.

"Ethan, what's wrong?" He catches me by the shoulders, and the rest of my friends huddle close. "Where's Sunny?"

"You have to get everyone out," I pant. "You have to evacuate everyone to the Mortal Realm."

"Why?" Jihun shakes me once when my eyes slide away.

"*Everyone* has to go," I growl, shoving his hands away. "No exception. And it happens *now*."

"But, Nephew—" the Queen of Sky begins.

"*NOW!*" I shout. "Everything burns. Please, Imo. Get everyone out."

"The prophecy of the End of Days . . ." she breathes, her eyes widening in fear. I can only nod. She gives my hand a firm squeeze and goes into action. "Bora, Taeyoung, and Jihun. Begin the evacuation. Without question, and without delay. Your king has willed it."

I feel my friends' questioning glances and the fear of those around me. I ignore them all. I summon my golden axe and silver axe, then stalk to the wall of the capital. Then I pour the force of my magic into my axes and slash an *X* into the fabric of the realm, making two realities flicker in the air.

How did I do that?

But I ignore even my own question and rip open another exit.

I am the King Foretold.

It is not my destiny to save the Realm of Four Kingdoms but to save the people. They are the soul of this realm. I cut another *X* into the boundaries of the Kingdom of Sky.

I will save them all.

I hear the din of shouting and the swoosh of wings as people make their way out of the realm. But I have no time to pay them heed. My aunt and my friends will evacuate the Shinbiin into the Mortal Realm.

I have to focus on creating more exits because only I can do that.

I carve one diagonal line down the fabric of the realm, then another on the opposite side. The newly added exit flutters, revealing a different night sky beyond. My arms tremble from bone-deep fatigue—my magic depleting with every tear I make. But I don't stop.

It is not my destiny that fuels me but my love for Sunny. It is my duty to save my people, but I have to fight for every life because Sunny will grieve even a single loss. I fall to one knee but push back to my feet. I can't stop, even if my body gives out.

For my people. For my fated love.

I will not lose a single life.

I don't let myself think about my other so-called destiny. I have work to do. I swing my axe but miss the mark. Thrown off balance by the momentum, I stumble and fall to the ground. I use my axes as my crutches and get up again.

I rip another exit in the fabric of the realm, and I do it again and again, until I can't lift my axes anymore. But with a hoarse roar, I swing my axes once more and slash open one last exit. Then I crash down on my knees, barely hanging on to my consciousness.

I don't know how long I kneel there, but then two strong hands lift me up by the arms. My head feels too heavy to lift, but I raise my eyes to meet Jihun's.

"I will see you in the Mortal Realm, Your Majesty," he says with a break in his voice. Hailey and Cheyun linger close behind him, worry saturating their expressions. When I don't answer, he shakes me once. "I will see you in the Mortal Realm, Ethan."

"Just go." I jerk my arms free and turn to walk away.

"Promise me, Ethan." He grabs me by the shoulders. "Promise me that I will see you and Sunny in the Mortal Realm."

"I . . . I will try." I blink, as though waking up from a dream. "I'll try, Jihun."

"Good." He presses our foreheads together, his hand heavy on the back of my head. "I will wait for you, Brother."

"Thank you." I pull him into a hug, my arms tight around him. "Thank you for everything."

"Everyone has gone through," Hailey whispers huskily.

"We have to leave, Jihun." Cheyun untangles him from my arms and takes his hand in hers. Then she reaches out and squeezes my arm. "It's been an honor, Your Majesty."

"The honor has always been mine." I nod solemnly at her.

Cheyun leads Jihun away from me, with him glancing over his shoulder every other second, then they step through a jagged exit together.

"Stay alive, Ethan." Hailey wraps her arms around me. "Bring her home to us."

"I will try," I say again.

Hailey bites her bottom lip to stem her tears and follows Jihun and Cheyun into the Mortal Realm.

Then . . . everyone is gone.

Thank gods I could do this much for Sunny. Because my other destiny can go fuck itself. There is no way in hell I would ever kill her—even to save her from herself.

THE END OF DAYS

Fire burns everywhere. Rivers run dry. Trees wither. The earth hardens and cracks. The very life forces of Mountains, Sky, Water, and Underworld feed the fire. Together they are infused with all the colors of light, and a blinding white gi—full and wild—is born.

The goddess of Light stands in the midst of the fiery ruin with her arms spread wide. Her snow-white hair billows around her head as though she's floating in water. Her eyes are closed, her expression serene, as though she is soaking in the warmth of the winter sun.

Suddenly, she opens her eyes, and white fire burns in them. Her face hardens even as tears stream down her pale cheeks. She clenches her fists and screams, a piercing sound of sorrow and defeat. White light bursts from her chest, wrenching her arms and legs apart in the shape of a star.

"Sunny," the King Foretold yells as he runs toward her. "I'm here."

"Is everyone gone?" Her voice echoes through the air as the fire lights up the night with an eerie white glow.

"Yes, we evacuated everyone to the Mortal Realm."

"Good." She closes her eyes once more, and the king sees a glimpse of the female he loves. "That's good."

"It's only you and me here." He struggles to swallow. "You don't have to be afraid anymore. You won't hurt anyone."

"Are *you* no one?" She pins him with her blazing white eyes.

"I am your fated love." He closes the gap between them. "Our love is destined by the heavens. If you die, I die. I am not no one. It's only that you and I are one."

The deafening silence stretches on until cold sweat slides down his back.

"No," she whispers. "That's not how it's supposed to happen."

"How what is supposed to happen?" the king asks.

"I can't control the Cheon'gwang, Ethan." Her eyes shift to a warm brown, her despair plain for him to see. "The prophecy of the End of Days . . . I am meant to be the End of Days, and you are supposed to be my salvation. I die, and you live. I die so everyone lives. That's how it's supposed to happen."

"I will never kill you." A tear rolls down his cheek. "I love you more than life, Sunny."

"If you love me, then you will never let me become the End of Days." White fire consumes the brown of her eyes again.

"But there is no one left in this realm." He spreads his hands. "You won't be hurting anyone."

"You don't *understand*." She breathes fire in her helpless fury. "I will not stop at destroying the Realm of Four Kingdoms. My powers will reach the Mortal Realm. *Everyone* will burn at my hands. *You* will burn."

"I don't care if I die as long as you live," the king shouts.

"But I am an immortal goddess." Her voice turns pleading. "You are asking me to kill you, and everyone else I love, and continue existing on my own in the ruins of my destruction. You are asking me to live with that unbearable pain. *Alone.*"

"Please, Sunny." He sobs. "Please don't ask me to do this."

"Ethan, I don't want to be alone again." She falls to her knees, fire burning around her, within her. "You promised me that I would never be alone again."

"Why does it have to be me?" He kneels in front of her. "Why, Sunny?"

She recites:

The true heart of the righteous shall
Shatter the light that reveals all paths.

"You are the righteous one. I know you are." She cups his face in her burning hands. "You are meant to shatter the Yeoiju. That is the only way to stop this."

"What heart?" He takes her hands from his face and presses them against his heart. "My true heart is not the one inside me. *You* are my beating heart. Sunny, you are my true heart."

"I . . . am your true heart?" She blinks, her eyelids fluttering like butterfly wings. She opens her mouth to continue, but a scream emerges instead.

She crashes to the ground, and the skin of her arms and face undulates like a snake is swimming through her veins. She kicks her legs and claws at her throat as though she cannot breathe.

"Sunny." The King Foretold frantically runs his hands over her body, not caring that his hands burn and blister. "What can I do? Tell me what to do."

Her eyes roll back into her head as she convulses, and her prone body levitates off the ground. And no matter how hard he holds on, the goddess of Light is ripped from his arms and raised into the sky.

The King Foretold takes flight after her, but a force, more powerful than him, slams him back. Even so, he tries again and again until he plummets to the ground, his body too battered to move.

It's okay, Ethan. I will come back to you.

The voice inside his head is warm and at peace. But the scream that rips from the goddess's lips is pure agony, and her body trembles violently from head to toe.

"Sunny!"

It's okay. She catches his eyes with her warm-brown gaze, blood dripping from one corner of her mouth. *Don't be afraid.*

Then she raises her arms, and the Shin'gwangdo appears in her hands, the blade pointing down . . . at her.

“No, Sunny,” he pleads, struggling to get up only to collapse again. “Please. Don’t do this.”

The goddess of Light raises the sword high above her chest, then she plunges it deep into her heart.

“No!” the king cries.

Her back arches on a choked gasp, and tears leak out of her wide eyes, then . . . she goes still. One by one, her fingers slip from the hilt of the sword until her arms drop to hang past her sides.

The King Foretold bows his head, pounding his fist on the hard ground, and weeps soundlessly with grief that penetrates the depth of his bones, his soul. By the time the sun rises, he is spent and motionless. Then . . . a calm settles over him.

He will be with her again. He will soon become untethered from this life, with his fated love gone. Before long, his heart will give out, and he will follow her into the next life. He will not need to be alone for long.

“Good,” he murmurs as he closes his eyes for the last time. “I love you, Sunny. I’ll see you soon.”

CHAPTER FIFTY-FIVE

Ethan

"Wake up, sleepyhead," Sunny murmurs. "It's time to wake up, Ethan."

Her voice sounds faraway. I feel as limp as a wilted dandelion, but I try to open my eyes. I'll do anything for her.

She's dead.

The thought pierces me like a bullet, and I cringe in pain, shutting my eyes tighter. *Why am I conscious?* I don't want to exist without her. I can't bear it.

"Ethan." Her warm hand cups my cheek. *Warm, not searing hot.* "What's wrong? Are you in pain?"

Isn't she here, though? How else is she touching me? How can I feel her if she isn't by my side?

"Nothing's wrong," I croak past my sandpapery throat, keeping my eyes firmly closed. "I'm not in pain."

But where . . . is here?

It doesn't matter. Wherever here is, all I need is to be with her. I should open my eyes. I would give anything to see her face again.

What if I'm dreaming? What if I open my eyes and she isn't here?

I trap her hand against my cheek, holding my breath.

Keep dreaming, Ethan. Don't wake up.

"You *are* awake." She drops a kiss on each of my eyelids. "Why won't you look at me? My feelings are about to get hurt."

My eyes shoot open. I would never do anything to hurt her, even if she's only visiting my dreams—even if she is only a figment of my imagination.

Sunny smiles softly down at me, her hair falling past one shoulder.

Gods, she's beautiful.

I want to smack my dream self in the head for keeping my eyes closed for so long. I could've been looking at her this whole time. I devour her with my eyes.

"Am I dead?" I honestly don't give a damn as long as she's with me.

"Nope," she says, popping the *P. Fucking adorable.* If I could move, I would kiss the hell out of her.

"A-are *you* . . . dead?" The air seizes in my lungs. Dream or not, I don't want her to be dead.

No, Sunny. Please.

"Breathe, Ethan." She kisses my forehead. "I'm not dead either."

If neither of us are dead, then this could be . . . real? Tender, vulnerable hope sprouts in my shattered heart. We could both be alive.

Can I really be this lucky?

"What happened?" With a grunt, I manage to flip to my side and push my torso off the ground. I squint into the distance.

How long have I been out?

The Kingdom of Sky is being ravaged by white fire as far as the eye can see. I try to bolt upright, then groan. I hurt *everywhere*, like I got reamed by a semi. But the pain makes this feel even more real. The Realm of Four Kingdoms is burning, and . . .

Sunny is here.

"Hmm." Sunny helps me sit up, and her touch makes every nerve ending in my body sing. "What do you remember up to?"

"You . . . you lost control of your power, and I evacuated everyone to the Mortal Realm," I hedge.

Inside, I am about to lose my shit. *Sunny is alive.* I shift my shoulders to see if I can manage a cartwheel or two. Maybe in a minute.

"And?" She raises her pretty brows. I want to kiss them. I want to kiss *her.*

"You a-asked me to kill you, but I refused." I jut my chin because I stand by my decision. Then my face crumbles because I don't want to remember the rest. "Then you . . . you killed yourself with the Shin'gwangdo."

Maybe I have this all wrong. Maybe we're both dead after all.

"So you basically remember everything." She leans her head against my shoulder. "But you got one detail wrong."

"Which part?" I gingerly place my cheek on top of her head.

I close my eyes and feel the silky strands of her hair beneath my cheek. I breathe in the fresh, warm scent of her. *My wife. My love.* I absorb her with all my senses.

"I *stabbed* myself with the Shin'gwangdo," she says matter-of-factly, and I flinch. "But I didn't *kill* myself."

I'm afraid to believe that we're okay. I'm terrified of the relief that wants to drain the tension and grief from my body.

I'm not strong enough to face my fury that she tried to sacrifice herself. I'm not ready to forgive her for doing what she had to do to save the worlds. I hate that she is good and noble. At the same time, I love her for it with all my heart.

I worship her.

"How did—" I push Sunny to the ground and cover her with my body as a piece of the sky plummets toward us after an earsplitting boom. I brace for impact, but the chunk of sky falls a few yards to our left.

"Oof," she grunts.

"I know. I know." I rise onto my forearms. "I need to stop using my body as your shield."

"Actually . . ." She pushes against my chest, and I reluctantly roll off onto my side. "I am no longer an immortal goddess. I don't even have the Yeoiju anymore. So I don't mind a little protection, especially when the sky is literally falling."

"What?" I shake my head, squinting in confusion. "I . . ."

"You were right, you know." She flips to her side and runs the pad of her thumb across my cheekbone. "*I* am the true heart of the righteous. It was never your destiny to shatter the Yeoiju. It was mine all along."

I hold my breath and listen.

"The Shin'gwangdo was the only weapon that could destroy the Yeoiju, and I was the only one who could infuse it with the power of the Cheon'gwang." Her hand trembles against my cheek, and I cover it with mine. "All I had to do was choose to give up my immortality and shatter the Yeoiju to release the four divine life forces back to nature."

More of the sky rains down around us, and a fist-sized chunk falls a foot away from Sunny's head.

Fuck.

"Maybe we should save this conversation for *after* we get ourselves to safety." I get to my feet and reach down to help her.

I think . . . we are alive. Both of us. Which means I have to get Sunny the hell out of this crumbling realm.

"My thoughts exactly." Ignoring my hand, she agilely hops to her feet, then turns toward the capital. "We have to get to the Mortal Realm."

"Where do you think you're going?" I catch her hand and give it a sharp tug, and she tumbles into my arms. Then I kiss her soundly on the mouth.

Gods, we really are alive.

With a moan that shoots straight to my groin, Sunny presses herself against me and licks the seam of my mouth. I open up for her with a groan and tilt my head to kiss her more deeply. The sky makes another ominous rumble.

"We might have to save this kiss for later, as well," I breathe against her lips, then pat her round ass. "Now step aside."

"Why?" she asks even as she takes two steps to the side like a good little wife. "The entrance between the realms is across the field."

"Have a little trust in your husband." I wink at her. I am far from fully recovered, but I don't want to lose the chance to impress Sunny.

I am truly a dingus.

I summon my axes and concentrate the gi of Mountains running through my veins into them. Spinning away from her, I slash a diagonal line down the fabric of the Realm of Four Kingdoms, then its mirror image cutting across its center, marking an *X*.

"Whoa," she breathes. "Did you just make a new gateway between the realms?"

"Yeah." I rub the back of my head, feeling sheepish postexhibition, and clear my throat. "But it's more of an exit from a disintegrating realm."

"Speaking of disintegrating realms . . ." She glances meaningfully at the white flames engulfing the Kingdom of Sky, as well as the sky about to fall on top of us.

"Right." I sweep her off her feet, and she wraps her arms around my neck with a little squeak. Before I'm tempted to kiss her again, I leap out of the exit and into the Mortal Realm.

I hover for a moment, high up in the sky—the mountaintop that marked the entrance to the Gray Void but a speck below us. But as I make a slow descent with Sunny in my arms, the lush mountains and blue waters sparkle in the sunlight.

"It's so beautiful," she whispers.

"Welcome home, Sunny." I kiss her softly on the forehead, lest she break. But I cringe when realization hits. "Shit."

We can't fly around in broad daylight. This isn't the Realm of Four Kingdoms. I hurriedly cloak us in invisibility.

"Shut. Up." Sunny smacks me in the chest. "Did you just turn us invisible?"

"Uh, yeah." I grimace. "I forgot to tell you about that, didn't I?"

"Yeah, you did." She smacks me again, then gives me a brilliant smile. "But we *have* been kind of busy."

"Kind of." I grin back at her. "We deserve a vacation. Where to?"

"Let's go to that cave near my childhood home," she murmurs.

"*That's* where you want to go?"

"For now." She rolls her eyes. "You're expending a lot of magic with the flying and the invisibility. We're in the Mortal Realm now. We don't have an unlimited supply of gi to fuel our magic."

"It's for the best." I sigh, some of my giddiness fading. "But it'll be daunting for the Shinbiin to learn a new way of life."

"It's not that complicated." Sunny shrugs in my arms. "In the Mortal Realm, the beings of the Shingae have three rules to live by."

"What rules are those?" Holding her close against my chest, I fly toward the mountain she grew up in.

"Never expose the world of gods. Protect the magic. And keep the Amheuk at bay . . ." She trails off. "I guess we just simplified the rules even more. We only have two rules to follow since the Amheuk is no more."

"You made sure of that." Pride and gratitude swell in my chest. "You saved us all, Sunny."

"And you saved me," she whispers.

"I can't imagine what it felt like to be the most powerful being in all the worlds. You were the goddess of Light. A god among gods." I shake my head in wonder. "It couldn't have been an easy choice to make."

"It was the easiest choice I ever made. Because it was the only way we both could live." She cups my cheek with one hand, looking at me as though I am her everything. My heart pounds so loudly that I almost miss her next words. "I'll always choose to be with you, Ethan. There is no other choice for me."

What did I do to deserve her?

I land in front of the cave and look up at the sky, gathering myself. With an unsteady exhale, I set Sunny down on her feet. But I keep my hands on her hips, because I can't stop touching her. When I finally meet her eyes, mine are filled with unshed tears—tears of joy, tears of gratitude.

"But you're not an immortal goddess anymore." My throat works as I hold off my tears.

"I don't want to be a goddess, Ethan." She holds me by the shoulders and pushes up to her toes. "I want to be your wife."

"You already are my wife." My fingers clench around her hips.

"Lucky me." Her soft laugh brushes against my lips.

"*I* am the luckiest bastard alive." I lose my battle against the tears. "I am yours, Sunny. Heart, body, and soul."

"Good, because I am never letting you go," she whispers. Her sweet kiss holds the promise of forever, and I kiss her back with all the love in me.

I am complete.

With Sunny—my wife, my fated love, my true heart—by my side, I can face anything that lies ahead. Even an uncertain world, filled with the divine gi of the flawed gods.

EPILOGUE

Sunny

"You are late," Cheyun clips out.

"I knew Ethan and I should've eloped," I mutter under my breath but offer my friend a strained smile. "Almost ready."

As annoying as the former suhoshin captain may be, I'm just fucking happy that she's alive. I've lost too many friends. The least I can do is appreciate the ones I have left. Plus, she's right. I am late.

For my own wedding.

I am apparently marrying my husband again because my father, Dangun, declared that our simple ceremony in the Kingdom of Sky was "not valid in the eyes of the god of Mountains." I might have gotten my goofy sense of humor from my old man. Still new to this father/daughter relationship, I didn't sass him by pointing out that he was no longer the god of Mountains.

As a matter of fact, the Shingae, the world of *gods*, no longer has any gods. I snort at the irony but sober almost instantly.

The collapse of the Realm of Four Kingdoms still haunts my nightmares. Even now, my stomach takes a sickening swoop at the reminder. I exhale slowly through my mouth, envisioning Ethan wrapping his arms around me, like he does every time I wake up gasping in the night.

I think of the smell of the dark coffee that he brings me in the mornings. The feel of his five o'clock shadow, tickling my cheek. The sound of our laughter as we watch our latest crap reality show.

He's safe. We're alive. We will share a life together.

Speaking of which, I am late for my wedding.

"Shit, shit, shit," I yelp, hiking up my floor-length gown and running out of Hailey's apartment.

I don't know how I got persuaded into wearing a fucking wedding dress. A lacy, strapless, mermaid gown at that. But I grin when I see my red Converse high-tops.

"I simply do not understand her attachment to that footwear." Bora crinkles her nose at them when she catches up with me at the elevator bay.

"At least she didn't insist on wearing her black combat boots." Hailey presses the Down button like she has a vendetta against it.

"I'm standing right here," I grumble crossly.

My friends, whom I appreciate and cherish, somehow got wind of all the Mortal Realm wedding traditions and made me sleep apart from Ethan last night. We survived the apocalypse, for fuck's sake. Who cares if it's "bad luck" for the groom to see the bride before the wedding? I would've slept better and wouldn't have been late for my wedding.

We pile into the elevator when it arrives, then rush out at the lobby even before the doors slide fully open. Out of habit, Cheyun leads the charge but hesitates when we step out of the building.

"Where is our ride?" She frowns.

"He's on his way." Bora looks down at her watch, then cranes her neck down the street. "There he is right now."

A black SUV turns the corner and crawls toward us at far below the 25 miles per hour speed limit. Taeyoung got his driver's license a few days ago, and from the looks of it, he is not exactly competent behind the wheel.

I hike my dress up again with the intent to walk over to the car—it would be faster that way—but Hailey places a hand on my arm.

"The Shin'gwangdo is showing," she murmurs in a low voice, sadness and understanding in her eyes.

I glance down at myself and see the tip of the dragon-scaled sheath lying against my outer thigh. With a small gasp, I let my dress fall back into place. The Amheuk is gone, but I still don't feel safe without the Shin'gwangdo. It's a regular hwando without the Yeoiju's powers, but I am pretty handy with plain ol' swords.

Before I can make an excuse that Hailey will see right through, our ride jerks to a stop at the curb.

"Your chariot awaits." Taeyoung bounds out of the driver's seat and beams at us.

Bora sends us a warning glance not to tease the former King of Underworld about his driving before walking up to him to peck him on the cheek. "You're right on time."

Cheyun, to her credit, refrains from calling out Bora's white lie and holds open the rear passenger door for me. I let her silently boss me around, and I take a seat as quickly as possible, while dressed in the most impractical contraption ever invented. Hailey scoots to the middle seat from the other side.

After closing my door harder than strictly necessary, Cheyun stomps around the back of the car to slide in next to Hailey, but she huffs an audible sigh when Taeyoung fusses over Bora's seat belt in the front.

"It's fine, Cheyun. We can be a little late." I lean forward to catch her gaze. "It's not like the world's about to end."

When Hailey flinches next to me, I cringe apologetically. "Too soon? Sorry."

"You're just nervous," Hailey says, excusing my loopy humor.

"Nervous?" I laugh too loudly. "Me?"

I am totally nervous. But more than anything, I feel . . . guilty. I am living a dream I didn't dare to dream.

I am supposed to be dead. Not Draco. Not Minju. Not Jaeseok.

I was a fucking goddess. How did I let Minju die right in front of me? Why couldn't I protect them? Impotent fury builds inside me, and for a fraction of a second, it feels as though white fire flares in my chest.

"Sunny," Cheyun says sharply enough to grab my attention. "Breathe."

I look down at myself in confusion for a second. *What the hell am I wearing?* Then I remember I am marrying my fated love. *Today.*

Not in a rushed ceremony with a bowl of water. Not while assuming one or both of us won't make it through the day. In a real wedding. Because forever is possible now.

Breathe.

I release a shaky breath, inhale slowly through my nose, and breathe out again. I know the drill. I have to remember to give myself grace.

Destroying the Amheuk didn't bring my friends back, but it saved everyone in the car and everyone waiting for us. As corny as it may sound, I can only honor the ones we lost by living my life to the fullest.

No more hiding from the worlds or from myself. No more dead-end jobs. No more pretending not to care about anything or anyone.

I have opened myself up and am vulnerable even when it terrified me. And I *care* even when it hurts. I am not overjoyed about being the queen of a lost realm, but I'm working on that. I even found a passion—investigative work, just like Ben and Ethan—and hope to build a successful career out of it.

Draco would've wanted that for me—just like I had wanted that for them.

We skid to a stop in front of the Bellagio Hotel on the Strip, and Taeyoung announces the obvious. "We're here."

Then, everyone is in motion at once. We jump out of the SUV, Taeyoung throws his keys at the valet, and we race into the hotel, toward our wedding venue—a small private terrace overlooking the Bellagio Fountains.

But as though choreographed, we screech to a halt at the exit to the terrace and look at each other like we've never seen arched French doors before.

"I have no idea why *I* am nervous." Bora shakes her head and reaches for the door handle, when a tall, distinguished male appears on the other side.

"Pardon me." My father steps into the hotel, wearing a stylish navy blue suit. He nods hello at everyone but falters when he sees me. Breathing out an emotional sigh, he takes both of my hands into his. "You look radiant, Sunshine."

"Can you not call me that?" I crinkle my nose, pretending not to like the nickname.

"What else would I call my sunshine?" Dangun gives me an indulgent smile and offers me his arm. "Ready?"

I put my arm through his and nod jerkily, because I can't find my voice. Taeyoung opens the door, and my father and I step out to the landing.

Ethan stands below the curved stone staircase with the morning light streaming down on him. He is sinfully beautiful in his classic tuxedo. He brushed his hair back for the occasion, which highlights his high cheekbones and strong jawline, but a stubborn curl falls endearingly over his forehead.

I know the moment he sees me. His lips part and his eyes widen, and he definitely stops breathing. How could I not love a male who looks at me like his world ends and begins with me?

I can't, of course.

I love him with all my battered heart and weary soul. He is my love destined by the heavens, and even death cannot sever the thread of fate that binds us.

"I'm ready."

For life. For death. For anything.

ACKNOWLEDGMENTS

August 2025, when I'm writing these acknowledgments, is a dark, dark time. My heart grieves. And I am weary, afraid, and furious.

But every book I write, especially the Realm of Four Kingdoms series, is a rebellion against the ugly voices that tell me Asian Americans don't matter—that we don't belong. It is my rebellion against the voices that tell me to stay in my lane, small and quiet.

And these are the people who lift me up and let me shine . . .

To Sarah Younger, my literary agent, you are my anchor in the turbulent world of publishing. You make me bold and strong, because I know you will *always* have my back. Thank you for supporting me through this roller-coaster ride, cheering me on through the rough times and celebrating the good times with me. I never have to do any of this alone because of you.

To my acquisitions editor, Megan Sakoi, you are a rock star. You went to bat for me to make *Light Burned* happen, and I am so grateful that I got to complete this series. Sunny and Ethan deserved to have their story told. The *whole* story. And my readers deserved this epic ending. Thank you for loving the Realm of Four Kingdoms as much as I do and squealing in excitement with me every step of the way.

To my developmental editor, Charlotte Herscher, thank you for your professionalism and dedication. I appreciate you squeezing in a down-to-the-wire third round of edits—or was it fourth round?

To Abigail Owen, the "she" to my "nanigans." Your dedication and sacrifice to help a friend in need—even when you are busier than Hades himself—is a testament to your generosity, loyalty, and kindness. I appreciate you, dear friend. Thank you so much for helping me make *Light Burned* the best version of itself.

To my family, the loves of my life, thank you for your understanding and support, even when I am a hot mess, stressed over yet another deadline. You are the reason why I can tell my stories. You are the motivation that keeps me going when I want to give up. You are my light.

To my readers . . . Good gracious, what can I say about you amazing people? Thank you for breathing life into my books by reading my words and filling your mind with my stories. Thank you for trusting me and sharing this journey with me.

GLOSSARY

- ajumma: A married or middle-aged woman
- Amheuk: Ancient force of true darkness
- banchan: Side dishes served alongside rice
- bojagi: A cloth used for wrapping items
- bomo: A child's nursemaid
- bujeok: A talisman or amulet (often a piece of paper with writings and symbols drawn by a shaman) to bring either good fortune or protection. It can also be used to bring ill fortune to an enemy.
- Celestial Palace: Royal palace of the Kingdom of Sky
- Cheon'gwang: Ancient force of true light
- Cheonji: Heaven Lake, a lake that lies on the border between China and North Korea on Mount Baekdu
- chima: A skirt worn as part of a hanbok
- cup ramyeon: A bowl of ramen made in the Korean style
- dakjuk: Chicken porridge
- dangui: A jeogori with an elongated front panel
- Dangun: The god of Mountains; son of Hwanung and Ungnyeo
- darisokot: A rudimentary string bikini
- ddeokbokki: Rice cakes popular as street food
- dobok: A martial arts uniform
- dokkaebi: A goblin from Korean folklore
- doksacho: A deadly poisonous herb
- dol: A first birthday

- Donggul: Building where the Suhoshin trial is held, nicknamed "the Cave"
- Donggul Monster: A mysterious entity that suhoshin cadets must fight in the Suhoshin trial
- dopo: A long outer robe worn by Korean nobility
- Dragon Palace: Royal palace of the Kingdom of Water
- Endless War: A war against the Amheuk that ended five centuries ago
- galbi jjim: A Korean dish of braised beef short ribs
- gama: A traditional Korean litter or palanquin
- gat: A traditional Korean hat with a wide brim made of black mesh
- gi: Life force, commonly referred to as *chi* (based on the Mandarin pronunciation)
- Goguryeo: An ancient kingdom of Korea
- Gojoseon: The ancient kingdom that evolved into Korea
- gomo: An honorific meaning *aunt*, specifically a person's father's sister
- gonggi: Also known as *Korean Jacks*; a children's game played with small stones
- goreum: A ribbon of cloth tied on a jeogori
- gukbap: A Korean dish of soup with rice
- gumiho: A nine-tailed fox spirit
- gungnyeo: A lady-in-waiting for royalty
- Gwangdo: Sword of light
- haejangguk: A soup, often containing seonji, used to help cure a hangover
- halmeoni: An honorific meaning *grandmother*
- han: Grief perverted by resentment and vengeance into something that haunts the soul
- hanbok: Traditional Korean clothing referring to both women's (a cropped top and a floor-length skirt that ties at the chest) and men's (a top and baggy pants)

- Hangawi: Also known as *Chuseok*; a mid-harvest festival celebrated on the full moon
- hanji: A traditional Korean handmade paper
- hanok: A traditional Korean house, single-story, with a stone-tiled roof and curved eaves
- hwando: A short, single-edged Korean sword
- Hwanin: The god of Heavens
- Hwanung: The former god of Earth, son of Hwanin and father of Dangun
- imo: An honorific meaning *aunt*, specifically a person's mother's sister
- in'eo: A merfolk creature in Korean folklore
- Jaenanpa: Faction of dark shamans whose primary purpose is to steal magic from beings of the Shingae
- japchae: A Korean dish made of stir-fried glass noodles and vegetables
- jeogori: A traditional shirt that goes with the skirt or pants of a hanbok
- jeon: A Korean fritter
- Jeoseung Palace: Royal palace of the Kingdom of Underworld
- jeoseungsaja: A being of Underworld who guides the souls of the dead to the Kingdom of Underworld
- jimil: Inner court
- Joseon: The last dynastic kingdom in Korea (1392–1897)
- jumeokbap: Rice balls
- kimchi: A seasoned dish of pickled or fermented cabbage and other vegetables
- makgeolli: A milky, lightly sparkling rice wine
- moonglade: A silver road, made from the elongated moon's reflection, that appears in the ocean on Hangawi
- mudang: A Korean shaman
- noona: An honorific meaning *older sister*
- oppa: An honorific meaning *older brother*

- saja: A shortened form of the word *jeoseungsaja*
- Samshin Halmeom: A manifestation of the Seonangshin in the form of an elderly woman
- sanggung: The most senior gungnyeo
- sanjeok: A mountain bandit
- Sanshillyeong: Spirit of Mountains, another manifestation of the Seonangshin in the form of an elderly man
- sayak: A poisonous elixir used for capital punishment during the Joseon Dynasty
- seonangdang: Tree shrine for the Seonangshin used by humans
- Seonangshin: The god of Mountains
- seonji: Congealed animal blood with a sweet taste and dense yet crumbly texture
- seonnam: A winged angelic being of Sky (male)
- seonnyeo: A winged angelic being of Sky (female)
- seungmacho: An herb used as an antidote
- Shin'gwangdo: The newly forged twin to the Gwangdo, forged of dragon scales melded with sacred ashes from Samshin Halmeom
- Shinbiin: Beings of the Shingae in the Realm of Four Kingdoms
- Shindansu: The Sacred Tree of Life
- Shingae: World of gods
- Shinsan: The divine mountain
- Shinsi Palace: Royal palace of the Kingdom of Mountains, located in the city of Shinsi
- somok: Traditional Korean joinery
- songpyeon: A sweet, half moon–shaped rice cake
- Suhoshin: Guardians of the Shingae
- uinyeo: A medical nurse
- Ungnyeo: In legend, a bear that asked Hwanung to transform her into a woman

- yeobo: A term of endearment used by married couples
- Yeoiju: Pearl of Light or Enlightenment (the last of the Cheon'gwang)
- Yeomla: The god of Underworld
- Yongwang: Dragon King, the god of Water

ABOUT THE AUTHOR

Photo © 2025 Alice Kuo Shippee

Jayci Lee is a *USA Today* bestselling author of sexy contemporary romance and epic romantasy, featuring Korean American main characters. Her work has appeared in *Cosmopolitan*, *Entertainment Weekly*, *The Hollywood Reporter*, *E! News*, *Women's World*, and *O, The Oprah Magazine*. Jayci is retired from her fifteen-year career as a litigator because she's a lover—not a fighter. She lives in sunny California with her husband, sons, and a fluffy rescue.